The Lantern
of
Dern Blackhammer

By

Lawrence BoarerPitchford

ISBN: 0-9850647-9-X
ISBN-13: 978-0-9850647-9-2

DEDICATION

To my wife who is the inspiration in my life.
To my friend Gary, whose passion for my work drives me on.
To my friend David, whose insight fuels my imagination.
Thank you all for being such a blessing.

CONTENTS

ACKNOWLEDGMENTS

Credits:

Cover Artist ~ Lawrence BoarerPitchford

Senior Editor ~ Wendy Schirmer

Editor ~ Julie BoarerPitchford

CHAPTER

1

Myth and Legend

In the hazy past

Bringing down his blacksmith's hammer, Dern felt the shower of sparks from its impact burning his forearms. The billet deformed with each successive strike as he flexed his muscles to apply more force.

He set the hammer down, then turned toward the forge and concentrated on the diamonds piled high. Wisps of red plasma extended from his fingers, hands, and arms penetrating the gems and making the crystals heat far beyond the temperature of a normal fire.

The stench of burnt hair filled his nostrils as a blinding light and shockwaves of heat washed over him. Plunging the metal into the fire, he watched it slowly grow to a bright red.

He strained, as his mind bombarded the diamonds with more energy making the metal transformed into a swirling white light. He pulled forth the glowing mass and relinquished his spell.

The billet was not of ordinary metal, but a combination of worldly and unworldly elements that would withstand the severe temperature and magical pressures soon to be contained within.

In a loud rhythmic chant, he called the words of magic and drove the hammer against the metal again and again until the billet was a thin sheet.

"This had better be worth the sacrifice and expense," he said in a low voice.

His personal fortune was now gone, all spent to make this one item. But there was little choice in the matter.

He glanced over to see the unfinished lantern, its brassy surface reflecting the light from the forge. Taking the sheet of hot metal, he laid it against the lantern and bent it to shape. The metals fused creating a seamless form, sending a wisp of smoke racing into the air. Once molded, it cooled instantly.

Droplets of sweat from his brow got in his eyes, and he wiped away the stinging fluid with the back of his hand. The work was nearly complete; just two more components to install and he could hoist a tankard of ale to his good work.

Dern licked his lips, as he imagined the dark and cold libation. He then turned to look at the wooden box near the lantern.

Such a simple box for such a rare treasure, he thought.

He walked over to it and opened the top. A highly polished lens of alumina glass reflected the ambient light. He ran his fingers over the red velvet that surrounded the treasure.

He took it from the box and fastened the lens to the lantern shell. He could almost hear the words of Pil'tuk, the goblin glass maker.

"The lens will not scratch and will take the impact of a god's battle hammer!"

"But do you think the lantern will work?" he had asked Pil'tuk.

"If the mad magician Valen of Del can produce us a Dark Star gem. But only chaos magic is strong enough to do the trick, and we both know what that means; if he fails to condense the energy just right, we might all be blasted into ash."

He glanced over his shoulder to the corner of the forge-room. Dern saw the large black gem locked between wooden pincers. A shiver ran up his spine.

The unnatural gem was the final touch, the power, the light, the quantillian dark stone with the power of a star. The magician had done his job all right, making something terrifying that did not belong on this world or any other, and for his trouble he was torn into atoms by the power of chaos.

Poor bastard, Dern thought.

He approached the gem. From the black surface, the reflection of his own eye looked back at him. For a moment the darkness was all-consuming, as if it was absorbing not only the light, but his thoughts as well.

The eye in the reflection blinked, and he shook his head in surprise. *Did he blink?* He didn't know. Looking at the surface again he seemed to be looking back at himself, looking into the gem, looking back at himself... his skin crawled and his hair stood on end.

He glanced away, concentrating on the lantern to clear his mind, then turned back to the wooden clamps. The thing seemed to be mocking him, trying to drive a wedge between his sanity and madness.

Carefully taking the gem, he carried it over to the lantern, opened the small door in the side, and placed it within the rectangular chamber— angling the gem so the flat surface faced the lens. Closing the door, he locked it tight.

"Now to ignite the flame!" said Dern, a slight headache forming in his skull.

He closed his eyes and envisioned the complex relationship between the geometry and the elements within, linking fields of force with the matter's energy channels. As he opened his eyes, a near blinding light dazzled him as a beam shot from the lantern onto the wall.

The atoms of the wall vanished, and a hole of pure blackness appeared. He secured the lens cap, careful not to expose himself to the light. As he looked at the contraption, he was startled by a sudden knock at the door.

"Blackhammer, is it finished?" said a soft feminine voice.

"Are you trying to cause my death?" he blurted. "I am as finished as this lantern. Let's hope it works."

She opened the door and came into the room, the light of pure energy taking shape into womanly form.

"The war is nearly won, and for all your sacrifices, you will be given rest and worship in the Netherworld," she said.

"You spiritual beings are all alike; bend us mortals to your will, then we are forgotten."

"Not so," she said. "We prize you mortals for the role you play in this universe. Besides, do you want to exist forever in this form?"

She laughed, and the sound lifted his spirit with joy. Bending down, she put her hands on either side of his coarsely bearded face making his skin crackle with static as she kissed him on the lips.

"The blood from my dry lips doesn't offend you?" he asked.

She smiled warmly. "Let me wet them with a flagon of ale, since my kiss did not satisfy you so."

She held out her hand and a container appeared with a dense foamy head on top.

"Drink and feel refreshed. Afterward prepare for battle."

He took the tankard, and she took up the lantern. Dern drank down the flagon and wiped his mouth with the back of his hand.

"How many will we be leading on this assault?"

"Two— you and I."

"Well, that's both disappointing and surprising... maybe even alarming."

"Take heart," she said. "A glorious death awaits us and a warm welcome in the Netherworld."

"Well, no mortal lives forever."

He picked up his battle axe and the runes on the haft glowed a radiant purple. He paused.

"War is a hot, thirsty business - you'd better make me two more flagons to slake my yearning." He looked into the empty mug.

She produced two more flagons. He drank both as fast as he could, then put down the mug.

"Now to put those demons into a bottle, and be done with it," she said while handing him the lantern.

He lifted it and strode to the door, then looked back.

"Coming?"

She smiled warmly, and followed him out.

"Hide within my cloak. When the time is right, step out and expose them to the light."

*   *   *

Five thousand years later

Ford was confused. Why take a walk when a perfectly good cab was at hand? But his father was fearless, sometimes at the expense of common sense, and Ford was willing to indulge him.

They were nearly to the park when a dark figure rushed toward them. Radcliff winced, clutched his arm. The figure in cowl and cape chuckled, turned abruptly, and dashed into an alley.

Radcliff began to fall.

"Father," Ford said, catching him and lowering him to the ground.

The elder Efferguard seemed to be choking and not able to respond.

"Help," Ford shouted. "Someone help me!"

A couple approached them from the park.

"Help – fetch a healer quick!" Ford called.

The gentleman rushed off down the street and the lady came toward them, but halted at the road.

Radcliff shook as if a sudden chill took him.

"Ford?" he rasped, his voice a hazy remnant of a once powerful man. "You must repeat to me the oath."

"What... the oath of Moore?"

Ford pulled the dart from the elder elf's arm and threw it to the ground. The poison was working quickly. Cradling his father's head in his lap, Ford began to sob.

"Speak it to me, boy. There's not much time."

"The honor of all Moorians..." Ford began, "is to protect Moore from enemies without and within." He wiped his eyes as the tears rolled down his cheek.

"To live without regret, to do my duty, to protect the weak, and to deliver justice when called upon."

"You're a good boy, Ford... I love you... We will meet again in the Netherworld..."

Gasping once, his father became rigid as the color drained from his cheeks.

"No," Ford sobbed with abandon, "it can't be, you can't be dead. A healer is coming! Father!"

A shrill sound made Ford look up. A constable approached, his whistle blaring as he ran.

"What happened here?" he asked.

"My father's been murdered," Ford said, the shock of the event growing within him.

"Who did this? I mean did you see who did it?"

"A fellow in a dark cowl and cape, standing across the street by the lamppost." He pointed. "He came and blew a dart at my father as we walked toward the park."

Several other elves gathered about gawking. Two more constables arrived, their batons at the ready.

"Let me pass, I'm a certified healer!"

A tall elf in a ruby colored long coat rushed to Radcliff. He knelt down putting his hands on either side of his head.

Saying a quick incantation, he checked for a pulse and peered into vacant eyes. He drew a glowing symbol in the air over the body that faded quickly, and then looked at Ford.

"It's not a healer you need, my lad, but a resurrectionist. This elf has passed over already."

Ford gently lowered his father's head to the cobblestones and stood up. Staring down at him he could almost believe, but for the pallor of his skin, he was simply asleep.

"What color was the cape and cowl?" the constable asked.

Ford looked at him and pointed at his breeches. "Blue – they were a darker shade of blue than your pants."

An older elf in a long tan moleskin coat approached from the darkness, passed the constable, and stopped at Ford. He spoke softly.

"You're Ford Efferguard?"

Looking up, Ford recognized him; a friend of his father's, Xavier Goldworm.

"Yes… I know you."

"And I know you, and your father. You, healer, can he be mended?" Goldworm asked.

"No, sir. He's beyond my services."

Goldworm grunted. "Has anyone called a resurrectionist?"

The constable shook his head.

Goldworm frowned and motioned to another elf standing on the sidewalk.

"Virgil, fetch a priest immediately – let's see if the old dodger is willing to come back from the beyond."

The elf took off like a shot and dashed into the crowd and the darkness.

Goldworm walked back to the body and shook his head.

"Damn shame. Your father was about to have Camber Delon arrested and charged with treason." Turning to Ford he looked grave. "Did you see the person who did this?"

Ford shook his head. "Not clearly, he wore a cowl and cape."

"Did he stand about so high?" Goldworm held his hand about shoulder height.

"Yes, I think so."

"And was he wearing an odd shade of blue?"

Ford looked puzzled for a moment. "How did you know that?"

"So he was?"

"Yes."

"It is my business to know things, young Mister Efferguard. The human who did this does dark deeds for pay. We think Camber Delon may have hired him."

The constable looked from Ford, to his father, and back to Goldworm.

"Efferguard?" the constable asked. "Lying there is Mister Radcliff Efferguard? The Minister of Prosecution?"

Goldworm nodded. "The same, and the Brood would appreciate it if you kept it to yourself. Take your men and shoo these looky-loos to the park and question them. See if any of them saw anything more."

He turned to Ford and put his arm around the young elf.

"I know that what I say now may not make you feel any better, but there will come a time you will want to right this wrong. Let it be handled the right way... by me."

He pulled a flask of liquor from under his coat and offered it to Ford.

"When you've come to grips with this, come see me. I think your father would approve of you working for me... I mean, the Brood."

Goldworm let go of Ford and walked to where his father lay.

A priest came from the other side of the street. He kneeled and set down a bag filled with tools that he promptly removed and laid out next to the body.

He mumbled and sprinkled something over Radcliff, then chanted and waved his hands around. The body glowed a ghastly green then shadowy images moved within the air.

This went on for some time, as the streetlamps were put out and the sun crested the buildings. Finally, the priest stood up and shook his head.

"I sent many messengers to find him. They tell me he's not coming back," he solemnly said.

Ford wiped his nose with his handkerchief.

"Mister Goldworm?"

"Yes."

"When I've seen to my father and family, I'll come by your office."

*   *   *

Ford held the dagger at his side, hidden by his thigh as he crouched in the darkness. Two years he'd worked for the Brood, climbing his way up to the position of Skulduggerer within the Shadow Bureau.

Two years had sharpened his skills to razor-like perfection in the dangerous environment of city-state espionage. In front of him stood a man wearing a green muffin cap, ruffled brown shirt, and gray trousers. In the man's hand he held a thin brown leather folder rolled into a cylinder and tied with a black velvet strap; but the folder did not belong to him.

It was by dumb luck that Ford was standing in the shadows ready with a dagger, for he had not intended on encountering any opposition this dark and crisp fall evening. He intended to meet a courier carrying a vital document for his employer.

When he arrived at the location there was no courier to be seen. It was just the hint of a sigh that made Ford take to the shadows. In the darkness a man emerged from the bushes replacing a bloody dagger into its sheath, looked about, brushed his trousers and shirt, and stepped back onto the cobblestone path.

In his hand was the leather folder, and Ford knew any search for the courier would only turn up a dead body. Keeping to the shadows, he followed the man to where he now stood within sight of the tallest relic in the city…the Helios statue.

The clopping of horse's hooves and the clack of carriage wheels echoed down the street. He looked on as the iridescent yellow lantern lights of a carriage grew larger.

The black cab pulled up along the stone curb across the wide street, but the door did not open, nor did the driver climb down from his perch.

Ford crept silently toward the man who held the documents. He too was watching the cab.

The man waited; anticipation apparent in his posture. Ford recited in his mind the oath of the Brood, *to live without regret, to do my duty, to protect the weak, and deliver justice when called upon*!

He waited, preparing himself. It was unclear if the man was biding his time for fear or effect.

"The long night waits for Jup," the cabbie said.

The man took a step; Ford pounced like a goblin on a sack of topus. Quickly he struck the fellow's throat with his left hand, paralyzing his voice while he pulled him to the ground.

The man rolled over in his grip and latched his hands onto Ford's throat. In the shadows they battled.

Ford grabbed the man's wrist, twisted his shoulders and stepped to the side, then locked the man's arm and flipped him onto his back. A blade flashed from the man's side as he dropped the folder and lunged for Ford, but Ford bent so the blade just missed him.

Striking with the pommel of his own dagger, Ford hit the man in the face. The man went rigid, a scream caught in his throat, and he limply crumpled to the ground. Ford stepped back and rolled him over. The man's eyes were now vacant.

From the darkness, he took up the document and looked across the street at the cab. The glass-paned window of the carriage door was down, and an arm hidden within a blue sleeve withdrew.

A muffled voice called to the driver. The cabbie snapped the reins and the horse drew the car forward and down the cobble street. Ford watched as the cab was illuminated by each successive lamppost, cloaked in a ghostly light, until it was out of sight.

He quickly examined the body for documents and a purse, but suddenly stopped. In the man's neck was a poisoned dart. Ford's blood chilled. *Could it be him,* he thought, *after all these years?*

Propping the body up against a stone wall, he stole away down a side street. A few blocks away, he crossed the vast city park. It sprawled out in a hexagonal pattern in the middle of the urban landscape.

People, some walking domesticated drogs, and others stealing kisses, littered the greens and paths, even as the city clock struck double six of the bells. Weaving his way through the park he made his way toward the office of his employer, Xavier Goldworm.

Ford emerged onto the avenue that intersected with the large white granite and marble edifices that made up the financial hub of Moore, the city's true power base. But he was not going into one of those exquisite buildings; he had another destination in mind.

Passing the Commerce Exchange, he turned down a dirty alley and stopped at a red door marked A23. Removing a small rune stone from his pocket, he held it up to the portal. A soft click echoed to his ears, and he pushed the door open.

Entering, he closed the door behind him, then turned to go up a long set of rickety stairs. A few light crystals provided just enough visibility to not break one's neck.

As he topped the stairs he heard someone clear his throat. Several doors were present and he moved to one that was faded green with no markings. Knocking, he heard Goldworm's voice ring out.

"Come!"

Ford stepped into a brightly lit room with a dirty brown desk at one end, and two wooden chairs flaking green paint. A hanging light crystal suspended from the roof by way of a black wrought iron chain, and an equally black chandelier, provided the room its modest light.

"Where the deuces have you been?" demanded Goldworm. He pointed at a small magic clock hung on the wall. "I expected you a half hour ago."

"There was a problem," Ford began.

"Problem? What kind of problem?"

"The courier is dead."

"Dead?" Goldworm pulled down on his doublet with contempt. "Who in the name of darkness did such a thing?"

Ford put the leather folder on the desk and sat down in the chair.

"I don't know, but the man who did it fought like a Bridge Troll for a fare." He pulled a white handkerchief from his pocket and mopped his hairline.

Goldworm looked down at the folder, quickly scooped it up and opened it. He thumbed through the documents, and then put it on the table.

"What about the villain who killed our courier?" Goldworm looked annoyed.

"Here's his coin purse," Ford said tossing the small black sack onto the desk next to the leather folder.

His boss dumped out the contents onto the table and gazed at the items. Ford saw a small gold pocket-clock, a few reading crystals, and a handful of various coins, some silver, some copper.

"Did he drop this as he fled?"

"He didn't flee. He was dealt with, but not by me," Ford said. "The city constables will find him soon. I trust you'll see that the news doesn't reach the papers?"

Goldworm fingered the items on the table, then said, "Clearly he was not paid in advance. Did you see who did the chap in?"

"Not clearly. The person was in a black cab, but I did see his arm."

"Arm?" Goldworm blustered. "What in the name of the underworld is that going to tell us?"

"He wore blue silk," Ford said.

"Blue silk you say? Then it's him," Goldworm mused.

"Raven Hill?" Ford asked.

"Raven Hill," Goldworm replied. "That collector of relics we've been keeping an eye on for the past few years. After Camber Delon was executed, he fled Moore. We've known for quite some time now that he's been trying to find relics that might help him."

"Help him do what?"

Goldworm frowned. "I guess in light of this development I can make you privy to this state secret. Raven Hill has aspirations of consolidating under one rule all the city-states and outer kingdoms."

"Including Moore?"

"Yes."

Ford rapped his fingers on the table.

"The man was killed with a dart," Ford added.

At this Goldworm looked at Ford as if considering his next words.

"A sticky hive, my lad, wouldn't you say? The dart is his signature when murdering."

"Like my father?"

"Yes, like your father. But, I hasten to say, you have taken an oath to serve the Brood, and this information should not interfere with this oath!"

He gave Ford a knowing look.

"The man is power hungry." Goldworm leveled his gaze on Ford. "We can't afford running off to do vengeance when there's more at stake!"

Goldworm handed Ford the folder.

"Read this. If Raven Hill gets his greasy mitts on this, he can destroy Moore, and any other city he chooses. That is, of course, if he understands how to use it."

Ford read for a few minutes, thumbing through the papers and a particularly old and worn brown parchment map. Putting the documents back on the desk, he smiled while shaking his head.

"It's real? I mean… how is that possible?"

"Yes," Goldworm said.

He sat opposite Ford across the desk.

"Ford…" he trailed off, his voice vanishing into the room. "When the Brood recruited you, it was with the expectation that you would serve the interests of Moore in defense of our many enemies. That interest now is focused on that relic."

"We need you to retrieve the Lantern of Dern Blackhammer before Raven Hill lays his hands on it! If he gets it, there will be some that'll immediately capitulate to his will, appeasing that bastard. There are others just waiting to join him, and still others he will crush into submission. In all, it will mean a war… a world war."

"What do we know about the lantern other than the folklore?"

"Nothing more than the legends, really. Supposedly it grants the possessor with certain powers making them invulnerable to defeat, or laying waste to enemies, or causing armies to vanish in a blast of lightning. You know the stories."

"Anything else you can tell me?" Ford persisted, knowing his boss's knack for playing it close to the vest.

"Well, there is one other thing. We recently got a translation of a Cuniaton text regarding the lantern. I'll have it sent to you after it is converted into Elvish."

"Why not just send a militia squad to arrest Raven Hill? Or, perhaps send an assassin to eliminate him?"

"Military? Assassins? We've tried killers already, but the man is cunning and shrewd. As far as a militia, far too many people would ask questions. If word got out that the lantern was real, by the gods, we'd have every thin-headed, round-eared, orc-brained fool seeking it out. That includes the governments of our rivals. Raven Hill is aware of this too, and I'm sure he doesn't want any interference either. We need to keep this on the quiet."

"So, you want me to handle this off the map?"

Goldworm sat quietly for a moment, deep in thought. Opening a drawer, he pulled out a bottle of spirits and two glasses. He poured three fingers of the amber liquid into each and handed one to Ford.

"Yes, outside the usual channels. The official word would be you're on your own."

Goldworm looked sheepish, downed the liquor in one draft, then refilled his glass.

"We have some ideas of what is needed, or rather who will be of help on this job, but we have to pull from outside the organization. You'll need to fetch them as soon as I have all the names and locations." He sipped his liquor for a moment. "I wonder if any powder-teleportus might be laid hands on?"

"Powder-teleportus?" Ford said surprised. "Rare indeed. The only jar of that I know of is in an iron vault, in the middle of the Mosul of Trent, guarded by fifty humorless men armed with hand-cannons."

"Good, you know where to get it then! And Ford, the clock is ticking, so don't dally about!"

CHAPTER

2

Osara Han

"Oh, yes, you were a very happy boy, born to parents who loved you!" Old man Jing told Han.

"But the goddess Quan Yi has a fickle hand and dealt you a severe blow, my boy."

He sat high on the rounded white stone by the side of the road. In his hand was a horse hair rope that led to a team of small ponies attached to a cart filled with pots and pans.

"How did you know my parents?" Han asked.

"They purchased many of my wares. Kindly and wise they were."

Jing smiled, then stuck his long-stem pipe into his mouth and puffed a few times. A long tendril of white smoke drifted up in the damp air.

"I was the first one to find your parents."

Han drew in the scent of the burning topus leaf.

"What happened to them?"

"Didn't Old Sun tell you?" Jing's eyes narrowed.

"He has never mentioned it, though I have begged to know."

"Sun… not the kindest man I have met. No matter, I will tell you what he has not."

Jing took another draw from the pipe and let out another long stream of smoke into the air.

"It was nigh on twelve years ago…" He scratched his chin. "I was by the Cho Wan River, on the road coming from the marvelous city of Liang. I had replenished my supplies and was heading toward your parents' farm.

"It was the smell of something burning that caught my attention, and I looked up to see white and black smoke in the distance. I rushed ahead thinking that an accidental fire had befallen your parents…"

He trailed off as if for a moment he was reliving the event.

Han shook Jing's knee.

"Go on, please."

"I'm sorry… but to think on this matter, after all these years, is difficult." He again puffed on his pipe. "I raced my cart up a hill that overlooked the valley where your family's farm was. What I saw made my heart stop!"

"What was it?" Han asked.

"In the valley were orcs putting your family's house to the torch. The field was burned, as was the barn."

Jing looked grave.

"What was I to do? I could not fight an entire company of rogue battle orcs. So I turned my rig around and raced for the village. There I summoned the elders and town watch, and we all rushed back to the farm. We found your parents and their servants all slain."

He smiled down on Han. "…But for one child."

Jing wiped a tear from his eye.

"It was a miracle one of the soldiers found the door against a large hill, obscured by brush and a large tree. The muffled cry of a child drew us all there. As the door was opened the wail of a babe assaulted our ears."

Again he wiped his eyes with his sleeve.

"Was it for fear of the orc raid, or to shield you from the mid-day heat, we would never know, but your mother had nestled you within the produce cellar, a babe in swaddling tucked into a bassinet."

"They were killed by orcs?"

Han's face was not sad, but curious.

"Yes, a raiding party from the Low-Land."

"How did I end up sold to Sun?"

Jing laughed.

"You were not sold; he is your uncle, your mother's older brother. Who told you you were a slave?"

"Sun," Han said. "He said that I was bought after my parents died."

"That split-tongued demon," Jing said. "You are an heir to property of which your uncle has been growing rich from all these years."

"What are you doing here?" shouted Sun coming through the tall green chola stalks and onto the road. "You are keeping my ward from his daily tasks, now get!"

Jing looked at Sun, then stood up and took his ponies and cart along the road. Over his shoulder he shouted, "Don't forget what we have discussed today, young Osara Han!"

Sun watched as the cart grew smaller in the distance and vanished over a hill. He turned to Han and scowled.

"Get back to work you whelp!"

The sky grew dark as Han put the plow horses to pasture. As he passed the barn he noted its black shape devoid of detail.

Walking up towards the house he heard the strings of a situ being strummed and gay laughter filling the air. In the window the lanterns produced an eerie glow of yellow light. The laughter of Sun's friends filled him with foreboding.

"Eyes of Lore!" shouted Sun. "Roll the dice again!"

"Where is that awful brat of a slave you own?" cried a female voice. "My wine cup is empty, and I need much more if I am to sleep with you tonight!"

Laughter and shouting echoed from the house again as Han approached.

"Han, where are you!" Sun shouted.

At the door, Han took off his shoes and entered the house. His muscles ached and he was covered in dirt, but there was no time to clean up.

The wood floor creaked under his weight. Sun appeared from a side door.

"Get Ms. Chew more wine! Be quick about it, you wretch, or I'll let her beat you with the bamboo pole!"

Han ran, sheer panic climbing up his spine. Sun did not make idle threats, and he felt the pole upon his back more times than he cared to remember.

He slid to a halt at the wine barrel and quickly grabbed an earthen pitcher. Filling it with the dark red wine he dashed back to the room, careful not to spill any. Quickly, he moved from cup to cup filling each.

"Who would like to beat my servant?" Sun asked, swaying from much drink.

"Let us roll dice for the pleasure!" Ms. Chew said with great enthusiasm.

The room held several of Sun's unsavory ilk. Several of the local town guards were there, along with six ladies-for-purchase.

Sun's favorite, the madam Chew, was sitting knees bent at the dice table and the guards were sprawled about on reed mats; a cup of wine in one hand, and a lady for pleasure in the other.

Sun laughed. "Throw your dice!" he said. "Highest point wins."

The clack of the dice hitting the wooden table shot fear into Han. With each roll his fate hung in the balance, and he already heard today the goddess was fickle.

Each man cast his dice, as did the women. The sound was unnerving.

"Fong, you are the winner!" Sun said to one of the largest guards. "How would you like to do it? I have a bamboo pole and a lash!"

"Go to bed, Han," Fong the guard said. "Just go to bed."

Han looked at Sun, then Fong, then his master again. Sun opened his mouth as if to say something, but fell unconscious to the floor, curled up into a ball and began to snore.

Ms. Chew leapt up and grabbed the bamboo pole and came at Han.

"Weak minded men will not save you from punishment," she yelled.

Fong's hand blocked the pole and he held it firm.

"Enough!" was all he said, as he took the poll from Ms. Chew.

"See to Sun; he's paid good money for you and your girls for tonight." He turned to Han. "Now, go to bed."

Han raced from the room and the house. He scooped up his shoes and ran barefoot to the small shack that was his home.

He was miserable, and cried as he lay on the brown sacks of grain that made up his bed on the storehouse floor. He lay awake looking at the stars through the slats of the roof, praying for deliverance.

Running away was often his fantasy, but he felt too weak from hunger to really do it. After what seemed like an eternity, he fell asleep.

"Get out here, you worthless dog!" Sun said.

Han woke. Something struck the wall of the storehouse, and he leapt up, ran to the door and threw it open. It was late morning and he had overslept. Outside he saw Sun staggering about, looking towards the fields, then at the butcher's shed, and then back at the storeroom.

"Where is it?" Sun shouted. "You ungrateful hobgoblin! You have stolen from me!"

Still drunk from the night before, Sun swayed this way and that. Stopping, he looked at Han and pointed his finger at him.

"There you are, you runt!"

"I have stolen nothing!" Han said.

Sun's face flushed red, and he came at Han shouting.

"You've taken my chest of gold coins! Thieves are punished by death as prescribed by the law, to be carried out by the elder of the house."

He stopped and staggered to the butcher's shed. Turning back, he held a hatchet in his hand.

"Time to trim that neck of yours." He came at Han.

Han sidestepped the attack, then heard the axe bury into the door frame. He scampered outside by the stone-mill and grabbed the chain-linked wooden handles from the milling stone. Sun followed.

Sun raised the hatchet, but Han brought the handles around and struck Sun on the side of the head knocking him to the ground where he lay unconscious and unmoving. Han dropped the bloody handle; staring for a moment, he was frozen with fear. Surely when Sun woke he would commence a savage beating, and probably flay him alive for his impudence.

He rushed to the house, kicked off his sandals and dashed inside. Gathering some food and a jug of wine, he quickly made a sack from a woolen blanket and tied it with some twine.

He ran to the door and looked out into the yard. Sun was gone. Panic filled him as he put on his sandals and began walking quickly towards the field.

His only hope was to hide in the tall stalks of chola; the stems stood ten feet high. It seemed a good place for a small child to vanish in.

He made it to the field's edge and looked over his shoulder. Near the butcher's shed Sun was tipping up an upside-down barrel. He hadn't seen Han.

Quickly Han slipped into the dense forest of stalks. The wet chola gave off a crisp scent he could almost taste, like the smell of wet grass in spring.

A clump of dark clouds approached and rain followed. The sound of the drops hitting the chola leaves made enough sound that he could slip into the field unheard.

The rows were muddy, and he took his time navigating from one to the other. He counted on confusion in the dense field of vegetation to give him time to formulate his escape.

He wasn't worried about getting lost, for his sense of smell, hearing, and sight was amazingly sharp. Stopping, he sniffed the air.

The river lay to the west and he could smell the mud. If he could make it to the river, he could find the road to Liang and be gone before Sun was aware.

Sun will never find me in such a large city, he thought.

Swiftly he moved through the rows, all the while terror gnawing away at his stomach. He knew well Sun's wrath could befall him at an instant.

Behind him, he heard the clopping of hooves.

Sun must have mounted the old plow horse, he thought.

It was abundantly clear that the horse was entering the Chola stalks, for they rattled loudly like a gourd full of beans.

"Where are you?" shouted Sun. "The demon's loose in you, boy! I shall beat the monster from your worthless sack of meat!"

Han kept moving towards the end of the field. He heard Sun behind him slashing at the stalks with a chet'ya, the farmer's reaping-blade used for clearing brush and Chola stalks.

"Curse you, Osara Han! Curse the blood for which your father sprung you!" Sun said.

The hairs on the back of Han's neck stood on end. He turned and looked down the row; Sun was staring back at him.

Driving in his heels to the horses haunches, Sun charged down the column. Mud flew from the horse's hooves as the beast closed the distance. He raised the chet'ya.

Fear melted away. Han felt his blood boiling with rage. A strange feeling came over him, the feeling that he was not himself.

Sun was growing larger, as the scent of flesh filled his nostrils. He looked from side to side; he was on all fours like a drog.

Sun pulled up his horse, tumbled over the creature's head, and landed heavily crushing chola stocks. His eyes were wide with fear, as if all his drunken mania were now gone.

The blade fell from his grip and the horse reared back in fright, striking Sun in the head with its hooves. He fell into the mud, his head fractured, and blood gushing forth. The horse ran off into the stalks, its cries of fright filling the air.

The smell of the fresh blood filled Han's nostrils. The scent was delicious as if he were eating some new delightful meal. He was tempted to lap up the blood, but thought better of it.

What has happened to me? he wondered. *Why can't I stand, why is the world larger?"*

He moved around his bundle of items. The wool smelled strongly of animal musk. The items hidden within identified by smell alone: bread, cheese, and even the wine.

He saw the rags that had been his clothes, the threadbare garments… mere shreds really. They were lying in the mud trampled by Sun and the horse.

Moving to Sun, he examined him closely. It was clear that Sun was not dead, but seriously injured, and unconscious.

Sun learned two lessons today, Han thought. *Don't underestimate the son of Osara, and Osara Han is no slave!*

He wanted to laugh at this thought, but nothing came out but a low growl. Looking at Sun he had a wicked thought.

He backed up to Sun's unconscious body, lifted his tail, and sprayed his musky scent all over him. It came naturally, and he felt elated to have done it.

That will let all know that I was here and had a hand… in this bit of justice, he thought.

Moving to where the bundle lay, he realized that he had no way of lifting or carrying it. He tried dragging it through the mud for a while, but the bundle unraveled.

The rain began to fall heavier, and the sky loosed a torrent. It was no good; he would have to take only one item. He decided to take the cheese and carry it in his mouth.

The bridge over the river was not far to the south, and he could shelter under it for a time.

But what will I do after that? Surely I have nowhere to go. Even his shelter in the storehouse now seemed like a palace. *What will I do for heat? I have no hands to make a fire! This new form was becoming quite inconvenient,* he thought.

Moving sleekly, almost effortlessly along the ditch by the road, he heard the rush of the small Cho Wan River. At the turn of the road, he climbed into a bush then surveyed the surroundings.

An arched bridge, made partially of stone and partially of wood, spanned the twenty foot wide river. The murky waters rushed by at a fast pace, choked with rain and debris. Quickly, he moved from the bush and slipped down under the bridge.

Lying there was at first uncomfortable. He could not brush away the small stones littering the dry dirt, and they jabbed him in his belly. His wet fur felt itchy, and had a strange musky odor that he did not care for. Laying prone he folded his paws, one over the other, and put his head down closing his eyes.

He was now without a home and too exhausted to care. In his mind he saw the simple desires he held in the past. He felt much older and wiser, but did not know why. Listening to the driving rain on the bridge above, he felt the bite of exhaustion overtake him.

The smell of rich, dark wet sod brought visions of playing in the new morning sun on a vast green field. In the distance he saw his father roasting half a muttonbux over an open fire pit.

His mother stood nearby, her apron white from the sun, and her hands dirty from having just come from the fields.

Orcs appeared, and grabbed his mother. His father changed into a large ferocious cat with claws like daggers and fangs like cow horns. The Orcs fell by the dozen, then one got a lucky shot with a spear – his father fell wounded. An Orc approached, lifted his sword and…

Han's eyes flew open. The rain had stopped, and there were people above… he smelled them. Looking down at the waters, he saw their shadows as the sun peeked through a break in the clouds. By his shadow, one of the men was large, wearing armor, the other thin and wiry with a big hat.

"So, how long do you think it will take to get to Liang?" said one of the men, his voice deep.

"No more than three hours," the other with the higher voice said.

Liang, Han thought. *That's where I need to go.*

Slowly he climbed to his feet, picked up the cheese in his mouth, and moved to the edge of the bridge. Looking down into a large puddle he now saw himself—a large cat's face, long whiskers, and stripped black and gray fur.

For a moment his own image frightened him. He felt the fear like needles stuck into the top of his neck, scalp, and along his back.

I've become a panfar! he thought. *They've not been seen here for a hundred years…*

Something fell from the bridge into the water— a small red paper boat. Quickly it was washed down stream.

"Clever," the deep voice said.

Turning away, Han looked up the embankment and moved to the road. Skulking, he made his way onto the road. Not far away was a two wheel covered cart pulled by horses.

The men were smoking pipes and looking into the river. One man was large, almost fat, with an ample belly covered with armor made from braided cord. His long black hair was braided and hung down to his shoulders.

The other was thin, wearing the Hack'ma of a learned official. He was bald except for a tuft of blond hair atop his head.

Han snuck up and stood on his hind feet and looked into the cart. It had a long bed filled with boxes and wares. He saw items labeled with wax, three trunks, a desk, several boxes filled with papers, all secured with rope to the wagon's wooden slats.

He gingerly lifted the round of cheese into the wagon and then jumped up into the back. The wagon creaked with his weight.

"What was that?"

"Could be a Bridge Troll. Let's get out of here before he asks us for a toll."

Han felt the two men climb aboard the cart and heard the snap of the reins. The cart moved and he felt each and every pothole and undulation as the cart moved down the road.

The cart was sturdy but noisy, and Han saw the bridge growing smaller and smaller as they drove away. He was still exhausted, and even though the wagon lurched and rocked, he fell fast asleep.

Han was in a deep black slumber. It was the muffled sound of voices that roused him. Slowly, his brain became aware of the words that were being used.

"I don't remember you packing this," someone said.

"A surprise to say the least," said someone else.

Han's eyes opened. He was staring at the two men from the bridge. The fat man was grinning. The skinny one was looking concerned.

Clearly they must be surprised at finding a large cat curled up inside their wagon, Han thought.

"Stay back or I'll bite you!" Han said, and then realized that he no longer was a cat.

"Our little waif is hungry it seems," the fat man said. "But, look you there, he's brought a whole round of cheese as a gift." He grabbed his belly and laughed loudly.

"Don't be foolish, Quan," the skinny one said chiding the fat one.

"Very well," Quan laughed. "The cheese brought him maybe?"

"You must excuse my friend. He is given to fits of much humor when he should be solemn and thinking." The skinny fellow regarded Han. "Behind you is a robe, you may want to put it on."

Han realized that he was nude. Looking back he saw a bit of green silk sticking out of a box. Pulling it he discovered a beautiful robe, quickly put it on, and climbed from the wagon.

"I am Chow Ti Gong. Who might you be?" the skinny one said while raising one eye brow.

"My name is Han... Osara Han."

"And who do you belong to, Osara Han?"

"Perhaps that cheese?" Quan blurted.

"Quan, leave off the cheese please," Gong said, exasperated. "Come now, my boy... you must have a family, friends, a home, a master?"

Han regarded them for a moment, fighting back tears. His lower lip quivered, and he felt ashamed.

"I have no... fam... family," he stammered. "I have no home either..." He began to cry.

"Nonsense," Gong said. "You were born of something. Unless you wish us to believe that you are divine and born from a rock?" He smiled. "Now, out with it. What happened that brought you to the back of my wagon?"

Han sniffled. "I… am an orphan. My father and mother were murdered by orcs. I fled the place where I was living, for the master of that house beat me constantly and was cruel."

"Did you deserve those beatings?" Quan asked.

"No, sir." Han looked down at his feet now hidden by piles of cloth.

"We will soon know the truth," Gong said, as he opened a leather satchel on a strap that he wore around his shoulder.

Fishing around for a moment, he quickly produced a dark black stone.

"Hold out your hand," he instructed.

Han looked on with suspicion. "Why?"

"Curiosity? That is good. But there is also obedience to be considered. Now, hold out your hand, palm up," Gong repeated.

Han looked about considering if he should run; they were in a dead-end alley at the far end, and the two men were blocking his escape. But if he did run, where would he go? He had no other option but to do as he was told.

Gong placed the smooth stone into Han's hand.

"Now just hold it there," he said. "Are you a bad child?"

Han stood stock stiff, his arm extended and his hand supporting the round shiny stone.

"No!"

"Did you run away?"

"As I told you."

"Were you beaten for no cause?" Gong asked.

Han face grew tense. "I told you, he beat me for no reason, and often!"

"And, are you lying to us now?"

Tears fell from his eyes as Han answered.

"No."

Slowly the stone began to change color from black to gray, from gray to dark green.

"What is this?" Han asked amazed.

"It is called a liar's stone. When the one who holds it lies, it will turn from black to red."

"But it's green," Han said confused.

"That's right. Green means that you have not told the whole truth, but you have not lied either." Gong smiled.

Han again looked down at his feet. "That is true. I…"

"It's alright young one. What has happened in your past is of no concern now. You cannot swim against a strong current like regret in the raging river of life.

"Just look at Quan and I. We learned very early in life that one must let go the past to embrace the future."

The sound of cracking wood echoed down the alley. A group of men approached, each with a weapon in hand.

"Now, now, now, what have we here?" said one of the men whose dark black beard was shaggy. "Seems these fools have parked their cart in my alley. You will need to pay the tax for such foolishness."

Gong did not turn, but addressed Quan. "Would you mind taking the boy behind the cart?"

Quan laughed. "My pleasure. If they're too much for you, just let me know."

He took Han by the hand and led him around the other side. Quan bent down and whispered in Han's ear.

"Look under the wagon and watch. If you are smart, you will learn something about people."

"Now, I think we'll beat you all and take your wares," the man with the beard said.

"Leave now," Gong said in a soothing tone. "You will be the wiser for it."

"Kill him first, but keep the boy to sell to the brothel-house!"

Two bandits rushed in. Han watched as Gong bent at angles that were unnatural. Each intended blow by the bandits failed to touch him, their edged weapons striking only air. As they recovered, Gong attacked.

He was a flurry of fists and kicks. The strikes were so quick that Han did not see them until they landed on a chin, knee, face, head, chest, or back. In a matter of seconds, all the bandits were injured.

Several men were incapacitated and lying on the ground bleeding. The ambulatory ruffians helped the ones with broken bones as they made a fast exit.

The bearded bandit stopped at the end of the alley holding one hand over his nose to stop the bleeding and the other raised in a fist.

"I curse you!" he shouted, then tuned and rushed off into the street.

Han looked up at Quan who smiled down with bright white teeth and warm eyes filled with life. Gong came around the cart and brushed his robe, though it was nearly spotless.

"How did you do that?" Han asked. "You were fast like a striking snake!"

"Are you truly interested?" Gong looked very serious.

"I am!"

"This is a path that will require the utmost resolve and commitment, for it is a lifelong pursuit."

"Yes, I will devote my life to it," Han said, his eyes no longer wet.

"The fighting style is called the Steps of the Jade Spider. If you choose, you may come with us and learn it."

Gong looked over at Quan, and then smiled broadly.

"Very well," Quan laughed as he took the horses by the reins and led it to the brick wall. "Another student, another path to rebirth. Why not?"

Han watched as Quan, the horse, and the cart vanished through the wall.

"Things often are not what they seem at first, young Han," Gong said as he approached the wall.

"Be ready for a new life. Once you pass through. You will learn more than you ever dreamt of…but you must choose your own way. No other can do it for you."

He turned then vanished through the wall.

Han stood there, looking back toward the street. He looked at the wall and took a step closer. For a second, he thought about running from the alley.

Such a commitment seemed terrifying. It was possible that he was making a terrible mistake.

He took in a deep breath and focused his mind. Within he sensed the other one, the panfar. A confidence filled his spirit and he made his choice. With no further hesitation, he walked through the wall.

*   *   *

Quan raised his head and Han bent down. "Seek your destiny to the west. A guide will reveal himself, follow… the lantern." Quan fell unconscious.

Han fought his sadness, trying to remain stoic as Quan lay dying. The old master's face became calm and peaceful.

Han stood over him, his hand clasping the old man's. It was best to keep a stoic countenance when guiding a loved one to the Netherworld. Fear or sadness could cause the spirit to become disrupted, filled with fear and longing for their former life.

Ghosts are made that way, he thought.

Quan requested no healer be present, or any magic used to prolong his life. He was committed to make the final journey. His breathing was becoming shallow, and it was clear that he was beginning to enter the land of the dead.

Han looked back at the assembled students. All looked mournful and drained. Some were orphans like him, and others from noble and wealthy families whose parents paid for them to attend the school.

Han had taught at the school for ten years. It was only twenty years earlier that he had taken his first step into the world known as the Quan Gong Chow Academy of The Jade Spider.

Han remembered his surprise when he appeared in the academy courtyard, the wall of the alley melting away. He was surrounded by students. Standing there was Gong to welcome him with a nod of his head and a hearty bow.

"You are born anew!" Gong proclaimed.

The feeling when Gong said those words washed over Han and remained in his heart ever since. That day he wept long and hard as the pain and fear of his old life drained from him. Gong put his arm around him and spoke.

"It is not every day that a boy is reborn into a new family and a new way of life."

The training was hard as was the discipline and the expectations of the teachers. Students had to display the highest level of ethics and honor.

Four bells of the morn woke them, and they gathered in the courtyard. They then broke up into ten groups of five and entered the temple for meditation and prayers.

At six bells, the students trained in the combat arts, first using hand to hand, than learning weapons. At the sound of the eleven bells, they assembled for reading and writing instruction, and learned the art of administration, oration, and negotiation.

By the sound of double three bells, the students cooked and ate their evening meal. By the time they had cleaned the complex from top to bottom, it was time to prepare for meditation and harmonization.

At the sound of the double five bells, Han crawled to his dorm where he fell into his bed, and slept hard – every night.

He loved the routine day in and day out, learning a little more each time. Gong taught the students the art of fighting in the style of the Jade Spider. Han would often train blindfolded, using other senses to avoid blows, and deliver devastating strikes.

Gong also taught weapons training, and he made sure that each student could use any weapon known.

"It is here deep within your mind that you are the master of all things," Gong said. "Slow down the world, slow down your opponent. By doing so, you will become faster, see the attack before it has happened, defeat your enemy before he knows his own mind."

Quan was the philosopher and scholar, though he was himself a warrior and well trained in the martial arts. But he preferred to use reason and persuasion over fighting.

He also taught the classes in writing, reading, history, philosophy, oration, and the art of public administration.

"Remember that the wiser man is the one who can defeat his opponent without raising a hand. Use your knowledge of history and the condition of living beings to provide the life of which you desire."

"But always do good to others, for if virtue and history is your weapon, one good deed can prove more powerful than an army of millions!"

Chow was a wiry man with white hair, a stern face, and goatee beard. He taught commerce, money, politics, and magic. Of the three masters, Chow was the most reserved.

"All races covet gold and thus if you know how to manage wealth, you can barter for much greater wealth. Money buys power, but power gathers wealth.

"Magic is that which makes all matter into objects. When one knows how to manage magic, and wealth, and power, he will be able to do good deeds. Use your training and knowledge to influence politics, and wield magic to build a chest of gold, so you can do much good in this world."

But out of the three masters, it was Quan whom he regarded as a father.

That's probably why they sent Quan to bring me to the reflection pool those many years ago, he thought.

There waiting was Gong and Chow. They stood there in their brightly colored silk robes. Each looked at peace.

"Do you know why we have summoned you, Osara Han?" Chow asked.

"I do not?" replied Han, his curiosity stirring within him.

"The secret for which you have hidden in your heart, it is time for you to bring it forth. It is the half of you that must be known," Gong stated.

"The cat?" Han said with surprise.

It had been four years since he had changed from a boy to a cat. He was beginning to believe it was just a dream.

"Not a cat, but a wild panfar," Chow said with a sideways glance. "A dire cat of the ancients."

"Change," Quan simply said.

"I don't want to... I'm not sure that I can."

Han stopped and brought his emotions under control.

"I will do as I am asked," he said.

"Do not fear the beast within, for none of us have feared it. The truth of it is you are a changeling."

Quan laughed, and suddenly was not there. His robe was covering something. Gong reached over and pulled the dark green silk robe from over Quan.

Standing there was a large and black bear. He shook his head and growled quietly.

Han looked on in amazement. "I... I can't."

"It's not a matter of *can't*," Quan said, as he took the robe from Gong and applied it over his nude body. "It is a matter of *will*."

"How do I do such a thing, master?" Han felt lost.

"I will teach you," Quan said. "You will learn how to stop being disguised as a man, and learn to assume your natural form. For you are a Masquian, born of the ancient peoples of this world, known now as the changelings."

"Am I magical?" Han excitedly asked.

"No, not like the raw magic that is channeled by a wizard or magician. But, your people have had a natural ability to shift your form from your human shape. Apparently, your form is the panfar. As old as the time of the dragon kingdoms."

"Can I change into an elf or ogre, or…"

"No. There has been none recorded that have been able to change into anything other than what they are known to be. But take care… You may suffer the prejudice of others."

"Our kind has always been bedeviled. You are not alone for those like us live in many different places of the world, and hold many different forms. Take for example the flying Masfalcons in the north who assume the shape of their halfling self when not the large flying predators," said Chow.

Quan cleared his throat. "Also, there are the Bear people, and the Fulkirk people, and the Mer people."

"There are many out there in the world who knowing or unknowing are of our kind. Some are evil, some are good, and some are uncaring. You will need to be wary and judicious of the use of your ability.

"You will need to be the master over your change, so you may be a man or your other form at will. There will be those who fear you, and if discovered, will try and kill you," Gong said.

"Ignorance is the destroyer of civilizations, Osara Han, and the murderer of all that is good," Quan said. "You will learn to be the master." He laughed. "You will learn!"

Han shook himself from his thoughts. Quan's breathing was now coming in staggered gulps, nearly gasps. He drew in deeply and exhaled… and then silence. A moment would pass, and then suddenly he would breathe in again, like a man struggling to rise from under the tidewater, getting his face just above the surface, then going down again.

Han leaned down and whispered in Quan's ear.

"You have taught us well, my master. It is time that you find your next world. We will be fine here. The school will live on."

Quan exhaled, his face fell pale as the blood drained from it. The man's body stiffened and Han fought back tears.

Quan's heart was solid gold, and now that gold was to be put back into the land. Quan changed form, returning to the shape of the bear. His fur was mostly gray, and he had grown shriveled and gaunt with time.

Turning, Han addressed the assembled students and teachers.

"The last of the masters is gone. Let us guide him through the catacombs of the land of the dead to rebirth."

Han fell to his knees and began chanting the ancient song of the dead. The detailed guide would help his spirit to navigate the pitfalls to the Netherworld.

It was only by giving back to the students that Han would repay those three masters for their guidance and kindness. Sitting back he realized that he was the master now.

*   *   *

As the years passed the school continued to flourish, even as the new emperor demanded all non-imperial schools disband. Han saw the truth: Emperor Qing's officious rules and regulations meant to destroy all independent learning.

The decrees had flowed from the imperial palace impacting all those who he thought a threat to his rule. One morning Han woke to the sound of hammering on the main gate.

The sky was dark, and the students were not yet awake. Walking down to the entrance he saw the banners of the emperor bobbing on poles just outside.

The hammering stopped, and the banners vanished. Reaching the gate, he pulled back the bolt and opened the door. No one was there. Turning, he saw a paper nailed to the gate: *By order of the emperor, all schools not sanctioned by royal decree shall disband immediately upon pain of death.*

He took it down and read it again. A flame of anger rose up from somewhere in his gut.

Why? he thought. *Why punish the children?*

A voice chimed inside his head.

"Han, you could choose to fight… but that would mean bloodshed and maybe the death of many of your students and teachers. Choose to bend to the gale, for hope dwells in the west.

"Close the school and let it blossom without walls, and when you return, your newly found wisdom will outshine the emperor."

He discontinued enrollment and concentrated on teaching the students to teach the art to others beyond the walls of the school. By the time the guards of the Qing came and nailed the closure notice to the door, it was only Han and his teachers who were present.

Han and the other teachers divided the school's wealth between them, then he laid a map of the provinces out on the library table and asked where each teacher would go.

One by one they pointed to different parts of the map, each swearing an oath to continue, in secret, to teach the art. Finally Han looked over the document, and pointed off the map to the west.

The other teachers looked surprised and concerned. He smiled warmly and spoke.

"I know you're worried," Han said. "It is only a matter of time before the emperor puts a bounty on all our heads. He can't risk us organizing a rebellion. I'm seeking a place in the west, in the lands of the dwarves and elves. If it is my fate to die, it is for the gods to say when, not the emperor"

He turned and retrieved a jug of wine from a shelf and several blue porcelain cups. Pouring each full, he looked down at the map and smiled.

Lifting his cup, he held a toast to his friends and their former life at the school.

"Let all here know that as Quan, Gong, and Chow were my adopted fathers, so you are my adopted brethren. Like a treasure hidden within a locked chest, I so keep these memories of my life locked within my bosom.

"Come morning, our new lives begin. Be wary of the Qing's men. I fear they are not done with us yet."

Each teacher offered a toast and in turn they all drank their fill until the bottle was emptied. They each left silently, back to their chambers for the last time.

Han, stayed staring out into the courtyard, his mind filled with the images of a twelve year-old boy standing, jaw open, and eyes wide with amazement.

The stars moved overhead, and the two moons rose and fell as he stared. The bells of the town clock struck five.

He went to his room, gathered up his belongings, secured his sacks of money in his saddle bags and retrieved his horse and pack horse.

Han walked to the wall in the courtyard where he'd arrived those many years before. It was an ancient anchor point; the end and beginning of a travel-portal.

Clearing his mind, he climbed into the saddle. He moved his hands in the air drawing glowing patterns that Chow had taught him.

The portal erupted in a red light that faded into a shimmering picture of an alley.

"May the gods watch over you, my brothers," he said, as he passed into the city of Liang. Behind him he used the sign to close the doorway, then walked his horses out of the alley and into the crowded streets of the city.

Han traveled for several weeks. The weather was changing, becoming colder along the Chir Chi Mountains.

Having left the comfort of the wispy green pines, he now approached the mountain summit; a barren place filled with snow covered stooped-trees, pitch black rocks, and alpine pools devoid of vegetation.

Once on the other side, he descended down towards the border town of Ho. Beyond Ho was the barbarian lands, the places of the dwarves and elves, and the beasts of the Outland.

He had never been outside his native lands before, and the legends told of cannibal women and boar-headed men waiting to devour any who were witless enough to encounter them. He chuckled at the thought.

Legends are rarely true, he reasoned in his mind.

Down the dirt road, he went into the valley. From his lofty place on the mountain, he saw smoke rising from the little stone chimneys that protruded from the middle of the round dwellings.

Ho was small, truly a village, far flung from the trading routes of the south. Surveying the fields he saw they were recently harvested, and the livestock seemed absent.

Halting his horse he pulled out a small leather codex from his pocket and opened the page to Ho.

"A small village that makes their living growing boc, ter-ter, and yehang, and they harvest oxen grass to make distilled hoopil – a powerful liquor with mystical properties," he read aloud.

Patting his horse on the head, he added, "Well, Wei, seems as good a place as any to rest up before going into the Outlands."

Wei snorted and shook his head. Han put his heels to his horse and began moving again.

Why are there no people out working? he thought. *If it's due to the chill in the air, why live way up here in the first place? Still…*

After a while, the switchback trail leveled out alongside pasturelands. The road was muddy and rutted, containing the occasional pothole.

Han's mount and pack horse leisurely maneuvered around them as it headed for the town gate. Taking in the visage, he saw the symbol for good fortune, made of wood, at the edge of town like a door-less gate. No defensive wall was visible, and Han saw the magic symbol to ward off evil lying in the mud.

As he entered the town he saw no people, and none came out. He thought this rather strange, for he had been through many towns of recent and the town's folks always came forth, if for nothing else but to try and solicit money for goods.

Bringing his horses to the watering trough he dismounted and let the beasts drink. The air was cold, almost chilled, and his breath hung in the air like a cloud of smoke.

In the air was the scent of fear. Listening closely, he heard someone whispering.

"Is he one of them?"

Han walked over to one of the homes, laid a three foot by three foot square rug down under the eaves, and sat down. Closing his eyes, he drove his mind into a deep state of meditation.

The world was but a shadow, an illusion of reality, and he was not connected to it, but for his extraordinary hearing. He became aware that a door opened, footsteps… maybe five people, approached. He felt their body heat and knew they were ten feet away.

They came closer. Only a few feet away now. One reached for him. He stood up.

Several men carrying rakes dropped them and ran towards the adjacent house. Han did not move; he stood there with his arms folded and his gaze upon them.

One man—an old gray haired elder— stayed, but stared in fright at Han's sudden move.

"Why are you fearful, gentle grandfather?" Han asked.

The man swallowed heavily. "We… the bandits…" he said.

"Bandits?" Han looked on. "I am no bandit. But, I see your fear clearly now. How long ago?"

"They left today. Took with them our food, our harvest, our livestock, and liquor all gone!" he said, his fear turning to anger.

"And where are the emperor's soldiers?" Han furthered.

"They do not come when we need them," the old man said.

"And the bandits left your village how long ago?"

"Not more than an hour. They said that if we make trouble, they will rape our children, both boys and girls," he said with fright.

"Which way did they go?"

"By the north road. They travel slowly with all our goods." The old man looked at Han with a frown. "But they were many, you are one?"

"Do bandits not travel as one? Do they not steal as one? Do they not make wickedness as one?" Han asked.

"I suppose, but they are many," the elder repeated.

Han smiled warmly and patted the old man on his shoulder.

"A man who is learned, does he not carry within him the knowledge of many?"

The old man now looked upon Han as if he were crazy.

"It's not books that will save you from swords and spears," he coolly said.

"If I do this for you, all I ask is that you provision me for a trip through the Outlands, you need not pay me other."

"Outlands? You are mad!" the old man said. "But if you dispose of our bandits, you will be welcome in our village for all time, mad or not."

"I fear, gentle grandfather, that I will not live for all time. Nonetheless, your open arms warm my heart. I shall do this for you." He moved to his horse, untied his pack animal and mounted his steed. "Did they have wagons?"

"Yes, several."

"Look for me by night fall," Han said as he directed his horse out of town along the north road.

The bandits were not hard to follow. They left a clear trail of broken liquor jars, fruit rinds and discarded clothing.

That's odd, Han thought. *These men do not fear for discovery.*

Stopping his horse at a fork in the road, he looked along one leg that extended into a long valley. It was clear that there was no debris along that path.

He looked up the other path that went north through black craggy rocks.

"Legion of Ching XI," he read on a tall wooden sign post.

He patted his horse on the neck.

"Well, Wei, it seems that these bandits might just turn out to be more than what they seem."

He mounted and headed north.

He began the ascent up to a narrow pass. The smell of smoke was in the air; a fresh fire with burning green bows.

The smoke was getting stronger and after a few minutes he heard men, their voices brash with arrogant arguing.

Finding a large crag, he tied Wei to a boulder and proceeded on foot. There was a narrow pass and a sharp turn with sheer cliffs on either side.

Peering around the corner he saw a broad opening covered in dark green grass, maybe a quarter mile wide. In the middle was a group of wagons and a few tents.

Smoke rose up from an unseen campfire somewhere in the middle. This was not a legionnaire's camp, but something more crude.

He began walking towards the camp. There seemed to be no lookouts, no guards, and no concern. The grass was moist and his foot falls made no sound.

The crackle of the camp fire snapped and popped in his ears, as did the dice rolling and men insulting one another. He moved cautiously, and closed the distance quickly.

At the camp's edge, he heard the men talking, making jokes and boasting of their theft. Peeking around a tent, he saw the bandits in the middle changing into Ching guardsman uniforms.

They were all big men, overfed and somewhat drunk. It was clear that they had no need for any of the food or drink, other than for want of greed.

The way of the world since the passing of the White Death, Han thought.

He cleared his mind of any anger or malice, and filled it with only kindness and compassion. Stepping out from the back of the tent he walked into the middle of the startled guardsmen.

"What in the name of the gods!" exclaimed a man in a captain's cloak.

"Where did he come from?" shouted one of the lesser soldiers.

"Imagine my surprise," Han began, "when I started to search for bandits and found the emperor's guardsman."

"What?" the captain said surprised at Han's impudence.

"Honor is a splendid thing, composed of a man's true self. Those who feel its pull may flee now, walk away, take nothing and go. Those of you who have no such feeling, pray now for the forgiveness of the people you have harmed," Han said.

"Is he joking?" said a soldier coming out of one of the tents and securing his sword belt around his shoulder.

The man with the sword drew it and charged at Han. Swinging as if Han was an easy kill, he found only a savage blow to the back of the head and darkness.

Han let the guard fall to the ground with a thud.

"You can't kill a guardsman of the emperor!" shouted the captain.

"*Kill* is for those weak of mind, and *can't* is only for those who are limited in their love for living," Han replied.

He put his arms at his sides and calmed his mind once more.

"Now, I offer again. Those of you who know you have done wrong and wish to atone for it, take flight, go to the temple and pray forgiveness!"

Several men turned and ran from the camp.

"Cowards!" shouted the captain. "You'll be boiled alive for your cowardice!"

"They were wise," Han said. "Now, for the rest of you?"

He moved with the swiftness of a master in the art of the Jade Spider. A kick swiftly planted here, a flurry of punches there, all the while bending in ways that men trained in the art of the sword could not strike.

One by one they fell to Han's fluid and surgical attack. Turning, he examined the field. Many men lay prone, several tents were a skewed, and the captain looked in shock.

"Now for you, Captain."

The captain held his sword at his side, his eyes wide with fear, his breaches wet from defilement. Looking from the left to the right, he considered his options and found only one.

Turning his sword on his chest, he threw himself upon it. The blade hit home and made a crunching sound as it pierced through his ribcage. He groaned loudly with the pain and rolled onto his side.

Han approached, and knelt down. "I was thinking of letting you go," he said.

"Why didn't you say so?" gasped the captain.

"I didn't think you so stupid as to kill yourself," Han answered with a shrug. "But you have proven me wrong."

The captain's eyes rolled up into his head and his body quivered with a death spasm.

Standing, Han drew in a deep breath—the smell of carnage filling his sense with a desire to feast, bathe in the blood, and let it wash over him.

It was the panfar within that demanded to be sated. Resisting the impulse, he began to gather up the villager's items into the wagons. He linked the wagons into a train and put the scene behind him as he headed back toward the pass and the village.

"Someone comes!" a child shouted, as he ran down the northern road into the village. "It is that man, and he has wagons!"

Han drove the wagons into the village. Coming to a halt he felt the energy from the gathering villagers. A young man called to him to tell them what had happened.

"They had a change of heart," Han said.

Villagers descended on the wagons and searched for their stolen items. Some carried away bags of grain while others, jars of liquor, and bundles of boc, ter-ter, and yehang. The elder looked up at Han in disbelief.

"How?"

"How can one man change the hearts of many?" Han smiled warmly as he looked about. "Just ask your fellow villagers, for when I came here their hearts were cold and now they are warmed again."

"A bargain is a bargain," the old man said. "Bring this man all the provision he can carry for a trip over the mountain, and across the Outlands. Spare nothing for him, for he is a hero!"

Han laughed softly. "Not a hero, Grandfather," he said.

"We will remember you as a hero for all time, you shall be a legend," the elder said. "Now, you shall come to the hall for a feast in your honor!"

"I am just passing through and—"

"Nonsense. We will not hear of it! Come and know our hospitality, since we did not provide much of it earlier. You can bid us farewell in the morn if you like, or perhaps you might like to make a wife of one of our daughters here?"

Han smiled. "I am a monk, old master," he lied. "I am sworn to poverty and chastity."

The old man looked on Han with some bemusement,

"Then let it be drink and food that sates your need, but know that if you decide to take a woman, let it be one of our fine daughters."

"I will keep it in mind, honorable grandfather."

It was a most exalted affair, as the villagers presented speeches and offered toasts, and the townspeople recited poems and odes to Han. All the while Han's true self was active, pacing within his mind, anxious for some reason.

He drank modestly, and ate well. He was hugged and bowed to, and even carried in a sedan car around the hall once. Finally, he retired to the home of the elder, where he made ready to sleep.

Propping his saddle bags near the hearth, he laid out a wool blanket. Folding it over so he would be sandwiched between the folds, he kneeled and warmed his hands by the fire.

A snorting sound caught his attention, and he looked over at Wei and the pack-horse standing in the small stable in the corner of the oval-shaped home. Several sheep and two goats were also there, snuggled down into balls of wool and coarse hair.

He was tired from the day's exploits and was just closing his eyes.

"Osara Han?" someone said aloud.

Han leap to his feet. There was an elf standing there in the room.

"Who are you?" Han asked in a low voice as to not wake the elder or his family.

"I am Ford Efferguard," Ford said with a bow.

"What is your business with me?" Han sensed no threat, though he remained in a defensive stance.

"I am here seeking your help, for we are bound by a common need," Ford said.

"Who sent you?"

"Those who sent me are offering to champion your cause for re-opening your school, and to build a temple to Quan, Gong, and Chow for their everlasting souls. They want to provide you with wealth, and a chance to fulfill your destiny."

"What do you know of my destiny?" Han asked.

Ford smiled. "I'll leave it to my employers to hash that out with you. I'm just the messenger."

"Who is your employer?" Han queried.

"You are invited to meet him, if you dare," Ford said. "You have but to agree to our terms, and we will be off."

"Terms?"

"You lay no claims to the object we are to acquire, and speak of this to none other than those you will be working with. You seem to have nothing to lose at this point in your life."

"The gods are fickle creatures," Han said. "It seems that my path is not my own."

"Is any of ours?"

Han chuckled. "I guess not."

He picked up his saddle bags and turned to his horse,

"Wei, you are released of my service. Take the pack horse and find a new master. Go your own way now."

He looked to Ford. "You are an elf, from the west?"

"I am," Ford said with a smile. "It is a wonderful place, the city that I come from."

"Are we to go there?"

"Not far from it," Ford said. "We don't even have to travel across the Scablands, or as your people call it, the Outlands."

"Really?" Han came closer to Ford. "Then do what it is you need to, for I'll come with you."

Ford nodded his head in agreement.

"Then let us away to finalize our arrangement."

He produced a jar half full of golden powder that glowed softly.

"We have a story among my people of the Emperor Po Chong, who used the Golden Vale to travel throughout the empire battling dragons."

Removing the lid, Ford tapped some into the palm of his hand and turned to Han.

"Nice story, but to tell you the truth I hate this way of travel. Be quick when I open the doorway, for if we are caught in transition as it closes, we might lose a limb, or worse."

Throwing the dust into the air the powder hung suspended for a moment, making a jagged golden mirror in the air. A flash of light illuminated the room and in the distance a crack of thunder echoed. The golden light vanished and a hole appeared.

Han saw a tiled floor, wooden table and three elves looking back at him.

"Now," yelled Ford as he jumped through the gateway.

Han followed closely behind. Another crack of thunder, and the doorway snapped shut.

CHAPTER

3

Aor's Child

Prince Volfgang Von Harigan looked down from the battlements of his castle over the green rolling hills of his kingdom. The new morning light shown with the luster of gold upon the Midlands, and he knew he would never tire of seeing such a sight.

Looking up at the azure sky, he mused.

"Rain to quench the land, pleasant lush green of hills, none tire of harvest and plenty, all hearts and souls the Midland fills."

He trailed off in thought.

"As close to paradise as a mortal can get," he finally said. Turning to his chancellor, he smiled a broad toothy grin. "What do you think?"

Lord Von Lay thought for a moment.

"My prince, it is your fairness, good judgment, and kindness that makes these lands seem so."

Harigan laughed. "Maybe so, but there is no other way to rule, is there?"

"It is for you to say, my lord," Von Lay said bowing slightly. "But your wife thinks over-kindness shows weakness, and there are many within and without who covet your stations and lands."

"I will always rule in the tradition of my family, who have

53

ruled the Midlands for more than a thousand years."

Your wife does not share your sentiments."

"My wife?" Harigan shook his head. "I can still remember the day of my marriage." He laughed. "I, a lad of two score and three, and my blushing bride only a score and eight."

"The castle was a flood with gifts from near and far," Von Lay said.

"Many oaths as well." Harigan chuckled.

"She was, and still is, the most beautiful woman in the kingdom." Harigan lost his smile. "Yet, her family ruled with beastly force."

He turned and looked out over the battlements again.

"After all these years she is still a cold, formidable, and often angry woman. I have had to reprimand her on many occasions for being abusive to her servants and looking down upon the peasantry as objects to use and throw away. She is quite unreasonable."

"Pity you had no say in the matter of your marriage," Von Lay said, standing next to him.

Harigan gazed at the horizon.

"An arrangement made at my birth. When I became ruler, she was brought to me. We had never met before. From the very moment of our meeting, it was clear that we were very different people."

"Differences of mind are always plain to see," Von Lay said.

"Differences of the heart cannot be seen so easily," Harigan added.

"There are some who say she makes the court decisions."

Harigan shook his head.

"Such nonsense. If she did, the peasants and nobles alike

would revolt."

"My lord, the princess has been keeping her company with the Earl of Westfax and his ilk," Von Lay said.

"What make you of these affairs?"

"A plot is afoot, my lord, the nature of which we do not quite know yet."

"Come with me," Harigan said.

Turning, he walked into the parapet and down the spiral stairs. Entering the courtyard he headed quickly to the castle. Von Lay rushed to keep up with the big man's long strides.

Inside the castle they moved up a set of stairs to Harigan's ample study. Stopping at his desk Harigan remained standing as he looked over many stacks of papers.

Pulling out a blank sheet, he quickly scrawled out an order and handed it to his chancellor.

"Take this – it authorizes you to have all resources at your disposal to discover if a plot is in action."

Von Lay took the paper, rolled it up and put it securely in his belt. Harigan turned away and walked to the window. For a moment the room was silent.

Looking down through the small circles of glass into the courtyard, Harigan saw several of his cousins playing corbitall—a game played with four rackets, two soft flexible balls and a net.

The two young men were frantically dashing from side to side, a racket in each hand, keeping each ball aloft while trying to make the other miss. He turned back to Von Lay, disappointment etched on his face.

"It is here in the Midlands that the heart truly resides. We buffer Moore from Carth, and Carth from Ter, and Hob from Mo'ab, and any number of competing city-states. Many would love to see our neutrality compromised, and the Midlands plunged into war."

"Like that fellow who came here craving admission to court. The one your wife supported... Raven Hill was his name."

"Yes. That man was infested with intrigue," Harigan said.

Von Lay laughed. "Yes, and you turned him out with your hounds at his heels - to the chagrin of the princess."

"Yes." Harigan laughed for a moment. "Continue to observe, and keep me informed."

"I shall indeed, my lord," Von Lay said as he turned and left.

Harigan sat at his desk, a mass of papers atop the smooth polished surface. Taking one document, he read it. He dipped his quill into the inkwell and scrawled out his agreement to send one hundred freemen volunteers north as soon as they could be recruited.

He took down another paper— a request that he commission repairs to the Westfax city water clock.

He signed the document, noted the cost, and listed his desire for a report of the repair after the work was done. And so it went, page after page, request after request, all the while the light outside dwindled.

He stood from the desk and lit his lamp. Walking around the table, he stretched his legs.

Looking out the window onto the corbitall field, he saw the net moving with the wind. The courtyard was empty and only a flock of thrushes littered the court chattering at one another.

"I've come for you, my husband. It's time to attend dinner. If you were absent, it would look poorly upon our house." The princess stood in the doorway.

Harigan smiled warmly at her, and for a moment he regarded her beauty and grace with admiration. She was a vision, and her lovely green eyes only served to enhance her pale and sharply defined facial features.

Her dark black hair hung down to her shoulders, and she

fingered it as she looked at him.

"Well," she said, "are you going to attend?"

She attempted to foster a smile; the tension in her face clearly showed that she was attempting a very unnatural action.

He grinned and boasted a great laugh at her attempt to be friendly. He thought, maybe she was finally making a transition, growing more cordial.

"No point in always looking as if you have just eaten a crabapple," he said, as he walked to her and laid his muscular arm across her shoulders.

She was rigid, but he knew in his heart she was trying.

The Grand Feasting Hall held the two dozen nobles of the royal court. Along one wall was a massive fireplace, filled with large boulders of white fuelstone providing warmth and light.

In the middle, a set of large oaken tables formed a square, and benches followed the perimeter separated only by the ornate chairs of the prince and his princess. Racks of candles were suspended by a chain overhead, and candelabras stood at intervals along each of the tables. All those who were seated came to their feet.

"Sit, sit," Harigan bade them. "Do not let me ruin your conversations with my entrance."

The throng again took their seats. Harigan took up his place at the table and waited for his wife to sit before sitting himself. For a moment he regarded his guests, then sat beside his wife.

Some he knew intimately: Fredric Redbreast of Stutgil, Sir Varance Goodall the Earl of Westfax, Lord Greenbourgh the Earl of Bottomslund, and many more all talked and ate. Beside each of the men were their wives with their resplendent dresses, fancy hair, and dramatically ornate hats.

Standing, he held up his chalice and all conversations stopped.

"What is it that makes a man noble?" he asked.

"Honor, my lord!" called out Fredric Redbreast.

"Obedience, my lord!" shouted Levon of Stutgil.

"Power!" said the Earl of Westfax.

"Justice and patience!" called the Earl of Bottomslund, the prince's cousin.

"It is all true," Prince Harigan said. "All true but for power. For it is my experience that unrestrained power leads to discontent and ruin. I toast all of you, for your honor, valiant service to our country, and patience in times of trouble. May the god Theodite lay blessings at your door, and great wealth into your coffers." He drank.

All assembled raised their cups and followed suit. Sitting again, he took up his dagger and fork. On his plate was a spiced ullius fowl, recently roasted on a spit over a kitchen fire.

The baked plat root was soft and tender and the meat of the ullius fell from the bone as he took one of the wings and stripped the meat from it.

As he reached for his chalice, he saw his wife. She was gingerly picking pieces of meat from the roasted bird. The princess looked over at him with what appeared to be her desperate attempt at a smile.

He looked into her eyes, and there he was struck by a dark malevolence hidden within. Her smile was icy and unwelcoming, as if she knew an evil joke at his expense.

Sweat began to appear on his forearms. He mopped his arms with is napkin. Sweat appeared on his brow and he mopped that too.

"It seems to be rather hot in here tonight." Her gaze never left him, as if she were studying him carefully.

Breathing was becoming difficult, and his throat felt swollen.

"More wine, my throat is parched," he gasped as he became dizzy.

The cup fell from his hand and spilled on the table. The talking stopped and he heard the sound of armor clanking.

His sight faded and his hearing too, but in the distance he thought he heard the Lord High Chancellor say loudly, "Seize the princess and Westfax; they are under arrest for treason!"

Harigan struggled against the imposing darkness, but to no avail. A clap of thunder echoed in his ears, and the darkness and silence fell in upon him.

*   *   *

The Lord High Chancellor caught the prince as he fell from his chair. Easing him to the floor, Von Lay kneeled down putting his ear to the prince's chest. He heard a faint heartbeat.

"You, Paige! Fetch the royal surgeon, make haste!" he commanded.

The Paige dashed from the feasting hall and vanished into the brightly lit corridor. In that moment the Earl of Westfax produced a dagger, plunged it into a guard, grabbed the princess by the arm, and fled over the table and out a side door.

"Pursue them, you fools, "Von Lay shouted.

The chase was short lived, for the princess and Westfax had vanished. Returning to the hall, the senior guard reported in.

"They are nowhere to be found, my lord. One moment they were there, and the next, gone."

"Take a detachment and start searching the gardens and the Downs. The passageway they fled down has a secret door. It leads to both," Von Lay said.

Levon of Stutgil balled his fist up and slammed it into his hand.

"They must be found!" His eyes were wide with rage.

Von Lay stood and raised his hand.

"Silence!" he commanded. "It's true that there has been evil done here tonight, but there will be no vengeance done until the Justice Knights are summoned. There must be a trial performed. Where is that surgeon?" he shouted.

"With the prince incapacitated, who will rule?" Redbreast asked.

"With the princess outcast and accused of treason, it falls upon the shoulders of the Lord High Chancellor, until a successor is declared," Stutgil said.

"Make way!" shouted the captain of the guard as he escorted the surgeon into the room.

"My word," the surgeon exclaimed as he looked upon the prince. "Look on his nails and his lips. He is poisoned. We must remove him to his bedroom."

"What sort of poison?" Von Lay demanded.

"I'd wager that it's gilliad poison. He's taken a dose fit to kill a dragon. I know of no cure, antidote, nor have I heard of anyone who's ever recovered from such a poisoning."

"Then your work is done here." Von Lay dismissed him. "If it's not in the hands of such a skilled man trained to help those mortal, it must lie in the hands of those skilled in other arts!"

"Other art?" the physician asked.

"The monks who reside on the mountain. Their art."

The doctor looked grave.

"The god they serve is beyond most rational minds."

"Aor is the name of their god," Von Lay said.

Two men arrived with a litter. Von Lay helped lift Harigan onto the stretcher.

Von Lay looked at the doctor.

"That religious order is said to know the type of magic that most healers don't dare practice."

Turning, he called over one of the guards.

"Listen carefully; travel to the east until you come to the base of Hillmound, the black mountain. Follow the road. You'll eventually come to a fork. One way is a craggy mountain path. Take that trail and you'll find an ancient gate. Summon the monks who dwell within."

Von Lay put his hand on the young man's shoulder.

"Tell them that your lord comes. Tell them that his illness is from gilliad buds. Say this phrase, *varius noctum etum derutus Aor vengata*. When they hear these words, they will change their countenance toward you. Now go, time is of the essence."

The soldier rushed out calling for the fastest horse.

"You," the chancellor said, pointing at a servant. "Wrap the prince tightly in his silken sheets, and have someone fetch ice from the cellars. We will need ten full buckets. Have the buckets delivered to the main gate portcullis; there will be a wagon waiting. Empty the buckets into the back of the wagon. We will be there shortly."

*　　*　　*

Harigan was falling through darkness. His body was filled with pain. Time seemed absent and he hoped to hear a familiar voice, a comforting word from a friend, a family member. There was only silence

For how long the silence and darkness encased him he did not know, but it seemed like an eternity.

Then, like a faraway burning candlewick in his mind, there was a light.

Feeling the pain subside, his eyes came open. A fuzzy image of white light and blurry colors assailed his senses.

He saw a beautiful river valley, green and lush. Animals

abounded, some grazing, some flying, some rushing this way and that. The colors were rich, richer than anything he knew, and in his soul he felt as if he had feasted upon nourishment he had never experienced before.

In the distance he saw a great mountain rising up, and at the top was a temple with a shiny domed roof covered in polished bronze or gold. Shielding his eyes from the glare, he felt compelled to go there.

"You are a miserable excuse for a subject," a low voice whispered in his ear. "Come to my house, and I will grant you audience and raise you up!"

"Why can't I move?"

"Pathetic creatures such as you have weak wills. You are pathetic because many of you call to me – pray to me – will me to pay them for work done in my service – and the reality is, they have done nothing for me… and I am a god," the voice said. "Exercise your divine will; you have the strength."

Harigan concentrated. The weight of his body vanished, and he was moving. His feet felt light as air and he moved swiftly down from where he was, across the grassy plain and to the mountain.

"You have surprised me, mortal," the voice said. "Most lack the will and beg me to help."

Harigan flew along a cobblestone road; he followed it up the mountain to the base of a broad set of stark white stairs. At the top, a massive forged bronze door was closed.

"Who have you come to see?" asked the voice.

"The master of this house," Harigan boldly stated.

The doors flew open, and the inside pulsed with energy.

"I have expected you from the moment the Realms were born," the voice said from inside. "Think you so powerful as a god?"

"I am no god!" Harigan replied.

He strode into the room. As soon as he crossed the threshold he felt the floor upon his feet. The stone was cold, smooth, finished with great skill.

The inside was lit by several floating orbs of light, the nature of which Harigan did not know. They moved from place to place illuminating the floor, walls and ceiling, but not all at the same time.

He walked for what seemed hours. Looking back he saw darkness, looking forward was the orbs' confusing light.

This is madness! he thought. *Where am I to go — lost as I am?*

He looked up and before him was a gigantic golden throne. Sitting in it was a creature six stories tall with a man-like body, brooding brow, and a long white beard.

In one hand he held a club, sporting a great root-like knob on the end. In his other hand he held a glowing golden chalice.

"Harigan, do you know who I am?"

"No. Some god of men?"

Laughter fell from the heavens like thunder.

"Yes, one of the gods of men. You call me Aor, Lord of Making, and keeper of the Cudgel of Retribution. You have come to serve me.

"Gifts given by the gods have been lost in your world and must be recovered. There are those in the Mortal-lands who seek these treasures to use to undo the making of the worlds. You will serve me, retake those lost items, and set all to rights again in your world."

Harigan shook his head.

"I'm a prince in my lands, a man with responsibilities."

Again the laughter fell upon him.

"Look you here!"

An image appeared around him of a woman and a man coupling; their sweaty bodies twisted together. The woman rolled to one side, and Harigan reeled back.

The princess sat up and wiped her brow with the end of a blanket.

"Westfax, you have always made me shake with pleasure. My husband was a fool, and I hope he's dead. Now you must do your part!"

Westfax stood up. "I'll raise an army and destroy that ass-leach, the chancellor."

He walked over to a bowl and poured some water into it. He cleaned himself then looked back at the princess.

"Are you ready to shake again?"

The image faded and Harigan balled his fists.

"Treason!" he angrily said. "High treason – and my wife!"

"Yes. Mortal business is an unpleasant affair. Now, look into the possible future."

An image again appeared, and Harigan saw the princess as she cowered. A large man approached her and pointed something at her. A raised scar developed on her face. She screamed, and smoke filled the air. The scar appeared as an H. The image faded.

"There will be a reckoning for you. But until that day, you must serve me."

*   *   *

William Hatly was a teamster, not a soldier. But when the Lord High Chancellor called upon him to drive the wagon that contained the prince, he could not refuse.

The prince was the greatest man he knew, and if it would help to save his life he would walk into the fires of the underworld for him. Looking back, he saw a complement of armed cavalrymen. To his right was the Lord High Chancellor.

The wagon jerked up and down as it rattled along the uneven road. William maneuvered around the largest of the potholes and ruts, but the smaller ones he felt would do little damage, and merely ran straight over them.

"Who are these priests we are to visit?" William asked.

Von Lay glanced back at the body of the prince, lying on a bed of ice, wrapped in silk.

"Warrior monks of old, skilled in mystical healing arts," he said.

"Dark arts?" William looked grave.

"No, not that sort of magic. They're more like experts in medical magic."

"How do you know of them?"

Von Lay felt uncomfortable. "You don't get to be the Lord High Chancellor and not know important things like who the Monks of Aor are."

"Aor?" William said visibly shaken. "I thought they were extinct or just a legend."

"There are some who still practice that form of healing arts, but they no longer perform… the medical experiments."

"My grandfather used to tell us stories of how those monks would steal men, women, and children, and do unspeakable things to them – unnatural things with herbs, medicine, and magic."

"True, but they were more than that. Many of them studied the arcane as a means for higher understanding. The monastery at Carborn near the Scablands contains a library that has scrolls as far back as the first Kingdom," Von Lay said.

"How do you know all of this?" William asked.

Von Lay realized he had said too much.

"From talking with many who are learned in these areas."

But the truth was very different. He was intimate with the inner working of the Aor church, for he was a monk sent to get close with the house of Harigan. Over several years, he worked his way into the royal confidence.

When a new Lord High Chancellor was needed, he was the natural choice. For twenty years he influenced decisions that would one day make bring the church from the darkness into the light; to put to bed the dreadful things his order had done.

William pulled up on the reins and the cart came to a halt. Down the road came the young soldier dispatched from the castle. He appeared dazed and only stopped his horse when he nearly collided with the wagon.

"Lord Chancellor?" he asked, surprised.

Von Lay reached out and grabbed the man's reins. "What happened?"

"They tried to turn me away, then someone hit me from behind." He rubbed the back of his head.

"Two bullish fellows grabbed me and raised their clubs to brain me, and I said the words. They stopped and a man spoke to me. I told them of the poison then he said to come tell you that preparations will be made."

"When we arrive, I will enter with the prince. You will lead the procession back to the castle. Be wary, I feel in my bones that there is mischief about," Von Lay said.

Looking back at the wagon the soldier seemed confused. "Is that ice the prince is lying on?"

"It helps slow the poison. How much further to the gates?"

"A quarter mile or so."

The teamster snapped the reins and the wagon thunked and

trundled up the pass. Black jagged stone lined the road and moisture leaked incessantly from the cracks.

Coming around a corner the weathered gate of the monastery came into view. Green tarnished straps held the thick dark brown timbers that blocked the roadway.

Slowly the behemoth doors opened, and on either side warriors with bows and crossbows stood. Armed men appeared from the darkness, swords and shields at the ready.

A man dressed in a mismatched and brightly colored doublet stepped forth. He looked at Lord Von Lay.

"Did you send the message?"

"I did," said Lord Von Lay. "Valitor mittendos, serif."

"You know the god Aor as a brother. Come in and have respite."

The man turned and took the reins of the two horses and led them into the monastery.

The chancellor spoke over his shoulder.

"William, you must go now. Brother, provide this man a horse that he might leave us."

The man waved over a monk and instructed him. A horse was brought and William mounted.

"Are you sure?" William asked, as he looked around nervously.

"Yes," Von Lay said. "Now, return to the castle and assume your duties."

William and the soldier turned and dug heels into their mounts and raced down the hill.

"He harbors much fear," said the man in the doublet.

"He knows the reputation of this house well," stated Von Lay.

*   *   *

"If I serve you, what do I get?" Harigan asked.

"If?" Aor laughed. "Why would you think that any one has personal choice? You have served me for a millennium now, but you just don't know it."

Harigan shook his head. "How is that possible?"

"Time is not what you think it is," Aor declared. "You have been here before, many times, and served me in several forms."

"What is it you wish of me?"

"When the universe was born, I and my kind knew only the true form; all that was and ever will be was known. For a billion years we traversed the many universes making things from the raw material we found.

"We bent folds into space, and made the servants that did our bidding as we grew fat on the power. Then came the change."

Aor shimmered in a golden light and shrank to the size of Harigan.

"The things we made to serve us grew jealous and rebelled."

"Rebelled... against gods?" Harigan's voice was filled with disbelief.

"Mortals have little understanding of the ways of gods," Aor said, then chuckled.

He moved his hands in strange patterns, weaving together strings of light into images.

"See before you the days long past."

Harigan reeled as he looked on. Waves of light and darkness encased him, passion and longing filled his heart, and fear and curiosity overwhelmed his soul. He shouted.

"I am all these things."

"You learn well, mortal. It is more than seeing… it is feeling deep in your core that you are connected to the divine. In this case, me."

"There was a battle between evil gods."

"Yes."

"They were destroyed?"

"Defeated."

"But what is this?" Harigan asked, as he walked among the images. "These two gods who chose to seize all the power. They are gathered into a vessel?"

"Yes. Know that for many millions of years we forged much of this universe and bid you mortals do our will. Three among you, with the help of a spirit, did make the final strike against them."

"I see now, the way in which you built those gifts."

Harigan marveled as words, figures, and images formed in his head. A flash of light blinded him and he recoiled.

"The light, the lantern, buried from sight it lingers still," he said.

"Yes. You mortals are resourceful, and now a man-beast seeks to release our enemy. Gather the lantern and other divine items back to us."

Aor took his cudgel and waved it causing the images to vanish.

"Now feast, you mortal fool, for when you have sated your soul's starvation, I will task you with the gathering."

*   *   *

The priest-healer administered a special tea made of herbs and rare minerals. The prince shuddered under the influence.

The priest waved his hands over the body and chanted in the

69

ancient tongue of Aor, then took out some green powder and dusted the body with it.

"He's far away, in a place that I cannot see. Take those copper daggers and lay them at the prince's feet," the priest commanded Von Lay.

He then took a sheet of white material and pulled it over the prince. Instantly the sheet adhered to the man's body. At places along the sheet a red liquid appeared to stain the cloth.

"Stay back, this is the gilliad poison!" the healer said. "One touch at this concentration could render you unconscious for a week."

He turned and pulled up a chair. Sitting, he looked up at Von Lay.

"You might as well get some rest, this will take some time." He took out a pocket clock and set it on the table. "He should have died," he said. "Something strange is going on here."

"He's a fighter that one," Von Lay added.

The priest smiled. "It's not his strength that's kept him among the living."

"What then?"

"I'll know more once the poison is out of him, but if I were to guess, I'd say he's caught in transition between living and dead."

"Like the living dead?" Von Lay looked concerned.

The priest chuckled. "What class are you?"

Von Lay looked surprised. "2468," he said.

"Educated in Prin?" The healer furthered.

"Yes."

"I thought so. I was brought up in the art of healing in the city of Flay, by the Southern Sea. The islands off the coast are populated with the undead. They roam around, their flesh rotting as time turns them into blind skeletons. The prince here does not suffer such an affliction. He is between worlds."

"Here and the Netherworld?"

"Or the Underworld," the priest said.

"Not Harigan, he is the salt."

"You love this man?"

The priest pulled out a pipe and stuffed it with topus. He put his finger in the bowl, conjured fire, and inhaled the smoke.

"In a way. I admire him greatly. He's a man of conviction and integrity." Von Lay leaned against a beam. "I was tasked by the brotherhood to influence him to promote the church."

"And now?"

"I've changed in all these years. I guess it would be fair to say that I am more chancellor than priest now."

The healer again drew in the smoke, held it, and then exhaled. He scratched his chin.

"Those of you who were dispatched to the lordly households have suffered much confusion, I've heard."

Von Lay looked annoyed.

"I am not confused. We cannot lose the prince. Do everything and anything that you can to bring him back."

The healer stood and put on some gloves. Removing the stained cloth, he rolled it up and put it gingerly into the fireplace. Slowly it burned.

Dark blue flames licked at the chimney until all were consumed. He moved to the table, took up his mortar and pestle, and mixed in a slice of black root, some insect pieces, and some brightly glowing dust.

Working the mixture he ground it into a paste as he uttered

some arcane words, making it glow a bright red.

"Hold him while I apply this."

He used the mix to draw complex designs on the prince's head and body.

Chanting and moving his arms and hands, he pulled tendrils of energy from the surrounding wood and stone and spun it around the prince. Harigan violently shook.

A smell like burnt hair filled the room. The priest collapsed into the chair and puffed his pipe.

"If we don't see any change within an hour, I'll try one other thing."

*　　*　　*

Harigan feasted on the foods laid out before him. With each mouthful his soul filled a little more.

Reaching for a glowing pear, the visage began to fade. Aor looked on and laughed.

"Someone tries to pull you back. Remember that which you must do. Destroy the Vulrich and retrieve the artifacts. Seek what we have lost, and do my will."

Harigan's eyes opened. The room was different. All around he saw patterns illuminated in golden light. There were things in the room, unnatural things that moved causing the air to shimmer and bend.

Numbers appeared in the cracks and crevices of the stone work along the walls. Colors filtered through the holes and cracks. There were strangers present also.

Two men were there, one asleep in a chair nearest him and the other sitting further away with his back to him by the fire. Harigan carefully sat up. He knew what had to be done.

"The Vulrich," he said under his breath. "The Scablands."

"Yes, and the plate and horn. Bring them to me," Aor commanded.

Standing, he quietly walked to where one of the men was sleeping. The chair was common, hand turned legs, wide base, covered in cloth and stuffed with cotton.

He saw the individual atoms and how they were told to clump together to form the chair. Glowing brightly red, the leg of the chair stood out.

It was for him to take. He bent down and grabbed the leg and tore it from the chair, sending the man flying. Harigan held the leg aloft and it glowed with power.

Von Lay climbed to his feet. The chair he was in now lay in ruins and the prince was standing there lighting the room with a golden glowing chair leg

"I think you used too much magic!" Von Lay said to the healer who was on his feet and trembling.

"The magic I used would not cause this."

Harigan spoke. "I am the instrument of Aor! I am he who delivers vengeance. It is time that I apply the Cudgel of Aor and smite thy foes."

"What foes?" said the priest.

Harigan laughed. "Come if you wish to see the ill creations of your god." He looked intently at the man. "But know that your doom will come to pass on the road that I travel."

Jerking his head to the side, he looked at Von Lay and grinned.

"I see you will come regardless. It is okay, for your way to salvation is with me."

Harigan walked to the door, threw it open, and exited.

Von Lay ran for the doorway.

"Send word to the other monasteries that we travel. Tell them to keep vigil for us if we enter their realm. I will keep watch over the prince."

He ran after Harigan and into the night.

*   *   *

Blasting steam from its nostrils and foam from its lips, the horse flew down the mountain road. Von Lay pulled hard on the reins and brought the harried beast to a skidding halt.

The prince was waiting there at the bottom of the hill, the fervent light now only a dull glow.

"You wish to see what lies in store for those foes of mine?" asked Harigan. "Then follow me to your bitter doom."

"Prince, what madness do you speak? Calm yourself and rest for a moment until your wits again take hold," Von Lay pleaded.

Harigan trebled a low laugh.

"What madness speak you of? My purpose has turned, and now I follow a different path. If you choose to follow, then do so, if not, stand by."

Bringing his horse around, Harigan headed along the road to the east. Von Lay followed.

For two days they rode both day and night. The horses seemed immune to fatigue. A great thunder storm materialized and rain fell in stinging torrents.

Von Lay pulled back on his reins as a flash of light revealed a scarred and twisted landscape. They were entering the Scablands beyond the eastern border.

"No towns, cities, or villages exist out here," he shouted over the gale. "Only wastelands and bogs we will find!"

"Turn back if you fear to tread in my footprints."

Harigan did not look back, but only pressed on deeper into

the devastated land.

Von Lay followed, led only by the subtle radiant aura from Harigan's body. Twisted brambles, deep and distorted gullies, and stinking bogs barred their path, but somehow Harigan found a passage.

On occasion Harigan would stop and dismount, strike his club against the ground and fresh water would bubble up.

"Take your fill," he told Von Lay. "It will refresh you."

Harigan slowed his pace. After three days in the saddle, he took pity on Von Lay and began making camp at night.

Night after night Harigan would wave his hand over the tan, dry, scrub brush and ripe fruits and nuts would appear.

"Eat until your belly bursts," he said.

Each night they slept in the foul, defiled lands, and at times Von Lay cursed his poor choice to follow the mad prince.

"I should have stayed and groomed the prince's cousin for ruling," he said under his breath.

"Do not quibble with your choice of companion," Harigan said. "We all must live with our decisions."

As the sun rose on the seventh day, a large dark fortress made of gray stone and wrought iron came into view.

"It is the Fortress of the Glen Brook Vale," Harigan said.

"This cannot be!" Von Lay rode up next to Harigan. "That place is fabled, a legend lost to time."

"You are a victim of time," Harigan said. "Do you not believe your own eyes? Behold the lands of the Kings of Lormor!"

"What happened to the lands? They are not lush and fertile as in the tales." Von Lay halted his horse.

"That's where the Vulrich dwells, and my task to be

discharged. Here lies the magical Horn of Endless Drink and the Plate of Endless Feasting."

"This cannot be," Von Lay repeated.

"Your lack of faith means you will not enter."

Harigan rode on.

Approaching the main gate, he saw the shifting image of the fortress, its mighty black walls rising hundreds of feet topped with black iron spikes.

"The walls breathe," Von Lay said.

"Not for much longer," Harigan stated.

Von Lay reeled. "What is that horrible stench?"

"The deaths of a million fallen souls, who even now are tortured for their arrogance. Their pain and suffering fill the air. Vulrich keeps the scent fresh for his pleasure."

The image of the fortress was twisting and moving. Von Lay felt as if he would vomit.

He shifted in the saddle, his eye unable to completely avoid the fortress visage. His head spun and he held on tightly to the horse's mane as not to fall.

He rode on towards the walls as the edifice loomed like a glowing vision raised from the Underworld. The iridescent colors of red and yellow rolled off the structure like smoke billowing into the sky.

Harigan raised his cudgel. Sparks flew all around, fire erupted from the ground, and he rode through the first defense.

Von Lay and his horse tumbled backward to the ground. Darkness colored his mind.

Nearest the massive gates, two large demons blocked Harigan's way.

"You man-beast with little magic," one of the demons said.

"You come to your end."

Harigan saw the demons, dressed simply with metal armor lashed to their limbs, and iron helmets formed to their heads; pawns left to guard the gate of Vulrich.

One demon was missing a tusk and the other an eye. They were the forward guard of his foe, and were in for a shocking surprise. Harigan leapt from his horse and with the force of his thought moved amongst the demons.

The two creatures jumped at the shock of Harigan's speed. One demon brought around his pole-arm, but he was now too close for the weapon to be effective.

The other loosed his sword and laid a downward strike upon Harigan. Glowing brightly in a golden light, his body went rigid. The blade bounced off casting a shower of red hot sparks over the ground.

Harigan raised his cudgel and shouted the charm of vengeance. The smashing of bone and the bursting of flesh happened quickly.

Harigan stood there, covered in the thick blue demon blood. Approaching the gates, he lifted his hands up and shouted.

"Open!"

The gates flew apart, tearing from their hinges.

Golden light radiated in every direction from him and filled the space from the gatehouse to the courtyard beyond. He looked upon his path and knew it was right.

Walking quickly, he sensed the attacks before they happened and twisted his body to avoid the magic projectiles. He spun and dashed towards the inner sanctum.

Winged creatures, scaly, half-human and half-bat flew at him from all sides, but he struck them down with ease one at a time. Red glowing darts shot from the drain pipes, and murder holes, but failed to penetrate his radiant glow.

The main door to the castle opened, and blackness raced from the chamber and fell upon him. His strength was tested and he felt his connection to Aor stretching thin.

"Shut!" he shouted, and the castle doors slammed together.

A groan of anguish erupted from within as Harigan threw off the dark vale and emerged unscathed.

"You think yourself strong? I speak for Aor!" Harigan said angrily. "I have come to take back what belongs to the gods!"

He tore the doors from their hinges and his golden light flooded into the main hall. In his mind he increased the illumination of his body, and the wooden frame on either side of him burst into flames. Entering the mighty hall he gazed upon a cowering creature of horrific proportions.

A hundred feet long and coiled like a snake, the creature squirmed and twisted. Its head was narrow with a circle of bloody fangs dominating its open mouth. Half in and out were a pair of legs.

Harigan raised his cudgel and slammed it against the ground. A line of light traveled along the floor until it hit the creature, cutting it in half. Fluid and bones spilled from its center.

The partially-digested creatures within, missing skin and dangling organs, fell to the ground and flopped about like fish stranded on the shore.

"Vulrich!" Harigan shouted. "Time for your punishment."

Vulrich lurched from the darkness, its tentacles appearing as lines of red light radiating in all directions from its scaly body. Harigan got a good look at the monster— thirty feet tall, covered in irregular black scales, a long serrated yellow beak, and hundreds of eyes spread out over its head.

Its tentacles barbed with poison pods struck Harigan, injecting him with fiery venom. Slowly, they began pulling him toward razor-sharp hooks extending from the beast's mouth. A blanket of black fell upon Harigan, smothering him.

He raised his arms, and a blinding white light filled the room. The creature bellowed in rage, fear and pain. Passing his cudgel in front of him, Harigan swept the tentacles away, swayed slightly, and staggered forward.

Energy burst from his limbs, and he raised his glimmering golden cudgel.

"I deliver the vengeance so prescribed by your maker!"

The voice blasted from his mouth, and the shockwaves caused the roof to shower down in fragments on them.

Vulrich cowered, throwing out wave upon wave of energy in defense. Fire erupted all around, and the cudgel fell upon the creature.

A flash of white light eclipsed all other sources as a shockwave radiated outward, causing the walls to crack and the floor to open below the creature. A deafening sound echoed into the sky, and Vulrich was gone.

Exhausted beyond words, Harigan fell to his hands and knees on the burnt floor boards. He collapsed, and fell into unconsciousness.

*   *   *

Harigan woke. "What am I doing here?"

Nothing seemed familiar. In the air he smelled smoke and the stench of death. Looking down, he saw his clothes were scorched. He got to his feet and staggered to the charred stone fireplace and looked around the room, confused.

"What happened here?"

Debris lay strewn about mixed with piles of ash. He didn't remember who he was, what he was doing in this place, or what had happened.

Exploring the castle, he found many crumpled suits of armor and bleached bones wrapped in frayed cloth and leather.

In a closet he found a dusty shirt, pants and doublet. Trying it on he was delighted to find it actually fit him and he took them, replacing his burnt clothes.

"To the dungeon."

Harigan jumped. "Who said that?"

"I, your master. Find the stairs that lead down, and find what is mine," the voice said.

He walked around from room to room, down dusty dark corridors, and through many service chambers until he came to a stairwell.

He pulled a sconce from the wall and it spontaneously lit as he descended the steps. At the bottom an iron gate barred his path.

He clutched the lock and it fell apart in his hand. Pushing hard the gate opened with a deafening screech. One of the cell doors hummed, and Harigan approached.

As he oppened the door he saw a skeleton curled up on the floor, in its hands, a white and brown drinking horn and a small round metallic plate.

Quickly he stuffed them into his shirt, then stopped. A yellow glint caught his eye. Something round and pointy was under a pile of filth.

He reached down and lifted it into the air. Dirt and straw fell from it revealing a golden crown.

"What masterful cruelty laid thee low here?" he asked.

He turned and went back up the stairs, passing back into the burnt and shattered hall. Before him was a path of destruction that led to the courtyard.

The fortress was crumbling, the stones completely shattered in places, large oaken beams and bronze columns lying as if tossed by giants. He found a horse wandering in the courtyard, and climbed into the saddle.

The main gates had been ripped from their hinges. He slowly rode out being careful, almost fearful, of something he could not quite put his finger on.

Ahead was a wasteland, and he halted on a stone bridge. There on the ground he saw an unconscious man. He dismounted and knelt down by him and shook the man gently.

"Who are you?"

The man looked up.

"My Lord?"

Something inside Harigan's mind snapped.

"Yes. I remember now... my name is Harigan." His eyes took on a glossy pallor. "I've traveled to the nether reaches, met a god, battled and defeated the Vulrich."

He helped Von Lay up on his feet.

"I was once a lord of men, but am that no more. You know me, but I do not remember you."

"My name is Kereel Von Lay, your chancellor, my prince, before—"

"Before what?"

"Before you were poisoned by your wife and her lover," Von Lay said.

"Why would they do such a thing?" Harigan looked confused.

"They conspired to steal your power... my prince."

"You keep using that word, *prince*. I was a prince once, but no more. I am a servant of Aor, and shall do his bidding from here on out."

"I don't understand," Von Lay said. "You have a kingdom to rule."

"Others will do better than I."

"What will you do then?"

"The world is awash with the property of the gods. I am to gather it up."

"You will not return to the Midlands?"

"No," Harigan said.

"Then what will we do?"

"We?" Harigan smiled.

"You don't expect me to abandon you now, do you?"

Harigan laughed loudly. "The way will be hard. Death awaits you down that road."

"I've already traveled the road of death with you once, why not again?"

"Then Chancellor Von Lay, mount your horse and let's be off."

Harigan chose the rout. They moved though the swamps and marshes toward the darkening sky. The stench of bog infected every pore, and Von Lay developed a discontented frown.

Looking over at his traveling companion, he frowned even more at the great grin Harigan wore.

"How can you smile with such a stink upon us?"

"Rot, decay, stale water, it is all the making of life in this world, you just don't recognize it."

Von Lay slipped and put his foot into a foul and dark trench of water. His horse pulled back hard on the reins and he nearly fell.

"Hold up! By the gods I'm exhausted and sick of this bog. I'm hungry, and need some sleep, and I'm damn tired of walking these horses and not riding them."

Harigan looked about and pointed.

"There, a wide flat spot we can make camp. I'm afraid that we have more bog to travel before we can truly rest, and we'll need these animals to carry us most of the way."

"And what about some food? Our saddle bags have no more rations, and our wine skins are empty. Can't you call upon Aor to wrap us in his light again, to help us get to where we're going?"

"Aor comes and goes as he pleases. I'm merely a servant, not the master."

"Then what do we do?"

Harigan led the way to the flat high ground. There he sat and brooded for a while. Finally he pulled out the horn and plate from his shirt. The symbols on both seemed to glow an eerie blue.

"That symbol," Von Lay said, "it means meal."

"I recognize this now," Harigan stated. "It is the Plate of Feasting."

He waved his hand over the plate and envisioned a meal. Steaming fowl and tubers appeared before them.

Von Lay quickly grabbed one of the tubers and devoured it.

"This is delicious, as if made in the kitchen of your castle."

"It's quite possible that is where it came from," Harigan said. "I think it makes food you remember somehow."

"What of that horn?"

"I thought this stink was making you sick?" Harigan asked.

Von Lay smiled. "Let's see what happens when you conjure a stout, or a brandy in that horn."

They ate and drank for some time as the glow of the sun

vanished from the murky gray sky. Von Lay gathered some scrub brush and made a small fire as the temperature began to fall.

Poking it with a stick, he sat back and stared into the flames.

"Where are we off to?"

"I've been promised revenge," Harigan said. "And the town where that revenge will take place is that way." He pointed into the endless plain of bogs.

"What revenge?" Von Lay looked surprised. "Do you mean the princess?"

Harigan chuckled. "She was a princess in name only. Truly she was a witch, an assassin, and an usurper." Harigan looked away into the darkness. "She tried to destroy the work of Aor, and now must be made to suffer."

Von Lay looked over at the man. He seemed less divine now.

"What of the Justice Knights? Surely they would be better suited to pronounce judgment."

"It's the will of Aor," Harigan said, then laid down and with his back to Von Lay added, "Sleep. You will need all your strength soon."

*   *   *

The town was not large, a hundred thousand people at the most. From a distance, Von Lay saw the stark orange glow of hundreds of lanterns and the stark white of the light stones mounted along the main gate.

Harigan rode ahead, a strange yellow glow radiating from his body. The night was clear and the twinkling of a million stars shown down upon them.

As they got closer to the city defenses, Von Lay saw the gate guards moving about checking riders in and out.

Harigan approached and the guards parted to let him in. Von Lay approached and they did the same.

They rode into town. The streets were narrow, and the acrid scent of urine and animal dung was suffocating.

Turning down a dark alley, the unnatural glow given off by Harigan illuminated the broken cobbles of the street, and worn red bricks of the buildings. Emerging from the alley, Von Lay found a paved street choked with pedestrians. The heavy smell of fuelstone hung in the air.

Men, elves, and dwarves mingled about traveling the streets from public house to public house. Some were sober enough to look up and see the glowing man and give him quarter; others were knocked aside, as Harigan pushed past them.

Von Lay steered his horse around the throng, following Harigan. Pulling up to a tavern, the glowing priest dismounted and went in. On the shingle was a picture of a pair of dice neatly carved and painted.

Von Lay dismounted, looped his horse's reins around a post and approached the door. Shouts erupted from within and grew louder.

He stepped back into the street as Harigan emerged with two people, one in each hand. He threw the woman onto the ground at Von Lay's feet.

Harigan turned to the man who fell to his knees.

"You provided the wood for the pyre and climbed up willingly," Harigan told him. "Now, feel my wrath!"

A boom of thunder rattled the windows of the public houses. The glow around Harigan engulfed the man on the ground and a scream cracked the air.

The light dwindled and a twisted and deformed creature writhed on the ground. Turning, Harigan looked down at the princess.

"For you, all shall know your deceit! There is nowhere you can go that those around you will not know what you are."

"It was not me, I was a dupe," she cried, her tears streaming down her face. "It was Westfax, he did this to you! My husband," she sobbed, "do not kill me; I was wronged as you were, betrayed by Westfax! I still love you."

She screamed as a large, black scar appeared on her face in the shape of a H. Clutching the raised mark, the woman cursed Harigan.

"Thou art a savage goblin and a weak man!" she said. "I should have killed you while you slept."

Harigan laughed. "Everywhere you go, from here until you rot, people will know who and what you are."

Her movement was quick. A dagger flew from her side as she attempted to drive it into Harigan's chest. But when the blade arrived, Harigan was not there. The knife turned red—she screamed and dropped it.

"Your lying ways have brought you nothing but pain, and that pain will continue until you dwell in morta," Harigan said from behind her.

Turning, she raised her hands to shield her eyes as the light flared around Harigan. Getting to her feet she rushed to Westfax, helped the twisted mass of flesh to his feet, and fled into the growing crowd.

People gathered around the gambling den forming a semicircle about Harigan and his companion.

"Call the shire reeve!" yelled a bystander.

A dwarf with a long gray beard tried to tackle Harigan, who sidestepped the attacker and delivered a disabling blow. Von Lay lurched forward and struck an oncoming man with his fist. The man fell to the ground.

From down the street he heard the clang of armor echoing as the town guard rushed to the scene. Von Lay scampered into the saddle and called out to Harigan.

"To your horse, my lord, they mean you harm!"

He drew his sword.

Harigan, his body glowing, calmly walked to his horse. The crowd parted as if pushed aside as he mounted. Holding out his hand, he waved it in the air. Thunder echoed and all the people in the street fell prostrated before him.

"You have tasted the vengeance of Aor. Remember it well, for if I return, each and every one of you will know the lick of fire and the taste of your own bowels!"

"Stop!" shouted one of the armored men.

Harigan turned and dug his heels into his horse's side. The beast let out a screech and bolted towards the gate. Von Lay followed.

Ahead, men were manning the walls and the gate was closing. Harigan lay down in the saddle and spurred his mount on. He passed through.

Arrows flew in every direction as shouts of anger and defiance were hurled down upon him. Von Lay passed next. As he did, he felt a stabbing pain in his back.

Exhaustion washed over him, as terror gripped his heart. Arrows flew past as he dashed into the night. Shouts erupted behind him, and in his mind he knew that there was no other option but to just keep going.

For what seemed like hours he rode, the horse stumbling across open pastures and rolling hills. In the distance he saw a campfire.

It was difficult to stay in the saddle, and the pain in his back was more severe. As he approached, a man at the fire stood up.

"By the gods! What has happened to you?" the man asked.

"I don't know. I can't seem to move. All the power has drained from me," Von Lay said wearily.

"It's not power, my friend, that has drained from you, but your blood," the man stated. "You've been wounded. In fact, you have three arrows in your back."

"Strange..." Von Lay trailed off.

"What is strange?" Ford asked rushing over and catching the man as he fell from the saddle.

"That I who served a great man should come to this end!"

Ford pulled the man to the fire and laid him on his side. "There is a town not far from here, I'm sure they have a surgeon-healer there!"

"I just came from it and these arrows are their gift to me." Von Lay felt the bonds of life slipping. "But he did warn me..."

Looking into the man's face, Ford watched his eyes turn to gray. He was dead and Ford had no idea who he was. Turning, he became aware that another horse was approaching.

"Von Lay, is that you there?" came a strong and powerful voice.

The horse stopped beyond the light of the fire, and Ford saw a man dismount. He came into the light. He was a large man, thickly muscled.

"What have you done to Von Lay?" he demanded angrily.

"Nothing," Ford protested. "The man rode up to me in the darkness and collapsed."

"Poor fellow, I warned him of his death."

"And who are you?" Ford asked.

"I am today a poorer man for having lost a friend."

"Do you have a name?" Ford asked, not sure if he would get an answer.

"Volfgang Von Harigan."

Ford nearly fell over. "Harigan you say?"

"Aye, the very same."

"What luck, I was in search of a Prince Harigan."

"Then I would be he, but no longer a prince. Now I am a servant to Aor."

In the distance came voices and the sound of hounds. Lanterns and torches were visible atop the nearby rolling hills. Ford estimated they were a mile away and coming his direction.

"Who would want to put arrows into your friend?"

Ford quickly kicked dirt over his fire.

"Infidels," Harigan stated, "sinners, fools, and stumblebums."

"They seem bent on finding you for some reason." Ford appeared concerned.

Harigan turned to him. "You look familiar. Have we met before?"

"No," Ford said.

"The fire was in this direction!" shouted a voice in the distance.

Now Ford saw more than a dozen lanterns coming his way.

"It will be a glorious death for you if you stay and fight alongside me. I will see that you are well provided for in the hereafter!"

"There is another way," Ford said while fishing out the jar of teleportation powder from his saddlebag.

"Another way?" Harigan came over.

"I am looking for the Lantern of Dern Blackhammer," Ford said.

"The relic?"

"The very same."

"I am to seek relics for my god. The door to the realm of the Netherworld must be closely guarded."

"My employers offer you something for your service."

"What is that?"

"To remove a curse that is upon you," Ford said.

"Curse?" Harigan laughed. "You have been misinformed. Nonetheless, I will accompany you if the Lantern is involved."

"Soldiers, this way!" shouted a man with a lantern at the base of the hill.

The rumble of men on horseback shook the ground.

"It is too bad that you, a mortal, will most likely die here before we can retrieve the Lantern," Harigan said.

"Actually, I have the means to get us clear of here."

He un-hobbled his horse and sent it off into the darkness with a slap. He took some golden powder into his hand,

"When I open the portal, we will have only seconds to pass through."

"Here they are. Release the dogs!" shouted an angry voice.

Ford threw the powder into the air. The portal ruptured time and space, and Harigan plowed his way through. Ford followed. Behind he heard the snarling of dogs nearly at the camp. A crack like thunder echoed and Ford again found himself in front of Goldworm.

CHAPTER

4

Justice Knight's Quest

Close up ranks!" called Guy. Looking back he saw the Justice Knights he led. "Not much further, my good knights!"

"Comes a man in headlong flight, my lord!" Valdar the Lord Prosecutor shouted.

"One of the brigands?" Guy asked.

"A caravan driver from the looks of him. There's debris in the road ahead and several bodies!"

A man in a long white robe and a black feathered headdress rushed at the column of knights.

"Good knight, brigands have made away with the whole train and its contents, including the beautiful niece of the prince."

Guy halted his horse and signaled for the column to stop. "Which way did they go?"

"To the east, my lord. They fell on us like killbees, decimated my guards, and stole the whole caravan. They would have murdered me too, if I hadn't fled into the woods."

"You were right to flee," Guy said. "Whose caravan were you in charge of?"

The caravaneer looked sheepish.

"The whole thing belonged to the Viscount."

"You say the Viscount?"

"His daughter, wards, and ladies were in a carriage train in the middle."

"Clairmont," Guy shouted.

A knight in greenish armor rode up from the column, halted and lifted his visor.

"Yes, my lord?"

"See that someone from the bailiff ranks takes this man back to the fortress at Brindlewood. Valdar, take a complement of knights in an arc around Blackburn Woods and cut off the brigands. We'll meet at Darning Bridge. I will take the rest and pursue the foe directly."

"Yes, my lord," Valdar said.

Guy turned in the saddle.

"Justice Knights! Fiends have made away with property of the Viscount. To your wits and weapons, Court Three and Four follow Valdar. The rest with me."

He spurred his horse and rode past the wreckage.

Guy led his men along the road through large rolling hills. Birds shot into the air from the tall grass as they thundered along the highway.

Cresting a low hill, Guy saw a train of wagons and men on horseback. Men with swords and polearms walked with the train, others were on horses.

"Form three squadrons," Guy commanded. "Tame the havoc and let justice be done!"

Lowering himself in the saddle, he raised his lance.

"Justice Knights!" yelled one of the bandits.

A motley group of roughs broke and rushed off in all directions. Several ogres with pole arms looked as if they were going to fight, saw the knights, and fled too.

The caravan slowed and stopped. The ground shook and dust rose like smoke from a forest fire as the knights bore down on the stolen train.

Guy split a squadron off and swung back. Wagons were abandoned and animals left to wander. Silverware and bronze bars where scattered all around.

Several open wagons had bound boys and girls, their pleading eyes wild. No doubt they were destined for the eastern slave markets. He approached the covered wagons, and a sound caught his attention.

"The door is bolted, let us out," came a woman's voice.

Guy whirled his horse around to look at the brightly colored wagon. Coming up alongside, he laid his lance across his lap.

A large padlock secured the door. Reaching back, he laid hands on his war hammer and raised it above his head. Down came the sharp pointed end into the lock, destroying the mechanism and freeing the door. The door popped open and a tall blond woman leapt out, dagger in hand.

"Who are you?" she demanded.

"I am Guy, Chief Justice Knight of Olbrook, lord of Valeshire. Who are you, my lady?"

She sat back on the wagon doorstep.

"I am the Viscountess of Mid Vishonic, my uncle is Prince Kiev of Vishonic."

"I know your father the Vicount," Guy stated. "And I know your uncle too. You are quite far from home, my lady. How is it you came to ride in this caravan?"

Standing up, she sheathed her dagger.

"I was traveling to see my father who is in Bon York, the walled city at the end of this highway."

"I've heard he is meeting with the Council of City-states," Guy said.

"Father didn't say what he was doing." She batted her long eyelashes. "I'm sure it has something to do with the unrest between the Outland Kingdoms and the Council. What did you say your name was?"

Guy lifted his visor and smiled.

"Guy," he said.

"And you're a Chief Justice Knight?" She fluffed her hair. "That sounds exciting. When did you take the oath?"

"Ten years ago."

"I'm sure your wife must be very proud of you."

"I've not been blessed with a wife yet."

"Really?"

"You can call me Verily, that's my common name," she said.

"I don't know you well enough to call you by your common name."

"I give you leave," she said.

Gazing into her green eyes, a strange feeling came over him.

"Verily?"

"Yes, Guy Knight of Olbrook?"

"Are you married?"

She giggled. "Why, my lord, I will soon be if you are bold enough to ask."

*   *   *

Guy waited for word from the midwives of his wife's birthing. *It seems so long ago that our lives were intertwined,* Guy thought.

The midwife came from the room.

"It is a boy!" she cried. "A beautiful boy!"

Guy rushed into the room and stood by his wife. She held the babe to her breast.

"Is he whole? I mean, is he complete?"

"Husband, you worry when there is no cause. Your son is perfect."

Boasting a tremendous laugh, he sat beside her and embraced both mother and child. Sitting back, he placed his hand on his son's head and caressed it.

"I thought that I had felt the hand of divine love the day I met you, my wife, but now I know it was only half a love."

She looked into his blue eyes and smiled.

"What name shall we call him?"

"Hugh," he said. "After my father."

"If only he had lived to see this day," she added.

"He was called away to the Netherworld too soon."

"Call for the wet nurse, I am too weary to continue feeding little Hugh. I must take my rest."

"Of course," he said. "I'll arrange for a great ball to ring in this occasion!"

Valdar appeared at the door.

"Guy, we have to get to Highland Hills to hold court."

Guy kissed his wife and child and went to the door.

"How many cases?" he asked Valdar.

Verily watched as the two men left and the wet nurse entered and took Hugh to her bosom. The babe cooed, cried, then suckled.

Verily closed her eyes and slowly drifted to sleep. Her husband loved her and their baby. She was in bliss as the dreams unfolded in her mind.

For the next four years she often woke alone, her husband gone on court business. He at times left late in the night not to return for weeks.

Violations of the law by men, dwarves, elves, orcs, goblins, and bandits, kept him away holding court in distant reaches of the Outland Kingdoms. Yet, his love for her never veered and always flowed out to her when he'd return.

"My lady?" the maid said. "Wake. It is time for your breakfast, you must wake now."

Verily opened her eyes; the light of morning was streaming in through the window.

"Where is my husband?"

"He was called away, my lady," the maid said. "He bade me give you this."

She handed Verily a rose.

"He said that in a fortnight he will return."

Verily sat up and put on her robe, then walked to the bath to prepare for her day. After the bath she dressed and began attending to the business of her family. The money and the resources of the shire had to be managed.

She worked throughout the day and skipped the midday meal. As the sun dipped in the east, she got Hugh out of the nursery. She held him up to the window.

"Look, Hugh, the darkness comes and we must have supper," she said.

Hugh looked at her with doe-like eyes as she led him to the dining room. A feast was placed out on the table, and they both ate.

After supper, she took Hugh by the hand and went up to her bedroom. Passing her personal bodyguards, she said good night and entered the royal apartment.

The room was lavish sporting intricate tapestries, ornate red marble columns, and golden draperies. The blue velvet curtains of her canopy bed complemented the polished stonewood, as did the rich silk pillows and cotton sheets.

In the room Hugh rushed over to the direbear rug and threw himself onto the head. Wrestling it for a few minutes he tired and rolled off staring up at the high open-beam ceiling. The free-standing magic clock struck double five bells.

"Come along, little Hugh, time for sleep."

She rose to her feet.

"No nursery tonight little one, we will stay together until daddy returns tomorrow. Now, let's take a bath and prepare for bed."

Hugh stood and loudly said, "No", then dashed off to the bed and scurried under it.

"Get your toy boats and come get clean," she said, as she made her way to the edge of the bath. Her robe fell to the tiled floor, then she selected some bath salts and perfumes.

Adding them to the water, she swirled her hand to mix the water with the scented sundries. For a moment she admired the tub— it was a very ancient relic, carved from a single slab of green crystal.

She knew that when the water was filled to the top, it would appear as though she was floating in a vast green sea. With a word she could produce colored lights that would flash on and off in a soothing pattern, and if she made the symbol of Crylan, the tub would vibrate gently making the water tickle her body in a very pleasing manner.

She was about to call for Hugh when a man stepped out from behind a tapestry. She grabbed a towel and covered herself.

The man was filthy, with a long face, sharp nose, and a dirty short brown beard. He smiled in an evil way, showing his yellow teeth. He approached halfway but stopped and looked around the room with greedy eyes.

"Who are you?" she demanded.

"You have such nice things here," he said his voice high and strained as if he had been choked recently.

"I especially like the shiny things." He moved towards the bed.

"Who sent you?" she demanded loudly bringing him to a stop.

He focused his attention back on her. His eyes were a dull yellow and his clothes common; a brown leather jerkin over a stained muslin shirt.

His breeches were also brown, torn, and covered with grime. Wiping his nose with his sleeve he looked at the bathtub with disdain, then eyed the Viscountess with a lusty look.

"I'm here for your jewels and gold and whatever else I feel like," he said, as he stepped closer towards the tub.

Verily moved further back; the intruder bent down at the water's edge, dangled his dirty hand in the water, and smiled.

"Nice – warm – smells good too," he said, as he peeled off his jerkin and shirt.

Taking two rusty daggers from his belt, he set them on the floor at the water's edge. He then stripped off his dirty boots and breeches and exposed himself to her.

"I like what I see," he said. "Lose the towel." He licked his lips. "I like it when a woman fights."

Verily pressed against the tub's edge contemplating jumping from the water and running to the door. But if she did, he might discover Hugh. She couldn't take that chance.

The villain bent down on his hands and knees scooping up some water and splashed it over his face. Dirt clouded the tub causing it to make a humming sound as it quickly filtered out the muck.

"Funny trick," he said.

From under the bed little Hugh emerged, a wooden sword in his hand. Verily's heart filled with terror. She locked eyes with the intruder.

"You are quite the man," she said.

He looked surprised. "What?"

She splashed in the water.

"So you think you are man enough for me?"

"You'll find out soon enough," he replied, not sure if she was mocking him.

Rushing from the bed, Hugh struck the intruder with the thrust of a duelist. The man screamed out in pain and fell head first into the waters as Verily leapt from the bath.

She ran dragging the soaking towel with her, grabbed Hugh, and dashed to the door. Throwing open the bolt, she screamed.

"Warfred! Intruder – help us!"

Armed men flew down the hall and into the room. The thief tried to climb from the tub, blood was mingling with dirty water. He was prone on the ground as the guards leveled their swords at him, but just as fast the room filled with laughter.

Warfred came out into the hall, his face red from laughing. He composed himself and looked at the Viscountess.

"Quick thinking, my lady. The toy sword, a very well placed shot!" He laughed heartily. "I trust he did not harm you?"

"He was hiding behind the tapestry. He had wickedness on the mind I tell you." She looked confused. "What do you mean toy sword?"

"Come look for yourself," Warfred said, as he escorted her back into the room.

As she entered the room, she let out an involuntarily laugh, for sticking from the rectum of the intruder was the hilt of the wooden toy sword.

"Get it out!" cried the man.

"Perhaps the dungeon keeper will remove it," Warfred said. "But I cannot guarantee you won't prefer that to what awaits you there. We have many questions to ask you."

"Warfred, take some guards and find out how he got into the castle. He emerged from behind that tapestry." She pointed at the wall hanging.

Warfred snapped into action. "You and you come with me. You three report to the captain of the guard, and have him lock down the castle and search the premises for any other intruders.

"You two take this lump of filth to the dungeon. Once you find out what he knows report to me."

The men quickly dispersed.

"Would you like me to have a guard posted inside the room, my lady?"

"Yes, until we make sure there are no other intruders and we know how the brigand got in."

Warfred strode to the tapestry and pulled it aside. A small hole, just big enough for a man, had been broken through the wall.

The guards followed it to a tunnel that led to the catacombs below the castle. By week's end, the holes were patched and the access in the catacombs sealed.

The intruder was held for judgment, and Hugh and Verily moved to another apartment in the castle. She waited for her husband's return. There was much to tell, and a painful longing filled her heart.

The end of the second week things at the castle seemed back to normal. She was in the main hall when a bailiff arrived.

He was escorted in and came up to her with some expression of pain on his face.

"What is it, Sir Bailiff?" she asked.

"It is the Chief Justice Knight, my lady." He glanced up at the celling, then at her. "I'm not sure how to tell you this."

She looked annoyed.

"Is he going to be later than tomorrow? Was he called away to judge in the Hinterlands or the Scablands? Out with it? Why is my husband going to be late in returning to me?"

A reckless jealousy bubbled out of her. His long trips and departures now felt as heavy as lead on her heart. She had much to discuss with him, and now he'd be postponing again?

The bailiff's eyes never left her as he sighed.

"Guy, Knight of Olbrook, the Chief Justice Knight of the Outland Kingdoms… was murdered two nights ago."

She fell to the ground in shock.

"What? How?"

"Treachery, my lady. By the time we made it to Whitelime Castle we were all exhausted. Guy retired to the Chief Justice apartment. He shed his armor to bathe when a villain fell upon him. He fought fiercely, but by the time the guards arrived, our lord had bled too much."

She began to sob. "He can't be dead."

The bailiff looked mournful.

"I assure you he is perished. The guards found him face down in the bloody water of his tub."

"No, no, no – he can't be dead – do you hear me - he can't be dead!"

Warfred came over, helped her up and put his arm around her.

"My lady, come and sit here."

He eased her into the chair and motioned for the Bailiff to exit.

"I'll have the healer attend you."

Looking at the door, he motioned for another guard to come near.

"Find the physician-healer and bring him immediately. Tell no one of the lord's death."

The guard dashed from the room.

"Whatever will become of us?" she asked.

"You have no need to worry, my lady. Your station will not diminish."

"But my heart will. Bring my son… I wish to hold him," she said.

The healer came in. In his hand was a cup of some liquid.

"The shock has unbalanced your humors. Take this quickly, and drink it all."

She consumed the drink, got to her feet and walked to the couch. A few moments later, Hugh came in and rushed into her arms.

"My little Hugh, my darling child…" She dried her eyes and looked down into his.

"You will one day be a great knight, I swear it."

*   *   *

Years passed, and Hugh grew into a sturdy young man. In

just a few days he would undergo the customary initiation to become a Justice Knight, and he so wished his father were there to see it done.

A black grief settled on him, and he became withdrawn. His friends, the first-born boys of the other noble houses, all tried in vain to comfort him.

Cedric came and offered him strong drink; he refused. Balto came and tried to get him to play fire ball; he refused. Culter came and brought him tapau root and mustard-seed beef; Hugh refused it all.

Finally, Veric came to visit. He strode up the stairs and knocked on the door. When no answer was given, he entered the dark chamber.

A sliver of light was visible where the heavy curtains were drawn. In the bed curled up under silk sheets was Hugh. Veric threw open the drapes and the light streamed in, exposing the dust floating in the air.

"Damn you!" cursed Hugh. "How dare you?"

"If damned I am, then damned I'll be!" said Veric, as he walked with purpose to the bed and jerked off the covers.

Hugh tried to claw at the sheets but they lay at the foot of the bed.

"Now, either you rise to meet the day, or I shall drag you forth and throw you into the fountain in the courtyard!" Veric threatened.

"Just leave me," Hugh grumbled, turned his back and gave a dismissing wave of his hand.

"Aye, I will after you've had a good and proper purifying at my displeasure!" chided Veric.

"Be gone!" Hugh furthered.

Taking up the sheets, Veric threw them on top of Hugh and then launched himself at him.

Wrapping Hugh up in the sheets, he hoisted him onto his shoulder and quickly moved from the room. He went down the many stirs to the hall, and out the front door.

"May the gods curse you!" Hugh blurted.

"I will not stand for you behaving like a Curi-loaf, steeping in your own juices and stinking up the air around you. None can take it any longer, so—"

The wind outside was gentle, but the air was freezing. Snow was coming, but had not yet arrived. The sky was overcast with a high white covering.

Veric hefted Hugh up and lofted him into the fountain. A great splash rose and water showered down around the fountain's base.

Huge struggled to get free of the wrappings. He stood up, his face a blazing red.

"I – you – I mean…" Hugh stammered.

He let out a tremendous laugh. Veric began laughing too, as Hugh sloshed his way to the edge of the fountain and sat down. Veric came and sat down next to him.

For a moment neither spoke as they chuckled about the event. The smell of winter-berries carried in the air.

"I was being a raving aunk!" Hugh said.

"Those big fat cows in the hills? You sure were." Veric nodded his head. "Your grief is shared, but it's the way of things. Your father now sits in the Halls of Valor with the noble families. He will look upon your knighting and revel," Veric said.

"True enough, you're right. It's time that I took up the mantle of my birth, for I know my father would not have mourned as I."

Verily came outside. She walked over to the two boys and stifled a laugh.

"You boys deal with your woes in silly ways."

She ran her hand over his wet hair.

"Hugh, it's time for you to start preparing, and you, Veric... your family will be looking for you for the same reason," she said.

"Two days remain, and you both must perform purifications, so be off now and may the gods smile on you both."

She sat down as Veric nodded and walked over to his horse.

"See you soon, Hugh, Associate Justice Knight," Veric said, as he galloped across the lawn and toward his home.

"Hugh, your father and I are so proud of you. You will make a masterful Justice Knight and one day may even be a Chief Justice Knight, like your father," she said.

"Let go that darkness which enslaves your heart." She kissed him on the forehead. "Come inside and warm yourself by the fire, and eat some bread, meat, and cheese. Afterward, begin your fast."

*   *   *

The carriage ride to the temple was short, and Verily stepped through the main door. Hugh entered through the garden and met his friends under the portico.

He felt strange in the ceremonial garb; a special blend of elfish silk, and dwarven wool. The slippers he wore were made of chonch leather and tanned with pixie hive resin.

The undergarments were equally as exotic—made from mountain spider silk and saple tree sinew, it conformed to his body tightly.

A procession of armed men came; the fathers of the other boys. This was the time to show the changing of the guard, the new blood that would champion justice for the next generation.

Again the sadness washed over him, then he saw the blue colored armor that his father wore. It was held on a litter carried high above by the elder knights. In an instant his heart became light and he smiled.

"Knight candidates, to your positions!" called the priest.

They filed into the building and stood by the dais. The priest waited for the knights to place Guy's armor at the altar and retire to the back of the room.

The crowd murmured as the minstrels began playing. Hugh saw his mother in the front. The priest came forth and stood by the armor and held up his hands.

The murmurs died and all eyes looked forward.

"Since the days before the first kingdoms, the role of knight has been a sacred one passed from father to son. Today, the Justice Knight is even more sacred, for it binds the Outland Kingdoms with the City States. There is nowhere within the Kingdoms that a Justice Knight does not hold authority."

He unrolled a scroll and lit a candle. Several monks came in and laid out medals. For some time the priest prayed and made sacrifice.

"Let all here be honest, and if there is reason to dismiss any of these candidate knights, let it be known!"

Silence filled the hall.

"By Tera, goddess of light and righteous moral grace, I will now call upon these candidates to step forth and assume the role of Associate Justice Knight!"

They came up one at a time. As Hugh approached, the priest held up his hand and pointed to the armor.

"This armor cries out for a man to fill it," he said.

Hugh shook his head. "I can't, it was my father's."

"Your father's will directed that when you were knighted, you would have his armor. It is yours, Hugh. Keep it on a pedestal, or wear it, that is your choice."

He then presented Hugh the Medal of the Law, and placed it around his neck.

"You are a man, and a Justice Knight with all the authority to keep and apply the law of the land. May Tera bless you."

Hugh stood to the side with the others until the ceremony was complete.

As the families left the temple, he sat next to the armor. It was a light shade of blue, and recently polished. He reached out and felt it.

Not since his father was alive did he ever do that. It was cold to the touch, and he fought back some tears.

"I suppose if father wished for me to wear this, I should."

Verily came alongside him. She put her hand on his shoulder, and he turned back forcing a smile.

"Your father is so proud of you. I know that I am."

She walked around the armor and caressed the helmet with her hand.

"I can almost see his face there inside."

She picked up the helmet. "It's time you took up your birthright."

She placed the helmet on Hugh's head and lifted the visor. "It suits you well." Her smile was warm and reassuring.

"I can't leave you, Mother, to gallivant about the kingdoms."

She chuckled. "This is your time, my son. Now go and fulfill your destiny." She helped him put on the armor.

As he put each piece on, it conformed to his body, snugging against muscles and skin. Each piece, when placed against the preceding one, formed a seamless connection.

Once all were in place, the inside of the visor illuminated with colors. Hugh marveled at the contraption as he tried walking. Getting around seemed nearly effortless.

"Your father left instructions," she said, putting some papers on the dais. "Read them thoroughly."

She turned and walked to the temple doors.

"I love you, my darling son. Do your duty, and come visit when you can." She left.

He moved toward the door, but saw his father's notes on the dais. He reached for them and opened the documents.

Son, if you are reading this, you have taken the oath of kinghood. I have left you my armor, a very ancient set forged by Grimly Moore himself some two thousand years ago. Follow these instructions: train with the armor, and as long as you wear it, remember, your greatest asset is your mind. Now, go to your courtyard and train.

*   *   *

Hugh rode all night. He changed horses three times and reached the Castle Cranvale mid of the second day.

"There is no worldly thing that can be done," the surgeon told him.

"Can I see her?" Hugh asked.

"You may."

The surgeon let Hugh pass and go into the Viscountess' chamber. She lay in bed; her pale features betrayed the dire state of her health.

"Mother? Can you hear me?"

She opened her eyes.

"What is this sickness that possesses her?" Hugh asked the surgeon.

"Don't do that," Verily said in a weak whisper. "If you worry, you will cause wrinkles in your forehead."

She struggled to smile.

"I'll travel to Moore if I must to get an elvish healer," he said as her eyes closed.

He turned to the surgeon. "What will heal her?" Tears welled up in his eyes.

The surgeon shook his head.

"She has Advol disease, very rare and lingering."

"There must be something we can do."

"I've sent word to my colleagues at the surgeon-healer academy in Bon. I'll know more by tomorrow if there is anything known that can help."

"Leave us," Verily said, waving the surgeon out of the room. She looked up into Hugh's face.

"I know this disease, and there is no cure."

"That's not entirely true," Ford said, as he stepped from the shadows.

Hugh jumped and drew his dagger.

"Who are you?"

"My name is Ford Efferguard," he said with a flourish of his hand and a bow. "My employer would like to help."

"You're an elf. How did you get in here?" Hugh demanded.

"My employer is very resourceful. I'm here to summon you on an errand. In return they promise to pay you with something that will save your mother's life."

"What is it?" Hugh asked.

"Your mother will remain in this state for quite some time. Advol disease is a slow, painfully slow death. It robs the victim of their ability to move, then feel, then their mind."

"She will be near death for quite a while. Your surgeon will learn from Bon just what your mother said; there is no cure, but he and his academy have not my resources."

"And you will provide me with a cure?"

"My employers will provide that. Will you come with me to meet him and hear his proposition?"

Hugh looked at his mother. Her breathing was shallow, nearly absent. Wiping a tear from his eye, he bent down and kissed her on the forehead.

"Mother, I must go away for a short while. I'll return and I swear I will cure you of this affliction," he said.

Turning to Ford, he drew in a deep breath.

"I'll do whatever it takes."

"Good of you to say. I have a feeling it will take whatever we got," Ford said with a wry smile.

"Nonetheless, if we are to keep the schedule, we must away."

Ford reached down at his side and opened the flap on his leather satchel. Withdrawing a glass jar of the golden powder he removed the top and shook out a sparing amount into the palm of his hand.

"Get what you need and come near to me. When I use this, we will have but a few seconds to jump through the gateway."

Hugh sheathed his dagger.

"I have all that I need," he said.

"Very well," Ford replied, and threw the golden dust into the air.

A clap of thunder echoed as if a far-off storm was brewing. In the room a radiant six foot high broken rectangle opened just wide enough to allow one person at a time to pass.

"In we go," Ford shouted, and pushed Hugh through the portal.

Following close behind, Ford passed through the gap, then it snapped shut. The landing on the other side was less than elegant.

CHAPTER

5

Chaos and Order

Standing at the edge of the door, Sark's parents were dumfounded. In the room, Sark summoned a fire elemental and was commanding it to move around without burning anything.

"What is he doing now?" Sark's mother asked.

"He's still reading the scroll from the study: Master Gob's Magic Elemental. He's only two," Sark's father whispered.

"What does it mean?"

"He's a prodigy, by the blessing of the gods, a prodigy," his father said.

They watched as Sark manifested an ice elemental, then air, then he used his clay to make a mud-golem. The Netherworld creatures regarded the child with some curiosity, but it was clear that they obeyed his every direction.

"What do we do?" his mother asked.

"We encourage him!" his father said.

*   *   *

"It is said that at age five, Mister Sark finished the five volumes of *Magic*. You know the books of The Three Disciplines?"

"I know from his papers that he quickly gobbled up books

on magic, engineering, and mathematics. Graduating from primary school, he entered the academy at age ten, and at age fourteen he had attained the rank of Maestro in Manifesting and Conjuring.

"At age sixteen, Master Sark was teaching at the Academy of Magic and Learning in the elven city of Frouhauf, a miraculous achievement for a human. At twenty he was the chair for the Department of Learned Energy Analysis. So what happened to the amazing Professor Sark?" Miss Blackbane asked.

She sat very rigidly and held her notepad and stylus on her lap.

The headmaster picked up his goblet of brandy and swirled it about in the glass.

"It's not simple. As far as we can deduce, he discovered two codices, long forgotten in the library basement."

"What were they?"

"Professor Yorg Hillflower's *Legacy of Chaos Magic*. He was somewhat of an eccentric back in the Dark Times."

Writing down his every word, she checked off the facts.

"Let me see if I get this straight thus far… Professor Sark, one of the most prolific and promising instructors of the art of magic, found two old books and suddenly vanished?"

"Not exactly," the headmaster corrected. "He found those tomes a few years ago. For the last two years he's been working on a formula to harness Chaos Magic, the forth state of magical energy."

"Isn't that dangerous?"

She sat forward and put her tablet of paper on his desk. From her bag she removed a long-stem pipe and stuffed it with dried topus, then lit a match and inhaled.

"I mean, the ancients knew how to harness it, but all those of recent times who have tried to use it… well, haven't they ended up horribly dead?"

"Yes." He took a drink and set down the cup. "Are you sure I can't get you a glass?"

"Not at this time, thank you."

She sat back and crossed her legs and put the pad on her knee. She looked thoughtful for a few moments.

"Is he dead?"

"Heavens, no!" The headmaster laughed. "Just not working here any longer. I went to see him recently and tried to get him to return to the school, to impart his vast knowledge to our up and coming student body. But it was clear that he was obsessed with Chaos Magic. He refused to come back."

"I talked with a Professor Hillmire, and he said something about an explosion here on campus a year ago. Was that due to Mr. Sark's efforts?"

"It was, but I hasten to add that we do not allow Chaos Magic to be performed here any longer and that all labs involved with alchemy are strictly supervised."

"Were there any injuries?"

"None save for Sark. When we found him, he was mumbling 'bloom, bloom, bloom'."

"Boom, boom, boom," she repeated as she wrote.

"No. 'Bloom, bloom, bloom'." He corrected, then took another drink. "See, he was trying to do Theocratus' Flowerpot Surprise using Chaos Magic. It surprised him alright..." the headmaster chuckled. "He grew a thick coat of white and yellow flowers all over his body."

"That doesn't sound healthy."

"They fell off him an hour later."

"You said that you went to him and spoke recently. Where

might I find him?"

"I'm afraid that I am not at liberty to say; he's a man who appreciates his privacy."

"Yes, a man. How was it working with a human? Did the elven staff get along with him?"

"Everyone liked Mr. Sark. There were no conflicts related to race."

"But there were conflicts?"

"Again, our legal counsel has advised me to not discuss such things."

"Well, Headmaster Williams, you have been most informative and the Warren Hills Tribune thanks you for your time."

She stood and walked to the door. Turning, she smiled warmly.

"Oh, one more thing. Did you know that Mr. Sark has not been seen nor heard from in five weeks? His home is empty, and the local shire reeve reported to us that his townhouse has been dark and silent."

"That is troubling. I hope he didn't rip a hole into the Netherworld. Perhaps he just moved away."

"Thanks again, Headmaster." She smiled, turned, and left.

*   *   *

The informant that Ford paid mentioned that Sark had purchased an old estate outside the city. Ahead he saw an ill repaired tower, and just beyond, a weathered old home with a slate roof.

Wooden beams on one side of the tower appeared to be the only thing holing it up. The roof tiles were somewhat askew, and a white vapor was drifting from the top window.

Not far from the tower was a three story country home, also in a state of disrepair. In places along one wall, the interior was visible. Over the front door, a copper done supported by four columns shaded the entrance.

As Ford approached an elf woman dashed from the front door, a flock of black creatures in hot pursuit. They grabbed at her clothes and hair, and from time to time would even envelope her.

She screamed as they harassed her. In short order, she dashed past Ford, as did the black specters, and ran to the main road.

Ford continued to the house. Under the shade of the dome, he raised his hand to knock. The door flew open and a man ran headlong into him.

Climbing to his feet, Sark dusted off Ford as he helped him up.

"Sorry, friend. Seems we were attempting to occupy the same space at the same time. I've done it once, but have not been able to duplicate it since," he said. "By the way, have you seen a woman out here – a reporter from some paper? I think I accidently conjured some harriers and they may have taken a liking to her."

"Yes, she fled south toward the road."

"Probably wise of her." He smiled at Ford. "My name is Sark. How can I help you?"

"I'm Ford Efferguard, and I've been looking for you."

"Ford Efferguard you say?" Sark asked, as he began walking towards the tower. "Sounds Moorish," he added.

"Indeed it is. I'm from Moore. I've come to seek your help," Ford said

"Walk with me; I have business in my laboratory in the tower," Sark suggested.

"Yes, of course. I bring a message from my employer, who seeks your help with a quest."

"A quest you say?"

"Yes, a quest."

"For what? I mean, what is the treasure sought?"

"I am only at liberty to say if you accept my offer."

"It must be important if you seek me. I think it a relic," Sark guessed.

"If you accept I will say."

"Please don't, it is much more interesting guessing. Now where was I? Oh yes, a relic that is sought by one or many?"

Ford looked annoyed.

"There will be more than you in the party."

"So, a relic that takes more than one to find it, and probably very rare. Yes... rare, I think."

"My employer has given me leave to offer you whatever you desire— money, lands, or power," Ford said.

"Ah ha!" Sark said, as he reached the door to the tower. "A relic that is sought by the powerful, who cannot search for it himself, who is offering any desire to those foolish enough to quest for it. That must be the armor of Vilhart the Lucky!" he said.

"No. Now would you like to join our party?" Ford said, sensing Sark to be possibly crazy.

"Okay, very well... it isn't the armor of Vilhart the Lucky. I have it," he shouted. "It's the Tent of Ten Castles of Yuri the Cursed!"

"No, we are not looking for that," Ford said, becoming very irritated. "All I want to know is, are you interested in meeting my master and talking about our quest?"

"It is a fool Mr. Efferguard that steps into a void without knowing where it leads. Though, I have done that recently... I'm still cleaning off those shoes. Could it be the spell of Father McLeland the Bold, and his Caldron of Never Ending Stew?"

"No... by the gods!" Ford said now angry.

"By the gods? There are many gods, and it seems that all of them had some mystical relic that's been lost. Which god do you mean? Oh wait, could your search be for the Lantern of Dern Blackhammer?" Sark asked.

Ford was quiet for a moment.

"I can't say at this time. If you'd just come and meet my employer, all will be revealed."

"Ah, yes, the Lantern of Dern Blackhammer. Lost for, nigh upon five thousand years or more," Sark said while standing in the doorway.

"Do you smell something burning?" Ford asked.

Dark smoke was now rolling out of the top story window.

Sark looked up, then shouted. "My experiment!"

He dashed into the tower and up a rickety set of rotted wooden stairs.

Following close behind, Ford was hard pressed to keep up. Sark took two steps at a time as he dashed up the helix shaped stairs.

At the top, they both entered a large round room. It was thick with smoke and a large glass bulb filled with a black goop.

Quickly, Sark moved the heating lamp then threw the shutters wide open to allow the acrid smoke to vent.

"Blast it!" he exclaimed. "So much for two weeks of work."

Sark walked over to the glass bulb and stared at it. "Curses," he added.

"If you don't mind sir, may I have your answer?"

"What? Oh, yes, Mr. Efferguard, you were saying something about a quest for Dern Blackhammer's lantern? My terms are, I will go if I get to have unlimited access to the relic... to study it thoroughly. It is fabled to be composed of Chaos Magic. Oh, and one other thing, one thousand pounds of gold," he added. "A man cannot live on study alone." He winked.

Ford realized that Sark was not as crazy as he appeared.

"Then we will need to talk with my employer," Ford said.

Sark started gathering items and stuffing them into a brown cloth backpack.

"Do you keep him in your pocket?"

"I beg your pardon?"

"Your master, or rather employer, is he in your pocket or do we need to travel to meet with him?"

"No, he is not in my pocket. But he did provide me with this."

Ford pulled forth the glass jar of golden powder from under his cloak.

"We can go to him right now."

"Powder Teleportus!" Sark said surprised. "I didn't think any of that was still available."

"It's not. This is the last that we know about," Ford said.

"You're using a priceless magic powder to transport us? This quest must be important indeed," Sark stated.

"You'll know soon."

Taking a handful of the powder from the jar, Ford quickly tossed it into the air.

"Get ready, we will have—"

"Only seconds. I know," Sark stated.

Ford jumped through the magic doorway.

"Pity," said Sark, as he leapt through the opening. "I would like to have studied that dust a while."

CHAPTER

6

A Case of Wet Boots

"Dern Blackhammer raised his hammer and brought it down upon the anvil with a crash," Dormer Friggand said.

"The red glowing sparks showered the stony ground upon whence he stood. He raised it again and again until the final piece of the lantern was forged.

"He commanded the glass to be polished by his servant, Squal'etmod; its twenty tentacles furiously moving over the surface of the thick disc of glass."

He leaned forward in his rocking chair and put a match into the embers of the fireplace. Removing it, he placed the burning end to the bowl of his pipe and drew in deeply. He exhaled, sat back, and smiled down at the two beaming upturned faces.

"Finally, once all the pieces had been assembled, Dern took a glowing ember from his magic forge and placed it in the case, blew upon it with the breath of life, and the lantern was forever lit. The light of which, if looked upon by a mortal, will transport them to the gods, where they can learn the secrets of the Charm of Creation."

Dormer stood up, brushed off his breaches and stretched his arms upward. The fire was growing old, and the last glimmers of flames were now dark blue.

"Off to bed with you, boys. In the morn, we will be on the

lake, and if the gods are willing, we will have a day's catch that we can sell for gold."

"Dormer?" called his wife. "Will you be taking your nightly tea?"

"I shall," he called back to her. "Now off you two, or by mighty Hoth's wrath your friend will not be allowed to spend the night again this season."

Sean stood up with a sigh. "Come on, Plutz. My dad is right."

He and Plutz made their way to the staircase and slowly climbed it to the top most floor. The house was modest, two stories with an attic. His parents occupied the second level, and Sean's room was the attic.

The first floor was reserved for the fireplace, kitchen, and in winter, the stable for their two horses. It was a fine house compared to others along the lake.

In fact, Plutz's home, an old longhouse, had only one floor and two rooms. Plutz had to share his bed with three other siblings.

Sean sat at the edge of his bed. "I've been accepted to the academy."

"Really?" Plutz said. "That's great!"

"After this season, I'll be traveling to Portmouth."

"Perhaps one day you'll even be a captain of your own ship."

"Most of the graduates become captains," Sean said. "What will you do?"

Plutz chuckled. "I'll do my pilgrimage to Moore to see the Temple of Yuel."

"Then what?"

"Either I'll be accepted to the Temple Parish, or I'll come

back here and work with my father." He paused. "Wouldn't it be great if we found Dern Blackhammer's lantern?"

Sean looked at him.

"It's just a story."

Standing, he walked to the window and looked out.

"Jup and Tiber are now spaced evenly apart in the sky and beaming brightly," he said

"They say if you look upon the two moons at the stroke of double six bells and make a wish, that wish will come true," Plutz said, as he pulled on his sleeping cap.

"Plutz, I see a bear out there."

"Really? Or is it that you're trying to play me with a prank?" Plutz said, as he yawned.

"No, really, I can see it clearly," Sean stated.

The bear transformed into a hunched old woman with a cane. She looked up at Sean, then transformed into a bear again.

Plutz got out of the bed, walked over and looked out the window.

"You're right, it's a bear. How interesting. They typically don't hunt in this area. Now let's get some sleep. You know how your dad likes to work us until we can't move the next day."

"But... it was an old woman... I mean it changed before my eyes!"

"Ha, ha. It's not enough that a bear is in your yard, but you have to try and goof me too. Sean, when will you learn?" Plutz said.

Pulling the drapes, Sean sat at the edge of the bed. For a moment he wondered if his eyes were playing tricks on him. He nervously chuckled.

"Ya, that's it, I was fooling you. Can't blame a fellow for

trying."

He laid back down, his thoughts filled with adventures he would have at the naval academy. Finally, he closed his eyes and drifted off to sleep.

The dream came quickly to him. It was daytime, and he was standing in a clearing in the woods. A small cottage, one that he had never seen before had smoke coming from the stucco chimney. It was shaped oddly; a little more ornate than he was used to seeing in the High-Lakes region.

The windows were leaded glass made up by small circles, and he saw the bear sitting out front on a three-legged stool with a pipe in its mouth smoking.

For some reason he felt compelled to walk out into the open and give away his hiding place. The bear looked up and stood.

It tapped the pipe on the edge of the stool. The ash fell like a miniature funnel storm and formed a tiny doll. The bear picked up the doll and quickly gobbled it up, then the bear began transforming.

The creature changed from a bear into a shriveled old woman. Her face was drawn, her nose pointy, and she was stooped with a walking stick.

"I do love the fresh meat of a tenderly roasted babe," she said.

She came toward him.

"Sean, I shall give you a gift. You will be a great captain, and in return, when I call upon you, you shall do my bidding," she said. "Would you like to be a sea captain?"

"I would," Sean said. "What do I have to do?"

"Just agree. I will make it so."

"Who are you?"

"A friendly spirit, like in your father's stories." She produced a leather-clad book. "Just sign here," she said, handing him a quill.

Sean took the pen and winced as if he were pricked in the finger with a needle. The tip of the quill became red and she motioned for him to sign. He hesitated.

"All your dreams will come true... just sign. Your father will never have to work again. Your friend Plutz will look up to you. Your mother will have servants, and all your friends will think you important."

She again motioned. Sean touched the pen to the leather and signed.

Sean sat up. The room was dark and Plutz was snoring. He stood and walked to the window. Opening the drapes he saw the moons were gone, and in the distance the new morning sun was coming.

"Lads, time to get up," shouted Dormer as he rapped on the door. "Them fish aren't going to jump into the boat willingly!"

Sean let go the drapes. On the edge was blood. He looked at his finger, and a small red dot was right at the tip.

He and Plutz came down the stairs to the kitchen. There the two boys warmed themselves by the stove and waited for Sean's mother to ladle out the porridge.

"Eat. You'll need your strength when you're pulling on those oars," she said.

"Mom, what do you know about dreams?" Sean asked.

"Not much."

She opened the oven and took out some biscuits.

"Did you have a bad dream?"

"No, not like that. It wasn't bad per say, but something

about it felt bad."

His mother wiped her hands on her apron and looked at him.

"Are you worried about the academy?"

"Not that I'm aware of."

Dormer got a bowl and filled it with porridge.

"Well, some good hard work will put your mind right. If we're to make any money at all, we'll need to have a good haul today."

"I'm ready to do my part, Mister Friggand," Plutz said.

"Yer a good boy, Plutz." Dormer scooped his porridge into his mouth and finished before the two boys. "I'll be down at the marina."

The door shut and he was gone.

Sean and Plutz quickly followed suit, tossed their bowls into the washing tub and ran out the door. The road to the harbor was straight and not long, and both boys hurried to get to work.

Soon they were at the marina rolling rope and preparing nets. Many boats bobbed up and down on the waves of the turbulent Warland Lake.

Dormer stood at the end of the pier; his boat showing the bright painted colors of red and green with a large white and black eye painted on either side of the bow.

"Come on, boys," he called. "The dawn's approaching and the fish are jumping!"

The afternoon sun beat down on the three elves as they bobbed on the waves. A gentle breeze washed over them, and a flock of lake gulls circled overhead.

Sean looked out toward the river inlet and felt an icy chill run up his spine.

"Do either of you feel like we're being watched?" he asked.

Plutz glanced over as he mended a worn net.

"So, I'm not the only one."

"What are you two talking about?" Dormer narrowed his brow. "Being watched? By whom?"

Sean shrugged his shoulders.

"I don't know, but I sure feel like someone is."

Dormer chuckled. "Probably some of the girls keeping tabs on you two strapping lads."

"Maybe." Sean sounded skeptical.

"Perhaps you'll feel a bit more at ease with some of your mother's vikenberry pie in your stomach."

Dormer moved to the cold-box at the aft. He opened the device and pulled out a pan of pie. Taking his knife he cut it into six mostly even pieces and dished out a slice to each boy.

"Now, let whoever's watching burn with envy at our treat." He took a bite.

They finished off the vikenberry pie and all the grape water that was in the cold-box. From here on out it would be merely dried meat, some roasted gable nuts and a cup of sweet red wine to tide them over until they returned to the marina.

"Let's get those nets in, boys," Dormer said.

Sean and Plutz moved to the larboard side and began harvesting the nets. Dormer grabbed up his gaff and reached out for the nearest float.

"There's that show-boat Yarle Valcurl coming towards us," he said with a shake of his head.

Yarle was waving his arms and shouting.

"What's he saying, Pop?" Sean asked.

"I'm not sure." Dormer put his hand to his ear. "What is it you're saying? I can't hear you, Yarle!"

He pulled up a corner of the net.

"Bring in the net, boys... I'll find out what Yarle wants."

"Dormer!" shouted Yarle. "Yohan's children are missing!"

"Children missing?" Dormer asked. "Yohan's children are missing?"

"Vanished from his house while his wife was cooking! All the boats are being called in to help search for them!"

"We'll be along directly!" Dormer yelled back.

Yarle turned his boat about and began heading in towards the shore. Dormer turned to the boys, his face grim.

"You heard Yarle; we need to get our nets up quickly and get back to town."

With each stroke upon the oars the boat drew closer to the shore, and in the distance the marina was visible. All around them were fishing boats in various states of return.

Sweat poured from Sean's brow as his muscles bulged and his arms burned with each pull of his oar. A slight breeze came up blowing shoreward and Sean was glad to see his father start to put up the sail.

"Stow your oars, boys, we have some wind," Dormer said, as their speed doubled.

As they approached the docks, Dormer dropped the sail. A small wave carried them to the wooden marina, and he jumped to the wharf and secured the boat with the aft rope.

Sean jumped to the dock and secured the bow line. Other boats were arriving and being tied, and a stream of men and boys were moving from the docks to the shipwright building just up the hill.

"Come on, Plutz," Sean called out.

Plutz jumped to the dock. "Right, let's go," he said.

The large barn doors to the shipwright building were open, and Lake Elves were gathering. The late afternoon sun was making long shadows, and the group of men and their sons numbered in the hundreds.

Plutz's father, Hinder, stood up on the decking of a half-finished boat.

"We must form into search parties," he shouted. "Those kids could be lost in the woods or worse! Gather your light stones, torches, and lanterns."

He pointed into the crowd.

"Friggand, you, Sean, Plutz and I will search the woods near Drain Marsh by the river mouth. Yarl, have your clan search the old hilltop ruins. Dongals take your clan and search the area near the caves to the east.

"Valcurl, take your clan and search the area to west of the road, Gunter and Brandywell take your clans and search the area north by the old tower. Miter, Vingret, and Hooltub, take your clans and search the swamp up the coast toward Bastard Rock.

"Blow your whistles three times if you find anything, and we will all converge there. Time is of the essence!"

He jumped down and grabbed a torch.

"Now, let's go!"

Hinder and Dormer led the way out into the darkness towards the river. The area was relatively flat and marshy, and the river moved slowly along a radial arc through the woods towards the lake.

Halfway to the river, Hinder stopped the group and pointed into the woods.

"Plutz, you and Sean take this lantern and head into the woods through there. When you get to the river, go down stream twenty paces and come back towards the fields, move twenty paces toward the lake and repeat. Dormer and I will go to the lake and work our way back toward you. If you find something blow your whistle twice and we will come."

"Okay, Papa," Plutz said. "Come on, Sean... you hold the lantern."

They moved toward the woods.

The moons began their rise into the night sky and the light was abundant. Sean decided to put the shutter down on the lantern, and they moved with little care for any unseen dangers.

Moving into the woods, they took a dirt path leading toward the river.

"I sure hope we don't see that bear from last night," Plutz said.

"Me too. Do you feel anything strange?" Sean's voice carried some sense of stress.

"Like?"

"Well, I'm not sure... sorta like there's this thing watching you and you can't see it."

Plutz stopped.

"Are you trying to scare me?"

"What? No," Sean said.

"I don't feel that way now. What could be watching us?" They began walking again. "Something bad?"

Sean shrugged. "I'm not sure."

It did not take long before they heard the sound of the rolling river. Sean saw it first.

A long silvery line thirty feet across shimmered in the

darkness. Here Sean knew the current was not strong, for he and Plutz had fished from the very spot and even swam in the cool waters. Across the river he saw something; a small rowboat partially obscured by some brush.

"Do you see that?" he asked.

"I do. Looks like old man Filby's boat."

"I don't think it's his," Sean said. "It's of a strange make."

"Orc marauders maybe?" Plutz mused.

"No," Sean said as he set down the lantern. "Let's have a look."

He moved into the river and began swimming across. Plutz followed.

On the other side they climbed out into a thicket. They examined the boat. It was not elvish in make.

Sean led the way into the brush. The dark green glossy foliage reflected the bright moonlight. Sean made his way into the surrounding woods, but stopped and looked over his shoulder.

"Plutz... do you smell that?"

Plutz sniffed the air. "Cooking fire, prazel weed and some jupjup seasoning," he said. "Delicious – whatever it is."

"There are no homes out here." Sean looked concerned. "Come on."

Plutz followed as Sean led the way through the dark woods, and they made their way towards the smell.

Piercing the dense flora, the bright moonlight illuminated patches of the forest floor. Sean stopped and kneeled on one knee.

He motioned for Plutz to get down. There was danger afoot, and Sean's body language radiated fear. He pointed past a bush into a dark glade.

"Who do you suppose built that?" he asked in a whisper.

On the other side of the bush was a wide green marshy meadow with a cottage in the middle. In the light they saw smoke rising from the chimney. In the windows were several lights, like lanterns or candles flickering.

The door opened and out came a person dressed in a dark black robe. Sean stifled a gasp. It was the hag from his dream.

She scanned the meadow as she stepped from the stoop into the grass. For a moment it seemed she was going to walk into the forest opposite them.

"Sean, what do you see?" Plutz whispered.

The hag stopped turned, and stared in their direction. Sean melted back into the bush and held still.

"Shhh." He barely made the sound. He bent over and whispered in Plutz's ear, "An awful looking hag, living in a strange cottage."

Plutz whispered back, "It's Bobka Yoshka, the witch."

Sean's blood froze in his veins. If it was the legendary witch, and she had come to their town, she was not one to be trifled with by him and Plutz.

Common sense dictated that they run, find their fathers and get help. But there was something else… a feeling of pending dread and horror that he could not dismiss.

"She's a cannibal," Plutz whispered.

"Indeed," Sean said. "Yohan's kids, Fifer and Kiefer, she has them."

"How do you know?"

"I just do – and she's intending on killing them and eating them this night." His voice was tainted with panic.

"What do we do?"

"Rescue them."

Peeking his head around the bush, Sean saw no sign of the witch. "Come on," he said.

On hands and knees, Sean made his way through the tall grass towards the cottage. He felt intense worry. It was a well-known fact that witches regarded children as a delicacy.

Or, at least, that was what the legends told. He moved swiftly to a set of small hedges that made a border around the cottage. Sean crouched down and peeked over.

There were no signs that anyone was there. Both he and Plutz slipped into what appeared to be a garden.

Evil stinking herbs and strange nettles grew here, some with an unworldly green glow. Sean moved to the door and listened. He heard some whimpering, as if someone were sobbing.

A strange feeling came over him, like an insatiable hunger for sweets. A scent caught his nose, and he leaned into the light brown shingles that made up the wall of the cottage.

Taking in a deep whiff he was pleasantly surprised to find it smelled like a cookie. He carefully broke off a bit and put his tongue to it. It tasted good, like a cookie.

"What do you make of this?" he asked handing a piece to Plutz.

"You remember the stories. She makes her house out of tasty treats to entice children to come and have a taste, then *wham*! She puts a spit through them and roasts them before they're dead." Plutz's voice was shaky with fear.

"I'm so hungry," Sean said, as his stomach growled.

"Me too. It must be a spell she's put on this place, to make us stay here and eat until she returns."

Sean closed his eyes and tried to picture where she'd put the spit to roast him; his mind quickly cleared. Still, the hunger persisted gnawing at his belly. Putting his ear to the door, he heard the sobbing.

He whispered to Plutz, "I'm going to go inside. If you hear or see anything, hoot twice like an owl and run for the cover of the woods. If we get separated we'll meet at the river by the boat."

"Aye," Plutz said, as he positioned himself near some vile looking plants.

Sean lifted the latch and opened the door. The whimpering grew louder and he saw a fire in the fireplace, a caldron in the coals.

Steam was rising from the pot filling the room with a scent of boiled tubers and broth. By the fire was a blood-stained wooden table crudely built, and hanging from the wooden beams of the roof were dead things; squirrels, frogs, and various body parts of animals.

As he entered he realized that there were two metal cages in the corner of the room. Inside were Fifer and Kiefer. They were both sobbing, and pale with fright.

Both children turned as he came in, and their eyes grew wide with hope. Sean put his finger to his lips.

On the table was a key and a long knife, and he grabbed both. Tucking the knife into his belt he moved to the cage. The lock was simple, and he quickly inserted the key and unlatched the cages.

Both children, five and six, came forth and clung on to him; then came the sound of hooting. Sean grabbed both boys and rushed to the door.

"A nice dressing of flambyu will go well with my sweet meat!" said a haggish voice from outside the door. "But wait! Who has been nibbling at my house?"

Sean threw open the door and dashed out, smashing into the witch and knocking her over. She fell back into her garden and looked on in shocked surprise.

"Sean," she hissed with a rage that ignited the air around her. "I did not foresee you doing this! You are my servant. Return my dinner!"

Sean ran for the woods with both children tucked under each arm. The witch sprang to her feet and screamed a litany of curses, some of which Sean had never heard before.

A crackling of the air erupted all around, and the grass in front and behind Sean burst into flames. He ran through, emerging on the other side of the fire in a dead sprint. Behind him he heard the angry witch hot on his heels.

"I'll have your eyes for appetizers!" she called.

Sean felt as though his feet did not touch the ground as he swiftly navigated the swampy turf. In a moment he would be in the woods, and in another minute to the river.

A bony hand clamped down on his shoulder as he reached the forest fence. Plutz was waiting with a tree branch and leveled the creature. He fell in behind Sean, and they both rushed to the river.

A bright blue explosion lit up the night sky. Trees were blasted flat, and a rush of hot air enveloped the four boys. A cackling filled the air, and the witch was on their trail again.

Sean, Plutz and the two boys crashed through the underbrush and tumbled headlong down the muddy riverbank. The rowboat was not more than twenty feet from where they were.

"Quick, into the boat," Sean shouted. "If we take her boat she will not come after us, if she gets wet she'll sink like a stone!"

They all climbed in and Sean pushed them into the current. In a matter of seconds, they were in the middle of the river.

The witch emerged on the other side and gave a howl of rage.

"Sean Friggand," she shouted. "I'll forgive you for stealing my dinner! Your worth to me will be revealed. You'll be of service to me yet. I've seen it in a vision. You signed the book, you belong to me now! When the time is right, I'll come to see you."

Sean got the oars, and he and Plutz set to rowing. The boat moved slowly towards the other bank. He looked back, and the witch was standing there on the other bank watching them.

"A bargain is a bargain, young elf, and I shall call upon you in time. As for my supper, I shall find fairer treats further north."

She laughed and the air around her snapped and crackled with fire, then she was gone.

Plutz twice blew the whistle as loud as he could. They heard shouting from down river. Their fathers were coming.

The next day the elders convened. A search of the forest was conducted. The house and the witch were gone. It was clear that something had crushed the meadow grass, but the garden and the house were no longer there. It was decided to send a dispatch north, to warn other villages and towns of the witch's appearance.

*   *   *

The Burning Cost Pirates had raided the walled city of Cun Tang and made away with the treasury gold. Sean was dispatched with a squadron of gunships to intercept the brigands.

Near the Crumbling Keys, the pirates ambushed the squadron. Five gunships and four pirate ships were sent to the bottom. Sean's ship came alongside the pirate's flagship. Grappling hooks were thrown, and the pirates stormed aboard.

The pirate captain swung across and landed on the deck next to Sean. He was a large seven foot tall orc with a nose ring. Their blades clashed, and in the background magically powered steam cannons exchanged fire as grapeshot raked both decks.

Sean and the orc stepped over broken and bloodied bodies as they exchanged furious thrusts and parries. The orc kicked Sean and drove him back against the railing. Sean ducked down, avoided a nasty slash, and rolled to the side.

Bringing his cutlass up, then down, Sean severed the pirate's left hand at the wrist. He grabbed the monster by his leather harness, threw him to the deck, and put his sword to his throat.

"Surrender," he demanded. "I have the advantage."

Leveling his dark yellow eyes on Sean, the creature nodded his head in acquiescence and clutched the stump of his wrist.

"Fling yer arms to the deck," shouted the orc captain to his crew.

The fighting slowed and stopped. Over the sound of the wind came the clanking of arms hitting hardened wood.

Dragging the orc to the railing, Sean issued more orders.

"Tell them they are under my command, and anyone who thinks other can take leave of the ship and swim for it. I'm sure that there are plenty of islands about to harbor rogues such as they!"

The orc shouted his command for them to obey Sean.

"Secure the prisoners," Sean shouted to his Second Mate Mister Harding. "Send over a crew to repair the enemy ship and sail her back to Green Port."

"Aye, aye, Captain," Harding said.

Sean handed the prisoner over to one of his crew and leaned against the railing.

"Thank the gods that's done."

Over the next few hours he supervised the securing of prisoners, and the repair of his own ship. As the sun began its descent toward the horizon, he retired to his quarters.

Sean sat at the captain's table in his private room. The night was coming. He took a fork full of mutton and put it into his mouth.

"What of the repairs?"

"Our ship is complete. The other ship will be a few hours more, but that will put us into twilight and the reefs around here are treacherous."

"Agreed," Sean said. "We'll stay here until morning, and then set out for Green Port." He took a drink of wine. "Double the watch."

Harding left the captain's cabin and the door locked shut. Sean got up from the table and poured himself a glass of port.

He looked down at his arms. No scars. It was truly unusual that for as many battles he'd been involved in, no weapon had ever touched him. He bore no scars for his victories, and to his men he seemed enchanted by some mystical power.

Never did he question this, and always in his mind he resolved it with justifications of training, speed, youth, or luck. He moved to the bed and lay down.

For a while he read, then reached over, put out the light and closed his eyes.

"You've been enjoying the fruits of my power for some time now," the old woman cackled. "Now it is time you fulfill your half of our contract."

"Am I dreaming?" he asked, confused.

"Less a dream than you think." She puffed away on a pipe. "But, that is of no accord, for we have business to discuss.

"On the ship for which you have taken, there is a treasure. In the belly of the boat sits among the gold and jewels a rare thing. It is shaped as a caldron, black and overused. Go there and take the caldron—bring it to me. I am on the island of Gorn and wish to make use of this relic."

"But I must away at first light to Green Port and deliver my prisoners and booty to the city council there. The treasure does not belong to me."

"Kill the prisoners, and do as I command!"

"I will not!" Sean said.

"You have an overrated sense of duty." She chuckled. "Don't prove yourself a fool." She looked stern. "Are you ungrateful for all that I have done for you?"

"What have you done for me?"

"My magic has made you. No scars do you bear, and you are a captain of a ship now. I have done my part, now you must do yours."

"What part is that?"

"Forever serve my will. You made an oath and signed in blood." She blew smoke out toward him. "You did sign the contract, did you not?"

"I didn't know that it was not a dream," Sean protested.

"Your ignorance is of no concern to me or my guild. Now, you are ordered to get me that cauldron."

"I won't," Sean said in defiance.

She laughed. "Such obstinacy with your master?"

"I am my own master!" Sean said.

"So that is how it shall be then?" Taking the pipe from her mouth she stared at him. "Your tongue may wag right out of its home sooner than you wish!"

"I do not know what foul plot you have for that cauldron, but I will not do the bidding of a spell hack."

Lightning shot from her fingers, and her hair stood on end.

"I take insults from no mortal! To temper your arrogance, I shall teach you a lesson. If by dawn you have not plotted a course to Gron, and are not on your way to me, this curse shall be. Your boots will be forever wet, your heart lost, and your wits tested."

She brushed back her gray hair. Putting the pipe back into her mouth she inhaled deeply, and then as she exhaled said, "It is by your will you shall be so cursed."

Sean jumped from the bed, his skin was tingling and his hair was standing on end as if he had seen a ghost. Moving to his desk and with shaking hand, he retrieved a goblet and filled it with wine. For a moment he was terrified, as his heart raced and his pulse pounded in his veins.

Dressing quickly he came on deck. He moved across the plank connecting the two ships, took up a lantern and descended into the hold.

The decks below were musty and the heavy musky sent of orcs filled the air. A young sailor stood watch at a thick wooden door secured with a padlock.

"Captain," he said, coming to attention.

"Open it!" Sean commanded.

"Aye, sir."

He entered the small chamber and saw stacks of chests and bars of gold. Shifting the containers around, he saw no large cauldron. He ran his hand through the gold coins and ingots. Nothing. He exited the room and stopped at the guard.

"Where is the inventory list?"

"Here it is, sir." The sailor handed him a tube of paper.

Sean unrolled the document and scanned it. Halting, he noticed the words 'large black pot'.

"Where is this?" He pointed.

"The cook took charge of it, sir," the young man said. "Master Rolland said it was okay."

"Yes, he was quite right to do so." Sean turned and walked

back to his ship.

Once in the galley, he saw the large black pot sitting in the middle of the room. It was made of black cast metal and was warm to the touch.

He looked into it; the bottom was rounded and shiny. He was lost in some dream like haze. In his mind came visions, disturbing visions.

A searing pain lay upon his chest and he felt dizzy. Grabbing the sides of the cauldron, he stopped himself from falling in. A horrible face looked back at him, as the stench of rotting flesh assailed his nose. The image swirled, iridescent colors mingling together to form something.

"Captain!" shouted a voice very near. "Captain Friggand!"

His hands came off the rim of the cauldron and he realized there were sailors standing there, including Mr. Rolland.

"Sir, are you okay?" Rolland asked, a tone of worry in his voice.

Shaking his head to purge it of the visions, he cleared his throat.

"Set a course for Green Port, and make full sail. We have not a moment to lose."

"But the night, the reefs?"

"We'll have to risk it."

"Aye, aye! You heard him, to yer post ye dogs!"

*   *   *

"Captain Friggand, enter and be seated," Admiral Hicrom said.

Sean entered the room and took a seat at a long table facing the three Admirals. He removed his hat and set it on the surface. The three men looked severe.

"This tribunal of the Admiralty is back in session. Captain Sean Friggand you are the subject of an inquiry to determine if you are responsible for the loss of cargo and crew of several ships of the Realm.

"By the official record, you are the only survivor from the wreck of the Bitter Bow, lost at sea six months ago. You attest that you managed to swim to an island in the Keys, and survive there for four months until rescued by the S.R Huntfield, which sank one day into its voyage after your rescue.

"You, again, were the only survivor, living on a piece of wreckage for seven days until rescued by the merchant ship the Piltdowns Hydra. That ship also sank with all hands, and you, again, were cast adrift on barrels that you lashed together.

"You floated into Blyth Harbor on the eve of Hill Dance and reported these events to the Naval Council. When questioned about these events at the inquest, you claimed that a witch cursed you and that these events were not your fault."

He paused to take a drink from a cup on the table.

"It is the opinion of this court, based on testimony and in-depth investigation by the Council, that the sinking of the three ships over the past six months is not mere coincidence.

"Therefore, it is the rule of the tribunal that you are relieved of your command and given dock-side duties until such time as the curse you are under is remedied."

Sean cleared his throat and stood up.

"It is true that I have had a patch of bad luck of recent—"

"Captain, lives, cargo, and valuable expensive ships have been lost under your boots. When compared to other officers of the Realm, this situation is unprecedented. It is clear that your curse is far too dangerous for you to remain on board a ship of the Realm. We don't want to lose your experience, but we cannot sustain more lost ships."

"What will I do now? All I ever wanted to do was captain

ships."

"You can teach at the academy, or be assigned to logistics."

Sean drew in a deep breath and let it out.

"If I can't perform as a captain, I'll seek my fortunes elsewhere." He grabbed his hat and put it on. "I resign my commission."

"So be it! Let the record show that Captain Sean Friggand has elected to resign his commission in the Realm's Royal Navy."

Stepping to the side of the table, he saluted the three Admirals and did a smart turn about-face and walked out. In his ears was a distant, almost imperceptible cackle.

*   *   *

Sean sat at a table with a ledger, stylus and inkwell. Men lined up and were signing the log. As each man came forward they put down their name, dependents, place of origin and signed the book.

"So, Captain Mullen," one man asked, "how is it that I've never heard of you before?"

Sean smiled warmly and shrugged his shoulders.

"I've plied me trade mostly in Calamalhun, in the Brightblue. Just so happens that after I delivered some goods to Oakenhalf Island the owner of this ship asked me to captain her to Underhall on Pilsh."

"Good'nuf for me," the man said.

A burly fellow in line stared at Sean. He looked away then back. Suddenly he cried out, "That's Captain Sean Friggand!"

Another man called out, "Dear gods, he's the kill'en captain, never to bring a ship or crew back to port!"

Another man yelled, "Friggand is the blight of the sea, flee for yer lives!"

Elves and men fled the line, rushing to get clear of the tavern.

"Save yer selves!" cried another sailor as he reached the door.

"Wait!" Sean called after them. "It's not true!"

"He's killed a thousand men!" shouted a dwarf who nearly broke his neck fleeing.

"Ye've emptied me bar!" the barkeep angrily said.

"Sorry."

Sean sat back with a mournful look on his face. It was true that he had been on a dozen ships since his resignation from the navy, and they all had been wrecked, or sank, but it wasn't his fault.

"An unusual turn of event wouldn't you say, Captain?"

Turning, Sean noticed an elf in a long-coat and knee-pants.

"Surely is," he said. "Why haven't you fled?"

"I'm not a sailor," Ford stated. "So tell me, why do you still ply your trade as a captain?"

"It's in my blood. There's no other place that I belong. But it seems that I don't belong..."

"Can I buy you an ale?"

"You know me, but who are you? I like to know who buys my drinks."

Sean looked at him with suspicion.

"To the point; a good practice when conducting business. I am Ford Efferguard, a representative recruiting for a task."

"Pleased to meet you," Sean said solemnly. "What task?"

"To retrieve an item lost for many a year." Ford raised his eyebrows. "I actually came here to ask if you'd be interested in being rid of that curse you're under."

"You've got my attention."

"It is no simple matter, but if you're willing, my employers would like to meet you to discuss terms."

"Captain Mullen!" shouted a man who entered the tavern. "May I have a word with you?"

Sean stood up.

"Excuse me. I must go speak to the man that I have a contract with."

"It has come to my attention that you are not Captain Mullen, but a Captain Friggand! I do not take kindly to chicanery! Friggand is a cursed name among these islands.

"No crew will sail with you, and your reputation for losing ships and cargo is well known. Consider our contract void! And if I were you, Mister Friggand, I'd get out of town fast, because I intend on notifying the town watch and the harbormaster, and they may not be as kind as I."

The man turned and stormed out.

Sean returned and sat heavily down.

"I'm sorry. You were saying something about a job? It seems that I need one now."

Ford smiled broadly.

"Indeed so, sir. My employers would like you to help us with a task. It may require a bit of sailing, and some other talents that you possess. Payment will be in gold and silver, and they offer you the ability to get out from under the curse you are a victim of. Think of it man, a chance to ply yer trade once again."

"Count me in!"

Sean grabbed Ford by the forearm.

"Where are these partners of yours?"

"Closer than you think," Ford said. "If you'll just follow me out here."

He led the way into the alley.

"This may seem strange, but when I cast my spell, we will have only a short time to jump through the door. Do not hesitate, for I've been told people have lost body parts if not fast enough."

Sean looked concerned, but shrugged his shoulders.

"Let's get this ship underway. If I lose my head in the process, I'll probably be better off!"

Ford reached into the pouch at his side. He removed some of the golden dust and cast it into the air. The portal opened and he shouted.

"Quick!"

CHAPTER

7

Journey's Beginning

"It is important that each of you understand that if you fail, a dangerous fellow will have possession of an artifact that might put him in a rather powerful position," Goldworm said. "Ford, tell them what we know."

"A mage called Raven Hill is after the Lantern of Dern Blackhammer. It has been lost for five thousand two hundred and seven years, but we think we know where it is."

"Why is the lantern so dangerous?" Han asked.

"Because it is one of several fabled artifacts that use Chaos Magic as an offensive weapon," Sark chimed in. "An energy source so powerful that it could destroy an entire city, a city like Moore."

"That is our concern," Goldworm stated. "We know that Raven Hill intends on rallying several neighboring provinces into one massive army. That army will fall upon the western city-states to reconstitute the ancient kingdom of Hoth."

"We believe he intends to make himself king in the process. I don't need to tell you what it would mean to each of your families and cities if this were to happen," Ford added.

Goldworm brushed some fluff from his coat.

"Our spies acquired, among other things, an ancient text that describes the power locked inside the lantern. We think that

Raven Hill believes it is the god Hoth inside there, but we're not sure."

"The translation can be taken in several different ways. What we believe it says is that if the beam is directed at matter, the matter is gobbled up."

"Gobbled up?" Sark asked.

"Yes," Goldworm said. "Gobbled up. You've been chosen for certain reasons that I am not at liberty to say now. But rest assured that when the time comes, you will know what to do."

"Why are we up here in the mountains?" Sean asked.

"It is our starting point. That is why the teleportation powder was bound here."

"If I'm not mistaken we are in the borderlands of Moore in the Higlite Mountains facing the Prin Valley," Hugh said.

Goldworm looked annoyed.

"Yes, you are in the Higlite. You will be traveling down the mountain to the Western Highway and on to Prin. The woods at the lower elevation are part of the Goblin Treaty Lands, so don't muck about. Those little green bastards won't mind cutting off your heads and putting them in their Longhouse."

"Goblins?" Sean looked worried.

"Don't worry Sean," Harigan said, "they'll probably just stuff yer guts with pickled gili meat."

"That did not make me feel better," Sean said to Harigan.

"Goblins don't typically eat Elvin flesh," Ford added. "Nonetheless, be on your guard as we descend, and while on this trip in general."

"Mr. Efferguard will finish the briefing and lead the expedition. Good luck, lads, the fate of all our civilizations hangs in the balance," Goldworm said.

Goldworm left the room via a side door.

Ford cleared his throat. "It will take us a few days to get to Prin. Once down off the mountain it should be relatively smooth travels since the roads are well guarded. Follow me outside and get a horse and a pack lagma. Let's get this trek in motion," Ford said.

Ford took his horse by the reins and led it from the villa onto a rocky path. A woolly yellow lagma was tied by a tether to his saddle.

The snow had fallen the night before and the cold was biting. The others did as Ford, leading their mount and pack animal from the stables and down the lonely gray mountain. They wound their way through the snow-covered trails and along the switchbacks.

"Stay close together," Ford called back from the head of the column. "These paths can be treacherous!"

"Is it always freezing up here?" Sean shivered.

"Most of the year it is. Glaciers dominate higher up where the snow never melts," Ford called back.

The air was so cold that it hurt to breathe. Glancing over his shoulder, Ford saw the smoky white mist shooting from the lagma's mouths as it labored under the weight of its load.

"Why do you think these lagmas look so amusing?" Sark asked Ford, almost as if he were reading his thoughts.

Ford chuckled under his breath for they did look completely absurd.

"The gods have a fantastic sense of humor?" Ford responded.

Sark laughed. "Perhaps."

He turned in the saddle and looked back at the animals as he spoke again.

"I believe the thick yellow wool keeps them warm up here, and their backward facing limbs allow for better stability on the slick rocky surfaces."

"But what of their two long necks and heads?" Ford questioned, a bit bemused at Sark's comments.

"To reach the hard to get spiny leaves of the catterwal plant. The two heads... well you know the saying."

Ford thought for a moment looking out at the rocky trail. "Seems quite logical," he added. "The two heads and all. But what of the colors?"

"Mating," Sark said. "The bright colors make them easy to see at a distance, and the multi-color of the females... around the back side, make it easy for the male to find his mark."

"I guess it's lucky that they have no natural predators up here." Ford looked back at Sark.

"True. I hear they have a foul taste that even a starving orc would not stomach."

Ford looked thoughtful. "Do you enjoy manipulating the power? The forces of magic allows your type to do extraordinary things right?"

"You might as well ask if I enjoy breathing," Sark began. "It's a natural thing that I can't stop doing!"

Ford raised one eyebrow. "When did you know that you had the gift?"

"At birth. My mother told me that upon exiting the womb, I snapped my fingers and the umbilical cord severed!"

Ford laughed. "Really?"

"No. At age two or three my parents caught me making elementals and telling them what to do. They knew I was going to do something special in the world. Did you study magic in school?"

"Not really," Ford said. "Other than, of course, the typical prank or two – you know, the itching spell, the sneezing spell, the water in your pants spell."

"Funny, most people I meet say the same thing." Sark shivered. "It sure is cold up here," he said pulling his cloak tightly about him.

"I sure hope that there are no Mountain Goblins lurking about," Hugh said from the back.

"They tend to keep to themselves these days. Most just hunt and fish up here and seek refuge from the winter storms in the caves," Ford stated.

"Cause much trouble to you elves?" Harigan asked.

"No, their mischief is with the settlers of the Prin Valley. Simple things like theft and rustling. We seldom have issues with them."

Ford faced forward again.

"I hear they like to bind their captives tightly and cut off pieces of meat over a long period of time," Harigan added.

"What?" Sean's eyes went wide with fear.

"Don't believe everything you hear, Sean," Han said.

"And they pull out your fingernails and make you eat them," Harigan persisted, a wide grin upon his face for the torment he was causing Sean.

"I really don't want to hear this, Harigan!"

"Enough!" Ford said over his shoulder. "Sean, don't worry… the Goblins don't do any of that stuff!"

"How far to Prin?" Sark asked.

"Four days, maybe five. We'll need to camp on the mountain tonight, but tomorrow, we'll make the highway and then it's a direct shot to Prin."

Snow fell off and on throughout the day, and the sun remained hidden behind dark gray clouds. Large white snowflakes and sleet fell making the worn smooth stones slick. After many hours on the trail, the path widened.

"The sunlight is failing," Hugh said.

"There is a hunter's shelter not much further down. We can stay in there for the night."

"I hope it has plenty of dry firewood," Sean said.

"And some cured meat," Han added.

A round, gray, felt structure came into view. It was sitting on the edge of a high cliff overlooking a pine-covered valley.

Ford tied his lagma to a hitching post and led his horse inside. The Yurt was fairly large, sixty feet in circumference, with an area for horses and an area for people.

In the center, a fire pit was dug into the ground surrounded by local rocks giving it a rustic look.

"Tie your horses over there, and lay down your bedrolls over there," Ford said.

Hanging in the middle from a crossbeam was several hunks of quartered and cured flesh. Along one wall were boxes of powdered meal and jars of flower and Jup leaf.

Cutting off a hunk of the cured meat, Ford put it in a pot.

"Sean take this pot and put some snow in it, and Sark see if you can get a fire going," he suggested.

Snapping his fingers Sark ignited the wood in the fire pit. The yellow flames leapt into the air and instantly the room was filled with light.

The smoke swirled and raced out the oculus at the top of the hut. Sean came back in with the pot and hung it from a three legged stand over the fire.

Soon the pot was boiling and the room filled with the smell of hot stew. Outside, darkness was taking over and a cold wind began to howl. Harigan said some strange words and hoisted a drinking horn into the air.

"What's that?" Sean asked.

"It's a magic horn," Harigan said and quaffed the contents in one draught. He said the words again.

"Here." He handed Sean the horn.

Sean put it to his lips and tipped up the container. Dark stout sloshed down like a punching fist into his face. He jumped to his feet coughing and choking.

"Well, it's for the appetites of men and not boys," Harigan said.

Sean wiped his mouth with his sleeve and sat back down.

"I'll remember that for next time you offer me a drink."

Sark came over and examined the horn.

"You wouldn't happen to have a plate of never-ending food too, would you?"

Producing the plate Harigan said the magic words and food appeared.

"I do."

"You've been to the Fortress of the Vale in the lands of Lormor!"

"That's just a myth," Hugh said.

"Nothing can survive in those barren bogs and forsaken lands," Sean added.

"I am not familiar with this legend," Han said. "Perhaps you could enlighten me."

Sark cleared his throat. "Well, it centers on the King of Lormor who is faced with the encroachment of the First Kingdom of Orc. He makes a deal with a Warlock to help him defeat the orcs.

"The Warlock called upon the god Aor, who in turn sent his master of war, Vulrich, to aid them. The Warlock lost control of Vulrich, and the beast changed the Lormorian lands into a terrible waste, killing not only the orc army, but the inhabitants of Lormor."

Sark turned the horn around in his hand.

"It is said that the elves of Lormor forged amazing tools of magic. One, made for the king was the Horn of Never Ending Drink, the second was the Plate of Never Ending Food – both imbued with chaos magic.

"Since the demigod Vulrich had no use for such magic items, they lay in whatever ill-use Harigan must have found them in."

"They were just lying about," Harigan added.

"Interesting. So, this Vulrich just left after a while?" Han looked curious.

"What of Vulrich indeed?" Sark said while looking up at Harigan.

"I disbanded him – sent him home," Harigan said, passing the plate around. "Take what you like."

"The stew will be done in a few minutes. Stuff yourselves well, because it gets cold at night," Ford stated. "Is there something you could do to secure the Yurt tonight, Sark?"

"In fact, I have just the thing," Sark replied.

Taking out a spool of what looked like thread, Sark exited the shelter and was gone for a few minutes. He came back covered in snow, and quickly went to the fire and warmed his hands.

"It's snowing hard now," he said.

"What did you do?" Sean asked.

"I put up a serial-screech-line. If someone touches it, a screaming sound will shatter the air."

The wind blew most of the night. A snowflake slipped past the smoke and fell through the oculus, landing gently on Ford's face.

He got up and put a few logs on the fire and put the leftover stew on the coals to heat. Slowly the rest of the party woke and soon they had eaten.

The early morning light was filtering in and Ford rolled up his bedding and packed his bags.

"Saddle up," he said.

Moving the door flap aside, he grabbed a bucket of grain and pushed his way through the three feet of snow to where the lagmas were. As he approached, one of the long wooly yellow necks peeked up.

Suddenly all of them stood, and the snow buckled and sloughed away. Each one shook it off, and then, as if on command, they began bleating for food.

He watched as each creature pushed and shoved their way to the bucket, plunging a head in, feasting heartily.

Making his way back to the shelter, he warmed his hands by the fire.

"When the lagmas have eaten we'll head out."

Ford again led the way. Lagmas trailed each horse. As they walked, one head kept a keen watch for trouble, while the other focused on the trail.

After an hour the trees grew in height, the snow thinned, and the shrubs became thicker and taller. Soon they found alpine vistas of dark green pines.

Many hours passed as the pines gave way to foothill forests of thick oaks. A raging stream appeared to the side of the rocky path and flowed like a frothy torrent paralleling them.

Soon they were in thick grassy hills sparsely covered in stout oaks, their leaves dripping and glossy from rain. Ahead, the path widened and emptied onto a well-traveled road. In the air the subtle sound of a drum rose from the woods. Ford pulled up on his reins and halted the party.

"Sounds like goblins," Hugh said.

"It's strange that they are even out of their caves at this time of year... isn't it?" Sean looked worried.

"Not that strange," Sark added. "It's the centennial festival of Helluvart, the ancient goblin king who demanded blood sacrifices."

"What?" Sean said with a treble of fright in his voice.

"I'm sure it's nothing to worry about," Ford said as he began moving again.

They moved through the tall grass and stands of oaks. The smell of smoke filled the air. The beating of drums was getting closer. The whooping and the chanting of goblin-speak seemed to come from all around them.

"This may not be good," Ford said. "I've never heard them so active before."

"How often have you been up here?" Hugh asked.

"Twice a year, to do some hunting. Typically the goblins steer clear of us though."

"Goblins up ahead on both sides of the path," Hugh said. "I can see them. They appear as shimmering purple outlines when my visor is down."

Han shifted in the saddle. "Goblins can be unpredictable," he said.

Ford indicated that the column should stop and dismount. Hugh climbed down and approached Ford. Ford raised his eyebrows.

"What do you think?"

Harigan folded his arms over his chest.

"If they mean business, we should oblige them," he suggested, then hefted his cudgel in one hand."

"I'm not a warrior, I'm a sailor," Sean added.

"Nonsense," Harigan began. "Aor has told me of your exploits on the sea fighting pirates. Just imagine these green scaly fellows as pirates and not tribesmen and you'll do fine."

"They have the advantage of numbers," Han said. "I can smell their musky scent from here."

"Can you flank them, give them something to think on?"

"I can," Han stated.

He quickly stripped off his clothes and shifted into his cat form and skulked into the underbrush vanishing from sight.

"Hugh, your armor affords better protection than our leather and cloth. Can you lure them into the open?"

"Easily. Perhaps they'll recognize me as a Justice Knight and flee."

"Not likely," Sark said.

Hugh moved ahead toward the tree line. A group of goblins broke from the trees and rushed at him.

One, brightly painted, thrust his flint-tipped spear into Hugh, but the blade shattered on impact against his armor. The creature lifted the shaft and drove it down upon Hugh's helmet; it snapped like a twig. The creature rushed back towards the woods.

A second goblin attacked, driving an obsidian knife into Hugh's midsection—the blade snapped off. The creature howled with rage and threw himself onto the armor, at which he was knocked to the ground in a flash of white light and bolts of electricity.

Others rushed out and spun slings above their heads, letting loose a volley of fist size stones. The projectiles bounced off his armor resulting in no net effect.

Emerging from the trees, an over-fed goblin dressed in a brightly colored headdress came. He held up a shrunken head affixed to a stick and made a low melodious chant.

"Get down!" Sark said pushing Sean to the ground.

All around the shaman the air erupted in a flash of light. A noise resembling arrows passed just over their heads.

Sark leapt to his feet and looked back at the opposite tree line. Long spears were embedded in several of the branches behind them.

"This will not do," he said closing his eyes and building a spell. "*The distance, sixty feet, the air 50 degrees, the atoms are…*" He waved his hands in the air.

Sark's body glowed red. Just in front of him a tendril of fog rose. The fog, grass, and dirt began to swirl about until a blur of white mist and debris was as high as a tree.

"Fetch!" Sark said, pointing at the shaman already in the process of another spell.

Moving towards the creature, the funnel zigged and zagged as if on the verge of being out of control. The swirling cloud hit the forest.

A blast of chilled air erupted and hail fell from the sky. In an instant the trees were covered in ice crystals, and the ground covered in fist-sized hailstones.

Goblins were knocked to the ground, many crying out in pain as they were pummeled by the large balls of ice. Some ran for the forest, others stood and took the beating.

A battle cry filled the air as several dozen goblins rushed from the woods. In a moment, they were upon the party.

Sean spun, striking one creature and knocking it to the ground. He turned and landed a punch on a second one who crumpled then ran away.

From the corner of his eye he saw Harigan lift his cudgel above his head, and half a dozen Goblins fell prostrate.

From the forest, quick as a flash, came a wild panfar leaping onto a goblin from behind. The creature screamed and was driven to the ground rolling and fighting.

Screeching in fear and panic, the goblin struggled with the panfar as fangs and claws raked it. Han let the goblin go. The creature ran in a blind panic back to the forest.

The other goblins stopped, looked at Han, and dashed back to the forest. Last to retreat into the woods was the shaman, who brushed off the ice crystals and rubbed his head where he'd been hit with hail.

Sark readied another spell, but the shaman bowed, nodding his head in recognition of his defeat, then melted back into the forest.

"You'll get no blood sacrifice here!" Ford shouted after them.

"That was invigorating," Hugh said.

"Let's hope we have no more of that today," Sark added.

Sean mounted his horse.

"Let's get out of here before they return with a bigger force."

"Aye, let's get out of here," Ford affirmed.

The panfar slowly approached, shifting back into Han.

"Ya may want to cover your shame," Harigan said.

"Yes," Han said, as he put his clothes back on. "They had little will to fight."

"Mount up and let's get out of here before they decide to return," Ford said.

Ford maneuvered down the road keeping a wary eye on the hill. After a few hours, the dirt road met the cobblestone Western Highway.

The smell of the rich grassy plain filled his nose. Moisture, heavy in the air seemed to hint at more showers; soon they'd come.

"The wind is biting coming from the south," Sark said.

"It comes from the Freezing Sea," Sean said. "It will most likely sleet on us."

"Most of us know the story of the Lantern," Sean began as he rode up next to Ford. "But what do you know about it – I mean, do you have some solid information regarding it?"

"Putting aside the hearsay and the legends, there is a precious little more out there," Ford said.

"Yes, that is all well and good, but what more do you know?" Sean pressed.

"There was this Vigor document recently translated."

"Vigor?" Sark asked. "They were known for their esoteric and philosophic writings, hardly technical in any respect."

"They did keep many translations of very old documents, such as a translation of several Cuniaton codices. We have it in the Hall of Knowledge in Moore."

"It says that in the year 1680 of the Old Kingdom a thief named Chirkak stole the Lantern from the Tower of Gray, where it was kept by the mage named Limbot. Chirkak carried it off to the city of Kumaton along the Eastern borders of Lieber.

"There he tried to sell it, but was murdered, and the Lantern was lost from record until 1711 of the Old Kingdom, where it surfaced in the hands of Sulliman the Great and Terrible Orc King. Sulliman commissioned several of his court wizards to learn the Lanterns secrets.

"They wrote two long scrolls of notes that detailed the construction and what they thought was powering the light. Several trials with slaves proved that if anything living, or not, were struck by the light, it vanished. Where it goes they only could guess."

"So where did they guess the stuff went?" Sean asked.

Ford shrugged his shoulders. "They used the word *xihito* as to where. We actually don't know what that is."

Sark chuckled. "The word is actually three words, *xi* meaning the void, *hi* meaning the god's realm, and *to* meaning the universe."

"What do you think they meant?" Ford's curiosity was peaked.

"I'm not sure they were in their right mind." Sark smiled. "But from the words, it seems there is a void god realm of the universe out there somewhere."

"Like a pocket in the universe?" Han questioned.

Sark looked thoughtful. "Yes – exactly."

Several wagon-trains pulled by oxen rattled along the cobblestone road approaching them. Ford pulled to the side to allow them to pass, then moved along the highway again.

"There are some who might argue with that translation," Sark added.

"True. Translations can be tricky," Ford affirmed.

"I was approached several months ago by a man in a blue robe," Sark said.

Ford halted his horse. "What?"

"A man in a blue robe came to see me. He had a translation of a Vigor document also. He asked me a flurry of questions regarding Chaos Magic."

"And you suspect he was interested in the Lantern?"

"Undoubtedly," Sark said. "He pressed me on several occasions regarding a powerful source of Chaos Magic that could be compressed into the form of a gem."

"Did he show you the translation?"

"Not as such. See, I made tea and when I fetched it and came back, the man was standing on my porch talking with one of his men. The document was amongst a pile of papers he'd brought sitting on my refreshment table.

"I set down the tea and quickly made a copy with an image stone. When he returned and sat down, he had no idea that I had made copies."

Sark smiled and then chuckled softly. "It is a fool who tries to keep secrets around a snoop of a researcher."

"What does this mean?" Han's brow wrinkled.

"I'm not sure." Ford looked worried.

"Well, later I read the documents, and one was a translation by an elf scribe named Hilgrow. The gist of it was the Lantern is a mighty weapon and the light remakes matter in the desired image of the possessor."

Sean looked confused.

"Remakes matter?"

Sark turned and looked back at Sean, Han and Harigan.

"Yes, like turning an apple into a drog, or lead into gold – transmutation I think you would call it." He turned back. "Shall we?" he said gesturing along the road.

Ford put his heels to his horse and the beast began moving forward.

"Perhaps Raven Hill's interest is more than just becoming a king?" Ford surmised.

"Why be a king when you can be a god?" Sark furthered.

Sleet began to fall as they rode, and in the distance a walled town came into view.

"Perhaps we should stop at one of these charming roadside inns; it would be nice to have a hot meal, cup of chi, and a hot bath," Sean suggested.

Speaking over his shoulder Ford replied, "We need to make it to Born before nightfall."

"Pity," Sean added.

"Here, have some roast fowl and a horn of ale," Harigan said, handing Sean the magic plate filled with steaming food and his horn filled with dark brown ale. "Try not to slop it all over yourself."

"I've never been to Born, is it elf or man built?" Han asked.

"Actually it was Orcish in layout and construction, but it is a Human city now. In a few hours you'll see the majestic details of the white walls," Sark said.

"What of bandits and highway thieves?" Han asked.

"These roads are well patrolled by town militia, shire reeves, and well-armed merchants. Not to mention, who in their right mind would attack us when we have a Justice Knight riding with us?" Hugh boldly said.

Freezing rain began to fall as Ford and his party came within sight of the white walls of Born.

They pulsated and dimmed, then became bright again. Ghostly apparitions appeared standing guard; in their hands weapons of the ancients.

"An impressive sight," Sark said to Han. "But just wait."

They rode toward the main gate.

"Look there." Sark pointed. Runes over the main gate glowed in a golden light.

"Thy Chiac Tum!" Ford said.

"Keep evil out," Sark translated.

"Runes of wishful thinking," Harigan said smugly.

"It actually trapped the evil inside," Sark added. "The city was once beseeched by a dark evil. They locked the gates, but instead of locking out the horror, they locked it inside with them.

"A hundred years later the gates were opened by some marauding humans, and only scattered bleached bones were found. It is said that the ghosts of those slain by the evil still prowl the ramparts." He pointed at the wall.

"The folklore says that an army of priests were employed to dispel the dark forces that dwelled in the under-halls of the town. After that, they opened the city for business again."

"Halt!" called a man clad in armor at the gate.

Coming to a stop, Ford saw a man in his twenties. His armor was a piecemeal from various armies, and rusted in several places. He looked tired as he looked up into Ford's face with a scowl.

"What's yer business in Born?"

"Travelers seeking shelter, food, company, and drink," Ford said.

"Company, eh?" The guard chuckled.

Standing behind him were several other young men; one in chain mail, and the other in leather with a short sword tucked in his belt.

Both seemed younger than the man who spoke, and they appeared to be waiting for the other's commands.

"Well, it'll cost ya a silver sestires to enter."

"Good Captain," Ford began, "you seem a reasonable man. We are but poor travelers in search of work, and our resources are stretched thin as it is. Perhaps you might consider a score of copper assilis?"

"A score you say? Well, seeing how yer looking for work," he looked back at his friends, "a score it is." He held out his hand.

Ford carefully reached into his shirt and pulled out a small sack. He counted out twenty coins and placed it into the outstretched palm of the guard.

"Is there a tavern or inn you can recommend?" Ford asked.

"Try the Wild Drog to slack your thirst, and the Raven's Roost to rest yer heads."

He waved them through the open gate.

Ford knew it was common in small towns for guards to shakedown travelers. Everyone was trying to make a living, either by commerce or robbery.

If it wasn't bribes or extortion, it could be a slit throat, or worse. He chuckled as he thought how commerce and robbery were pretty much the same thing, except one was legal and the other punishable by death. He steered his horse along the main street. Shops and homes lined each side.

Large droplets of moisture fell from eves plopping down into brown puddles and onto the wooden boardwalks that bordered the street. A thin vale of smoky haze lingered in the air. Shingles hung every so often indicated the type of business they represented.

"They have nice cobblestone streets here," Harigan observed.

"They do," Ford affirmed. "Born is the first town along the Western Highway as you come from Moore, so there's money here."

Han sniffed the air. "A mist will rise tonight. I hope the place we stay has a warm fire."

Down the street, Ford sighted a shingle with the picture of a bed on it. Stopping just in front of the sign, he took the reins of his horse and tied it up to the hitching post.

"I'll secure us lodging and food for the night. Han, take a look and see if you can find that tavern, the Wild Drog. Sean, see about finding a stable to keep our horses and lagmas safe for the night."

Han rode further down the road. He noticed a group of people coming from a stone and wood building. Several horses were tied up out front, and the soft glow of light from the two windows indicated it was open for business.

Approaching, he saw a tankard painted on the shingle. A name was also painted at the bottom in medium size letters.

"The Wild Drog," he read aloud.

He dismounted and tied up his horse. Grabbing the latch, he entered the dimly lit tavern.

A smoky haze hung in the air; some from the fireplace and some from patron's pipes. The room was not large, forty feet long and thirty feet wide, with a wooden bar at the far end.

Square wooden tables lined the walls, and the middle of the room. In the back corner he saw a fireplace producing a warm glow and occasionally a bit of black smoke.

Silence fell about the room as the patrons turned and examined him. Slowly the din of the tavern began again and Han walked up to the bar.

"Barkeep, a tankard of bitters," he ordered as he put his back to the bar.

The tables along the walls were filled; some containing men, some with elves and dwarves. A few had only one person sitting, shrouded in darkness, sipping their ale, wine or mead.

Each flat surface had a small lantern with low illumination, keeping the patron in shadow. Stoneware pitchers and tankards, some upside down and some right side up, sat in front of each.

"I'll be on me way, Sandy," said a burly human as he stood up and staggered out the front door.

"Here's yer bitters, mate. That'll be a copper," the barkeep said.

Han tossed the coin on the counter, took his mug, and sat at a vacant table along the wall by a large leaded-glass window. He set his cup on the table and watched the door and the bar.

Drinking his beer, he observed the nearest group of people: one human, one dwarf, and one elf. Each were dressed in sturdy leather and quilted cloth, and a cloak hung over each chair-back.

A human was smoking a long steamed pipe. The strong, but beguiling smell of topus leaf filled the air as the man took a long draw from the stem, and exhaled a plume of white smoke toward the ceiling.

A strange feeling came over Han, as if he was being watched. Casually looking about he noticed no obvious onlookers, but the feeling persisted.

He spotted a figure along the far wall looking his way. The person glanced down at their tankard. Gazing out the window into the street, Han saw the distorted reflection of the stranger; his cloak like a blob of red ink. He looked over at Han again, just for a moment, then again turned back to his beer.

Han finished his drink and stood up, leaving the tankard. Walking to the door he felt eyes upon him again.

Lifting the latch, he felt the strong cold wind blow the door inward. A chill swept over him while he stepped outside.

Once on the stoop, he pulled the door shut, took his horse by the reins and walked down the street toward the inn. As he approached the entrance Sean came down the stairs.

"There you are. We were getting worried," Sean said.

"The taverns down there," Han pointed. "Where's the stable?"

"This way."

Sean walked with Han to a long building made of stucco and wood.

"The stable master has added extra security for our mounts. How was the tavern?"

"Typical. Most of the bar-creepers were sitting with their backs to the wall, hiding in the shadows… you know the type."

Sean snickered. "Yup, in every port they're the same."

"But I think there was this one sitting in the back who kept looking over at me."

"You are a bit different."

Han stopped.

"Did you hear that?"

"What?"

"The faint sound of footsteps; someone is following us." Han looked around.

"I don't see anyone. They could be down one of those alleys, though."

"Perhaps…" Han replied.

They walked over to the stable and Han handed over his horse. The stable master saw them out and closed the door behind them locking it tight.

Sean shrugged and began walking back toward the inn.

"Ford said that we'll probably take in some drinks at the tavern if it meets with your approval," Sean hinted.

"I didn't see anything obvious to be worried about."

Sean stopped.

"Now I feel like someone's following us."

Han took a sniff of the air. "Topus leaf... and something strange, like perfume." He looked around.

"A woman of pleasure perhaps?" Sean asked.

"Could be." Han began walking again.

It took only a few minutes to reach the inn. Opening the door, they stepped inside. The room was well-lit with a parlor on each side, one for males and the other females. Mounted directly in the middle of the hallway was a set of stairs leading up.

Sitting in the male parlor were Ford, Harigan, Sark and Hugh. A tall man dressed in a yellow robe was also sitting and pouring tea from a teapot.

"And you'll be staying only a single night?" the man in the robe asked.

"Yes, just one night. We'll take the rooms at the top of stairs," Ford said.

"A very good choice." The innkeeper stood up and pulled from his robe a leather book. "Now if you will just provide your names, I'll be happy to have you stay here at my inn."

"Names?" Harigan said, looking suspiciously at the man.

"It's a common practice in these parts to provide one's name to the innkeeper," Ford said taking the ink stylus and scribing his name. "Each of us must do so."

"If it's the *common practice* I shall do so," Harigan said.

One by one they each signed the book.

"That is fine."

The innkeeper smiled as he looked over the ledger.

Ford handed the fellow a silver sestires."This should cover the cost."

"More than adequate. I'll make change for you."

"No need, keep it as compensation for any inconvenience," Ford said.

The innkeeper looked surprised. "You're the second one this day to overpay and say that to me."

"Second one?" Sark asked.

"We get nobles and rich travelers from time to time. They pay a little extra for any *inconvenience*." He folded the ledger closed and hid it under his robe. "The rooms have blankets and sheets, and there's one lamp per room. I provide evening meals. My wife is a good cook, and we have a contract with several farms in the south for produce."

Ford nodded his head. "Yes, that will do nicely. Thank you."

"I lock the doors at four plus five bells, but there is a cord outside that you can pull if you get locked out. I or my wife will open the door for you."

"That's fine," Ford stated.

"Good evening to you then." The innkeeper left the room.

Ford looked over at Han.

"So what did you find?"

"The tavern called the Wild Drog is just down the street."

"Good. Let's go and get some drinks," Ford said while rubbing his eyes.

"There's one thing," Han added. "A figure was watching me, a fellow in a dark red cloak. And after depositing my horse at the stable, I could swear that Sean and I were being followed."

"Did you see who it was? Was it the same person?" Ford looked concerned.

Han shrugged his shoulders.

"That topus leaf must have fouled my sense of smell because I thought I smelled latvita flower perfume, and only heard what I thought was a footfall behind us. Yet, when we turned there was not a soul to be seen."

Ford stood up. "But, no one accosted you or made themselves known?"

"No."

Ford thought for a moment then said, "We'll go to the tavern, but remain on our guard."

"Indeed," Harigan said as he rose to his feet and made for the door. "I'm sure there are tithing's to collect and spirits to be had at that libation trough."

As Ford opened the door to the Wild Drog, the sound of dice, the stench of topus, and soured beer hit him all at once. The din of chiding, and laughter filled the air as he stepped inside and scanned the room.

Shady and enigmatic characters lined the walls and corners, while the locals seemed relegated to the tables in the middle of the room. Two large leaded glass windows faced the street and acted more like mirrors than widows.

Making for the bar, he ordered a tankard of dark stout. The crackle, hissing, and spitting of the fire drew his attention.

Empty chairs were spaced in a half circle in front of the fireplace. He took his beer and retired to one of the chairs.

Leaning toward the fire, he warmed his hands as he checked over his shoulder for the others of his party. Harigan sat at a table near the door with several unsavory-looking fellows. He put down some money and took up a pair of dice.

"Slivy Bones!" he cried out, and tossed the dice on the table.

"Brine," one of the men at the table said.

Harigan threw the dice again. "Drums!"

"He seems to be doing well," Sark added while sitting next to Ford.

Ford smiled wryly as he noted Sark's remark. Han and Hugh approached, each with a tankard in hand. Sean came last and sat near the hearth, cross-legged on the floor.

"Prin is three days journey from here. I've been there several times," Ford began. "The road is well-patrolled and the incidence of robbery is pretty low. The city of Canaric is the next stop and is a bit smaller than Prin; we'll be staying there one night

"From there, we'll be on our way to Maubury, where we'll hire a river boat to take us to Prin. Once in Prin, the island of Brule is our destination and it lies squarely in the middle of the Green Serpent River. The Keep of Tallibach is on that island. The city has grown around the ancient fortress which is now only a tourist destination."

"The fortress?" Han asked.

"This fortress was built on top of several ancient fortresses from time before written history," Sark said. "It's said that the Black King Vericornius built it to guard against human invasion from the west."

"We're going to raid the crypt below that Keep," Ford stated. "It seems the king gained possession of the item we seek a thousand years ago and was buried with it. He built a burial chamber especially for the protection of his remains, and the... item."

Ford looked around. The noise of the tavern was loud. In the back of the room were several people: a dwarf, and a human, and a slender fellow wrapped in a reddish cloak and cowl.

Turning back to his companions, Ford pulled from his pocket a stonewood pipe, the bowl and stem polished to a white luster. From his other pocket he removed a leather pouch filled with shredded dark black topus.

He dipped the bowl of his pipe into the pouch and packed it with his thumb.

"Han, do you feel like you're being watched now?"

"No... but—" He casually glanced about the room. "That person in the back with the red cloak is the same that was here earlier."

"Is he in the same spot?"

"Yes," Han said.

"Then he's probably not the one who followed you."

Ford took a match and lit his pipe, drew in deeply and exhaled a white plume.

"Is it still there, the item I mean?" Sean asked.

Ford pulled out a tattered parchment from inside his coat. He unrolled it and passed it around the party.

"A map?" Han said surprised.

"A map indeed," said Sark with a grin. "I hope it was not bought on a Prin street corner."

"It wasn't," Ford stated.

CHAPTER

8

Born

"How did you come by this map?" Sark asked as he tipped up his mug of ale and drank.

"The Brood acquired it from a group of tomb robbers," Ford said.

Sark narrowed his eyes. "Then how do you know it's authentic?" He raised one eyebrow.

"The map was scrutinized by experts who vouch for its authenticity," Ford added.

"Our lives depend on the accuracy and validity of that map," Sark said. "I would hate to think that we were played fools for lack of research."

"I assure you that this is from a group who delved into the mines below the fortress." Ford furthered. "They stumbled across the lower entrance of the castle, and survived, extricating themselves from the tunnels."

"All of them?" Sark pressed.

"Well, some of them," Ford said looking from man to man.

Sean took the map and examined it.

"Underground?" Sean asked, worried. "How will we know what direction the map is pointing?"

"The map has been imbued with glowing scribe marks about the compass rose," Ford said. "They glow with the orientation of the map towards north."

"Convenient," Han stated while stoking the fire.

Harigan came over and stood next to the fireplace. "Made me a tidy sum," he proclaimed.

"Was it luck or divine help?" Sark asked.

"Aye, I'm lucky enough."

Harigan held the horn in front of him and said the words. The horn filled. He laughed a jolly guffaw and tipped the horn up to his lips and quaffed the entire contents. The dark beer spilled over his ample beard and down on his shirt, adding to the various stains.

"Those sheep did not like the fleecing I gave them," he added.

The party sat silent, as the din of the tavern vibrated all around them. Warmth from the fire emptied into the room as the logs were consumed by the blaze.

"You son of an orc!" shouted a large man with a black beard at the dice table.

"To yer mother's paid services. I curse you," yelled back a red haired dwarf.

A fight broke out and Ford watched, as did everyone else in the bar. Black Beard was large and thickly muscled. The other cut to the left, then right, then ducked a wide hay-maker punch. His wild and unkempt hair tussled about, and it was clear that his lean stature gave him an advantage.

The dwarf landed a hard blow to the man's midsection. He crumpled to the ground and held up his hand in submission.

"You win - you win – it's I who is to pay..."

He gripped his stomach as he stood up and tossed several coins on the dice table. The dwarf scooped up the coins and put them into his leather pouch at his side.

"So be it," he said as he swaggered out the front door.

The black-haired man sat down and hoisted his mug up to his lips. Looking around, he fixed his eyes on Ford, lifted his tankard in a salute, and drank deeply. Laughing heartily he stood and made for the door.

"Common bar fight," Ford began as he turned to the party. His voice cut off as he saw Sean, unconscious on the floor.

"The map?" Ford gasped.

Han looked at Ford. "Sean had it."

Ford rushed to Sean and searched him. Finding the map missing, he frantically looked around the room.

"Gone! Curse my foolish ignorance," he chided himself. "We have to find that map!"

"Right!" Harigan pulled out his cudgel and moved to the front door.

Ford watched in surprise as Harigan began asking questions and bashing patrons with his cudgel. The first fellow didn't even get to answer when Harigan's brass-colored cudgel fell upon his head knocking him off his chair and unconscious. The priest moved to the next man.

"Where's the item stolen from us this night?" he demanded.

"Uh, I don't know what you're—" The man fell to the cudgel.

Several men along the wall drew weapons, but Harigan somehow, someway avoided their attack and laid man after man low with the crunch of his mighty club.

Within the course of a few moments the tavern was in complete pandemonium as people leapt to their feet and either spoke frantically or pointed to someone else. When one elf in a brown leather jerkin pointed at Ford, Ford shouted.

"Enough! This is getting us nowhere, and fast."

The tavern fell silent as everyone looked at him.

Harigan halted, and looked down on a stout fellow in a chainmail coif. He raised his cudgel high.

"Stop!" cried the burly fellow.

Harigan was perched over him ready to deliver a mighty and potentially lethal blow.

"I know what happened to your property," he quickly said, his hands up to protect his head, fear written upon his face.

"Speak and I shall let you live further," Harigan said, his voice deep and menacing.

"It was a comely-looking fellow, in a rust-colored garment. He was sitting over there. He paid them fellas to get into a fight. When the fight happened he vanished."

"Where did he go?" demanded Harigan angrily.

"I don't know," the man said. "He just disappeared!"

Harigan's expression betrayed his intent to deliver the blow anyway.

"Wait-wait-wait! I suspect he snuck out with one of the fighters; that's what I'd do," the man added.

Harigan turned to Ford with a bearded grin.

"There, simplicity at its best," he said, as he put his cudgel back at his belt and turned.

"Damn," Ford grumbled.

"They haven't left yet," Sark said. "I can feel the energy of the abeo cloak they're wearing."

"What did you say?" Ford asked, stopping in his tracks.

"That guy who stole the map is still here. I can feel the energy from the cloak he's wearing." Sark pointed toward the far corner of the room. "He's got a rare cloak of abeo, a vanishing garment. I haven't seen one of those in years. That's why I didn't recognize the feeling earlier."

"How can you be sure?" Ford asked.

Sark looked confident. "It was one of the first chaos relics I handled in my earlier years. I'm sensitive to the energy field. He might be invisible, but I can feel him nearby."

Ford spun around and stared into the darkest part of the tavern.

"You, there in the back, you're not a local and not one of these mercenaries. Who are you?" Ford demanded.

Harigan rushed at the corner with his cudgel held high. "You," he said angrily.

"No - Harigan!" Ford called. "Harigan, you block the front door. Hugh, block the door behind the bar to the storeroom!"

Ford removed his dagger.

"Han, check the ash-pale by the fire. Is it hot?"

Han reached over and felt the pale.

"It's cold as a stone."

"Fetch it to me, quickly," Ford said.

Han brought the pale.

"A strange request," he added, bemused.

Taking the bucket, Ford reached in and threw ash all about the room: the floor, the unconscious men, tables, and chairs. From one end of the bar to the other, Ford dusted every surface with the white ash.

"Hey!" shouted the barkeep. "Yer making a mess of me tavern!"

"Shut up!" commanded Ford. "Turn up the lanterns until we have some good light in here!"

Harigan turned up the wall lantern nearest him. Hugh increased the light by the bar, and Sean turned up the lantern on one of the tables. The light illuminated the room.

"Now, none of you move," Ford said.

CHAPTER

9

Game of Hearts

Harigan's eyes scanned the room. Every few seconds he'd slap the head of his cudgel into the palm of his hand.

Hugh stood at the back door, his short sword at the ready. Ford stood watching the floor, focused on the area towards the back of the room.

"Whoever you are, there is no escape," Ford said. "Unless you can tunnel under the floorboards."

Ford took a handful of ash. Walking towards the front door he spread the ash into his footprints as he went.

"If you surrender the map, we will let you leave. Just put it on a table, and I'll give the order to unblock the doors," Ford sincerely stated.

"Let's bash his head in!" Harigan suggested.

"No – if he does as I say, he has a safe passage out of this tavern. If not, you're at liberty to do as you will with him."

Harigan scowled through his beard at Ford. "You would do well to learn the teaching of Aor!"

Eyeing the dust-covered floor, Ford searched for signs of movement. He waited quietly.

"Ye've bashed me patrons and dirtied up me tavern, when do you expect to be on your way?" The barkeep looked angry.

"Just as soon as we have our property," Ford reassured him

while still scanning the tavern.

Suddenly dark black smoke began rolling from the fireplace, filling the room.

"The flue, he's shut the flue of the chimney," Ford cried out.

"Oh, me bar! Yer making a mess of it," shouted the barkeep as he rushed to the fireplace and wrestled with the chimney flue.

Ford fell to his knees to avoid the thick black smoke. Ahead he saw footprints with no feet leading towards the door. Harigan was swinging his cudgel wildly. Ford crouched, and sprung.

Grappling with the invisible thief, he tried to secure the man's arms. He was strong and wise in the ways of fighting.

A quick strike to Ford's throat froze him for a moment. The man stood up, and the cloak parted down the middle. The cowl fell away revealing a beautiful elven woman with long black hair.

She quickly pulled the cowl back over her head and vanished again. Ford struggled to his feet, staggered to one side and leaned heavily against one of the tables.

Sark called out, "Ferimus, acris, tumbu!"

The dark smoke swirled like a cyclone, and funneled up the chimney clearing the room. The sound of smashing wood and glass filled the air.

Harigan shouted several curses as tables and chairs toppled while he rushed toward the broken window, but the person was gone.

"Curse that harpy," Harigan swore.

"Yes... a woman." Ford's voice was strained.

"A woman?" Sean said surprised.

"She... is... cunning," Ford choked out.

"We should pursue her," Han said as he dashed for the door.

"No," Ford called. "She's of little concern now." He pulled out a roll of parchment from under his cloak. "I retrieved the map. She'll be displeased when she discovers it missing." He rubbed his throat.

Sark came along side Ford and looked at him with some curiosity.

"I see in your eyes a spark of recognition."

Ford said nothing, but continued to massage his throat.

"It's no denying it; it's written upon your face my friend," Sark whispered.

"Perhaps after we get back to the inn," Ford said.

"You, sir, are a man of many talents," Sean said then laughed, slapping Ford on the back. "I thought I had foiled our chances with my carelessness. Glad you had fast hands."

Ford moved to the bar and took a tankard. Handing it to the barkeep, he motioned for the man to fill it.

As he stood there he tried to get the image clear in his head.

Willowfern... after all these years. But why? Why was she a thief? Why was she after the map?

Ford finished his drink. "Let's get back to the inn. We have many miles to ride and need to get an early start." He moved toward the door.

Harigan put his cudgel down at his side and moved some of the broken tables from blocking the entrance. Smoke and ash hung in the air, and blood stained the floor and a few walls. The broken window looked like the open mouth of a monster.

The barkeep frowned deeply, his eyes narrowing with anger as he looked over the wreckage of his tavern. Ford reached into this leather pouch and produced several golden coins and laid them on the bar.

"For the damages," he said, knowing the amount was more

than enough to have new furniture made and the window replaced.

The barkeep's eyes went wide with greed. "Yes, for the damages," he repeated back to Ford.

"And to keep this out of the purview of the local constabulary?"

"Yes, I've no idea why them mercenaries tore up me bar, but they've all left for parts unknown to me," the barkeep said with a crooked smile.

"Good - then we do understand one another." Ford turned and made for the door.

The slap in the face of cold air sobered Ford as he stepped outside. Some sooty foot prints led away from the broken widow, but the sleet and cold rain had obliterated where they went.

"Is it like that all the time with you, Ford?" Sark asked.

"No - this is the first time anything like this has happened."

Sark smiled. "You handled it pretty well, if you ask me."

"Thanks - it was all off-the-cuff." Ford nervously chuckled.

Once back at the inn, Ford went to the parlor and picked up the whiskey decanter pouring himself a full glass. Drinking down the amber liquid, he sat on a red-striped chair, savoring the liquor. He looked from man to man.

Harigan said, "I'll have some of that," and poured himself a glass.

"I thought that horn of yours made any type of liquor," Sean said.

"No, just mead and beer."

Harigan drank down the whiskey.

"Now what?" Hugh asked.

"We be extra careful. Raven Hill has made the first move," Ford told them.

Han crouched down by the fire and warmed his hands. "It's clear he needs the map."

"What do you know about this woman?" Sark asked.

"She and I were lovers many years ago in Moore. I met her when I was thinking of settling down, raising a family... you know, the fantasy."

Ford took another drink.

"Why is she here trying to steal the map?" Hugh asked.

"She and I had a falling out. I was sent on assignment out of the city. She thought I should quit and take up a decent job." He looked around the room. "She and I argued before I left. I told her if she couldn't handle my career, she should find someone who better suited her. She was gone when I returned."

Ford took another drink, then stood and refilled his glass.

Sark chuckled softly.

"Ford, judging by tonight's exploits, you made the right decision. She might have killed you at some point."

Smiling, Ford shook his head. "She wasn't like that then."

"Nonetheless, she's involved," Sark said. "I'm sure her appearance doesn't change things, right?"

"True. Strange events though. Why she's involved with such a nefarious characters as Raven Hill, I'll never know."

"She could be working on her own," Sark suggested.

"No. Someone knew we'd be here, and when. The only other one we know of looking for the item is Raven Hill. She's working for him, alright. But why?"

Han stood up and turned toward Ford and Sark.

"In my land we have a saying: *in the midst of chaos only the gods know the outcome.* There is also another saying: *when the heart is bitten by love, for every ounce of bliss there is a pound of suffering.*"

Looking up at Han, Ford nodded his head.

"It's a good saying."

Sark stood up. "Do you think there is a celestial hand in any of this?"

"I doubt it," Ford said. "Anyway, we'd better get some sleep. There's a lot of miles we need to make tomorrow."

"That's a capital idea. Sleep well," Sark said.

"Until the morn." Ford stood and made for the door. As he walked to his room he heard the voice of Harigan arguing with someone, but both the voices were Harigan's. He stood there for a second listening, and then entered his own room.

Ford woke on the ground, the back of his head aching. His eye caught the flicker of the lamp on the desk. For a moment he wondered if he had drunkenly slipped and knocked himself unconscious.

Getting to his knees he rubbed the bump on the back of his head. His balance was missing, and he felt as though the room was wobbling.

A sound caught his attention, and he slowly turned to the dark corner of the room hidden by the back of the door. There, a crossbow was pointed at him from the shadows.

"Willowfern?" Ford asked in surprise, not sure if he was hallucinating.

"Yes, none other," she said.

"I don't understand. I haven't seen you in years…" He saw the malevolence in her eyes now.

"We have been watching the messages of the Brood," she said.

Ford rubbed the back of his neck. "Impossible. How?"

"Never you mind the details. Suffice to say my master knows many things," she said as the corners of her mouth twisted up slightly.

"It was you, in the tavern…" he began but faltered feeling as if he would blackout.

"Yes, isn't it obvious?" She chuckled. "Now, the map if you please?" She held out her hand.

"Or?"

"Or I'll kill you."

"I think you mean to kill me regardless."

"Perhaps," she said.

He made a move to stand, but she shook her head and motioned with the crossbow for him to remain kneeling. She took a step forward.

"So, it's not just the map, or power you seek… you want revenge?"

"Revenge is a fool's errand. If I kill you, it's only out of necessity," she said.

"Pity. I loved you once," Ford said with a sigh.

"Loved me!" She realized her outburst, and controlled her volume. "I will tell you only that we have come to be here together out of professional necessity." She held the crossbow steady. "Some might even call it the will of the fates."

"Fates? When I knew you, only peace, magic, and enlightenment were your calling. Now you appear here as a thief and assassin. You have come by this profession through some lapse in reason, me thinks," Ford said.

"When you shunned me I was devastated. For some time I didn't eat, drink or sleep! I didn't even leave my apartment for many days. I wandered in a haze for weeks and maybe months - I really could not say.

"One day I looked up and found myself in the city of Torrence." She leaned against the wall and rested the crossbow on her knee. "There I woke from my nightmare with a hunger that was all consuming.

"Without coin I begged for help, but none would listen. I threatened, but was only beaten and raped by the town guard. I cried out for salvation, but the gods only rained licentious punishments upon me.

"Finally, I resolved to steal. In the crowd I saw a well-dressed man, his blue robe shimmering in the early evening lamp light. I bumped against him, and came away with his purse."

She chuckled softly, all the while watching Ford intently.

"I ran as fast as my tattered shoes would carry me. I came to a tavern and opened the purse to discover it contained gold coins. I bought ale, bread, sausage, and cheese. I ate until my belly was stretched tightly.

"Then a voice whispered in my ear, 'My child, what will you do for me now that I have advanced you your first salary?' It was the man in the blue robe."

"Is there a point to this story, or are you trying to allow old age to kill me?" Ford quipped.

She took another step and leveled the bow at him.

"If I were you, Ford, I would weigh my position more carefully. I think it will do my soul well to send you into the Netherworld knowing what harm you did my heart."

Her eyes blazed with vengeance.

"So," she continued, "the robed man found me, by his magic or wits. In exchange for him not calling the town guard, I swore a faith to serve him. At first I was afraid he would want sexual favors, but he never asked or forced himself upon me.

"He instead asked me a flurry of questions about my past and what I knew. Soon I was sent on errands for him, simple at first, then of greater complexity. Before I knew it, he was tasking me with responsibilities that required particular talents.

"I retrieved many a relic for his personal use." She scowled. "Then he asked me to retrieve a map from a group of travelers. When I saw you, my heart was stricken again. I chose to take the map and not kill you in the tavern; I was confused and weak like the day you left me." She put the door at her back.

"Do you think it by chance that Raven Hill sent you here?" Ford asked.

"A powerful magician like Raven Hill knows much. He's determined to find that lantern at any cost," she said.

"So, you know what it is?"

"Of course… he keeps nothing from me."

"I fancied marrying you once. You didn't wait for me."

"You chose to leave me," she replied.

"I was locked in the dungeon of Khail Hillkeep. The dwarven king had me kept there for a year while he decided if he'd have me executed. It makes little difference now, but I had no contact with the outside. I could send no notes, letters or messages of any kind."

Looking thoughtful she cocked her head slightly. "What were you doing there?"

"Spying," Ford said.

"For the Brood?"

"Of course."

"Damn you for your frankness!" Her anger was bubbling

over. "All these years I thought you just left."

Her lips grew tense.

"It's still like a poisoned dagger in my heart. And it's time I plucked this dagger from my chest once and for all," she said. "My master was clear on what must be done." Her finger tightened on the trigger.

The door flew open.

"A pox upon thee!" Harigan shouted, as he dashed into the room knocking Willowfern to the ground.

The bolt fired and struck the small end table. The room filled with a light so bright it was blinding for a moment. The end table turned black and quickly decomposed. Ford rolled to one side, not sure what just happened or why he was still alive.

Striking out with the cudgel, Willowfern rolled to the side and jumped to her feet. Harigan's weapon connected with the floorboards, splintering one at the joint.

Harigan grabbed and picked Willowfern up off the ground. She struggled wildly as he flung her into the wall. She was stunned and slid down to the floor.

The cudgel rose above Harigan's head then down it came to deliver a killing blow. Ford launched himself at Harigan's arm, freezing it in place.

Harigan's strength was enormous, and the cudgel was moving slowly towards Willowfern's head. Ford struggled to keep him from killing her, as Harigan applied more force.

"Flee!" Ford called to her.

She looked at him, her eyes filled with tears and disbelief. For a moment she was frozen, and then she climbed to her feet and dashed from the room.

Ford let go, and Harigan slowly put his cudgel at his side. He looked at Ford with a sour expression, but behind his eyes was a glimmer of humanity.

"You still love her," he said. "It is the will of Aor that she still lives, I see. She still has a part to play."

"How did you know she was in here?"

"The god told me," Harigan said with a dour look. "Perhaps I should tell you of the wonders of Aor."

"That won't be necessary. And…" he paused, "thank you."

For a moment Harigan was taken aback.

"You, master Efferguard, are a fool," he flatly said. "It would have been better, I think, to have delivered her to the arms of Aor with a good old-fashioned braining!"

"I couldn't let that happen."

It seemed that Harigan was about to say something, but instead turned on his heels and walked out of the room leaving the door open.

CHAPTER

10

The Road to Canaric

They woke early and ate. Han and Sean retrieved their party's mounts and pack animals and brought them to the inn. Ford looked about, but knew that if Willowfern were following, he'd have little hope of noticing her.

"Do you feel any strange magic in the air?" he asked Sark.

"No abeo cloaks, if that is what you mean..."

Ford smiled. "I'm not sure what I mean."

"If she follows us, we'll not know it." Sark replied, then looked around, and mounted his horse. "When there is no control, it is best to just let go of the illusion."

"Illusion?" Sean asked.

Sark snapped his reins. "The illusion of control."

"Traveling this early without a second breakfast seems barbaric!" Hugh said.

Harigan turned slightly in the saddle and looked at Hugh.

"For a Justice Knight, you certainly complain much."

"I don't!"

"We'll see." Harigan turned back to the dark path.

A glimmer of light was on the horizon as they traveled northwest. The lands around were flat and green with many irrigation canals feeding thirsty fields.

A strong smell of tilled dirt hung in the cool air, mixing with the moisture from the ditches. Ford inhaled deeply, his memories racing back to the days he spent with Willowfern in the Moore Park Gardens, reading and dreaming, and laughing.

"These small, round, sod-and-timber farmhouses look like giant mushrooms," Han said.

"Certainly there's no end to chimneys belching out smoke," Sark added, waving his hand in front of his face. He turned to Ford. "Where did you study magic when you were a boy?"

"In Moore. That's where my family is from. I took a class in incantations and cantrips at my local school. I tried my hand at it, but had little talent."

Smiling, Sark said, "Perhaps you just needed to practice more?"

"It was no use. Even simple stuff, you know… lighting candles, moving light objects about on a table, childish things… I wasn't good at it."

"Pity. It can serve a man well if only to enhance his career."

"I suppose it could help me sometime, hopefully for things other than lighting a candle for a date, or making someone sneeze."

"You should let me teach you a few things when the time is more convenient."

"If you think I'd not be a waste of your time," Ford said.

Hugh pointed into one of the fields.

"Look, a dwarf farmer tilling the soil with a steam-oxen."

The mechanical device was belching out smoke from its stack, and steam pumped from several valves. The furrows it dug were a dozen at a time, and as wide as twenty feet.

Sean nodded his head toward one of the houses.

"There around the home, his wife with a bucket feeding hogs."

"I didn't know that dwarves farmed in this region," Hugh said.

Ford pointed ahead along the road.

"There'll be many farms like these. The Hotep dwarves settled this region a dozen years ago. They were driven from the Sawtooth Mountains in the east. Cattle, herbs, and vegetables are their chief production now," he explained.

As they approached the boundary of the next farm, Ford halted the column. "Dismount and take a break," he said.

A caravan of swarthy Bottomland elves approached.

"I have roast fowl and melie bean cakes!" the dark-skinned elf said.

He was tall, over six foot, and his eyes were almond shaped and dark as brass. His long, flowing black hair was contrasted with his receding hair line, and his brightly-colored clothes flapped in the wind.

Leaning down from his horse he spoke directly to Ford.

"You fellows look as though you could do with a meal and some drink. I'm Bilidonius, road caterer from Canaric."

"How fresh is the food?" Ford asked.

"Killed this day and cooking in a kaylee pot."

Sark looked surprised. "Kaylee pot? Where in the world did you acquire one of those?"

"It's been in my family for generations, keeps food fresh and hot."

"Might I see it?" Sark asked.

The elf looked at Sark with some bemusement, then smiled.

"If ye buy a pie, ye can gaze upon it all ye like."

Sark quickly produced a few coppers.

"I'll take one," he said.

"Filici, give this fellow a meat pie and show him the pot."

"Really, Papa – let him see the pot?"

Bilidonius looked annoyed. "That is what I said, now do it!" He turned to Sark. "It's kept in the middle wagon."

He raised his voice. "It's okay that this man sees the pot, but that is all!"

Sark walked back to the wagon. A young girl pulled open a purple velvet curtain and Sark gasped with surprise.

"It is a kaylee pot!" He returned to Bilidonius. "You have a great treasure there. Guard it well."

Bilidonius raised an eyebrow.

"That is why I told my family to only let you see the pot and nothing else." He smiled then laughed. He turned to the rest of the party. "Now, loosen your purses and prepare for a feast."

The side of one of the wagons came open revealing a wooden serving bar. Two young elven women worked within, and in short order a wooden plate of fowl and two cakes were sitting on the counter. Soon, everyone in the party were ordering and eating.

"What's the big deal with this pot?" Sean looked curious.

"All you have to do is make a kill. You don't have to dress it or prepare it, just shove it in and it comes out prepared and delicious," Sark said with giddy excitement. "But, what's more, you only have to make one kill. The pot makes duplicates of the meal, as many as you like."

"Why don't they make those now?" Sean asked.

"The magic formula has been lost." Sark stated.

Han approached the wagon and turned to Sark. "We have a legend in my country of the magic oven. It is a similar thing, but we say it is possessed with the spirit of a demon chef who does the bidding of the oven's owner."

"I've never seen a kaylee pot, but I've read stories of them," Hugh said.

Harigan laughed, stuffed a leg of fowl into his mouth then followed it with a horn of ale.

"I know where there are two of those pots!"

Sark's expression betrayed shock. "Where?"

Harigan eyed Sark carefully. "In a place you would not wish to travel."

Tearing the meat from the bone, Sark chewed for a moment. "So tell me."

"The ruined hill fort of Hidelbrow, and the dungeon of Keep Slayerlow."

"You're right – I don't want to know any more."

Harigan smiled from beneath his bushy beard. "You would be wise to listen to me more often."

Once Bilidonius finished serving, and saw that no more money would be made, he called for the wagon to be closed up.

"We're off. Good travels to you and your company," he said to Ford.

"Fair travels to you and yours," Ford replied. Turning, he remounted his horse. "We have more miles to ride before we reach the safety of the city. Let's log some miles."

*   *   *

The road was straight, and the city straddled it like a mounted rider. A long line of travelers were crowded onto the road all converging on Canaric.

"You there, mind your horse," called a teamster with a steam-powered wagon-train as it pushed its way past the crowd. The five long enclosed wagons trundled by, their wheels clacking along the flagstones. Ford moved to the side as it passed.

The road was choked with traffic as farmers, vagabonds, merchants, and nobles alike, all vied for room on the narrow highway. Pedestrians weaved in and out of the cart and horse traffic adding to the congestion.

"Watch yourself!" Hugh called down to a woman in a dirty dress pulling three small children by the hand.

She looked up at Hugh with malice, and then turned her attention back to the road and her dust-filled path.

"The noise is rather deafening!" Sark shouted to Ford.

"It is the bustle of commerce," Ford said. "Business men from the west and north bring goods to trade and money to spend. The river is not far away, and it serves as a vital link for the movement of that wealth."

Han removed a handkerchief and wiped some dust from his face. Carts filled with fruit, and vegetables were in every direction.

"There's a lot of money to be made in this town," he said to Sean.

"Look up there—" Sean pointed to the side at drovers herding livestock towards the town. "The inns here probably have a full kitchen and bountiful menus!"

"Caravan coming up on our left," Harigan shouted.

"The gate guards follow strict city procedures by recording every person, every cart, and its contents. Stay together," Ford called back over his shoulder.

Removing his handkerchief, Ford blew his nose. The mucus was black and filled with dust. He wondered what that gunk was doing to his lungs. The stench of animal dung, urine, and human filth was growing ever stronger, and he knew they were getting close to the city walls.

Tucking the cloth back into his belt, he stretched, extending his arms upward and allowing himself a vigorous yawn. Suddenly, an army of men dressed in the livery of Canaric appeared.

They moved with deliberate speed, using shovels and brooms to clear the debris and animal defecation into gutters at the side; it was carried away by filthy ditch water. Then these vigilant cleaners of Canaric vanished into the dust.

"Who was that?" Sean asked.

Ford turned in his saddle. "Civil servants of Canaric."

The gate was several hundred feet away. Its colossal size was impressive. Two mighty gates forty feet wide and sixty feet tall were open.

They were made of bronze, inlaid in ivory and polished to a bright reflective luster. Sark leaned over toward Ford.

"I have read that a man can stand on the top of Thurmond mountain as the sun rises and be blinded by the reflection from the eastern gates of Canaric."

"They are impressive," Ford said.

"They were forged with the magic metallurgy of the Old Kingdom. I read about it in a codex when I was a boy," Sark replied.

"I'm not familiar with the history of Canaric," Han said.

Sark turned slightly in the saddle.

"It was originally a Goblin town, during the Old Kingdom. The dread King Hollowbeck was approaching from the east with his army of five hundred thousand orcs. When he arrived, he found those," he pointed at the gates, "barring his path."

"Impressive isn't it, the gates of Canaric?" Harigan asked.

"They are massive," Han said while wiping dirt from his nose and mouth.

"Anyways," Sark continued, "the king laid siege to the town, and for a year he tried to batter down the gates with rams made of iron and lead. He even employed a mercenary force of ogres to smash the gates, but to no avail."

"Did the city ever fall?"

Sark smiled. "Not to the Dread King. After the year of siege, the wall guards recorded that the king's army was dwindling. At first they thought it was desertion, but they found out it was disease.

"When they opened those mighty gates and came out to investigate they found empty tents, rotting bloated carcasses and dying orcs. The goblin scouts returned and all the population of Canaric died weeks later.

"The scribe Goh'golac called it the Shadow Sickness; it was the last entry in his journal and found in his skeletal hand."

Looking up at the walls, Han saw men in armor moving atop. "When did the men come?"

"The town was skirted by the caravans and forgotten for years, until it was finally settled again by a band of Commersarians who didn't know the legend. It's been going strong minting coin from trade ever since."

"Get ready, we're coming up on the gate," Ford shouted back.

Through the haze Ford saw the individual guards waving carts and people forward. With one hand they motioned for a person to come forth, with the other they took the fee.

Another guard just beyond handed the visitor a printed paper, and yet another guard verbally told the individual what to expect if they made trouble.

A tall, thin guard dressed in polished white armor waved Ford up to the checkpoint. He held up his hand for the payment and then eyed him with dark blue eyes in a most curious manner.

"You look familiar to me," he said. "Your name wouldn't be Ford Efferguard, would it?"

Ford was shocked. He rapidly searched his memory for any recollection of the voice. He was taken back and hesitated to answer.

"It's me," the guard said taking off his helmet. "Marconius Guntervos!"

Ford let out a tremendous laugh.

"Marconius, you old broadnober!" He got down from his horse and embraced the elf. "I didn't know that you were a guard here in Canaric."

"Not many people do. Sort of a career by chance one might say." He held his helmet at his side. "What brings you here?"

"Talk on your own time!" shouted a frustrated teamster driving a tri-wagon pulled by two large tuluk oxen.

"Damn!" Marconius said. "He's right. How about you and I meet at the Milking Maid near the town forum across from the Temple of Shu later?"

"What time?" Ford asked.

"Say double three of the city bells?" Marconius grinned.

"It's a contract," Ford said.

Taking out a sovereign gold coin, he handed it to Marconius. "Those five fellows behind me are part of my group. This sum should cover us all."

Marconius shouted out, "Let these men go. They're paid up!" He waved the rest of the party through the gate.

"The Milking Maid, right?" Ford shouted to confirm, as they moved past the arrow coves and portcullis of the inner defenses.

"Yes, at double three bells!" Marconius called back.

Slowly Ford navigated his way through the throng of pedestrians, teamsters, and carts that choked the boulevard. Moving through the mass he headed toward the qasba. It was the only way to reach the forum and the noble villas beyond.

Rounding some apartments, the road widened. They were on a hill overlooking the chaos of the city. One-story buildings were visible in the distance and sparsely placed around the city center. Multi-storied buildings dominated, and the temples looked like mushrooms in a vegetable garden, randomly placed.

"What in the name of Hoth is that?" Hugh said pointing at several tall structures that wound around the city like two snakes.

"The fabled aqueducts of Canaric," Sark said.

"They're huge! They must channel whole rivers of water," Sean said.

"They do." Sark chuckled.

Ford pointed towards a set of domed three-story buildings gleaming with gold and silver. "Those are the public bathhouses, famed for their healing properties, and fed by several effervescent hot springs."

"They are co-ed," Sark added. "But be wary you don't violate any taboos."

"What?" Sean said. "Men and women together?"

Harigan looked at Sean. "Come now, you're an elf of the sea and the world, don't tell me you've never seen the intimacies of the female animal before?"

Indignantly, Sean said, "I am quite familiar with women, but I just have never seen them in a bathhouse with men before."

"Right…" Harigan said and maneuvered his horse away from Sean and up in front of Hugh.

"What does that mean?" Sean was annoyed.

Harigan smiled under his bushy facial hair.

"Fine, you fuzzy faced lunatic, don't tell me," Sean said under his breath.

"Up on that hill are the large estates," Ford said pointing across the city.

"Ah, yes, the wealthy Commersarians. Those who founded their fortunes here. The potential to be rich and affluent is not predicated on nobility in this city," Sark said.

Ford turned in the saddle. "But being of noble blood doesn't hurt."

"Why do you admire these people?" Sark asked Ford.

"They are not bound by convention here. You know that. Women hold power, property, and more than one husband. Whole buildings are dedicated to pleasures of suffering. Drink and dream-shrooms are used for pleasure, as well as various smoking herbs.

"Men marry men, women marry women, and both orc and goblin can marry who they like here. It is money that drives this city and not confined cultural tradition. "

Sark looked contemplative. "Don't fool yourself; they are bound by conventions of another sort."

"Perhaps…" Ford turned back. "These villas we are heading toward are quite opulent. Luckily we'll be staying in one tonight."

"Really?" Sark asked, surprised.

"Indeed so. The Brood has made many friends in the city states. These friends are both rich and powerful."

"Where is it that we're heading then?" Sark's curiosity was peaked.

"The house of Vilicor vin Delecor. They have an ample estate on the hill where we can refresh and acquire fresh mounts."

"And next on our itinerary?" Sark inquired.

"To Marbury, and then to Prin. Once in Prin we will seek out the cavern entrance to the catacombs under Tallibach."

"The map is our only guide," Han said. "What should we do to secure it? There was an attempt to steal it once."

"Twice actually," Sark corrected. "But I agree with Han, that the map must be protected. We may want to make a copy of it before it is stolen," Sark said.

"I thought of that, but it has a magic component that I'm at a loss to get duplicated," Ford said.

"I can do it," Sark smiled.

"Wise idea, but then we would have two maps to lose," Ford added.

"This copy would be harder to lose," Sark replied. "If it got more than a few yards away from me, the detail will vanish and become useless."

Sark looked thoughtful. "That does pose a challenge, though. I will need some items that I do not currently carry."

"Where would we acquire those items?"

"An apothecary shop or the local Magic Guild would have them," Sark said.

"I don't see how you'll do it. Our magicians in Moore were unable to duplicate it."

"I have a way," Sark said. "When we get a free moment, I'll fetch the supplies and copy it. But be aware there is an inherent risk."

"I don't like the sound of that."

"Without great risk there is no great reward," Sark said. "Do you really want to know?"

"I'd better," Ford said.

"The map is much older than you know. The parchment is made of dragon hide, and the ink is from the blood of a demon; demons and dragons don't give up their mortal substances so easily. But the real risk is in the form of magic needed to copy it. I'll need to invoke a weave of Chaos Magic and Elemental Magic." Sark smiled confidently. "The two don't really go together, and if I weave poorly, well the map may dissolve, jump to another universe, or get cursed and be un-usable."

"What are the odds?" Harigan asked.

"Three to one normally, but since you have me doing it, it's one to three." Sark smiled.

"You're proving your mettle," Ford stated with a chuckle. "But even one to three is more than I think we can risk."

Harigan shrugged his shoulders. "I don't like those odds. I'll see what I can do to help."

"Okay, let me know if you change your mind. I'm aware that this city has a rather fine apothecary shop," Sark added.

The road turned and widened, emptying out into the qasba. Here was a large market square and many tall four story buildings.

The market was more than two hundred yards long and a hundred yards wide. Awnings and carts lined the edges, and wide doors granted access to the various buildings from the market.

The sun was shining down, but the air was cool. People moved throughout the square wearing cloaks and quilted doublets with breeches, or the more common jerkins and trousers.

Wares of every description were being hocked and buyers from every part of the civilized world seemed present. Ford saw the swarthy people of the south gathered near an ornate set of blue and red tents decorated with gold tassels. They were selling spices and herbs, and amber.

Next to them were Lake Elves selling fish sauce and marugo puddings, glazed pottery and elvin ale. Down from them were the humans— brawny men selling sausages and breads, Darkmountain stout and bitters, black enameled metal wears and cobalt blue glass.

And near the men were Quarry Dwarves, stout and fiery in temper with long beards, selling scale armor, short swords, and jewelry. Stacked up in front of them were pig-iron billets, and rare mixed metals like everstrong, white steel, and never-rust. The list of merchants seemed endless.

At the end of the qasba they passed the working class tenements— three and four-story structures made of timber and cement, often without kitchens, heat, or running water.

Ford heard babies crying, women shouting at derelict husbands, and the occasional caterwaul of a house serpent. The smells of animal dung, human waste, cooking food, and sweat assaulted his nose.

People looked down on them from second floor windows and watched as they passed. Several times children rushed from side passages into the street, nearly colliding with them. The little scamps looked up annoyed, then dashed off into a darkened alley or doorway.

They came out from the apartments into a wide street leading to the forum; the center of the city and the seat of public buildings. Down each side street were shops, taverns wine bars, brothels, tea houses, and temples all commingled.

Emerging into the forum, Ford admired its size, a mile long and at least a mile wide. A broad avenue went down the center, and all around were impressive edifices made of stone.

There were other buildings there too, some made of stucco and painted red and black, topped with wooden or slate roofs. Most were painted on the sides with images of heroes and beasts.

The roadways were all paved with large black paving stones and down the primary avenue, on either side were massive stone aqueducts three stories tall.

"I've never seen such things!" Sean said, pointing at the waterways.

"Built by the genius architect Fenius Hargus the Younger, and his mountain giant stone masons. The stark white stone aqueducts are legendary," Sark said.

"Designed to carry massive volumes of water, they make a circle following the layout of the city's defensive walls," Ford added. "Hidden within each estuary are two canals ten feet wide flowing in opposite directions, serving two purposes: one, to provide drinking water, and two, to provided fast transportation around the city. It's said that a messenger can get on a canal gondola at one end of the city and be at the other end in ten minutes, and return again in another ten. In fact, I have tried it just to test the legend, and to my surprise, it was true."

"Can we take a ride?" Hugh asked.

Ford shook his head. "Unfortunately, this trip, we won't have time to travel the canals."

They traveled down the long avenue past the lavished temples and columned public buildings. Massive bronze doors of the mystical temple to Titrius loomed in majestic beauty. Intricate scroll work and filigree showed the magic goblin words for strength and honor.

Looking ahead, Ford saw the great vertical wind-spiral atop the ten stories high, shocking pink Guia de Timoria building. The spiral was spinning in a slow fashion driving the many machines within that did sewing and weaving.

All around the perimeter of the building were dark green hedges and brown glazed pots filled with yellow and orange flowers. He admired the magnificent foliage that adorned many of the buildings and side streets.

Purple, red, blue, and yellow flowers blossomed from many a dark green bush, often just in front of the well-manicured hedges that lined the street-paths. Down the sides of the streets, strips of grass lay like great green sleeping serpents between cement and stone walkways.

Sean again spoke excitedly. "What are those?"

He pointed at a checkerboard pattern laid out over rolling hills as far as the eye could see.

"Estates, each with its own manor house," Ford said. "They stretch for miles and take up thousands of acres."

The rolling hills went on for many miles towards the horizon. It was clear that the city walls had been extended to encompass the estates.

From his vantage Ford looked down at the second closest manor house still a mile off.

"Valicor vin Delecor," he said aloud.

"That's the home of your friend?" Sean asked.

"Yes, they're friends of ours. It's good to have such friends," stated Ford.

It took thirty minutes to get to the road that led to the estates. They moved along a high wall made of gray stone and red stucco.

After some time, Ford came to a halt in front of an archway with a name-stone at the top where the keystone was. Dismounting, he walked up to the gate and found a rope hanging from one of the pillars and pulled it.

The sound of a bell rang from beyond the wall. A man in polished brass and steel armor carrying a sword stepped out and jumped with surprise.

"Master Efferguard!" he said with some amusement. "You're the last person I expected to find pulling the bell rope. How wonderful it is to see you again."

"And you, Guard Master Hall. Your employer is expecting me and my party. Would you be so kind as to announce our arrival?"

"Indeed I will, sir," Hall said with great enthusiasm.

He disappeared behind the wall, and Ford heard him talking to someone. A moment passed, and Hall appeared again.

He unlocked the gate and said with a flourish of his hand, "You are expected at the main house. You know the way, I trust."

CHAPTER

11

Old Friends

Valicor was standing on the portico waiting when Ford arrived. A small army of gardeners were all around. Some pruned fruit trees, clipped grass, and trimmed the six-foot-high hedges that made a small maze.

Valicor stood tall, nearly seven feet, thin and fit. His long golden hair came down to his shoulders and his high cheeks gave him the appearance of being a mirthful elf, though he was human.

As he descended the stone staircase, he opened his arms and threw them around Ford much like an octopus surrounds its prey.

"Ford, by the gods, it is good to have you back!" he said. "We got word of your travels only yesterday."

He eyed the others.

"And who are these fine looking fellows with you?"

"May I introduce Osara Han, Captain Friggand, Father Harigan, Sir Hugh – a Justice Knight—and Sark the magician?" Ford said.

Valicor let go of him.

"Well, quite a group you've brought. Beerdon will be excited that we have some interesting guests finally. None of you worry… there is plenty of space here at our little house. None of you worry one little bit. All preparation have been made for your stay." Valicor took Ford by the hand and ascended the stairs.

"Beerdon will be so pleased. He was just saying the other day that all we ever do here is entertain the same boring old friends."

"We'll only be staying the one night. We have business in Prin," Ford said.

"Prin? What a wonderful place with respect to cuisine and culture, but it is a hole when it comes to safety and manners. Why Prin? "

"Business," Ford said.

Turning, Valicor let go Ford's hand and shouted to two servants standing in the entry.

"Fetch the personal belongings of these men. Also, take these worn-out horses and pack lagmas and pick out some fresh mounts for my friends. They'll be leaving on the morrow."

He turned to the group. "Come everyone, let's get refreshments and some rest, and I'm sure that you are all eager to meet Beerdon!"

Valicor turned and started into the villa. As he walked he leaned over so Ford could hear him.

"I'll have to show you the new rug we purchased just this week. It's just the most darling of accoutrements— magically heated and even glows in the dark." Valicor let go a childish giggle.

As the evening light diminished and the estate lamps and lanterns were lit, Ford sat feasting in a large, bright, and lavishly-decorated hall.

The floor was hidden by ornate rugs covered in bright reds and dark black abstract patterns. Rich tapestries hung from every wall depicting woodland scenes or seascapes.

Brightly polished brass lanterns were suspended from the ceiling. Upholstered couches, polished wooden tables and large blue velvet pillows were all about.

Many colors, reds, gold, blacks, whites, blues and purples were mixed together; all coexisting without offense. Even the incense was colorful as whiffs of white, green, and blue fragrant smoke rose into the air.

"Can you see…" Valicor said to Ford, "the rug at our feet was the one that I was mentioning earlier today. Notice its subtle patterns, and delightful colors. Put your bare feet on it and feel its warmth. And, if the light was dimmer in here, you would see its luminescence."

Ford looked down. Indeed the rug was a masterwork. Circles, crescents, and chevrons were arranged in groups throughout. A slight iridescence radiated from it.

As he felt it with his hand the patterns shifted and contorted to form other patterns.

"They move," he declared.

"Yes! Quite so!" Valicor said with a laugh. "Enchanted – and expensive."

Servants came from every direction bringing fresh food and drink, and clearing away finished plates and empty tankards. Roast fowl, and suckling pig were brought and devoured. Grilled and marinated vegetables were brought with a complement of baked tubers, herbs, and auroch butter.

Loaves of bread were piled high on the table, as bowls of olives, and pickles were set out. Looking about the room Ford saw Han eating modestly, taking a small amount on a plate.

Beerdon smiled. "It's not often that we have a holy man dine with us. It is pleasing to see that you eat like normal men."

"Normal? There is little that is normal about me," Harigan stated.

"I'll say," Sean added.

Harigan grunted, then pushed more food into his mouth.

Ford sat back and observed. He knew Valicor Delecor, the son of a wealthy commerce family. Also, he'd met Beerdon Glikenspear, the proprietor of one of the biggest breweries in Canaric.

The Brood had sent him several years previous to ship hundreds of kegs of beer to the island nation of Gool. All the libations were intended for the wedding of the King of Gool's daughter.

Valicor's father controlled several cold-ships making them available to the Brood for a price. Ford quickly forged a contract, promptly filling each with barrels of fermented dark stout.

At the reception, Ford waited for the partygoers to slip off into drunken slumber, and stole the plans for a naval steam ship the king's Minister of War had in his safe.

When Ford returned from Gool, he stayed at Valicor's city townhome. It was there that he noticed the young Valicor preferred men to women, though he did not seem particularly attracted to Ford.

Ford had to meet with Beerdon; Valicor tagged along. He noticed that Valicor and Beerdon seemed enchanted by one another.

Beerdon, unlike Valicor, was a man short and thickly muscled. His bald head was large and his full black beard made him look older than he really was.

His taste in clothes was clearly more conservative than that of Valicor's, and his reserved and modest behavior made him liked and respected by many of the noble families of Canaric.

The two men wedded a few years later, and Ford remained friends ever since. Now they were kind enough to allow him to use their villa as a resting point for his mission.

Harigan stood up and lifted his horn into the air. He said the magic words, and a frothy head formed at the mouth of the horn.

With little hesitation he turned the horn up and quaffed mightily, the dark contents sloshing down his beard and onto his shirt. Wiping his beard and mouth with the back of his hand he looked over at the two hosts, stood, and spoke.

"By the breath of Aor, yer both men!"

"Well of course, silly," stated Valicor with a laugh. "Where have you been?"

Harigan quickly sat back down. "Obviously not here. I need another drink."

He spoke the words and filled his horn again.

"So, what is it that you are doing here, Ford?" Beerdon asked. "Or, should we discuss other topics?"

"Perhaps other topics will suit us better," Ford smiled.

"Don't be foolish," Valicor siad. "Can't you give us a hint? We won't tell."

"I trust you implicitly, but right now suffice it to say that we're on an important mission for the Brood. A business trip one might say."

"Will you be staying in Marbury at all?" Beerdon asked.

"One night perhaps. But our destination is actually Prin."

"I hope that you'll visit the fortress," Valicor said excitedly. "I hear that they've done lots of repairs on it since the quake."

"Repairs?" Sark looked surprised.

"Yes, I've heard that they had to shore up the foundation."

"When was this?" Han sat forward.

"Last year I think," Beerdon said.

"This may not bode well," Hugh said to Ford.

"So, you're going to the old fortress?" Beerdon's face betrayed subtle bemusement.

Ford was quiet, lost in thought.

"Do you know if they worked down in the catacombs below the structure?"

"There are catacombs below the dungeons?" Valicor asked surprised. "They didn't take us there on the tour."

"Val, they're not going on the tour I think," Beerdon said with a knowing shake of his head. "Mister Sark, what form of magic do you practice?"

"I am proficient in all manipulations of the power, but of late I have been interested in the Chaos energy."

"That can be dangerous."

"Indeed," Sark said.

Valicor cleared his throat.

"Your armor, Sir Hugh… does it have some intrinsic meaning?"

"It was my father's. The metal was forged by the Gillivox elves of old. My father once told me that it was designed by an elven master smith called Grimly Moore."

"Grimly Moore?" Ford said, surprised.

"Do you know of him?"

"Indeed I do. Your armor is an artifact."

"I have yet to discover all it does," Hugh said.

Beerdon shifted in his seat.

"Captain Friggand, what seas have you sailed?" he asked.

"I've been upon the Alliabas and even spent some time on one of the islands there. I've been to the western sea of Corinth

and even Corinth Minor, and I've sailed the Atlas Ocean and…
visited several islands there too."

"And you, Master Han? What talent do you lend this
fellowship?"

"Sailor, warrior, healer, or priest?" Beerdon said with a placid
expression.

"Perhaps I'm more philosopher?" Han suggested.

"I be the priest on this trip," Harigan mumbled, as he stuffed
a roasted bird leg into his mouth and bit through the bone.
Chewing loudly, he seemed preoccupied in thought.

"A priest of which god?" Valicor asked.

"Aor, the vengeful and righteous," Harigan said in between
bites.

"Aor? Were they not the healer priests who were fabled to
kidnap villagers and perform unmentionable experiments with
them?" Valicor asked.

Harigan turned his gaze upon the flamboyant man and
visibly shivered.

"The world will come to an end one day," he said as he held
up the horn, spoke the magic words and drank. He wiped his
mouth. "Aor has room in his realm for you and yours too, I
suppose."

Valicor sat back, a quizzical expression on his face.

"A robust group you have, Ford," Beerdon said. "I wish you
luck on your trip, whatever it is that you're doing."

Ford glanced over at a tall black clock standing in the corner.
"Gods, I nearly forgot! It's getting close to double three," he said
as he jumped to his feet. "If you'll excuse me." He politely bowed
to Valicor and Beerdon. "I must meet a friend."

"Where are you off to?" Beerdon asked, getting to his feet
and drinking down the last of the liquor in his glass.

"I ran into a friend at the gates. I swore to meet him this night at the Milking Maid."

"I know of it. It can be a difficult part of town. It is not far from the Saburo," Beerdon warned.

Sark grabbed ford by the arm.

"Don't be a fool with the map," he said. "Leave it with me, and I'll ensure its safety until you return."

Ford hesitated for a moment, but then turned the map over to Sark. If it was not safe with him it would not be safe with anyone, he reasoned.

"Be very careful with it."

"You are assured," Sark said.

"Let my chariot driver take you to wherever it is you are going. I'll give him orders to stay there and bring you back safely when you're ready," Valicor said, walking Ford outside.

"I appreciate that."

Valicor shouted for his servant and sent him to fetch the charioteer. In a matter of minutes, the chariot arrived.

"Sestius, watch after Master Efferguard," Valicor ordered. "Now take care. Canaric can be a tricky place at night, as you know."

"My friend, your hospitality is grander than the King of Rogert," Ford complemented.

Valicor smiled, turned on his heels, and vanished inside the villa.

CHAPTER

12

The Milking Maid's Secrets

"The Milking Maid," Sestius said, gesturing up at the large mural depicting a woman milking an auroch. "I'll pull up to that turnout and wait for you there."

"Thank you, I won't be long," Ford said.

Climbing down from the chariot, he eyed the crowd. The place was bustling with activity.

Patrons were so numerous that they had spilled out from the front door and were socializing in the street. Burly men mingled with loose women, and burly women mingled with loose men.

Each patron held aloft a tankard, goblet, or glass as music played from inside the tavern. Pushing his way through the crowd, Ford entered and looked around.

The smell of sweat and cooking meat mingled with the smoke from pipe and fireplace. Dice tables were crowded, and players harangued each other as the dice were thrown and fortunes were won and lost.

The small round tables were taken up with more people than they could support. All around conglomerations of patrons gathered, while the many waiters and waitresses rushed about serving libations.

Ford scanned the room. Through the smoky haze and dark shadows he saw Marconius waving him over.

Making his way across the tavern, Ford kept one hand on his coin purse and the other on his dagger. After ten steps, he arrived.

"My friend," Marconius said loudly. "I have a tankard of ale, a hunk of local cheese, and a loaf of the house bread ready for you!"

Ford reached out and shook Marconius' hand. Sitting down, he looked at the many tankards on the table.

"I see you got a head start on the evening," Ford said.

Marconius pointed at one. "Those were here when I sat down. I had to fight off several bands of tavern-creepers seeking a table before you showed up." Marconius laughed. "For you, mate." He nodded at a full mug.

Ford eagerly quaffed several gulps. "Good beer! Must be a Beerdon Lager."

"What brings you to Canaric?" Marconius asked.

"You know, the usual - business."

"Business?" Marconius gave him a knowing look and laughed. "It's none of my *business* anyway."

"How did you end up in Canaric?" Ford asked back.

Marconius laughed again. "I found myself here five years ago on *business* too."

"A woman or a man… or other?" Ford tipped up his tankard.

Marconius guffawed so loudly that several patrons turned to look.

"A woman! But not just any woman. I met the daughter of Salva de Medigeons."

"The human that runs the port business here?" Ford was surprised.

"The same."

Marconius finished his tankard of ale. "At first it was a very naughty affair, and seamy." He chuckled. "She asked if I would stay. Her father got me a job at the gate, and I've been there ever since."

He waved over the barmaid.

"Two more ales."

The serving wench quickly cut through the crowd toward the bar.

"Women can have that effect on a man," Ford said.

"A spell is more like it," Marconius retorted.

A large burly man came around and scooped up the empty tankards into a bucket and vanished into the crowd. The barmaid returned and plunked down two more drinks. Marconius paid with a coin and she, too, vanished into the throng.

Leaning in, Marconius looked about cautiously.

"A man came to see me the other day. He asked me about you. He said at first he was a friend, but then added that if I were to see you that it would be worth gold coin to tell him." He drank some ale. "You know fellows like that, mysterious and evasive."

"What did he look like?"

"He stood slightly shorter than you and wore a short trimmed black beard, neat appearance and well spoken; educated somewhere. He was a human, but dressed elvish and had a strange golden amulet around his neck the shape of a Trilip containing a blue gem in the center."

He took another gulp of ale. "He was traveling with a woman; tall, dark hair, lovely really. She stood back eyeing the crowd... a bodyguard, perhaps. The fellow had done his leg work, for he knew who and where I was, and that I knew you."

Ford tipped up the tankard and took a healthy drink.

"Was he wearing a blue robe?"

"Indeed," Marconius said. "Do you know the fellow?"

"By reputation," Ford said, as he finished his tankard and looked around. "Did he ask anything else?"

"No," Marconius added. "But after he left I asked a friend of mine to follow him. A few hours later he returned and told me the man's name is Raven Hill, hailing from Hillmount. Supposedly selling and buying antiquities. He's put up at an inn in the Suburo called the Jolly Palace."

"What of the woman?"

"He didn't find out anything about her." Marconius finished his ale. "Oh, also my friend discovered that this Raven Hill was heading to Prin soon. Take it from me, he's up to no good and you're on his list of mischief."

"I appreciate the information," Ford said. "If my business in Prin comes to any money, I'll see that you get some of it."

Marconius laughed heartily.

"My woman keeps we well stocked with gold and silver. I have more than I can possibly spend. Just do me a favor..."

Ford sat forward making sure he could hear the man.

"What is it?"

"Don't get killed!" He laughed again.

"I'm afraid that might not be up to me," Ford said.

The town water clock chimed loudly. Ford stepped out onto the street and sucked in the cool night air. A slight haze had settled around and the streetlamps appeared to have halos surrounding the dim yellow lights. Pulling up to the corner, Sestius stopped the chariot.

"Back home, sir?"

"No," Ford said. "How well do you know the Suburo?"

"The hand of death lingers there, sir. I'd suggest we go in daylight and with an armed escort."

Ford climbed up. "If it makes you nervous, you can drop me at the entrance and I'll walk in."

"You know I can't do that. I am responsible for you." He jiggled the reins and the cart began to move. "I'll take you there, but be ready to make a fast exit."

Ford smiled. "It's late; most easy prey have passed out or are in brothels now, and the blockmen gangs are probably not out anymore."

"But if they do come out, we'll be in for it," Sestius suggested.

"I'll only be a short while," Ford said, as he watched the buildings go by.

The cool breeze felt good on his face. Moisture in the air was beginning to cause pools of water to form at the base of buildings and light poles.

After a few minutes they came to an archway. Beyond the arch was the narrow streets of the Suburo; a warren of tenement apartments, small shops, brothels, and gambling dens.

"We can still turn back," Sestius mused.

"I know," Ford added. "Nonetheless, take me to the Jolly Palace."

Darkness was all-consuming as they maneuvered through the tight streets. Tenement apartments, three stories high, showed little sign of light as few exterior lamps were lit. Only infrequently was there the dull glow of candlelight from a covered second or third story window.

"Here we are, sir."

Sestius pointed to a lantern illuminating the sign as he pulled up near the main door of the inn.

"Take us up to that corner," Ford said. "Let me out then find a place to turn around. Wait out of sight until I signal you."

Driving the chariot to the corner, Sestius let Ford get off and then maneuvered down the street looking for a turnout. Ford quickly moved into the shadows.

The cry of a baby echoed down from some unseen hovel. The stench of urine and filth was strong, as he found what he was looking for.

The mortared bricks of the adjacent apartment were inlaid with less than perfect precision. Enough of a gap remained where he could get a finger hold. Slowly, hand over hand, he climbed up the wall.

Easing himself over the lip of the rooftop, he rolled onto his back, sweat covering his face and shirt. The smell of cooking meat wafted to his nose, and for a moment he entertained the idea of stealing a bite from that unseen kitchen.

Somewhere in the darkness a woman's moaning filled the air. He looked across the gap, and saw it was about ten feet to the other roof.

It was a bit too far to chance jumping. The rooftop was solid looking, but if he landed wrong, he might end up crashing through the roof and into a bed with two surprised lovers.

The roof he was on was wide, made of cement or thick plaster with a small shed near one side. Creeping over, he opened the door and noticed various tools.

Nothing useful stood out, so he stepped back and closed the door. Above, he noticed a ladder on the roof of the shed.

Taking it down, he pulled and pushed on it. It seemed stout, but would it take his weight? He stood at the edge of the building, then slid the ladder across the gap and made sure it was secure on the other side.

Applying his weight to it, he slowly moved out over the drop-off. The wooden joints creaked loudly. He stopped and waited. When he didn't plumet to the street below, he moved across again. He climbed atop the opposite roof and wipped his brow with his sleeve. Ford hooked the ladder with his hand and pulled the ladder across.

Below, inside the inn, he heard the sound of a door shutting and locking. In the distance he heard the sound of dice hitting a table.

Over the side, he saw a balcony. Latching onto the ledge, he descended down and put his weight on the veranda. It creaked slightly, but held him.

Shutters were closed and he removed his dagger, put it between the two halves and lifted the latch. He looked inside.

The room contained a rope bed, rolled mattress, and a few other furnishings; clearly not occupied. He stepped onto the floor, and moved to the door where he put his ear to the wood and listened. No sound.

He opened the door and headed out onto the third floor walkway. The center of the building was open down to the bottom floor, where a courtyard was laid out with tables and patrons. A meal was being served, and a man in an iridescent blue robe was standing holding up his drink.

"A toast to a successful trip and profitable venture," he said.

A goblin dressed in a porter's uniform approached the man. "The item you asked for arrived today, sir. Where would you like us to put it?"

"In my room, of course."

"Yes, sir."

Ford watched the goblin go to the stairs, closely followed by two youths with a large crate. Up to the second floor they went, then they went to the next set of stairs.

Ford ducked back into the empty room and listened. Soon the footsteps approached and waned. He peeked out and saw the three enter a room at the corner of the walkway.

A moment passed and they came out, closed the door and walked around the opposite way to the far stairs and descended. Ford moved to the room.

The door was not locked and he slipped in. The crate was in the middle of the room; a subtle green glow emitting from the crevices between the boards.

A quick search of the room revealed little of importance. Turning, he looked at the crate again, removed his dagger and put it between the boards on the top, prying upward. The top slipped its nails, and he pulled it aside.

"An oculary?" he said quietly.

"Yes - that is correct Mister Efferguard."

Ford spun around and Raven Hill was standing in the doorway, two large human brutes behind him.

"I wondered when you might come a-calling. You must think me a true idiot that I would not safeguard my room with magic. No mind...you are here, and now I must do something about it."

Taking a step back, Ford felt the box at his heels.

"And, not just any oculary is it?" he asked.

"No, it is the oculary of Crill Pitnic the Stenchful. It's fabled to be linked to the jewels used in the eyes of the statues that overlook the crypt of King Vericornius. I assure you it does."

"King Vericornius?" Ford looked confused. "Vericornius is a myth."

"Where is it you think old Goldworm's sending you? That map you carry spells it out."

"Now what?" Ford asked.

"Kill you, don't kill you?" Raven Hill put his finger to his chin. "Quite a quandary."

Ford quickly palmed and threw his dagger. Raven Hill moved almost faster than Ford saw, stepping aside and letting the dagger strike the overly muscular man behind him.

The beefy fellow looked at the dagger stuck neatly into his bicep and gritted his teeth.

"I'll pull you apart," he said.

Leaping over the crate, Ford dashed to the window and kicked the shutters open. Stepping out onto the wooden balcony, he felt it give slightly under his weight.

A high-pitched screech erupted and a flash of bright light blinded him. He reached up for the roof ledge, found the lip, locked his fingers onto it, and pulled himself ungracefully up and onto the roof.

"Kill him!" shouted Raven Hill.

"To the roof stairs!" yelled a voice from below.

Ford's vision returned, as green spots littered his sight. He got to his feet and ran toward the ladder. Suddenly his legs were stuck together, and he fell heavily to the rooftop.

"You didn't think it was going to be that easy to escape, did you?"

Looking back, Ford saw Raven Hill standing on the rooftop. From under his robe he produced a slender twig like item and pointed it at Ford.

"Don't worry, this will be incredibly painful until the fire destroys your nerves," Raven Hill said.

The two ruffians arrived and the man with the wound grinned malevolently at Ford.

"I wish the boss would let me make the pain last for months," he said.

Something landed on the wounded man with a roar and spattered blood all around. The man screamed, as a struggle began.

The other man turned to help his mate, then burst into flame. Crying out in shock and horror, he fell to the ground and rolled about to put the fire out.

Raven Hill turned to the opposite rooftop and pointed his wand.

"To oblivion and darkness with you!" he shouted.

"You're an unbelievable hack," Sark shouted back.

A cone of blackness extended from Raven Hill's stick toward Sark, but a flash of amber light blazed into the sky and the cone vanished. Ford heard alarmed voices from below in both buildings.

"Now run, Ford," Sark called.

Ford's legs were free, and he got to his feet and dashed to the ladder and threw it across the opening. The fury creature passed him in a bound, landing on the other roof and skidding to a halt.

The creature growled loudly then easily jumped down to the ground from the top of the building. A chariot appeared below and the driver called up.

"Quickly, sir, the watch is coming!" shouted Sestius.

Sark waved his hand and a tube of shimmering light ran the height of the building.

"Follow!" he said.

Grabbing onto it, he slid down to the ground. Ford did the same. Both men leapt onto the chariot, and Sestius cracked the reins.

The cart shot down the cobblestone street at breakneck speed.

"Hold on, sir, this will be tricky," Sestius shouted.

The chariot rocked up on one wheel as he took a corner, then fell back to the street just as he made for the archway. Slipping back into the commerce district, the chariot headed towards the estates.

"Good thing I decided to visit the apothecary shop," Sark laughed. "It's right across from the Milk Maid Tavern. Han and I saw you leaving, and we noted you were not heading back to the villa."

"I felt a bit of snoopery was needed," Ford said. "He has an oculary, some way of seeing the vault where the lantern is buried."

Sark said, "And Vericornius was laid to rest in a vault where the gems of Crill Picnic stand watch; to be watched by the Stenchful."

Sark tugged on Sestius' doublet.

"Would you mind pulling over up here? We need to pick someone up."

"What?" Sestius said.

"It's okay," Ford reassured him.

Bringing the steed to a halt, Sestius waited as Han appeared from the side; his clothes in his hands. Jumping into the car, he quickly set about putting on his clothes.

"We can go now," Sark said.

Ford looked concerned. "The map, is it with you?"

"I left it with Hugh until I returned. Who better to guard it than a Justice Knight?"

"Good point," Ford said. "Take us back."

The chariot moved again along the road toward the villas.

They entered the villa, and Valicor was sitting in an overstuffed black leather chair waiting. He rose and looked at Ford.

"Thank the gods you're alright. We saw a flash in the sky earlier, and I thought some ill deeds were at hand. I was worried to death. And you, Master Sark and Mister Han, when your friend the Justice Knight told me you had ventured into the city, I was a fright. You could have been killed or worse."

Sark smiled. "Your worry is appreciated."

"Sestius did an excellent job at rounding us all up. But I don't see what all the concern is about. It was a rather boring evening," Ford added.

"An easy walk to the apothecary shop," Sark affirmed.

Han looked at both men, then at Valicor. "Not a worry to be had," he said.

"Now that I know you're safe, I'll bid you good night." Turning, Valicor waved and left down a marble hallway.

Ford looked at Sark and Han, then spoke in a low voice,

"If Raven Hill has an oculary, do you think it will aid him?"

"He doesn't have the map. But an inside view of the crypt may provide invaluable information, perhaps even life saving information," Sark said.

"Ancient crypts are often protected by powerful magic," Han suggested.

"The map you can drop off to me in the morning," Ford commented. "I'm too exhausted to get it now."

"Yes, in the morning then," Sark said, as he turned and went down the hall.

"It was an interesting evening," Han told Ford, then turned and left for his room.

Ford moved to his quarters, checked behind the door, then closed it behind him. Once satisfied he was alone, he disrobed and climbed into the bed.

Sleep overtook him, and he fell into a deep and dark slumber.

Ford woke realizing that the room was bathed in golden light. He moved to the side table and completed a whore's bath, dressed, and fitted his leather belt around his waist.

Checking his coin purse, he looped the leather thong around his belt, and tucked it into his pants and left the room. Harigan was outside in the hall, and he smiled at Ford.

"Come along, Harigan. We must make good time today."

"Good time?" Harigan laughed. "There is no good or bad time, just time." He followed.

Once outside, Ford saw that the horses were saddled and waiting. He made one check of his items and mounted his horse. The others quickly mounted and made ready to travel as well.

Ford led the party down the road to the villa's main gate. Sark rode up next to him.

"It wasn't easy."

"Wasn't easy?" Ford asked.

"I made a copy." Sark handed him the map

"What?" Ford had a look of concern.

"Including the imbued compass," Sark added.

"You could have destroyed it," Ford said while turning to look at Sark.

"The chances were good that I wouldn't. Nonetheless, as you can see," Sark produced another parchment from under his cloak, "I was successful. Here's the copy," he said.

"I'm not sure if I want to kill you for taking such a risk, or just hug you for doing so."

"No need for hugs, and killing would only sour the mood of our journey." Sark grinned.

"I guess I have much to learn about risk and reward," Ford said as he turned back.

Glancing up into the dark sky, he saw scattered clouds. "Looks like it might rain," he added.

They rode out the Canaric west gate and onto the north-west road heading to Marbury. Looking down, Ford noticed a small sack tied to a brass loop on the saddle.

He untied it and looked inside. It was sausage, bread and cheese. Smiling he knew it was Valicor who had made sure they had food for their travels.

The man was considerate if nothing else. He also knew that in a few hours the food would be well received in his stomach.

CHAPTER

13

Marbury: Gateway to Prin

By midday the clouds had rolled in from the plains. Heavy and black, they dumped their contents in a furious barrage of large, overripe droplets.

The cold and damp weather made for miserable riding. A signpost lay ahead etched with the word 'Marbury', and Ford instinctively looked in the direction of the arrow.

"Not far now," he said.

"These pasture lands are never ending," Sean mused.

"Be thankful for them." Ford smiled. "They provide most of the produce and livestock for the surrounding states."

"I'll be glad to get out of my armor and into a hot bath," Hugh complained.

"Raven Hill still poses a threat," Sark said. "We should be doubly on our guard."

"With such a party as we have, he would be foolish to try and rob us on the highway. Not to mention it's patrolled by glider-guards."

Sark raised an eyebrow. "I've heard of them. Are they effective?"

"Quite."

Ford grabbed up the sack of food and opened it.

Slowly the sun peeked out from the clouds and all things wet began to emit a vapor of white mist into the cold air. Traffic grew from a few farmers on foot or with a cart, to caravans and traders, pilgrims, and merchants.

The smell of lavender and dew berries filled Ford's nostrils as he traveled lazily along the road. Traffic was not intolerable yet, and the sun was infrequently obscured by the broken gray clouds.

Ford stood up on his stirrups and looked ahead past the traffic. "I can see the city walls," he said.

"I'm glad the dust is absent," Sean admitted.

"The Tribur River Bridge is not far away now," Sark added.

Stacks of hay piled up in the pastures looked like little tan-colored hills. Several farmers stood by the piles, their pitchforks methodically moving up and down as they tossed loose golden stalks up on the mounds.

"There's something wrong here," Han said.

"I agree," Harigan added, then lofted his horn up in the air and said the magic words. He guzzled down the contents. "There's an evil intent lurking close by." He wiped his mouth with the back of his hand.

"Yes, I have a strange feeling too," Sark added.

A wagon and twelve tough-looking fellows were approaching from the bridge. At first they seemed ordinary travelers from the city making their way to Canaric, but the lead man's cloak looked bulky, and the man behind him seemed nervous.

"What do you suppose their game is?" Sark asked.

Surveying the nearby area, Ford planned his next move.

"We need to split up. You take Han and Sean over towards those stacks of hay. I'll take Harigan and Hugh across the road. If they mean us harm, they'll be compelled to divide their forces." He turned to Sark. "If they make a move on us, let loose with something powerful."

"Will do," Sark said. "Han and Sean you're with me." He led the two men to the hay piles.

Ford took Harigan and Hugh, crossed the road, and moved toward the ruins of an old crumbling aqueduct.

The approaching wagon stopped. Looking at Sark, then at Ford, the man with the reins hesitated. Turning his gaze upon Ford, he pointed.

"Get 'em!"

Eight men jumped from the cart and ran toward Ford. A thunderous blast of energy washed over everyone. Men, horses, and even the wagon were tussled about.

Several of the rough-looking men were blown head-over-heels into the meadow by the river. Ford's horse reared up and cried out in fright.

The smell of burnt hair filled the air, and a loud buzzing sounded in Ford's head.

"Ride - make for the bridge," Ford shouted.

As he spurred his mount, he saw the disarray all around. The twelve ruffians were laid out like felled trees, the cart was blackened, and the two oxen pulling it started to run.

Sark was standing on the ground near the hay, his hair smoking and his clothes singed. Han and Sean were staring in disbelief, but immediately began riding as soon as they saw Ford. Glancing back, Ford saw Hugh and Harigan both moving toward him.

"Sark, come on," Ford called.

The magician looked up, then scrambled to his mount and dug in his heels. He rode fast and recklessly toward Ford and the bridge. The main gates of Marbury were not far beyond.

Ford looked back; all of his party was in tow. But, in the distance the glider-guards were descending on the roughs. After a moment Ford raised his hand, and they all slowed.

Sark came up alongside him.

"That was unexpected," he said.

"Amazing, powerful, I've never seen anything like it. I'm still seeing green dots in my eye," Ford said.

"I used the chaos force, just trying to draw their attention with a flash of light. I got more than I bargained for."

Han approached. "Ford, what happened back there?"

"Ask Sark."

Sark shrugged his shoulders.

"When dealing with chaos magic, you take your chances."

"You," called a voice from above.

Two glider-guards swooped down and landed in front of the column.

"Who's in charge here?" one of the things said.

Ford had never actually seen a glider-guard up close. It was made of wicker with a wingspan of fifteen feet. The wings themselves were made of some sort of sewn fabric.

It had two dark black crystals for eyes and no mouth or ears. A subtle green glow danced about it as the two things positioned themselves in a staggered formation.

"We do not allow threats to commerce or common travel along this road," it said.

"I know this. We were accosted by those ruffians," Ford stated.

"Maybe so, maybe not. You will take a test to prove if you speak the truth." It stopped and looked at Hugh.

A moment of silence passed. The thing emitted a strange ticking sound.

"You are a Justice Knight?" it asked.

"Of course," Hugh said.

"This has occurred in our jurisdiction. Do you claim authority?"

Hugh looked intrigued.

"Yes?" he said, and asked at the same time.

Another moment passed, followed by the ticking sound.

"Central Dispatch has ruled – you may take authority outside the city. You have the authority here. What is your ruling?"

"It is as Mister Efferguard said, we were accosted. The men behind us are sentenced to five years hard labor for attempted robbery," Hugh said.

The glider-guard hummed, and vibrated. "You have spoken. We will remember you and your party for five months. Do not break the law along this road. We will take care of the robbers back there. They will pay a heavy price for such behavior. Safe travels. This message brought to you by the Council of Prin!"

It turned and nodded to its counterpart. They expanded their wings and rose into the sky, then glided off on the breeze. Ford looked back; the roughs were chained now and being marched off to parts unknown.

"That was inconvenient," Sean said.

"Let's get on to Marbury," Ford replied.

"Look at that," Sean pointed at the massive statues on either side of the citiy's gates. "They must be at least thirty feet tall."

One moved its arm and a shadow fell over the travelers waiting to gain entrance.

"Did you see that? It moved," Sean excitedly said.

Sark chuckled. "An exciting sight to be sure. They're ancient, enchanted, and still working after all these years."

"Safeguards ensuring two things: enemies will be met with immediate destruction, and the city entrance fees will be collected without corruption," Ford said.

"How do they do that?" Han came closer.

"They're enchanted. The process is simple enough," Sark began. "As a wagon driver approaches, he places the fee of a silver coin in a slot along one of the golem's legs. The visitor is allowed to pass if the coin is indeed silver, and of the right weight. If not, he is denied entrance, and very few are foolish enough to argue with a massive stone golem armed with a twenty foot long everstrong sword blade."

"So, what is the history of this city?" Han asked Sark.

"Stranger than you know. Originally built by goblins before the Big Frost and right after Furl Haptilsh the Pig Slayer conquered the area, Marbury was built. The name means in goblin, butcher-river, and was built as a trade town.

"Haptilsh built the city using his newly enslaved inhabitants. They constructed the walls, and buildings, dug the trade canal and constructed the outposts. After a few years he realized that true power lay not in battle, but in commerce and established accords with the neighboring kingdoms.

"The rich fertile adjoining kingdoms needed to go through Haptilsh's domain to trade with each other." Sark steered around a large pile of animal dung. "It lasted for ten generations until the tribes of man began encroaching and settling in the valley.

"Descendants of Haptilsh had no interest in mingling with man-beasts, or others, so they declared the city purged and moved all the goblin inhabitants east over the Gorin Mountains."

"They left a whole city?" Sean asked.

"Haptilsh was dead two hundred years and they had no stomach for battle anymore. They took their wealth and left," Sark concluded.

Ford maneuvered between some people pulling a cart and a rabble of women carrying urns on their heads.

"It's rumored that they built a magnificent city somewhere in the east," Ford added.

"Yes, somewhere," Sark said. "But no one's found it yet."

"Master Efferguard – welcome back!" said one of the golems as Ford approached.

Ford looked up at the great gray stone behemoth. The creature looked down, its massive everstrong sword at rest with the tip on the ground. He waved up at the thing but said nothing.

"A coin if you please," it rumbled.

Putting a silver coin in the slot, he heard it fall into what sounded like a pile of other coins. He waved his men forward adding a coin per man as they passed.

Traveling through the gate, he saw a wide cobbled avenue. The buildings on either side were for the city guards, and the next set of buildings were the stables and administrative offices.

Inns and pubs were the next layer of buildings. More stables and animal pens followed. They progressed toward the inner ring and central commerce zones.

As he rode he looked up at the lavish homes situated on several small hills surrounding the canal. From the lofty hilltops, the barons and moguls could watch and keep track of their trade moving in and out of the city.

The town was modest when compared to Canaric, Prin or Moore, but still elegant as it was egalitarian. Products from all over the river valley flowed through it, so it was no wonder that the caravans plied their trade from Marbury to the hinterlands.

Many a traveler could book passage on barge or caravan to destinations far flung. Marbury's importance was clear.

Ford, halted in front of a dark brown wooden sign depicting a mythical hourt—half man and half deer with antlers—leaning back with a tankard in one hand exposing its ample member.

"The Inn of the Rutting Hourt. We'll stay here tonight."

"Looks respectable enough," Sean said.

Harigan dismounted and walked up to the door. "Aor sees all."

"What do you mean?" Hugh asked.

"This!"

Harigan moved his hands as if parting a curtain. The air shimmered, and a black shape lurched from the space and fled down the street.

"What in the name of the Netherworld was that thing?" Sean shouted.

"A shadow-specter," Sark said. "They are often bound to locations to spy for mages."

"Raven Hill?" Ford assumed.

"Yes, without a doubt. He really would like to have that map."

"He'll not have it unless he takes it from my dead hand," Ford declared.

Sark dismounted and patted Harigan on the back.

"Good work. You really do see much."

Harigan stood for a moment, lifted his horn and made ale. Consuming it, he then wiped his beard on his dirty shirt and opened the door.

"I approve now," he calmly said.

"Won't it report to Raven Hill?" Sean looked worried.

"No. Harigan pulled it from its envelope. It's no longer bound to Raven Hill's will. He will know that one of his agents has stopped working for him, but he will not know why."

"I'm going in to get us some rooms. Han and Sark take the horses over to the Danbrish Stable. Ask for Frin Glarworm, and tell him you represent me. He'll buy the horses and tack. Tell him nothing more, for he can be a talkative fellow."

"We'll do as you say," Han said.

Ford entered the inn. The proprietor cleared his throat from behind the desk. He held a metal stylus in one hand freshly dipped in ink.

"Master Efferguard I see," he began. "So wonderful to see you again. What sort of accommodations will you be pleased with?"

"I am traveling with some business acquaintances this time. We'll need enough rooms for six. Can you accommodate us?"

He looked over the register and flipped a few pages forward, then back again.

"For you, anything is possible. I have many vacant rooms. How long will you be staying with us?"

"One night," Ford said, as he pulled out his coin purse.

"Three sestires shall be fine," said the innkeeper.

Ford laid them on the desk.

"Would you like to see the rooms?"

"Yes, please." Ford turned to Harigan. "Get the saddle bags."

"'Tis thirsty work doing mortal business," Harigan said.

They stowed their gear in the rooms and ventured down to the dining room. The room was full, and patrons ate and conversed contentedly as the courses were served and drinks were poured.

A man with a crooked nose sat next to Ford at the long table and commenced discussing the economic issues of river trade. Ford examined the man carefully as he talked; a little taller than he, a gray beard, and a patch over one eye.

He wore a large gold hoop earring in his right ear, the display of a sailor who sailed to the port of Mirth and back. His face was craggy and his grin filled with yellow and missing teeth.

After the main course the servants brought more drinks. Jars of distilled spirits and pitchers of dark red beer were poured. Conversations began to gather even more momentum.

Patrons' voices rose to a din, and those who were in search of quieter surroundings excused themselves and made their way to the parlor. Ford, too, headed towards the soft chairs of the sitting room.

When he arrived he noted that the man who had sat next to him at dinner was sitting near the fireplace in a dark red velvet chair. The fellow turned and waved him over.

"Master Efferguard, so pleased that you decided to take in the parlor," he said. "Come sit by me!"

"In all our conversing I don't think that you introduced yourself," Ford said.

"Ah, you are right. Indeed, I have been remiss. I am known as Kaleb Greegal. I own several barges that transport local produce and livestock up and down the river from port to port.

Today I am here for business, and tomorrow I shall be away back to Port Vallance at the river mouth."

Ford sat across from the man. Holding his drink with both hands, he leaned close to the fire. He felt the warmth and watched as more people came in. Ford sat back into his chair.

"It seems to me," Kaleb began, "that you are a man of commerce. Am I right?"

"In a manner of speaking," Ford said.

"What would you think the value of this ring is?"

He handed Ford the ring then sat back.

Examining it, Ford saw it was made of multi-metals and set with a large yellow gem in the middle.

"Seems to be made of some metals I don't recognize. The gem is large, two carats maybe, and the cut is very accurate."

He held the ring up to the fire for a closer inspection.

"The color is excellent. There is an inscription along the band, but the language I am not familiar with." He gave it back to Kaleb.

The man took the ring and held it up to a lamp near him. He laughed and then handed it back to Ford.

"The truth is, master Efferguard, that this particular ring is a cheap bit of jewelry. I've had hundreds made for sale here in Marbury and Prin, and a dozen other river towns. It fetches a few coins from unsuspecting tourists wanting to impress their lovers, or wives. Keep it as a reminder that things are not always what they seem." He guffawed.

Ford took the ring and put it into his pouch, then sat there for a while consuming his drink. The topic of discussion drifted from politics to business, then to lost loves as the two men chatted.

Finally, Ford stood and put down his empty glass on a small round table.

"You'll have to forgive me sir, but I'm quite weary and will bid you a good evening."

"Pleasant dreams to you," Kaleb said.

Exiting the parlor, Ford walked to a set of stairs and ascended. On the second floor he walked to his room and entered.

Lighting the oil lamp on the small table, he dumped his coin purse out and took account of what money he had left. Twenty gold coins, seventeen silver coins, two dozen copper and the cheap ring that Kaleb had given him.

He put the coins back into the bag, but kept the ring out so he could copy down the inscription. From his pack he took a thin tube that Sark had given him and set it against the door.

Finally he placed the ring back on the table and crawled into bed. His eyes were heavy and he quickly found himself in a deep slumber.

It was a strange dream; a gigantic rabbit was hopping about with a saddle on its back. He reached up and took the reins and petted its twitching nose.

Finally, climbing on the rabbit, he began hopping about through a thick rain forest. Four-armed apes lurked in the trees, and gourd-shaped yellow fruits hung low in the green canopy.

As he turned a corner, a man stepped out wearing a blue robe and laughed.

"Ford, only a fool would take a gift from a stranger."

He woke with a start. The oil lamp was burning still, but the reservoir was low. He sat up and noticed that his room had been searched.

The contents of his pack lay on the floor, and his clothes had been turned inside out. Springing to his feet he searched for the map. It was gone.

Bolting from his room, a screech broke the silence. He quickly grabbed the tube from the floor and pressed the button to make it stop.

He walked out into the hall. There was no telling how long ago the thief had made away with the map. He calmed himself, went to Sark's room, and knocked.

"Come in," Sark said.

Ford opened the door. Sark was standing and had a dagger in his hand.

"What's going on?"

"Son of a drog," Ford cursed. "I was robbed."

"Robbed? Sark said. "When?"

"Sometime in the night."

"What did they take?" Sark rubbed his eyes.

"Guess." Ford's face was angry.

"Good thing we have a copy," Sark added.

"The theft is bad enough, but I'm at a loss as to how they did it!"

"How did the thief get in?" Sark asked.

"I don't know," Ford replied. "The door was locked, the window bolted, I even put that screech rod you gave me by the door. I really don't know. I'm typically a very light sleeper."

"Did you drink anything strange-tasting?"

"No, just the spirits from last night."

"Anything out of the ordinary?" Sark pressed.

"Nothing I can think of…" Ford stopped. "A ring."

"A ring? What ring?" Sark looked concerned.

Ford quickly left the room and returned. "This ring," he said, handing it to Sark.

"Blast my soul," Sark said taking it in his hand. "An entropy ring, and it's all used up."

Ford realized the stone was now red.

"That gem was yellow last night," he said.

"They're yellow when unused, but red when spent." Sark shook his head. "A priceless relic, actually. How did you come by it?"

"An old businessman…" Ford's voice trailed off. "Damn, what a fool was I!" he chided himself. "I should have known better. Of course, he completely lulled me into his confidence and then… wham - conned!" He slammed his fist into the palm of his hand.

"Raven Hill is in possession of the map now. He'll know exactly our approach," Sark said. "Except…"

"Except what?" Ford asked.

"Well, the night I made the copy, I built in a little insurance knowing that Raven Hill was after the map. I added a layer of ulrich blood over the path to the tomb. It can only be seen in the light of the full moons, or with a moon stone, which I have."

"Why didn't you tell me?"

"I figured I would reveal it when the time was right… Seems a good time now."

Ford's face changed from anger to mirthful. "So Raven Hill can't see the path that leads to the lantern?"

"No, and without knowing what I did, he'd be at a loss to discover the subterfuge!"

Chuckling, Ford sat down on the small stool by the writing desk. "You aren't seeing into the future are you?"

"No, but we have been somewhat reckless of late."

Both men sat in silence for a few moments then Ford got up.

"We're helped by this turn of events."

"I provided only the option to succeed," Sark said. "That's all."

"What time is it?" Ford narrowed his brow.

Rummaging through a sack on the nightstand Sark produced a small travel clock.

"Nearly four bells," he said.

"No point going back to bed. I'll see if the kitchen-keeper has tea yet."

"And see if they are going to serve lumb cakes too?" Sark patted his stomach. "I do love fluffy lumb cakes in the morning."

CHAPTER

14

Curse of Wet Boots

Stepping out into the street Ford smelled the fuelstone fires of the bread mills and the corner cafés. The sky was deep blue with just a few large white clouds floating in the distance.

A man with a wide push broom slung over his shoulder strolled by, stopped, swept some debris into a drain, and then moved down the street.

"This way leads to the barges," Ford said.

"I don't want to be a wet blanket, but you said barge?" Sean looked concerned.

"Yes," Ford replied.

"You do remember that I travel under a curse, right?"

"Yes," said Ford.

"That curse causes any ship that I sail upon to sink."

Ford smiled. "Sark and I have come up with a solution."

"If we can't cure you of the curse, we can trick it," Sark added.

"Trick it?"

"Of course. A witch's curse is rooted in logical spell construction," Sark said. "I've read of those who were able to live relatively normal lives with terrible curses upon their heads just by learning to manage it."

"So what does that mean?" Sean was curious.

"You see, if one knows the nature of the curse, he or she can set up events that allow the curse to execute and think it has accomplished its destructive function."

"Like?" Sean said.

Sark shrugged his shoulders.

"It's quite simple really. Your curse has to do with your being aboard a ship and that ship sinking." He smiled. "So, we'll simulate a ship at sea."

"How do we do that?"

"You'll see," Ford said. He led the way past many storehouses where sailors, river dregs, and drunks all commingled. Approaching a long river boat he spoke with a sailor for a few minutes.

The sailor disappeared into the pilothouse and came back with the captain. Ford gave the man a gold coin.

"Ah, yes, anything you need steward," the captain said.

"How long to the city?" Ford asked then took out his pipe and lit it.

"Six hours to the wharves of Prin. Load your party, and we'll get underway."

Ford summoned a few sailors and had them fetch a large tub, place it on the deck, and fill it with canal water. Getting a smaller tub he had Sean climb inside and he, Hugh and Harigan carried Sean onboard, placing him in the larger tub.

"We're hoping that the curse's logic path computes that you're the only one in the floating container. It will start to sink the bucket, and when sunk it will stop working and go no further," Ford said.

"You really believe this?" Sean looked quite skeptical.

"Yes," Ford responded. "Sark knows his business."

"It has a sixty percent chance of working," Sark added.

"We have a galley below. Would you like me to fetch you some food?" asked a young sailor who was watching with amusement.

"Oh, the captain says you have the run of the ship. He's the best pilot there is, so don't you worry. We'll be in Prin in no time."

The sailors cast off the lines and pushed the boat into the current with poles. The canal was wide, ninety feet from side to side, and constructed so the water flowed gently, and ever so slowly toward the river. This made it easy for boats to sail up and down with relative ease.

Ford sat on a barrel eating some bread and hot soup as the docks of Marbury grew smaller. The dirty gray-green waters of the canal passed as the pole-men pushed the boat along.

Ahead were miles of gently curving countryside with small farms and their docks that extended into the channel.

"How's the bucket doing?" Ford asked.

Sean looked skeptical. "Not a drop yet."

"Give it some time," Sark reassured. "Curses often are designed to give the victim a false sense of security."

"I hate witches," Sean grumbled, then folded his arms and looked dour.

Harigan drank down a horn of ale. "Life is a funny thing. When I was a prince, I had much wealth and love of my people. My wife and her lover tried to kill me, and in many ways succeeded. Now I serve Aor in search of divine relics. But the funny thing is that I feel richer, happier than I ever did as a prince."

He said the magic words, filled his horn and handed it to Sean. "Drink and you'll feel better."

"Thanks," Sean said. "Do you feel cursed?"

Harigan chuckled. "Not in the least. I have a blessing upon my soul, not a curse."

Sean drank the ale and handed the horn back.

"Now you see, some water's seeped into your bucket," Harigan said.

A small amount of water was beginning to pool in the bottom.

*   *   *

Moving in between the large crates tied to the deck, Ford made his way to the pilot house. The wheel of the craft was firmly in the hands of the captain as he adjusted their course ever so subtly.

"How much further?" Ford asked.

The captain adjusted the wheel again.

"Three hours, maybe four."

"Excellent."

Ford turned and walked back down the ramp to the deck. Old imperial mile-castles, mostly crumbling and collapsed with rotted wooden roofs, loomed like ancient sentinels of the old world.

A few times he saw a water serpent crest the surface, and then descend down; no doubt hunting fish to feed its insatiable appetite. Harigan seemed engrossed in something along the bank.

"What do you see?" Ford queried.

"Not what I see, but what I feel. Raven Hill is on the move to Prin along the road!"

"Will he be there ahead of us?" Ford stood by him and looked out.

"No, but it will be close."

Hugh walked over to a group of reserve pole-men. It was clear that they were much impressed by the blue armor he wore.

"Where did you get that fancy armor?" one man asked.

"It must have cost much!" another added.

"It was a gift by my late father. He was a Justice Knight," Hugh said.

"A Justice Knight?" a fellow with a scar along his cheek repeaated. "I 'ave a problem with me wife, can ye help me banish 'er to Snowbound?"

The other pole-men laughed. A whistle blasted from the wheelhouse, and the reserve took up positions at the edge of the barge. The whistle sounded again and the fresh sailors took over moving the boat.

Glancing over at the front of the craft, Ford saw Han near the bow practicing his fighting arts; he moved with a fluidity that was captivating, and at times, disturbing.

Ford walked toward the port side and saw Sark leaning against the railing, a stylus in one hand and a wax-pad in the other. He was furiously scrawling notes of an unknown nature.

"What are you working on?" Ford asked.

Looking up, Sark acknowledged him.

"Just compiling a list of artifacts that Raven Hill has used to thwart us."

"He's a dangerous fellow," Ford said.

"No doubt, but he is also arrogant, and that means he's over confident."

Ford put his elbows on the railing."What do you really know about this guy?"

Sark looked surprised.

"What do you mean?"

"I get the impression you know more than what you've spoken of." Ford's eyes betrayed his suspicion.

"Okay, you're right. I know much about Raven Hill, but it is bad form to discuss it with non-members."

"You mean non-members of the Magician's Guild?"

"Exactly," Sark said. "You see, if I reveal some information about Raven Hill, you could use it later after this assignment to harm him. I can't be a party to that. In fact, it is part of our oath that we behave very judiciously when discussing members." He looked up and watched the scenery pass.

"I understand the nature of secret societies quite well," Ford added.

"But, as I've said, Raven Hill is flawed."

"If you say so."

Ford looked out at the bank.

Sean waved and called Ford over. "Look," he said, "the tub has some water leaking in."

"Seems that Sark was right; it's a logical spell," Ford commented.

*　　*　　*

A boatman brought a cauldron of stew up on deck for Ford and his party. The sun was at the midpoint, and the river gulls were swirling overhead.

The dark green waters of the Serpent River were just ahead, and the captain maneuvered the boat out into the current. Immediately, Ford noticed the strong rich scent of the river mud that lined the sides of the waterway.

"Wow, look at those outcroppings of pink and red stone," Sean said.

"Further along the river you'll see the Prin villas, many made from that same pink stone," Ford told him.

As if on cue, the classical old homes began to appear. The villas were perched along the muddy banks, each with a dock extending into the river.

The homes spoke of the prominence of the region and the wealth that Prin represented.

"In my homeland, we have such monuments too," Han said. "But, I must admit these homes are magnificent."

"There, behold the walls of Prin," called one of the boatmen near the bow.

The sight was awesome. The great soft pink walls of Prin were a hundred feet high and breathtaking.

Ford admired the incredible architecture; the impressive carvings etched into the walls depicting the many battles and heroic events of the city.

One of the most impressive was the reliefs depicting the digging of the Grand Canal that led to all the farmlands east of the river and the bounty therein.

"Watch yer port side," the captain shouted at a fast approaching barge.

"You watch it," yelled back the other captain.

"If you strike my boat, I'll have you to task in Prin for it."

Slowing slightly, the other boat veered off. The other captain made a rude gesture, and his boat crew all dropped their pants and exposed their behinds to Ford and the crew.

"Suck on that!" the other captain yelled.

"Damn you, Willits! If you wanted to pose for a picture, you should have shaved first!"

Again the other boat captain held his fist in the air, but the pole men of Ford's barge had stepped up their poling and the boat moved swiftly away from the offenders.

As the day wore on, the boat traffic grew heavier. It took an hour to just get a berth at the busy marina.

Slowly the barge was maneuvered by pole into position. Boatmen took up the rough horse-hair rope.

Bow and stern lines were thrown to the dock workers who quickly hooked them to large yellow oxen. Inch by inch they were drawn into the wide berth by the scruffy long haired beasts.

The crew rushed about throwing sacks of grain to dockworkers on the wooden boardwalk. Several cranes on the dock were maneuvered into position. A stout ogre in an apron and rolled sleeves cranked one of the hoists, lifting cargo nets filled with goods from the barge to the dock.

The boat crew maneuvered wheeled carts and dollies across planks to the dock delivering the precious cargo to waiting buyers.

Stepping from the bucket, Sean put his wet boots on the deck.

"I'm amazed that worked," he said.

"Like I said, curses are logic based and can be circumvented sometimes," Sark said, as he walked up to him.

"Come on, let's find a suitable inn," Ford suggested.

"You, Ford," called the captain from his wheelhouse.

"What is it?"

"Be wary. Prin's warehouse district can be a bit rough if you're not used to it!"

"We'll take heed." Ford replied, then stepped onto the gangplank and onto the shore.

Mobs of warehouse workers dashed this way and that carrying crates of vegetables and carts filled with wares. The workers were burly men, elves, and even a few large muscular orcs. Most scowled as Ford passed.

Not far down a cobble street stinking of rotted produce, was an archway. Along the top was raised letters.

"Plitius twenty ten," Sark read.

"Who was that?" Sean asked.

Sark gave Sean an expression typical of a teacher to a student.

"You really don't know?"

Sean looked uncomfortable.

"No."

"During the Old Kingdom, Plitius was a noble who paid to have this district built. Originally, it was used to ferry supplies for the rich and powerful to and from the fortress. Now it serves those in the commerce trade."

"Oh," Sean said.

They made their way through the streets of Prin. Ford was careful to avoid the rabble. Once into the less grubby commerce district, he gave a sigh of relief and headed towards the inns and hotels.

Cabs and carts moved in mobs of thick traffic. Pedestrians flowed like sorghum; globbing up in corners, and slowly moving along sidewalks.

Ahead he saw the fluted columns and grand archway of the Prin Hotel. The amazing structure had only been built a few years earlier, but was renowned for its opulence and hospitality.

"Are we going to be staying there?" Hugh asked while pointing at the hotel.

Ford continued moving forward.

"No. We need a smaller inn, out of the way and closer to the fortress."

"Yes, one that will take wretched fellows such as we," Harigan added with a wink to Sean.

"What wretched fellows?" Sean challenged.

Harigan did not reply, but did tap the side of his nose with his index finger.

Not far from the large hotel was a set of smaller inns. These inns catered to the odd pilgrim, middleclass tourist, and small-commerce traveler. Ford stopped in front of a simple, yet well-kept establishment.

"This one looks good," he declaired.

Hugh examined the raised letters of the shingle.

"Siru Heftus," he read aloud.

"The resting place," Sark said with a smile. "It's a play on words; from the tome Higgle's Humers. You know, 'when a bawdy young lass in body and face, takes yer coin in windowless space, you find yourself wound in soft frilly lace, lay thee down in the resting place'."

"I never read Higgle," Hugh said. "But, it seems that I should."

Ford entered the establishment. An overly large fellow sat behind a desk near the far corner of the room. A small light crystal hung suspended in the air just above his head illuminating the few papers laid out before him.

Looking up, he narrowed his gaze and smiled. His jowls acquiesced to gravity as his mouth forced its way upward.

"How might I serve you?" he asked.

Ford removed his coin purse and set it on the desk.

"Rooms for six for two nights."

"Traveling through, are you?"

"Here on business," Ford said, as he set down two silver coins. "And no more questions."

The innkeeper looked at the coins and continued to smile.

"As you wish, young steward. Who shall I put down as my visitors?"

"Willverly Davenport and associates," Ford said.

The man jotted down the name and then handed out six key-stones for the rooms.

"The room number is on the stone. Don't lose them, for the magician's guild charges an arm and a leg to have someone come replace them."

Han, Harigan, Sean, Hugh and Sark each took a stone.

"The rooms are on the second floor," the innkeeper stated. "Dinner is served at three plus four bells, and drinks are served in the parlor afterward."

He stood up revealing his immense girth.

"Enjoy your stay with us here at Siru Heftus."

Ford stopped as he approached the stairs. He turned to his company and looked thoughtful.

"Stow your stuff in your room and return to the parlor. We have some work to do," he instructed.

CHAPTER

15

Skeletons in the Cellar

They met in the parlor and Ford laid out their tasks. He then told them he had to take a look at the Fortress and left the inn.

He waved his arm as a red painted cab passed him by. He hailed another, and another, and yet another, but all were filled with passengers and passed him without even a look from the driver.

Stepping out into the flow of traffic, he waved his hand at an oncoming coach.

"Cabbie," he shouted.

The black and brass open cab cut through the throng and stopped. The driver, a thin man with a round baled head, looked down.

"Where ye both be going?" he asked.

"Both?"

Ford looked behind him, and Harigan was standing there.

"What are you doing here? I thought you were going with Sean."

"Nope – with you," Harigan said.

"Okay." He turned back to the cabbie. "To someplace where I can get a nice view of the fortress," he ordered.

"Aye, my good steward," the fellow said. "I know of a place. It be not too far, made of wood and comes with tankards. One silver," he added.

"I want to see the fortress, not own it," Ford countered. "Maybe five coppers."

"Make it half silver and we have a bargain." The cabbie's squinted eyes widened a bit.

"We'll pay you ten copper, and you'll live to take another fare," Harigan said climbing up into the cab, his weight causing the carriage to tip to one side.

"What!" the cabbie said, insulted. "You threaten the likes of me? I'm Zelanian and don't take kind-wise to such clap." His face betrayed the insult. "To yer hobnails boys, and be off with you!"

He made ready to snap the reins of his horse when Harigan, towering over the cabbie, grabbed the man by his shirt collar and lifted him from his driver's seat—the reins dangling in his hands. The man's legs kicked wildly as Harigan examined him closely.

"Do not try me, Zelanian. For your sacrilege I should pull out your intestines and strangle you with them, Harigan said.

"No, sir, I'm ready to take this fare to their place of respite," the cabbie acquiesced; sweat pouring from his scalp.

"Good," Harigan said putting the man back down gently on his seat. "See to it, and then we'll decide if we'll pay for the ride at all."

"Pay after, that's fine, fine indeed fer the likes of me, good sirs."

The cabbie released the break and took them into traffic.

"I like a cabbie that can see reason," Ford said, sitting on the soft red-cushioned seat.

"Yer more than fair, me good sirs… more than fair," the cabbie said over his shoulder.

"This city air will do us both good, meist thinks," Harigan said, as he adjusted his position on the seat, folded his arms and closed his eyes.

"Are you sure you want to come with me? All I'm doing is going to take a look at the fortress."

Harigan opened his eyes and sat forward.

"You mortals are all alike, talk much, but see little."

He said the magic words, turned the horn on end and consumed the contents.

"As you wish," Ford replied.

The carriage traveled down several long blocks passing shops and warehouses. Pedestrians crossed the streets this way and that, sometimes leaping out of the way of a carriage or cab just in the nick of time.

Other carts and wagons bustled about adding to the madness of the street mob. After a few minutes the cab came to a halt and the Zelian glanced back.

"Here it is, the place we talkied about. Not jostled meist hope; good ride yes? Some copper for the effort?" he asked.

"Pay him," Harigan said, as he climbed down.

Ford fished out the coppers and handed some to the man.

"The place you wanted, it's behind the tavern," the cabbie said, as he snapped his reins and moved out into traffic again.

Turning, Ford walked around a wooden decking that surrounded the tavern. The boards creaked as he made his way to the back. Through the slats he saw the dirty waters of the river.

The awful stench hit him, and he covered his nose. He saw the fortress. The outer walls were large, made of dark black stone fitted together with white mortar; a contrast to the reddish pink stones of the surrounding area.

The foundation was clearly visible, connected to the white bedrock along the bank of the river. A thick layer of cement was built up rising from the rock to the base of the fortress.

As he looked on, what appeared to be a body floated by, and for a moment he thought he saw an arm, but then the mass was gone from sight.

"So that's the fortress?" Harigan asked while coming up behind him. Tipping up his horn, he quaffed down the contents.

"It is," Ford said. Turning to Harigan he asked, "How can you eat or drink near this stench?"

"It's not easy," Harigan said, then consumed more ale.

Ford shook his head. "You're an odd individual."

"To a mortal maybe. You know, you'll thank me later for coming."

Ford looked up at Harigan.

"What do you mean?"

Harigan boasted a tremendous laugh.

"You are a funny creature." He chuckled. "Now, for more important work!" He walked to the building's edge and vanished from sight.

Again, Ford turned to look at the fortress. He knew they would not visit it like so many tourists. Their destination was deep below those impressive battlements.

Judging by what he remembered of the map, when they reached their destination, they would be directly under the dungeon vaults that housed the royal jewels. That could spell execution if caught, or worse, torture and then more torture, before execution.

Reaching into his satchel, Ford removed a round piece of glass that looked like a magnifying crystal. He held it up to the base of the fort walls as a faint glowing dot appeared on the glass.

"It's there," he said quietly, but surprised. "I'll be damned."

Replacing the glass, he walked to the edge of the building and onto the main road. Harigan was nowhere to be seen.

"Harigan!" Ford called, but no reply was made. "Where did you get off to?" he said under his breath.

Strolling across the busy street he made his way past some warehouses and toward one of the larger streets of the city. He hoped he would be able to hail a cab and make it back to the inn with plenty of time to freshen up for the mid-day meal.

The walk was uneventful and he was careful to look back from time to time to see if Harigan was following. But in such a crowded environment it proved difficult to identify any one person or creature. In fact, if he was being followed, he was at a grave disadvantage.

After navigating a few blocks he arrived at a corner that was relatively clean and free of animal filth. Hailing a cab he watched the black enclosed vehicle push through the crowd and come to a complete stop curbside.

The cab was detailed in dark wood fitted with glass windows. He pulled open the door and climbed in, sitting with his back against the small circular rear window.

The opposite door opened and a man entered. Ford was about to declare that it was his cab when the man pulled out a magic hand-cannon and pointed it at him.

"Drive," the man shouted out the compartment door. "Now for you, Mister Efferguard. If I were you, I'd just keep my mouth shut while we take a little scenic drive."

Ford made no moves; he just sat and observed. The man was robust, wearing a sturdy leather vest over a dirty yellow shirt tied with a leather cord at the neck.

His black breaches were dirty and in places showed threadbare, and his shoes were of a common leather variety, worn and cracked. Ford turned his attention out the window. He watched the store fronts pass.

After a few minutes the cab turned down an alley and stopped. The door opened on his side, and a man motioned for him to step out.

Stepping down onto the cobblestone alley, he was pushed from behind toward an open door. Once inside, the smell of lamp oil was present and oak panels lined the dimly-lit hallway. At the opposite end was a faded red door and it was opened.

"Down there, through the door. There's someone who wants to talk to you," the man said.

Ford moved down the hallway keeping his eye on the door. After a half a dozen steps, he was at the portal and quickly took a peek inside.

It was an empty clerk's room, just a desk, a bookshelf, some chairs and several lamps.

"Go on, get in there, we ain't got all day," the man said, as he shoved Ford through the door.

He heard the door close behind him. The office was warm and comfortable and two glasses of liquor were sitting on the desk. He walked around the room examining books and documents lying about.

The sound of the door opening drew his attention, and he turned to see a man dressed in a vibrant green and black doublet, dark red breeches, polished black riding boots, and a dark blue cloak. It was Raven Hill.

Reaven Hill walked up to Ford and extended his hand in greeting.

"Sorry for the theatrics, Mister Efferguard, but it is important that I be sure that the nest of fools you have surrounded yourself with wouldn't interfere with our meeting."

He walked around the desk, picked up one of the glasses of liquor and handed it to Ford.

"Viro Tu Vac," he said. "I know that you will appreciate it."

Ford sniffed the glass, half checking for poison or drugs, and the other half curious as to what vintage it was. He raised his eyebrows.

"A Vac 6024. Quite a fine distilling."

"Excellent, Mister Efferguard! You know your liquor well. Please be seated. Our meeting at the inn in Canaric was not satisfactory, and perhaps I was hasty in wanting you dead. As you've guessed, I am the other one interested in the item you seek."

Ford said nothing. Swirling the amber liquid in the glass, he surreptitiously glanced at the ring on his left hand. The gem was still red, indicating no poison, and no drugs in his drink. He tasted the liquor and the corners of his mouth twisted up.

Raven Hill smiled knowingly and continued.

"You see, we've been at odds you and I. Competing interests if you will. We have no need for pretense here, Mister Efferguard. I know the item and its power well. Those you represent want it to block my rightful claim as lord over the western provinces. After all, who are they to deny me? I deserve it."

He moved the chair back and crossed his legs. Lifting the glass to his lips, he drank it with an expression of ecstasy.

"As you so astutely pointed out, it's a Vac 6024. I believe when you possess something it should be the best, and that is why I want you to come to work for me."

Ford was taken back for a moment. He regarded Raven Hill with a contemplative expression and then took a sip from his glass.

"Work for you?" he asked, as if he had not heard the man correctly.

"Yes." Raven Hill smirked. "I have your map. It is only a matter of time before I have that lantern in my possession. I've spoken to a few people, and they seem to think highly of your talents."

"Perhaps you would like to change teams? Be on the winning side. Those bureaucratic fools care nothing for you."

He stood up and set his glass on the desk.

"Mister Efferguard, let me be frank. I don't want to kill you. You are of some value to me alive, and, I might add that my associate Willowfern agrees. Oh yes, she did make a good case for your life. Strange though, I gathered that at one point she wanted to see you stretched over hot coals; at least when I first spoke to her."

He raised an eyebrow. "No matter though, she convinced me that you would make an excellent addition to our little group. Rich, powerful, and immortal a team, if I might be so bold to say?"

"Immortal?" Ford said surprised. "That's an odd inturpetation."

"Come now, Mister Efferguard, surely you know that the power of the lantern can lay waste to regions, making he who holds it immortal?" He picked up his drink, sat down again, and took a sip.

"Gali trump tit ex emor, sarum, ex emor, loch ve luminous, sach," Ford quoted from the ancient text of *The Legend of the Lantern*.

"Excellent, Mister Efferguard!" Raven Hill grinned. "I see that Willowfern did not exaggerate your qualifications. So you know the legend and the true words of the lamp?"

Ford took a dramatic pause as he sipped his drink.

"The words could be translated into invincible, immortal, or unstoppable," Ford said. "But, it could just as easily mean something else. It was written in polysyllabic characters, of the

Old Kingdom, of which there were peculiar added script accent marks to the right of each. Those marks have been in question for hundreds of years."

"Nonsense," Raven Hill scolded. "It means exactly what you said— invincible, immortal, and unstoppable. Now, are you willing to leave the employ of those who would see you little more than a clerk, and work for someone who will truly appreciate and reward your talents?"

"What are your terms?"

"Other than your life and the lives of your companions, whom I'm not sure you actually care about; how could you care for them?" He chuckled menacingly.

"They're just idiots with little value, except for that damn Sark. He's a thorn like no other. Nonetheless, you are a true man of action, and that complements a man of vision such as myself."

He smiled while holding his glass with both hands and peering into it as if it were a crystal ball.

"My terms are these: slaves, servants, women, land, riches, power unlike any chancellor has ever had. And the option to retire, live out the rest of your days fed, pampered, and satisfied!"

Ford regarded the man for a moment, all the while thinking that Raven Hill was overselling it. The truth probably was that once he had retrieved the lantern, Raven Hill would have him killed.

"Those are very good terms. What is it you wish me to do for you?" Ford asked.

"Direct, I like that," Raven Hill said with a laugh. "Do the same work you are doing for those idiots in Moore, and of course, retrieve the lantern. Oh yes, if you were to kill Sark, I would not be bitter."

Ford smiled. "Very generous terms, indeed."

"So we have an agreement?" Raven Hill came to his feet.

"We—"

Ford heard shouts from the hallway. The door smashed inward splintering into a hundred pieces. Ford jumped up. In the doorway was Harigan holding a bloody cudgel, and in the hallway behind him were bodies.

"Who here needs to be taught the meaning of the word vengeance?" Harigan asked, his hand clinched on his cudgel and his shirt covered in bits of bloody matter. "I have a recipe for thee." He grinned malevolently.

Ford turned to see Raven Hill slip out through a secret passage, a common conveyance for most business owners. Surely he would have locked the passage and set a trap behind him.

Striding into the room, Harigan stood towering over Ford.

"I see that you're still alive," he stated.

"Let's get out of here," Ford said, as he quickly moved into the hallway.

Looking out into the alley, he noticed that even the carriage was damaged from Harigan's assault.

"Quickly," he called to Harigan, as they moved out into the main street and down several blocks.

"Was he going to torture you?" Harigan asked.

"No. He wanted to offer me a job," Ford stated over his shoulder.

"A job?" Harigan laughed loudly. "A funny way to make an elf a job offer."

"It actually happens more than you would know," Ford said. "But it was no offer. There was no choice in it. I'm sure he intended to kill me and the rest of you as soon as he had the lantern in his possession. He does not strike me as a man who would share power."

"You are an astute elf," Harigan said, as they slowed to a walk.

"How did you know where to find me?"

"I move in mysterious ways," he said with a wild look in his eyes. "It also helped that I saw the carriage pass by with you and a potential convert riding within. I said to myself, '*Harigan ole boy, that human in there with Ford is in need of some salvation*', and so I followed. I applied the appropriate salvation." He held aloft the bloody weapon.

"We need to get back to the inn." Ford said, as he flagged down a cab.

"I sense Raven Hill is on his way to the fortress even now," Harigan added.

"Then we haven't a moment to lose!"

CHAPTER

16

Vue Caverns

The street led to a bridge a half mile from Prin.

"Halt," called a large and rugged-looking bridge-troll.

He eyed Ford and his party only for a moment, then held out his hand. "Five copper per horse!"

Ford removed his coin pouch and paid the appropriate amount. The troll examined the coins and put the pieces of copper into the box that he carried around his neck. Pulling on a chain, he lifted a wrought iron gate allowing the party to travel to the west bank of the river.

"May your journey be pleasant," the troll said as they passed.

The road beyond the bridge was well traveled, and as they came over a rolling hill the surface changed slightly. No longer were the paving stones even or often.

Ford steered his horse around large potholes and ruts. It seemed that the old highway had fallen victim to stone thieves. A half mile from the bridge Ford came to a crossroads.

"That way," he said, pointing along the worse of the two roads.

A man and a boy came toward them. The elder carried a cage of chickens, and the younger pulled a two-wheeled cart topped with greens.

"Are you off to Bealtown? If you are you're on the wrong road," the man said.

"No," Ford replied. "But perhaps you could tell me how far to the Vue Caverns?"

"Four miles hence." He pointed back the way he had come. "They're closed to visitors this time of year. The city hired a complement of ogres to make camp there to keep the curious away, until the season opens again."

Sark looked at Ford, then down at the man.

"Ogres? Are they gypsy ogres, or guard ogres?"

"Gypsies," the boy said.

"Come along, son." The man began walking again. "If you're thinking of going to the caverns, you might want to think again," he said over his shoulder.

"Ogres could mean problems." Sark's brow furrowed.

"Gypsy ogres are notorious at drinking and fighting amongst themselves." Ford looked back. "Don't worry, fellas... they're not war hardened battle ogres at least," he said. "Let's move on."

He slowly moved down the road.

They rode for an hour. Sark, Sean, Hugh and Han made small talk. Harigan rode beside Ford, ever watchful for trouble.

In the immediate distance, Ford saw the rolling hills with tall yellow grass waving in the gentle breeze. Every now and then he saw a small animal leap above the grass then vanish again.

The road turned towards a hill that seemed higher than the others, and they began a slow and steady climb to the top. At the top Ford halted.

"Do you see that jagged black outcropping about a mile away?"

Harigan studied it. "Those peaks are volcanic rock," he said.

"Yes, and in some places volcanic glass. The brochure tells of whole portions of the mountain being dark glass," Ford explained.

"The road winds down this way." Han pointed at the zigzagging road. "And there's smoke by those black rocks."

They traveled for a while, then a musky scent filled the air. Sean came alongside them. "Must be the ogre's camp," he said with a sigh.

"Don't worry, Sean, just stay behind me if there is any roughhousing," Hugh reassured him.

"There should be no trouble. Those ogres will never know that we were ever here," Ford added.

"They have a keen sense of hearing and smell," Sark said. "It's going to be a pretty trick to slip past them."

Ford glanced back. "We can have Han—"

A white flash of light domed over the black rocks. The sound of yelling and then screaming filled the air. A few curses in Ogrene floated to Ford's ear as a concussion wave rolled away from the spot.

"What in the name of the dark lords happened?" Sean said suprised.

"Raven Hill," Ford said. "Quickly!"

He spurred his horse and dashed down the hill at breakneck speed.

Rounding a curve, he rode toward the caverns. Trees and bushes grew thickly and the road was bordered by thick brambles and dark tree trunks. A clearing came into view, and he slowed and stopped.

Carts and wagons were overturned, and the bodies of a dozen ogres lay sprawled out or slumped over.

"Sark, are they dead?" Ford called.

Sark climbed from his horse and moved to one of the ogres. Putting his ear to the creature's chest he listened.

"Both of his hearts are still beating." He looked at the other ogres. "They're just stunned and unconscious."

He moved back to his horse and removed his saddlebags.

"We'll need to move fast I think!"

"Grab all you can carry and let the horses go. We'll not be returning this way." Ford grabbed his saddle bags, pack, rope, and lantern.

He watched as the horses galloped back up the road. Turning, he moved up the hillside and stopped at the cavern entrance. Sark quickly ignited several lanterns and they proceeded into a dank and musty cave.

CHAPTER

17

Under the Fortress

Ford held the lantern low, shielded his eyes and peered into the darkness. No sign of light appeared. A faint hint of dust hung suspended in the air leading down into the cave.

Ford's free hand moved to his dagger. He knew what dwelt within caves, and how they prayed on civilized creatures. Beasts such as harpies, grogs, slimes, and many other monstrous creatures lurked under the ground.

"They must be moving fast," Sark said right behind him.

"Too fast to lay traps?" Ford asked.

Sark closed his eyes and clapped his hands together and sat on the ground. A shimmering humanoid shape appeared and moved down the tunnel.

A few moments later it came back.

Sark got to his feet, and dusted off his trousers.

"No traps up to a dozen yards ahead," Sark said, then staggered and leaned against the cave wall. "Doing that sure takes the energy out of me."

Unrolling the map, Ford was amazed at the brilliance of the glowing marks. He looked up to see two gaping openings.

"Sark, come here and look. These markings seem to be directing us through the larger passage."

"I agree."

Ford ran his finger along the glowing line on the map.

"It looks like there's another set of passages ahead. The map says for us to take the middle one."

"We're losing precious time," Sark said.

"Okay, follow me." Ford led the way.

Dust was still in the air ahead of them, and fresh footprints were embedded in the dirt. He moved into a jagged chamber with stalagmites, stalactites and large yellow crystals that protruded from the walls and ceiling.

The sound of something scurrying in the darkness caused Ford to pause.He held up the lantern and glowing eyes retreated into the darkness.

"Gremlins," Sark said. "They're just curious of what we're doing. Be careful they don't steal something from you as we move through here."

Ford moved on. In the distance he heard running water, and once in a while, he saw the reflection of his lantern light in the black pools of standing water.

He made his way through minor cave-ins and rubble that littered the floor, all the while noting the dust and footprints. After some time, Ford saw that the rough and jagged cavern path was changing.

The walls here were smooth light red limestone blocks, fitted together with expert precision. Along the walls were runic symbols.

"Similar to Yule, but more like Hargrove pictographs. Not magic, unless you say the words," Sark said.

"What does that mean?" Hugh asked, the glow of his blue armor fostering a soft illumination.

"It means, don't speak the words," Sark reiterated. "Best we move along and not dawdle."

Ford held up the light as he came to a place where the floor was uneven. A strange musty smell lingered in the air.

"Don't move," Sark said putting his hand on Ford's arm. "The map denotes danger here!"

Looking down at the map, Ford saw a box with a skull in it. He knelt down, noticing some faint footprints in the dirt that suddenly ended.

"Tripped recently," he said quietly.

Sark knelt down near the last footprint. He examined the walls of the tunnel and then the edge where the print disappeared.

From his side pouch he produced a small glass vial and shook up the contents; it glowed a ghostly green. He held the vial over the area where the print ended and opened the top.

The vapor spilled out and fell to the floor. It hovered over the dust for a moment but then settled into cracks that became visible. Outlined on the floor was a pattern, two slabs, measuring ten feet long and four feet wide.

"It's hollow below, but I don't know how deep. The dimensions are clear, but I can't tell you how the trap is sprung or reset. There seems to be no trap immediately beyond," Sark said, as he continued to examine the area.

"But I can tell you that the poor bloke who triggered it didn't live to tell about it. Look at the ceiling and walls. That's not paint."

Ford held up the lantern and was surprised to see the blood spatter on the walls and ceiling.

"The end was not good," Sark added after a long pause.

"How do we get across?" Ford asked.

"Jump?" Hugh peered over Sark's shoulder.

"Too far," Sark said.

"Could you levitate us across?" Sean looked at Sark.

"Levitation takes too much time."

"Is there nothing that you can do?" Sean furthered.

"It would take hours to muster a proper spell to get us all across this gap, and I dare not try any chaos magic in this confined space. We could end up submerged in sewage, or killed and buried by rubble in a sonic blast. Chaos magic is a little unpredictable, as you know."

Hugh moved back down the tunnel, and then returned.

"No lumber, so we can't lay planks across."

"Han," Ford said, "can you leap across?"

"I can in my true form."

Han stripped off his clothes and changed shape. He vaulted over the trap and landed without kicking up any dust. He shifted back.

"Throw me my clothes."

Harigan wrapped Han's clothes around his cudgel and tossed it across.

"Cover yer shame," he said. "Oh, and you forgot to take the end of the rope across."

Ford shook his head. "We'll just toss it across." He unraveled the rope.

"So, what do I tie the rope to?" Han asked.

"Have you not seen? All the while we've been down in this underworld, there have been iron sconces placed at regular intervals along the walls," Harigan said.

"By the gods, I didn't," said Ford.

Sark chuckled softly and scratched his head.

"We were so concerned about being killed that we overlooked the obvious."

Ford coiled the rope and tossed it across the span.

"Secure the rope to one of the sconces," Ford said. "How in the blazes did Raven Hill get across so fast though?"

"He lost one man at least," Sark reminded them. "Perhaps, somehow he was prepared with a ladder or levitation boots… or something else."

Han caught the rope and pulled several yards across. Moving to the wall, he felt around until he found one of the ancient iron sconces.

Pulling on it he made sure it was secure and looped the end of the rope around it making a knot. He then pulled on the rope applying as much force as he could; the rope did not budge.

"Good on this end."

"He's clever, that Raven Hill," Sark said. "If only we knew how he got across."

"Are you coming across or should I jump back?" Han asked.

"Aye," came the voice of Ford. "We'll be across in a second."

Slowly the rope's slack was pulled tight across the trap.

"Come across when you're ready," Han said.

"I'm coming across now," Ford called out as he handed the lantern to Sark.

He grabbed the rope and swung his feet up and locked them around the strand. Slowly, he pulled himself along as he dangled only a few feet from the top of the trap.

As he got to the other side a screeching sound filled the air and the sconce on the opposite wall ripped from its moorings.

Ford landed with a thud on the edge of the trap. Han quickly grabbed him and pulled him from danger.

The rope landed on the slabs causing them to move; one spinning counter clockwise, and the other spinning clockwise. The rope was dragged below into gears and spinning blades.

"By the gods! That scared the evil out of me," Ford said.

Sark took the lantern and angled the lens down into the pit. At the bottom he saw metal, some rusted and others shiny, all pilled like trash.

At the top of the heap was a metal helmet, crafted in the old style— rounded top, with cheek protectors and a nose guard. Clearly the helmet had been severed from the rest of the armor and was neatly sitting with the head still inside looking up.

"Poor fellow," Sark said as he peered across at Ford.

Sean looked into the pit. "Now what?"

"Seems the device is stuck, so I guess you'll have to crawl across the slabs," Ford said.

Sark handed the lantern to Hugh, grabbed onto the edge of the nearest slab and pulled with all his might; it was stuck fast at a steep angle. He pulled it again to see if it would move; it did not.

Leaning out, he dangled his legs into the pit and quickly moved hand-over-hand across. Once on the other side, Ford helped him onto stable ground.

"Out of my way!" commanded Harigan, as he moved to the pit. He clamped his hands onto the slab and did the same as Sark.

The slab moved slightly under the priest's excessive strengh. As he got to the middle, the slab moved even more causing the gears to wind the rope tightly into the mechanism.

Harigan looked down and saw the blades cutting into the rope. He scowled. Sweat began to dribble down his face. He got to the other edge, got his legs onto the tunnel path and pushed himself onto solid ground.

"Easy as eating dangle-root pie," he exclaimed while wiping the sweat from his face.

"Toss me the lantern, "Ford called to Hugh.

Hugh cradled the lantern in his hands, bent at the knees, and lofted it across the pit. Ford caught it and put it down next to him.

"Come on across," he said to Hugh.

Even before Hugh touched the trap, the slab moved again. The Justice Knight readied himself.

Leaning out over the pit he gripped the edge of the slab, and let his legs dangle down into the hole. The slab began to rotate, but stopped. Hugh was now at a thirty degree angle.

A look of panic fell across his face.

"There's nothing honorable about falling into a trap made to kill thieves," he said as he continued to move, his hands inching their way to safety.

Getting his feet onto the ledge, Hugh thrust himself off the slab and threw his arms out for balance. The slab gave way and rotated.

Han grabed and held him tightly. "Hold on," he said as he pulled Hugh away from the pit.

Hugh steadied himself. "Thank you, I thought I was done for."

"What about me?" Sean said on the other side.

"Not sure," Ford replied.

Sean vanished into the darkness.

"Do you think he's leaving?" Hugh asked.

Sean reappeared, his feet pounding the dusty floor. He came to the edge of the trap and leapt.

"He's not going to make it!" Han yelled.

"Nonsense," Harigan said, as Sean was engulfed in a golden bubble of light.

Instead of landing on the slabs, he floated over the trap and gently down between Harigan and Ford.

"Aor watches out for drunks, fools and children," Harigan said.

Sean exhaled and fell to his knees. He looked up, his face pale.

"I thought I was a dead elf."

Hugh pulled off his helmet. His face was soaked with sweat. Pulling a cloth from a leather pouch at his side he dabbed his brow and neck.

"Harigan, why didn't you use that magic bubble for me?"

"Aor also likes his entertainment," said Harigan with a smile.

Sark motioned toward the darkness.

"We need to watch the map closely," he suggested.

"The map doesn't indicate any other traps, but there's a fork ahead," Ford said, as he pointed into the darkness.

The smell of the tunnel was changing and there was more dampness in the air along with a rich odor of river mud. From time to time they trod through puddles of water, and stepped over roots that crisscrossed the tunnel.

Heavy cobwebs contained small wrapped silken bundles that hung from them. Mouse and rat bones stuck out of some, and littered the floor.

Ford stopped. "Ahead, marked on the map is an obstruction."

"What sort of obstruction?" Sark asked.

"The map doesn't say."

"Look at this," Han said pointing at footprints in the muddy floor. "Fresh."

Cautiously Ford moved along the tunnel into a chamber the size of a small parlor. Two openings were visible as he held the map in front of him.

"The floor is clean," Sean stated.

Ford angled his lantern down and indeed there was no layer of dirt.

"That blackheart cleaned off his footprints," Ford said.

"So, we know he knows we're behind him," Sark said as he stood next to Ford. "Let's see what this obstruction is on the map."

"You're not worried?" Sean asked, looking concerned.

Sark chuckled. "He's moving fast, and his attention is focused on the tomb. He'll not be focused on ambush."

"The map shows the tomb down the left tunnel." Ford moved that way.

"He knows what's waiting inside that tomb," Sark said.

"I hope whatever it is, is not made of chaos magic," Ford added.

"Maybe..." Sark trailed off. "At a bare minimum, I hope it doesn't kill us."

They continued down the tunnel a hundred yards, and then Ford stopped. "Look at this." He pointed at a figure carved into the stonework of the wall.

Sark took the lantern and angled it at the carving,

"There's more lining the tunnel," he said.

"I have a creepy feeling about these carvings," Sean said.

Han came close and pointed down the tunnel.

"There's a body down there."

Ford took back the lantern and held it out as far as he could. At the limit of the light he saw a pair of boots.

"What do you think killed him?" Hugh asked.

"Wait, I know what…" Sark pulled out a small booklet and flipped to a page. "Yes, here it is. It's a cuvette-lay, or rather a watcher-lurker in the stonework. They were one of the ancient world's tomb guards."

He reached into his pouch and produced a slim red candle. "I need to build a vortex or one of these carvings will kill us."

"How long?" Ford asked, annoyed.

"Five minutes."

He lit the candle and began grinding some herbs between his hands. A dark mist rose from around Sark and crept along the walls. A bitter taste assailed the party.

"What in the name of Gor the Great is that?" Sean asked while spitting out the acrid taste.

"A byproduct of the spell. It sometimes leaves a nasty acrid taste in everyone's mouth."

The mist formed into a tube of darkness.

Sark took a few steps.

"Stay near me and within the darkness," he said.

They all moved down the hallway and past the body. The carvings ended and Sark disbanded the black hazy tunnel.

A white glow, faint and pulsating like a heartbeat, appeared in the distance. As they moved closer, Ford saw the tunnel end and an archway leading to the ruins of the fortress under-halls.

A wrought iron gate was bent and twisted as if rended by some powerful force. A body lay to one side, a man recently deceased.

"The walls glow here," Hugh said.

"Much like your armor," Sark suggested. "They're imbued with magic."

"Looks as if Raven's been through here," Ford added. "Any magic surprises ahead?"

Sark stepped up and without touching the remains of the gate, examined it and the rocks.

"It's a composite metal, neither of which is iron. It's a Folio-elctro-piazo-portus," he said.

"And what in the name of holy Aor is that?" Harigan looked curious.

"It's a surprise gate. If touched it'll deliver a lightning bolt of electricity into the thief – or whoever is trying to thwart it."

He pointed to the body lying face down.

"These stones around the bars are casement warning stones… they are very old. When did you say the map was made?"

"The map is sixty years old as far as we can tell," Ford replied.

"What are casement warning stones?" Sean asked.

"They give off a harmonic vibration sending a signal to a guard house or command center," Sark said. "Most likely they're vibrating in some dark and dusty broom closet or larder now."

Ford secured the lens cap on the lantern.

"Let's hope so," he said.

Beyond the gate light stones embedded in the walls illuminated their way. Just past the wrecked gate was a row of dirty benches covered in cobwebs. A stairwell of gray, unkempt stone lead upward. Ford moved to the landing and listened, then went up.

At the top of the stairs there was an arched entrance into a dark room. Removing the lens cap from the lantern, he shined the light into the hallway. A thick growth of green fungus clung to several wet area near the roof.

The stench of fungus and mold was heavy. Holding up the lantern he could just barely make out the other side where the tunnel continued.

"Slime," Sean shouted, as a glob of glowing green gunk emerged and moved slowly toward Ford.

"Damn slime," Ford said.

He kicked at it; his boot sunk into it leaving a smoking slippery goop on his shoe. He dunked his boot into a puddle of water trying to wash off the acidic slime.

Sark reached into his side pouch and pulled out a vial of white powder. He opened the bottle and tossed the dust on the closest slime. The creature quickly shriveled and turned black. Another slime moved towards Han and Hugh.

Hugh crossed the water, removed his sword, and cleaved the slime in twain. The creature quivered, then both halves started moving towards them.

"Hugh, you idiot," chided Harigan, "those slippery slimies can't be chopped like common kindling."

Calmly Sark walked to the slimes, tossed some powder on the two halves, and watched them shrivel up and turn black as a stone. Sean poked at them with his dagger.

"Disgusting," he said.

Putting the bottle back in his pouch, Sark looked at Ford.

"We'd better move before other nasty things come to investigate."

"Let's move," Ford said, and again headed down the tunnel. "By the way, what was that stuff you used?"

"Basilisk dung," Sark said, "ground into powder. A sure remedy for slimes."

The tunnel narrowed for a short distance and then came to a chambered intersection.

"Now which way?" Han asked.

Looking at the map and down the right shaft, Ford pointed.

"This way."

"What's that stuff?" Sean pointed at the ground.

Sark knelt down, then grabbed Ford's leg."Don't move." He examined what looked like reflective glass particles.

"I'm glad you said something. It's what we in the magic business call pixie dust. Good thing you saw that or one of us would be missing a leg," Sark warned.

"Is it really pixie dust?" Sean asked.

"No," Sark replied, as he searched through his bag. "It's a chemical compound that will explode when disturbed."

Producing a small glass orb, he cracked it like an egg and let a blue smoke seep out falling over the sand-like crystals.

"There, the gas has stabilized the compound. We can cross." He tossed the expended orb to the side and stood up.

"Raven Hill is one sneaky bastard," he added.

Ford took a step on to the shiny crystals and they crunched under his weight.

"That's reassuring," he said.

"Let's hope he's out of tricks for the moment," Sark said.

They continued down the tunnel. The stench of river mud was again in the air. The tunnel changed again to an older, less-refined cut stone.

At last they came to a black wooden door, cracked by time, damaged by moisture, and eaten by insects in places. Still it was fastened together with rusted wrought iron straps. An iron ring hung down on the left side, red with rust.

Ford reached out and pulled gently on it. The door moved and creaked loudly.

"It doesn't matter," he said. "They know we're here already."

Holding the lantern up, he saw a square chamber a hundred feet wide and fifty feet long. A door was placed in the middle of each wall. He deftly moved to the door opposite.

"The map says through there," he said, shining the lantern light on the long neglected wooden door.

Sark reached out and gently pulled the metal ring. It broke from the rotted wood and he held it up for Ford to see.

"I doubt they went this way," he said.

A sound came to their ears; metal clanking, pottery breaking, and an anguished cry.

"Then what way did they go?" Ford looked uneasy.

"Perhaps my subterfuge worked and they abandoned using the map, thus the sounds of battle and cries of doom," Sark suggested. "They're lost and wandering."

Ford pulled the door all the way open. Beyond was another hallway. At the end of the hall was another door covered in a faded peeling green paint.

Past the green door was a wide hall supported by tall white columns. On the floor were fragments of pottery covered in thick brown dust, and fragmented remnants of wooden chairs and tables.

Plates were smashed on the floor along with broken tankards. Long brass candelabras had fallen to the ground and were lying at odd angles.

Sark bent down and examined the dust on the floor.

"Strange," he said.

"What?" Ford held the lantern low.

Sark looked up then pointed at the falling dust in the soft light. Ford tilted the lantern up.

The reflective eyes of a harpy startled him. The creature was high up resting on the roof timbers and was observing them.

Ford quickly went to the other end of the room.

"I don't like such creatures," he said and moved through an archway.

Sark and the party followed into what appeared to be an ancient kitchen. Pots and pans, spits and kitchen implements lay all about.

Sark scanned the room and found two doors, one on the right and one on the left.

"What does the map say?"

Ford put down the lantern and held the map out. "Through that door."

"The open one with light coming from the crack?" Sean mused.

"Yes," Ford replied.

Ford opened the door and stepped in. At the end of the hall a door made of bronze glowed with golden light. An inscription was carved in the stone along the frame above the door.

"Le'mon, bourges, Sulemond!" Sark said.

"What does it mean?" Sean's face betrayed his curiosity.

"Protect he who rests inside," Sark said.

"The light of Aor fades beyond this doorway," Harigan explained. "I can see nothing of the other side."

Han stepped forward.

"What does the map say?"

"There is no other information, the map is at its end," Ford stated.

Reaching into the leather pouch at his belt he pulled out a golden amulet studded with blue and green jewels.

"But there is a place for this to fit," he told them, as he inserted the amulet and said some words under his breath.

The brass door shook causing dust and dirt to fall from the seams. Covering his nose, Ford stepped back as the gray particles hung heavy in the air.

The door swung inward; it was several inches thick and made of one piece. Ford carefully stepped inside.

A room at least a hundred feet long and sixty feet wide came into view. Seven massive pillars supported a high ceiling. Magic torches hung along the walls each burning red making the stone look crimson.

Along the ceiling he saw moving images of an afterlife. At the other end two large stone statues dressed in black ring mail stood guard over a sarcophagus made of white marble.

"A crypt," Sark said as he stepped into the room.

"Excellent work, Ford," Raven Hill said from behind them.

Spinning around, Ford saw four large orcs holding hand-cannons.

"Easy, elf-meat, don't do anything that you'd regret," one said.

"Ford, what should we do?" Hugh asked, as he drew his sword.

"I'm sure that Mr. Efferguard would suggest that you all do just as I say." Raven Hill smiled. "Now, let's all go into the crypt so I might get what I came for."

"Move along," the other orc said waving the cannon towards the door, and each of them headed into the chamber.

"It stinks of dust and age," Raven Hill said. "But also power." He laughed and removed the amulet from the door. It closed behind them. "Now we're all inside, nice and comfy."

"Now what?" Harigan asked.

"Now, you bring me what I want, and I want that lantern!"

"Why don't you get it then?" Sean motioned with his hand.

"Good question. The answer is, I'm not as stupid as you, and I happen to know that this crypt has security built into it. The deceased was not only rich, but wise to grave robbing. So, Mister Friggand, if you would do the honors…"

Sean looked to Ford, who shrugged his shoulders.

"Go easy," Ford said.

Slowly, Sean made his way toward the sarcophagus. Lightly putting his foot down on the floor next to the marble coffin, he looked over his shoulder and smiled.

"That was easy," he said.

The two statues quickly moved to guard the King's body.

"Sean," Sark shouted. "The statues are golems, and they don't look happy!"

CHAPTER

18

The Lantern

"Sark, I hope you have something up your sleeve," Ford said, unnerved, "or we may be permanent residents here."

One of the gray golems rushed toward Ford, its metallic sword raised over its head. Ford dove to the side as the blade bit into the floor.

"Let roots bind you," shouted Raven Hill.

The golem stopped as plant roots shot out of the ground and entwined it. Just as fast, the statue broke the rope-like restraints, letting them fall to the ground. It looked around, raised its sword and swung it at Raven Hill.

Ducking just in time, the magician rushed between the giant's legs and was confronted by the other golem. Two thunderous blasts echoed in the chamber and the second golem staggered back, bits of stone fraying from it.

Its gaze turned to the orcs and their hand cannons. Two orcs rushed to the right while the others reloaded their cannons. The golem took the bait, and in two strides cornered the running orcs and thrust his sword.

One of the creaturs cried out as they were spit on the end and lofted into the air. The other orc primed his cannon and fired. Chunks of stone frayed away and cascaded around the golum's feet.

The stone monstrosity spun and cut the second orc in half. Next it surved the rest of the interlopers.

"Sean, get to the sarcophagus," Ford called out.

Sean tumbled across the floor coming up at the coffin. The second golem came at him, but the nimble elf was too quick and dove around a column. The golem slashed at him striking the pillar and chipping stone from the support.

Ford looked across the chamber and saw Raven Hill; the man moved stealthily along the wall in the shadows toward the marble encasement.

A golem's blade passed just above Ford's head and he rolled to the side. One of the other orcs yelped, as the golem's sword connected and cleaved his head from his shoulders. The last orc ran to the door and beat upon it with his fists. The golem rushed toward him and crushed him with his foot.

Sark shouted, "Feeze!" Ice formed all over the golem, starting at its feet and stopping at its neck. The room turned frigid. The golem turned its head to look at Sark, clearly straining within the block of ice trying to break free.

Rushing over, Ford did a tumbling roll and came up short of the sarcophagus. His eyes locked with Raven Hill's. Raven lifted a mace high and smashed the corner of the coffin. The active golem turned and came at them both, raised its sword, and brought it down.

A blue flash appeared, and Hugh's sword connected with the golum's, deflecting the attack into a column. Grabbing him by the shirt, Hugh pulled Ford out of the golem's reach.

"But Raven Hill," Ford shouted.

"Let the golem dispatch him," Hugh yelled.

Raven Hill vanished behind the coffin; the golem turned its attention on Hugh. A thundering sound echoed loudly in the room as the monster's blade struck Hugh's sword again. A blinding flash of white light erupted.

Dust and debris from the shockwave rained down from the ceiling, filling the room with a brown haze. Hugh parried the next attack as the creature nearly stepped on him as it moved past.

He tried to strike the behemoth from the side but it thwarted his attack, side-stepped, and brought down its blade again.

Hugh blocked with his sword, causing the air to ignite with another white flash. The golem's sword ground against his, as the creature forced him back.

Hugh focused his strength and stepped to the side causing the golem to falter and stumble. He deflected it with his arm buckler, spun and struck the golem in the leg causing sparks and stone chips to cascade into the air.

Ford dashed over to the coffin, but Raven Hill had secured the treasure.

"Looking for this, Ford?" Raven Hill asked while holding up the rectangular metal container. "Take a good look, for it's the last you'll see of it!"

He tossed the mace away, then held a small golden rod up above his head, made a low musical note, and the roof exploded making a hole. A rope unfurled, and he grabbed it.

"Be so kind as to die soon, won't you?" he said as the rope retracted, and he disappeared through the hole and into the darkness above.

"Curse you, Raven Hill!" Ford yelled after him.

The golem's sword struck next to Ford. The monster repositioned and raised the blade. From the side Han appeared, planted a kick to the incoming sword and redirected the blow.

He spun and grabbed Ford, pulling him to safety. The golem lunged and tried to stomp Han who twisted and ducked under, then appeared on the creature's back.

It spun to the side trying to fling him off. Hugh rushed in, striking the golem again in the leg chipping more stone from the thing.

Harigan walked through the mayhem to the sarcophagus and stopped below the hole.

"Here's our exit."

He lifted his cudgel, and like an arrow, shot straight up through the hole. A rope unraveled from the ceiling to the ground, and Harigan looked down.

"Your stairway to salvation," Harigan said, then laughed loudly.

Hugh stepped to the side, slashed the golem, and its arm fell away. It turned, unfazed, and swung its sword again. Hugh spun left, then turned right and brought his sword down on the creature, cutting it in twain.

Sparks flew into the air as his blade hit home and came to rest stuck in the side of one of the columns. Hugh stood back and pulled the blade free, causing some column fragments to fall to the floor. The two halves of the golem lay immobile.

"The frozen golem," warned Sean.

The golem began moving within the ice, and the ice was cracking.

"Quickly, up the rope," Ford yelled.

Sean rushed to the rope and began climbing hand-over-hand. Han grabbed onto the end, anchoring the rope so the captain could climb faster.

Deft from years climbing the riggings of ships, Sean nearly flew up into the hole. Hugh took the rope and played anchor as Han began to climb.

Soon, Han was at the top too. Up went Sark as he nimbly climbed the rope like a spider on a silk thread. Ford looked at Hugh. Hugh looked at Ford and shook his head.

"I'm better protected with my armor than you. If the creature should get loose, it will take him more time to kill me than you." He pointed up the rope. "Now, up you go."

Ford grabbed the rope and scaled it as fast as he could. Once up on the next floor, he organized the men to pull up Hugh.

"Tie the rope around yourself," he shouted down.

"Already done," Hugh said.

Ford heard the sound of shattering ice. He grabbed the rope, followed by Han, Sean, Sark and Harigan. They pulled with all their might, and the blue knight began to rise.

"Hurry – it's coming," shouted Hugh.

Ford was straining; his muscles were burning as he pulled. Suddenly the rope was jerked down. They pulled up, but it went down again. Ford moved hand-over-hand to the edge of the hole. The golem was hanging onto the heels of Hugh.

"He's got me," shouted Hugh. "Leave me and save yourselves!"

"Pull, damn you!" Ford ordered his crew.

Harigan started to speak in tongues and shake. A wave of golden light engulfed them all. Ford felt as strong as a team of oxen. He saw the golem still hanging from the knight's legs, its sheer weight causing the rope to begin to fray and come apart.

Hugh groaned as he was pulled up into the hole. His visor was down, but Ford saw the man's eyes through the slits; strained as if he were in extreme pain.

Harigan tied off the rope to one of the columns in the room and dashed to the hole. He raised his cudgel and brought it down on the head of the golem with such force that the statue's head exploded. The golem's body stripped away from Hugh and plummeted.

It landed on the sarcophagus smashing it and the golem to rubble. Harigan looked satisfied and mumbled something that sounded to Ford like, 'Shear the sheep, reap the wool'.

They pulled Hugh up through the hole. The golden glow faded. Ford collapsed and gasped for air.

His hands were in pain as were all his muscles. On his hands and knees, he looked up and noticed a door open with a light beyond.

Struggling to his feet, he staggered over and peered out the portal. Footprints, widely spaced in the dust, went down the dimly-lit hall. It was the direction his adversary had fled.

"He went this way," Ford said, stumbling out the door and into the hallway.

CHAPTER

19

Daring Do

It was a beautiful day for a tour. Pushing aside her long golden bangs, Sheala looked over the dozen children and adults in her group.

"I am one of ten trained historians from the Prin Library of Antiquities," she said with pride. "You are about to embark on an odyssey into the past – mingling with the vibrations of history that are the Tellibach Fortress."

She smiled at the children.

"I'm sure that all of you will find it illuminating."

She led them down a wide columned hallway to a large hall with a fireplace at the head. It was her favorite room in the fortress, filled with the very best of the tapestries and art, statues, frescos, and the great oil painting of the Black King Vericornius.

"The gold and silver used for the friezes and gildings were all mined locally. The Vue caverns, not far from the city, is where they originally harvested the gold. When there was no more gold to be found in the caverns, the dwarves found silver and gold in the hills west of the city."

"There they pushed back the goblins and giants, and forged great masterworks of art for the Black King."

She paused for a moment while she walked to the fireplace.

A young boy with his parents was pointing at the painting over the fireplace.

"Who was that, Ms.?" he asked.

"Vericornius..."

She heard the sound of plaster crumbling to the floor. The frame was moving, and as she turned to look at it, the painting came crashing down on top of her.

Struggling to free herself, she squirmed out from one side and looked on in shock and dismay as a man in a blue cloak dashed through the crowd and down the hallway.

She turned to address the child when several other people leapt from the hole and rushed down the hall, nearly knocking her down.

She was fully stunned. In all her years taking tourists into the fortress she had never before had such a thing happen.

She immediately ran to a window and pulled the locks off and opened it. Shouting down to a guard in the courtyard, she cried out for help.

"Some men just ran out of a passage destroying a painting. One is dressed in a blue cloak!"

"We'll get 'em at the gate," the guard said, as he ran from the courtyard.

*   *   *

Ford skidded to a halt at the opulent and massive bronze gates. An open carriage was racing away from the fortress with Raven Hill snugly and smugly sitting within.

Several other carriages were sitting there waiting for patrons. Ford dashed to one, leapt in and tossed several gold coins to the driver.

The man grinned a toothless smile.

"Follow that carriage," Ford said pointing at the fleeing Raven Hill.

"Aye, little master," said the driver. "No carriage is faster than mine."

The party climbed into the conveyance, and the man snapped his whip. The cart began rolling.

Voices erupted behind them, shouting for the cab to halt.

"Stop that carriage!"

The carriage driver glanced back once, but paid no heed and drove his horse on faster.

He snapped his reins and cracked his whip several times, and the cart careened down the road after Raven Hill. Pedestrians jumped to the side as the carriage flew past along the cobbled streets.

One moment Raven Hill was in sight, the next he turned a corner, only to reappear on the straightaway. Both cabbies were skilled, but Ford's cabbie seemed a bit more, as he extracted every bit of power from his beast.

The other cab rolled up to a building and stopped. Raven Hill jumped from the carriage and rushed into the multi-story structure vanishing from sight. Ford followed.

Up the stairs he flew, his dagger in hand. Raven Hill, just feet away, turned and dashed up another flight of stairs.

Four stories Ford ran, until he came to a metal gate. Raven Hill ran past and slammed it shut, turned and smiled. Ford reached the door and grabbed the handle.

Ford woke up, a taste of metal in his mouth. He felt strange and smelled burnt hair.

"What happened?" he asked.

Sark kneeled down next to him.

"Don't move. You were hit with a static-electric spell delayed and put on the metal door. You're lucky to be alive."

"The lantern? Where's Raven Hill?" he asked.

"He had a carpet up here," Sark said.

"A carpet?"

"A magic flying carpet." Sark sat down. "He raced away to the northwest floating on the air."

"Damn," Ford said. "Northwest?"

"Yes, we saw him sail over the wall from here."

"I guess that's it then. We're doomed," Ford stated.

"Not quite. Before he got too far, I threw a viola worm onto his carpet." Sark laughed as if he had said something funny.

"I'm not familiar with that. What is it?"

"It's elementary really," Sark said with a grin. "The worm loves to eat magic thread, and as we all know, magic carpets are woven with magic silk."

He laughed heartily. "Oh, I suspect he'll get fifty miles at the most before his carpet falls to pieces."

"Where did you get a viola worm?" Ford was surprised.

"I own a rare placet ring. The worm boars into the sap of the placet tree, and the sap covers the creature. Over the years the sap turns to amber, and the worm can remain dormant, encased for millions of years in the placet amber. If one has a placet ring, he is able to release the worm to do its dirty little business. An old trick used by the ancient Morganites to escape after being bound by magic ropes when captured in battle."

"Sark, you never cease to amaze me," Ford said. "We have a chance. But let's not run off without our heads. We'll need to gather some supplies for traveling over the coastal mountains."

"Also," Sark began. "Raven Hill dropped something in his haste."

"What?" Ford silently thanked the gods at his good fortune.

"These," Sark said, holding out a green gem, a piece of paper with some writing on it, and a small mirror.

Ford looked at the objects. "Unimpressive things," he said.

"Except for the paper," Sark added.

Ford took it and read it aloud.

"Dock 52, berth A4, the Downing Crown."

He looked puzzled for a moment, and then shook his head with delight.

"He's booked on a ship, the Downing Crown."

"And that ship is a sailing ship and not a river boat. The only sea port that is close is Darkwater," Sark said.

"Yes, of course."

Ford's mood changed and he stood up. He staggered a bit, but remained on his feet.

"Let's get back on the hunt," he said.

Back at the inn, Ford pulled out a map and laid it open on the table. He drew a line with his finger along the map.

"We need to get across the mountains of the Westlands to the port city of Darkwater. It's a relative straight shot and not more than seventy miles. At a brisk pace it should take us no more than two days, barring any unforeseen issues. With a bit of luck, Raven Hill has fallen to his death. If we're not so lucky, he landed and is on foot. By horse we should be able to close the distance."

"Isn't that giant territory?" Sean asked.

Harigan smiled. "And you all know the Westland Giant's disposition well; they did not take kindly to elves or humans intruding into their land."

Sark shrugged. "We're not traveling off-road. It's the commercial highway. Giants won't bother us. Also, there's still snow on the ground in the mountains, and the giant clans move to the high country hot springs to ride out the cold weather. It's as good a time to travel without a caravan or contingent of city soldiers as we could ever hope for," Sark said.

"Regardless of giants or other, our path now runs through those mountains," Han added.

"Yes," Ford said. "Let's get to our horses and be away."

They headed for the northwest city gate. Ford saw dark clouds brooding over the hills. It was most likely going to sleet if not snow on them over the summit. He prayed that Sark's trick had worked and Raven Hill had fallen not too far away.

CHAPTER

20

To Darkwater

Large green oaks littered the rolling hills. A thick carpet of clover and grass filled in between the trees.

From time to time Ford saw large wooly aurochs grazing, as well as deer and mutton ox. The temperature was falling as they wound their way up the rutted switchback road towards the summit.

By nightfall, sleet and ice were forming and sticking to their clothes and animals. Ford called a halt to their advance and dismounted.

Leading his horse off the road and into the woods, he pushed away the thorny brambles and underbrush until he emerged into a clearing where the only thing lining the forest floor was thick grass and large ferns. The strong smell of rich, wet ground and foliage filled his nostrils, and he drew in the heavy scent.

"What is it you're remembering?" Sark asked coming alongside.

"My garden at home, just after a good spring rain."

"A good memory," Sark affirmed.

Ford removed his saddle and bags, bed roll and supplies, and hobbled his horse near a plethora of ferns and grass. Sark and

Sean did likewise as Harigan brought the string of pack ponies to the site and began removing the tent and extra food supplies.

"See if you can't find some large pieces of wood," Sean told Hugh.

"Aye." Hugh hurried off. Returning a few minutes later, he laid the firewood by a shallow pit Sean had dug.

"At least we won't freeze to death tonight," he said.

Soon the camp was established and a cooking pot was on the fire boiling some stew made from salted meat. They all huddled around warming themselves as a biting cold set in. The only one who seemed unaffected by the cold was Harigan.

Ford made a check of the camp then returned to the fire.

"I'll take the first watch. Who'll take the others?"

"I'll take the next," Han said

"And I'll take the next of the next," Harigan asserted.

Sean went next and then Hugh. Lastly, Sark volunteered, saying that he wanted to collect some herbs that only bloomed in these particular mountains, in the cold, and under iridescent clouds of the early morn.

After the other's had gone to bed, Ford sat on a gray log by the fire pit. He took a long stick and poked at the embers watching the shifting patterns of the simmering red heat.

Sleet began to fall, and he pulled his cowl over his head and rubbed his hands together while holding them over the yellow flames.

He was deep in thought when he suddenly felt a hand on his shoulder. Spinning around, dagger in hand he leapt to his feet.

"Sorry, that was unintended," Han said.

"I could have killed you," Ford said, as he replaced his blade and rubbed his eyes.

Han nodded."Perhaps. I'm pleased that you didn't."

"Your stealth can be a hindrance sometimes," Ford declared.

"I see that now." Han sat down. "You'd better get some rest. I'll take the watch."

Ford moved toward the tent. "Good advice. See you in the morn."

Entering the tent he found the empty spot were Han had been sleeping and laid out his bedroll. The sound of the sleet hitting the tent roof was pleasing and lulling, and he quickly fell into a deep slumber.

Ford woke, sat up, and slowly climbed to his feet. His bones ached with the cold, but he felt relatively well rested.

He rolled up his bedding and set it by his saddlebags. Quietly exiting the tent, he saw a thick fog. He walked a few feet, then saw the fire and Sark.

The magician was calmly sitting near the fire. Ford approached and knelt down, poking the low flames with a stick.

"It's cold mornings like this that make me thankful that we're not wild animals," he said.

"Those animals have better sense than we, for they're still resting in their dens, warm and sleepy."

Ford laughed a soft chuckle. "Indeed, but when they arouse themselves, they'll be looking for food, and we have ours here ready to eat," he said, pointing at the black pot filled with leftover stew sitting in the coals.

Ford sat down. "We should get to Darkwater by nightfall, save any unforeseen issues," he said.

Sark stirred the pot. "Raven Hill is without his henchmen, and on the run. I don't think we have much to worry about for the moment regarding him."

"True, but he is not the only danger lurking in these mountains." Ford looked about.

Harigan stepped out from the tent and came to the fire.

"Raven Hill is halfway to Darkwater. I saw it in a vision. Take heart, for there is an obstruction that is baring his path. He will have to move slow and stealth."

The Aor priest looked in the pot and frowned. "I'll invoke the plate this morning," he stated.

He produced the magic plate and said the words. Steaming meat and tubers appeared.

Han, Sean and Hugh came from the tent.

"A good morning meal will do us well," said Sean.

All of them sat around the fire eating. Once the group finished, they broke camp.

The mist was lifting, and Sean secured the small cauldron to one of the pack ponies. Moving to his horse, he climbed into the saddle.

Ford led the party from the woods back to the road, and over the summit. The snow was high here, but the warm magic stones that lined the road kept it clear and dry.

Down the hill they traveled following the Westland's highway as it meandered this way and that. A ray of sunlight appeared as warming snow fell from the trees.

Emerging from the treeline, Ford saw a broad valley made up of strips of grassland and dark green oaks. The Western road snaked like a scaly brown serpent though the expanse. On the horizon, a small dimple of dark angular shapes stuck out from the natural topography.

"The city of Darkwater," he said.

"It's a long way off still," Hugh added.

"Look there." Harigan pointed to a strange shifting pattern in the valley.

"It seems to be moving," Ford said.

Sark pulled out his spyglass and extended it.

"An army of giants," Sark calmly stated. "With siege engines and flying banners of several clans."

"Are they heading toward Darkwater?" Sean asked.

"It looks that way," Sark added.

Ford's face looked stressed. "How many giants?"

Sark shrugged. "Maybe ten thousand."

"There's no way we can get past that," Hugh said.

Sark got down from his horse. "There's something I can do. I can make it sleet and snow on them. They'll be forced to make camp to wait out the storm."

"How long can you sustain that?" Ford asked.

"I'll have to use the chaos magic, since they're so far away."

Ford thought for a moment. "If it works I don't care if you summon Greenbaum the Pain Merchant," he said.

"Okay, this will take a few moments," Sark advised.

Harigan laughed mightily as he dismounted. "This should prove to be entertaining," he said.

Sark rubbed his hands together then shut his eyes tightly. The air around him became luminous and snaps of electricity popped everywhere. Orbs of light flew this way and that, and shimmering blue streaks raced from Sark and into the sky.

Sark opened his eyes. He looked around as if confused.

"What happened?" Ford asked.

Harigan laid on the ground covered his head with both hands. A bubble of golden light formed over him.

"I don't know," Sark began. "Like I've said, chaos magic is unpred—"

In the distance a flash of white light blinded everyone. The ensuing shockwave rippled across the ground setting fire to the grass and plants in the valley.

The party was blasting flat against the ground. The horses were blown off their feet and tumbled up the hill. The party tumbled after them as the heat singed hair and flesh.

A deafening roar echoed throughout the mountains, and a cloud of debris shot into the air. Ford struggled to his feet, his ears ringing.

Han's mouth was moving, but he couldn't hear his words. After a moment he heard a faint voice.

"What happened?" Han was asking.

Sark struggled to his feet. He stuck his finger into his ear and wiggled it around.

"That was unexpected," he said loudly.

"What in the name of the Underworld was that?" Ford demanded.

"I'm not sure!" Sark shouted.

"Look—" Sean pointed into the valley.

The clouds formed a halo around a clear blue sky. The ground where the giants once were was turned black, reflecting some of the sunlight like a bowl of glass.

Streamers of steam rose from the burnt soil and rushed up into the atmosphere. The giants were nowhere to be seen; in fact there were no bodies, no trees, no grass, nothing left but black glass spread out like a dollop of cream in a cup of tea.

Sark brushed off his robe. "I'm not sure how that got away from me..." Glancing at Ford he added, "You look a bit sunburned."

Ford looked at Sark. "I now understand the danger of the lantern."

Harigan got to his feet.

"Now you all understand my mission. Such power should not be left in the hands of unstable mortals." He whistled, and his horse came galloping down from the hill. Taking the reins, he looked at Sark. "Even the gods frown upon your genius, but for all your ability you still don't know what dragon you have by the tail." He smiled and mounted his steed.

As he slowly meandered away, he spoke over his shoulder. "I have one more thing to do, but we'd better take our time and let the area cool a bit."

It took only a short time to police up the horses. The beast's singed hair stunk terribly as they rode with care into the valley toward the black stain. It stretched a mile across, and Harigan was waiting right at the edge of the shiny glass.

"What is it you're doing?" Sean asked.

Harigan pulled a wooden plaque from under his shirt and retrieved a wooden pole tied to his saddle.

"I made this last night just for this occasion."

He fastened the sign to it and stuck it in the ground.

"Where did you get that?" Ford asked.

"While you were sleeping last night, Aor bade me to make this sign as a warning to you mortals. This place will be known as Sark's Plane," he said admiring the sign that read the same. "I came up with the name."

"Sark's Plane? I like it," said Sark, as he approached the sign.

As he got closer, the letters on the board glowed brightly with a white light.

"It's imbued," Sark said looking at Harigan who was smiling back at him. "How did you... I mean, it takes weeks to make a magic sign that can do that."

"Time is not what you think it is," Harigan said. "Weeks, months, years... it means nothing to the gods. You, Sark, must learn more control. Today, you made Aor and his brethren nervous."

He took up his horses reins. "The surface here is thick and will be slick, so you'd better lead your mounts across."

He walked out into the black surface.

The clouds reformed above, and the cold returned. Rain fell. It felt good on Ford's skin. For hours they traveled past the black scar and into the surviving woods beyond.

As the late morning came, the great walls of the city of Darkwater were visible. Though they were still several miles away, they saw the gigantic white lighthouse rising above the protective walls, hundreds feet into the air. By the afternoon they had reached the gates.

"You, traveler," shouted a gate guard. "Did you see what that flash in the sky was?"

"What flash?" Ford asked.

The man in armor waved them through without further questions.

"They don't know anything," he said to someone hidden behind the battlements.

Ford entered the city. The many carts, equestrians, and pedestrians moved through at a steady pace. He followed the signs to the marina.

As he passed through the double white marble arches that marked the entrance to the shipyards, he found berth A4 empty, and the Downing Crown sailing out of the harbor.

CHAPTER

21

The Elusive Downing Crown

Ford leapt from his horse and walked to the harbormaster's office. The harbormaster was a big man, overfed with a round head with a wreath of brown hair.

He wore a thick red mustache that hung down below his square chin and a neatly trimmed goatee that came to a well-groomed point.

"Sir, the Downing Crown, what is its destination?" Ford asked.

The harbormaster looked up from his paperwork.

"What business is it of yours?"

"I've an important message for the captain of that ship and it must be delivered to him with all haste."

The harbormaster eyed Ford for a second.

"The captain is piloting to Glumly Island in the Western Sea not far from Brin," he said.

"Is there another ship set to sail there today?"

The man looked irritated.

"Let me look."

He opened his ledger and thumbed through it. He took a pair of wire rim glasses and held them a few inches away from his eyes. He stopped and looked up.

"The Comely Lady is set to embark at the next tide. That should be around double three bells," he said.

"The captain is a Mister Huron—a barnacle encrusted half-elf with a taste for salt air and a nip of the bottle," said the harbormaster.

"Captain Huron," Ford repeated. "Is he game for taking passengers?"

"If he has room and you have coin. He sails a small cargo ship."

"Is it fast?" Ford asked.

"Compared to the Downing Crown?" The man chuckled. "Not nearly. But with all sails set and a stiff wind at her aft, she can maybe make ten knots."

"The Crown will do easily twelve, but she's laden with cargo too so if your intent is to catch her, you stand a fair chance."

"For your trouble," Ford said, as he put down two silver coins on the desk.

The harbormaster looked at the money. "Seems a bit light for such sport as we've had," he said.

Ford placed down one more coin. The man's eyes narrowed as he reached for the money. Weighting it in his hand, he smiled.

"Fine enough. I'll have the good taste not to mention that we spoke," he added.

"Where do I find this Comely Lady?"

"Berth C17. And have the good sense not to mention we talked," said the harbormaster.

"Not a word." Ford left the building and rejoined the party.

"We need to find a ship called the Comely Lady," he told them. He took his horse by the reins and led it through the mass of long-shore workers."It's at Berth C17."

They walked down to the docks, and Sean boldly stepped forward.

"Ahoy," cried Sean as he approached the gangplank. A sailor stood up from scrubbing the deck and came forward.

"What be yer business?" he asked.

"Passage to Glumly Island for me and me mates," Sean replied.

"Passage? I'll inform the Boatswain-mate. He can see if the captain is taking passengers," the man said. "Mister Foely, would you come here please?"

A gruff-looking sailor came over; a piece of wood in his hand, and a fish knife in the other. He whittled on the wood, slicing off strips into the water between the ship and dock.

"What is it, Mister Torance?" he asked while eyeing Sean and the party.

"These men here want to book a passage to Glumly."

"Aren't you Sean Friggand?" Mister Foely asked.

His eyes narrowed, and he looked severe.

"Uh... no, my name is Marsh Hill," Sean replied.

"Obviously you don't remember me, but I was the rigger's mate on the Hydra. I remember seeing you on the wreckage floating against the current to the south as I floundered on a barrel going north."

His face betrayed a look of rage.

"I found out later who you were; a scourge of the sea I hear. If we had known better, we'd never picked you up from that decking you were clinging to!"

"I think you're mistaken, Master Foely. I'm Captain—" Sean stumbled over his words. "Captain Hood," he finally said.

"Hood – Captain, eh? You just told me your name was Marsh Hill."

Foely waved over a burly man.

"No, you're Captain Sean Friggand the cursed alright. And I'd not let you within a league of this boat, even if you offered all the jewels of the Nine Jins." Turning to the man he added, "Don't let any of them on board!"

"That didn't work out well," Ford said.

"We're not sunk yet," Sean said pointing at a small steam tug moored down the wharf.

"With that little beauty we don't need wind to propel us. And it takes a small crew such as us. We can sail now before the tide."

Ford looked skeptical.

"But they're designed for local trips, short routes, and take have a shallow draft. The magic stones used to heat the water only keep their heat for a short time."

"Unless they're powered by chaos magic," Sark said.

Ford considered his position for a moment. It was clear he struggled with the thought of Sark using chaos magic again.

"Come on," he said, as he moved down the marina boardwalk and stopped at the tug.

"Ahoy!" he called out.

No reply came. He rapped on the saxboard.

"Ahoy!"

Still no answer.

A young elf with a bottle in hand approached them.

"They're at the Sea Beast Tavern," he said. "A game of chipping is underway. The captain will be along shortly, I'm sure."

He tipped the bottle up and drank heartily.

"Last I saw 'em, he was losing a week's wage. A word of advice though; when they do show, tell'em that Gill Hammershot says their boat is a mud-skipper river wreck."

He laughed for a moment, then staggered down the boardwalk to a similar craft and boarded.

"Let's get underway," Ford said, as he loosened the aft ropes.

Han untied the fore. Harigan pushed off the dock with a pole, and Ford and Han leapt to the deck.

Sark opened the aft hatch and descended, followed by Hugh.

"Ah, a two hundred gallon boiler. This shouldn't take but a moment," Sark said.

"Sean, can you actually pilot this thing?" Ford asked.

He laughed. "At the academy, they started us out piloting one of these. It'll be no problem."

Sean move into the pilot house.

Green smoke billowed from the steam vents. The boat shook once as a minor rumble emanated from the hull.

A host of green glowing fairies swarmed from the opening in the deck. Hugh ran up from the hold and furiously waved his arms as the creatures enveloped him then flew off into the sky.

"Hey," shouted a lanky fellow from the docks. "By the Underworld, what are you doing with my boat?"

The fairies suddenly noticed the men on the dock and swarmed them; biting and pulling hairs out.

The men ran up the walkway waving their hands about. As fast as they attacked, the fairy swarm flew into the sky and vanished.

The captain waved over a harbor constable.

"They've bloody stolen me tug!" he shouted.

The constable rushed off up the docks toward the harbormaster's office. Ford knew this meant trouble.

A moment later several bright flares illuminated the sky. Horns were sounded, and along the shore men were pointing and calling.

"He's going to summon a police sloop," Ford said.

"I've almost got it," Sark shouted from within the hull.

Sean looked out from the pilot's cabin.

"To port, a patrol boat."

It was the police sloop; several fellows dressed in uniforms pointed cannons at them.

"Sark, if ever your magic worked – make it work now!" said Ford.

A burst of steam shot from the stack, and the boat lurched under their feet. The gears inside the boat were moving, and so was the tug. Faster and faster they cut through the water as the police sloop came in behind them.

Sean pulled at the wheel steering them towards the mouth of the breakwater and out into the open sea. The tug picked up speed.

"We're losing them," Han said, as the sloop fell away behind them.

"We'll be fine if there are no storms," Sean shouted out from the pilot house. "These tugs don't do well in open seas."

314

A cannonballs from the sloop landed just short of the tug's aft.

Before the sloop fired another volley, the tug slipped through the breakers and into the blue and churning sea.

Sark came up on deck, a red lump on his forehead.

"I hit my head on a pipe," he said. "Nonetheless we're up to a full head of steam now.

He rubbed his head.

"Not much room down there for all the mechanisms and me."

Looking to aft, Ford saw the sloop exiting the breakwater and coming out, then veer to starboard and begin coming about.

"They've broken off it seems."

"Glad to hear it," Harigan said. "They came ever so close with that shot."

"Now what?" Hugh asked.

"We let Sean do his thing," Ford said while looking at the pilot house.

Sean stepped out and put his pipe in his mouth.

"Plenty of charts in here. We're on target for Glum."

He lit a match and drew in some smoke.

"At our present pace, I'd say we'd catch up to the Downing Crown in four hours or so, barring of course any sea monsters or pirates."

Sean went back into the pilot house and stood there with the wheel firmly in his hands. Ford took up a position on the bow keeping watch for the Downing Crown as they cut through the waves at great speed.

Han stood on the deck near the steam vents trying to keep an eye out for any other ships, and Hugh moved to the starboard side to keep watch.

Walking to the port side, Sark sat down against the railing and opened a small codex. As he read, he felt the misting of the sea all around him.

"If it's going to be four hours until we see the Crown, you might want to relax a bit," Sark called to Ford.

Ford came over and sat down beside him.

"What are you reading?"

"Coldwaller's treatment on Chaos Magic," he said. "Interesting stuff."

"To some I guess."

"Here, read this." Sark handed Ford a small scroll. "It's all about casting the perfect party trick."

"I see. Amaze your friends and such?"

Sark smiled. "Exactly so." He went back to reading.

Darkness settled over sea. A white glowing mist rose from the waters. Ford saw the fog hovering at the level of the tug's main deck. In the distance he saw the Crown's aft lantern.

"Probably another hour," Sean said, stepping out onto the deck for a smoke.

"Then what?" Ford asked.

Sean took in some smoke and exhaled.

"I don't know; I'm not running this game."

It was clear Ford had better come up with a plan.

"What about coming up alongside, and we board her?"

"I can do that. We have enough steam in this beast to do the trick," Sean said.

"Then what?" Ford mused aloud. "We might be in for a fight."

Sean shrugged. "I'm just getting us there; you're the one who's got to figure out how to get on board."

The Downing Crown was not far ahead. Ford saw her deck lights clearly. They had not been spotted in the misty darkness, and Sean was maneuvering the boat to come along side.

Sark appeared next to Ford with a grim expression.

"The hold is filling with water," he said.

"What?"

"Sean's curse, we all forgot in the excitement."

"How bad?"

"We'll be sunk within the hour."

Sark looked at the small dingy tied up at the aft of the tug.

"We can't all fit."

"By the blackness of Haig's Hall," Sean said loudly and pointed. "Look at that!"

Ahead of the Crown was something massive, green, and glowing. An iridescent fog was billowing up from the sea. Electro discharges flew in every direction as if a violent and destructive tempest were brewing.

Ford watched as the Downing Crown vanished into the boiling clouds of the storm.

"What is it?" Ford asked.

"I'll be damned if I know! Not like any storm I've ever seen, or heard about," Sean declared.

"Look," shouted Hugh.

Ford watched as what looked like a giant spectral hand reached from the fog and laid hold of the tug. All who were standing fell to the deck.

Sean latched onto the wheel as the tug pitched upward slightly, then came out of the water completely.

"Profits of Yam," screamed a distant voice somewhere in the darkness of the storm.

"If nothing else, he's theatrical," shouted Sark over the gale.

"What? Ford shouted back.

"Raven Hill! He's quite the showman!"

"He's responsible for this?" yelled Ford.

"He is," Sark shouted. "A portal has been ripped open by Underworld magic, and we're being pulled in. Good luck for us, really. If we had been a mile further back, we might have missed it all together."

A flash of bright yellow light surrounded them and then darkness enveloped all. Ford felt like the ship was spinning around.

In the utter blackness several bright blinding blue flashes burst forth, then darkness again. The howl of the wind was deafening and cold rain and sleet smashed against them burning any exposed skin.

Someone in the darkness cried out a terrible sound, then bright blue sky and a hot sun shown down on them. The ship tilted nearly ninety degrees and then sprung upright. Ford's head hurt and his eyes were seeing green spotty blotches.

"Land ho," said Sean. "Off the starboard bow!"

Ford saw a dense green tropical island. He rubbed his eyes, then looked again.

As he oriented himself, he noticed a tattered ship just vanishing around the landmass. It was the Downing Crown missing its main mast and all manner of debris hanging from her decks.

"There," Ford called. "That is where we need to go. Follow that ship!"

"Aye," Sean said as he scrambled to his feet and grabbed onto the wheel.

Hugh stumbled up and lurched to the railing and vomited over the side again.

Han looked into the hold.

"The belly of this ship is nearly filled!"

The ship shuddered and the sound of cracking wood seemed to come from all around them. A massive crack appeared along the deck as the ship tore in half.

"Seems that Friggand's bad luck is at work," Harigan laughed.

The ship split; the bow and pilot house sank immediately, followed by the aft.

Ford, Sean, and all the others were flung into the emerald waters. Ford bobbed to the surface, coughing as he began to tread water.

He looked around and realized he was in a calm sea void of heavy waves. The water was very warm and the clear shimmering green of the water lent itself to being nearly translucent.

Fish darted this way and that. Even some large beasts appeared lurking just below their feet, stalking the lesser fish.

A piece of floating debris bumped against Ford; part of the ship's decking. He scrambled atop it, steadied himself and looked about.

Ford called to Han. He saw the man bobbing in the water not more than a few dozen yards away.

"Over here," he called.

Han swam over, taking only a few powerful strokes to reach him. Climbing onto the decking, he rolled onto his back.

"It doesn't seem possible," he said.

"Anything is possible," Ford countered. "Probably had quite a lot to do with Sean's curse."

"No, I mean that storm and suddenly being here, wherever here is."

Sark was holding onto a half-submerged barrel in one arm and his backpack held aloft with the other. Sean swam around the man.

"Don't be afraid," he called to Sark as he rode a shallow wave up and down. "The water's quite fine for swimming!"

Sark looked desperate as Ford paddled close and pulled him and his pack onto the makeshift raft. Harigan approached slowly, floating on his back and gently paddling with his hands.

"Where's Hugh?" Ford asked.

"Gone to the briny deep I would suspect with all that armor," Harigan said with a boastful grin. "All that armor and only the ocean to fight. He was doomed from the start." He chuckled.

Harigan put his hands on his chest, closed his eyes and with no effort, quickly drifted toward the island faster than they could paddle.

"We need to make for that island. I saw the Crown headed around the corner." Ford pointed at a jungle encrusted finger of land protruding from one side.

Some long fragments of decking bumped up against the raft and Ford picked them up. He and Han used them as paddles and began paddling towards the island. Sean grabbed on to the back and pushed the raft from behind.

"Look," shouted Sark, as he pointed into the water.

Looking down, Ford saw Hugh below them in his armor walking towards the shore. He glanced up and waved at them, then pointed at the island and strolled into a seaweed grove vanishing from sight.

CHAPTER

22

Island Surprise

Ford saw the island was large and expansive.

"Look at those great dark green mangroves covering the beach," he said.

"And those mountains topped with mist," Sark replied.

"Those are some high mountains," Han affirmed.

Sark pulled out a spyglass and extended it.

"It seems the jungle is made up of many different types of trees and large ferns. I can see palms by the shore, but very strange trees inland."

The raft shifted under them, and the rolling waves carried them a few hundred yards. Sounds of the water crashing into the beach were not far off.

The raft tipped down. Ford, Sark, and Han held on for dear life as the wave propelled them towards the beach. Below them the waters seemed to recede as they climbed higher and higher into the air.

"Hold on," shouted Han, as the raft tipped forward and down.

Tumbling from the wreckage, they fell into the churning waters towards what looked like jagged pink and white coral. The raft came apart, sending its occupants smashing into the reef.

Ford hit against the jagged rocks, slicing his leather vest, shirt, and pants. He bobbed to the surface, white bubbles flowing all around him.

Gasping for air, he struggled to keep his head above the water. Another wave tumbled his over. He was rolled, then tossed about like a cork. Another wave crashed on top of him driving him into a sandy sea floor.

He again struggled to get to the surface, and then was hit from behind by Sark. Both men hit the sandy beach hard as the water drained from over top of them.

Ford clawed his way up onto the beach and fell heavily onto the warm sand. He tried to speak, but only succeeded in coughing and vomiting.

Han staggered up the beach and up to the treeline. He fell to the black rocks and rolled onto his back. Hugh emerged from the surf, water draining from his seaweed-covered armor.

He walked to the trees before sitting down on a large tree root. Off came his helmet, and he looked at Han and Ford.

"The air was getting pretty stale in here," he said.

Sark dragged his wet backpack up above the surf line and collapsed. His labored breathing came in gasps.

"By the gods, I thought I was done for."

A mighty wave crashed on the beach. Sean landed on his feet and declared, "Refreshing. What a grand swim."

Ford slowly looked up with an annoyed expression at the Lake Elf. "Did you really need to say that?" he rasped.

"I guess I didn't." Sean looked around. "Where's Harigan?"

As if on cue, Harigan came from down the beach. He walked around piles of drift wood and seaweed.

Coming over by Han he sat down and hoisted his horn, said the words, and drank deeply.

"Nothing like a good ale to quench one's thirst after such exercise," he said. "How is it that you didn't drown Hugh?"

"Somehow air was trapped inside, and I could breathe without a problem," Hugh said. "By all the gods, that was quite an experience – I mean walking down there under the water!"

Sean lifted his nose and took in a deep whiff. The smell of brine and foliage mixed with something more.

"Smoke," he said. For a moment he looked around, then pointed into the jungle. "That way."

Han stood. "I smell it too, and someone is cooking something delicious. Some sort of fowl and maybe auroch too."

Sean pushed his way through a large fern and stumbled onto what looked like an ancient roadway.

"I seem to have discovered an abandoned road," he said. "It's in a desperate state of disrepair."

He looked up. "Strange creatures are lurking in the trees too."

"By Aor," Harigan said. "Creatures not seen since Hoth and Aor were young."

"They look like apes, but they have four arms and lots of snow white hair," Han said.

Ford moved along the road.

"Let's get going."

"Raven Hill must have been heading here with some purpose in mind," Sark stated. "He's the sort of person who isn't particularly spontaneous, or at least that's what I've heard."

"That's good to know," Ford added.

They moved between several large fallen branches laden with bright yellow fruit; strangely shaped with a long neck and bulbous bottom. Harigan tore one from the limb and shook it.

"There's some liquid inside," he said.

Sean snatched one up and shook it. Taking his dagger, he sliced off the top and sniffed, then took a sip.

"It's like the liquor that the natives of Broom Island make from sugar weed."

He consumed the remainder. Harigan followed suit.

"I hear the sound of voices," Han said. "I don't recognize the language. I can also hear pots and pans, and a babbling brook. It must be a camp."

Stopping at a large yellow and orange plant, Ford heard laughing and chatting on the other side. He motioned with his hand for Han to come forward. Leaning in, he whispered to him.

"Quietly see what is going on beyond this plant. Don't take too long, and if you're spotted, we'll meet you back at the beach where we started."

Han nodded. With great stealth, he vanished into the foliage. Ford turned to the party.

A hand fell upon his shoulder from behind and he nearly yelped with shock. Turning he saw Han.

Han motioned for them to be quiet and held up one hand over his eye, then he held up all his fingers.

Ford wrinkled his brow. He turned back to the others, and realized standing there was a cyclops, his feet planted wide and his arms folded over his chest.

The creature was at least twenty feet tall and thickly muscled. His one eye was glaring at them with what Ford though was malice.

The cyclops' leather jerkin hung over a puffy red silk shirt. The creature's dark green breeches were pantaloon-like, bulging at the thighs and neatly fitted into large black leather boots.

"Shy more seely fog," the cyclops said.

They all looked at each other. Ford shrugged.

"We don't understand," Ford said.

"Oh, you're from the hills. I said, why are you skulking about here?" He used a deep and authoritative voice.

"Uh, we… were…" Hugh began.

The cyclops pointed up into the trees.

"You know the gorochs lurk in these trees and are fond of bashing unsuspecting travelers with yam-yam fruits. Now, get you back to the party, and wander not in these dark woods anymore," he said.

"Party?" Han asked.

The cyclops looked curious.

"Yes, the festival of Ge Hi Mo! The yearly faire."

He waved his arms and shooed them past the large plant as if they were geese.

Ford stumbled forth into a large glade filled with brightly colored tents, cooking fires, banners, and people. He saw dark elves, forest elves, western elves from the Steppes, and elves from the Downs. A family of well-dressed orcs passed by, their children well mannered.

A large ogre was pushing a massive swing that seated a dozen people; some human, some goblin and even a dwarf. Food was being purchased, drink was being consumed, and in the distance, near the forest fence, Ford saw a band of goblin minstrels preparing to play music.

"What in the name of the Netherworld?" Ford said, shocked.

Tumbling into him, Hugh, Sean, Han, Harigan and Sark all came from the bush. They gazed at the festivities with expressions of disbelief.

Han leaned into Ford. "That's what I wanted to tell you. It's a faire, attended by a cacophony of creatures, hosted by what looked to be a contingent of finely dressed cyclops!"

"Most extraordinary and unexpected," Ford stated under his breath.

Bursting from the foliage, the cyclops chuckled.

"Now, don't wander from the faire again. I take it your ignorance of the gorochs are because you're from the high country?"

"Yes, the high country," Ford confirmed.

The cyclops nodded his head.

"I see. Your accents are strange and that's what's confusing me. Well you've been warned about the forest. But don't worry, the gorochs never venture from the trees."

"Pardon me," Hugh began. "Do you know a Raven Hill?"

Putting his finger to his chin, the cyclops looked thoughtful.

"Ah yes, I seem to recall that there is a fellow named Raven Hill who showed up here ten years ago. Keeps to himself mostly. A strange chap indeed, and not too chatty. I've been told he's friends with Count Dulopolis the Second."

"Count Dulopolis?" Sean asked.

"He, of course, is our most famous, or shall I say infamous, vampire. Raven Hill has been known to attend the Count's vampire's ball that's given annually. All the best people attend."

"Where does this Count live?" Harigan asked.

"He owns the castle on the smaller island at the west side of our island, near Quimby cove and the ruins of an ancient port."

He suddenly noticed a patch of fluff stuck to his vest and brushed it off.

"Any other questions?"

"Not at the moment," Ford said.

"You hill folk sure are secluded," the cyclops stated.

"What's your name?" Han asked.

"Nevile Gile Theronius of the Mistytop Nevile's, not the Bottoms Nevile's. We still don't speak to them… since the incident. Anyway, I am at your service."

He turned to look into the crowd. "Now, I see that the iced-cream vendor has arrived, and I should go help keep the children from looting his cart. Good day to you."

Nevile walked away towards a giant, dressed in a rainbow colored dragon costume fitted with tiny wings, pushing a cart.

Ford, Han, Harigan, Sark and Sean stared.

"What in the name of the Underworld is happening here?" Harigan asked, seeming just as surprised as the others. "Our world is upside down."

"Why don't you ask Aor? He seems to know everything?" Sean jibed.

"That, my friend, is a capital idea," Harigan said, "I'll ask."

He sat down and fell into a deep meditative trance.

"Perhaps if we mingle, we may find some answers too," Sark suggested.

Han, Hugh, Sark, Ford and Sean entered the crowd. Ford saw a long line of people coming from one direction. It was hard to see far, but he had the advantage of being on top of a berm.

A small orc child came up and pulled on his trouser leg.

"Parador mi sur."

Ford looked down. "Yes?" he said.

"Oh, my apologies," the child said. "I didn't know that you spoke the hill tongue." He smiled showing his sharp fang-like teeth. "I'm studying it at school. My teacher says it's a very old way of speaking."

The youngster appeared to remember what he wanted to ask Ford. "I was wondering if you could help me find my mother?"

"Sharigee mortu." A frantic orc woman came and latched onto the child's arm. "Yigi herothi," she scolded.

"Mommy, this elf speaks hill talk," the boy said.

She looked at Ford then also smiled a mouth full of fangs.

"You speak the hill language? We do not get many who do these days. Welcome," she said and pulled the child into the crowd vanishing from sight.

"Ford," called Sean, as he came up alongside. "There is a city called Viroteleius not far from here. The sausage vender told me that we should take the glide-coach there. I'm not sure what that is, but it seems to be located in that direction." He pointed.

"What about the vampire?" Harigan asked coming up.

"I didn't ask," Sean replied.

"Aor has spoken to me and informed me that this island is quite old. It was once ruled by dragon lords who vanished several thousand years ago. Their slaves are the ones who inhabit it today. The vampire's castle is not far from that city you mentioned, Sean." Harigan hoisted a flagon of ale to his lips.

"Why don't you just have Aor transport the lantern into our possession?" Sean mused.

"It is not that easy," Harigan said. "The Lantern contains a powerful gem. He cannot set his hands about it. Thus, he needs mortals to do this work."

Harigan lifted his horn in his other hand and said the words.

"Plus he's a busy god you see, and can't be holding our hands every second of the day."

He drank down the contents of the horn.

"I also found out that the name of this land is Bri Zeel. It's a Dracon word meaning land of fire fruit," Sean added.

"I suggest that we find this glide-coach and make good use of it," stated Ford.

"The coach is that way beyond those trees," Sean said, pointing again. "The town is ten miles or so towards that high mountain, the one capped with the mist."

The smells of cooking pastries, meat pies, sausages, and fowl filled the air. As Ford walked he kept his eyes shifting about, ever vigilant for any cut-purses in the crowd.

It was strange, that all these people were not only mixing together, but were actually social with one another. He saw Han near a booth that was selling leather goods, and he was haggling with the vendor.

Ford made his way there, but then saw the shimmering blue armor of Hugh approaching. The man was chomping on a wide piece of dark bread topped with cheese, and in his other hand was a tankard that he gulped down.

"We're going to a town nearby called Viroteleius," Ford said. "Raven Hill is staying at a castle owned by a vampire."

"I've never met a vampire before." Hugh looked concerned. "We'd better get going then." Hugh then tried to fit the large wedge of white cheese into his mouth.

CHAPTER

23

The Count, The Glide Rail, and the Tower

Ford stood staring at the strange contraption. He had never seen anything like it before. It was twice as long as a city omnibus and more ornate.

Two doors allowed entrance into the interior which was covered with a gray metallic shell detailed with decorative metalwork. Along the shell were holes cut into the sides fitted with glass and sealed.

People were getting in and out of the cars from the side doors that opened and closed by sliding along the shell.

"What do we do?" Hugh asked.

"Get in," Sark stated.

Ford approached and looked inside. It seemed roomy and plush with cushy seats covered in red velvet with gold embroidery. He climbed in and found the seats set close together.

Sitting in one he felt as if the chair hugged his butt. Sean, Harigan, Hugh, Sark, and Han also entered and found seats.

A man with a large bushy brown mustache looked in, counted the riders, and stepped back outside the car and shouted loudly."Yi ot shey!"

"Must mean 'all on board'," sark said to Ford.

The door closed and Ford heard the sound of a lock being set. After another minute the vehicle lurched forward and began moving at an impressive pace.

The shell pitched forward and down, as Ford's stomach lurched up into his chest. The car plummeted, came right and level, then down again. It passed into a treeline, came right and then leveled out.

He looked out the window and the scenery blurred together; a turn to the left, a rise upward, and then a turn to the right. All the while he remained affixed in his seat.

The vehicle slowly stopped and the doors opened. Another man looked in; his black beard trimmed neatly to a point. He shouted loudly.

"Dolche!"

Ford looked over at Sark. "I take it that means disembark?"

Sean looked around. "Are we there?"

"Ah, hill speakers," the man with the beard said, as Ford's party stepped out of the car and onto the platform.

"Viroteleius is small but has a wonderful charm. I'm sure you'll enjoy your stay."

Ford followed the man along an arched hall lined in white and blue porciline tiles to a set of stairs going up.

"Just go up the stairs and you'll be bathed in the heavenly warmth of Viroteleius," the man added.

Once outside Ford saw a typical country village.

Small cottage-homes appeared along the street, as were small businesses and offices. Ford strolled out stepping over the gutter and onto the cobblestone street. A few people were coming and going, but for the most part, the town seemed deserted.

"Lovely cottages," Han said.

Harigan walked up alongside Ford.

"Some stone-and-timber buildings and a small stucco temple." He looked disappointed. "It's not a city, it's not a town, It's a village."

Ford approached one of the shops that had an open door. Looking in, he saw an elf kneading a large lump of white dough.

The smell of yeast and baking bread filled the air, and Ford's mind raced to a time when he sat outside the Brindlewood Café in Moore eating fresh baked hard-bread, slathered in butter.

The proprietor looked up expectantly and stopped his work.

"Seli de finde?"

"We're not from around here," Ford explained.

The proprietor smiled. "Ah, you are commoners from the hills." He wiped his hands on his apron. "I said, not at the festival eh?"

"Actually, my companions and I just came from there," Ford began. "I'm in search of an outfitter. Do you know where I might find one here in town?"

"Going back to the hills so soon? Well, no mind; all you have to do is go down Main Street, near the glide-coach station. The shop is called *All Things*," he said, gesturing toward the street and to his right.

Wiping the flour off his face with the back of his hand, he smiled again.

"Hope that helps."

"Much appreciated," Ford said.

Turning back to the party, Ford pointed down the road. "Somewhere down there."

They walked down the street a few short blocks until Ford spotted a blue spade shaped sign that identified the street as Straus Min, and below it *Main Street*.

Not far from the sign was a wooden shingle hanging in front of a small timber and stucco building that read, Yungs Comp/*All Things*. He approached and opened the door.

"We speak hill," he said loudly.

Immediately a dark haired gnome in a purple shirt and blue trousers rushed over and stopped just in front of him.

"Can I be of service?" he asked while adjusting his small wire-frame glasses on his tiny beak-like nose.

"I'm in need of some camping supplies. Can you provide such?" Ford asked.

"Can I provide such?" The gnome seemed offended. "It is the nature of my business. Did you not see the sign outside?"

"Then would you be so kind as to see if you have a tent, some travel pots and pans, rations, and bedrolls?"

"Of course I have such on hand. Would you be requiring lamps as well?" the gnome inquired.

"Yes, that would be handy."

"Very good."

The gnome clapped his hands, and from the back came two dwarves with the exact supplies as Ford requested.

"Would you require changes of clothes too?" he asked reaching up and pulling on Ford's vest. "Seems a bit worn and threadbear. Let me make you and your friends some fine garments of spider silk and wool."

"How long will it take?" Sean asked.

"Not long. I have a very smart spider; he weaves very quickly and precisely."

The gnome took off his glasses and cleaned them on his shirt.

Looking at his team Ford realized the truth of what the gnome said. They did look shabby now, and no wonder after being in tunnels, tombs, drowned in the ocean and pulled through a portal.

"Very well. Will this cover all our expenses?" He handed the little fellow two gold coins.

"Let me weigh it, since this is not a coin of the island. But, gold is gold," he happily said, and took the coin to a set of scales. "You'll get a silver havoy back."

"That's fine," Ford said.

"If you don't already know, there is very good camping at the ruins. All you have to do is take the coach to the ancient port of Neonbo. Stay wide of the Count's castle. The new resident has been known to be disagreeable."

"New resident?" Hugh asked.

"Some fellow from a remote continent."

The gnome held up a slate-like tablet and fitted in some gems into the frame. A flash happened, and the little fellow smiled.

"That will do nicely. I have all your measurements. Now if you just give me your names I'll have all your clothes finished in short order."

"That was simple," Han said.

The gnome laughed. "You don't know the half of it! In the meantime you may want to freshen up. Are you staying at the hostel two doors down?"

"No. We're just passing through, to the ruins," Ford said.

"Oh, then you may want to take in a cup of ale or wine. The tavern is next to the hostel; they have a bath for travelers there too. Also, the next coach going to the ruins departs in fifty five minutes. I'll have the clothes and your supplies brought to you."

"Thank you. You'd better have the clothes brought to the glide-rail station," Ford said, as he turned and headed back out the door.

"Well, at least we won't stink anymore," Sean quipped.

"If we have less than an hour, we'd better get to that coach."

"Yes, good thinking," Ford said, and turned back to the gnome. "Pardon me again, but which way to the coach that goes to the ruins?"

"When you leave my shop, turn left. About two blocks you will see a set of stairs going down with a sign. That leg of the coach-line they built in one of the old cliff caves. It was the place with enough energy to power the car."

"Thank you again."

"Make sure you mention *All Things* to your friends and family," the gnome shouted after them.

Turning left out of the shop, Ford walked briskly down to the coach access. Indeed, there were a set of stairs descending into a tunnel.

The stairs were white stone, but the walls of the tunnel were made of copper with sculpted beams of brass. Every few feet a light stone hung down from the roof providing ample luminance.

A black iron sign with gold letters directed them toward the glide-coach platform. As he stepped off the stairs, he was amazed at the structure. In fact, it was less like a cave and more like a modern market.

"Are those shops?" Sean asked pointing at the spaces where there was a window and door carved into the rock.

Walking over and peeking inside, Sark nodded his head.

"They are, but they're all closed."

"Come on, let's see about this coach," Ford said and walked down the platform. "Looks like we're in for a wait."

"Be patient, Ford," Sark told him. "Perhaps we should play a game of guess the poem."

"I don't think so," Ford replied.

"I'm glad we don't have to pay for the ride," Hugh said.

"Now what?" Sean looked bored. "Should we go to that tavern the gnome talked about?"

Shrugging his shoulders, Ford pointed at a set of benches.

"We wait."

The air swooshed around them as the coach rode up to the platform and gently came to a halt. Ford stood up from the bench and approached the car. The doors opened and no one got out; it was empty.

"Everyone is probably still at the festival," Sark suggested.

"Sir!" called a voice from down the platform.

The two dwarves from the gnome's shop had arrived carrying a box of clothes, the tent and a sack of goods.

"I'm glad we caught you. Here are your items," one dwarf with a black beard said. He looked around. "But I fear there are no places to dress here."

"We'll dress in the coach," Ford suggested.

Both dwarves laughed. "That is one crazy thing to do," the black-bearded one said.

"It will be the least crazy thing we've done all day," Ford countered.

"Enjoy your trip," the other dwarf said, as they both turned and walked back down the platform.

"Don't let the Count bite you."

They both laughed again.

An elf in a uniform appeared down the platform and walked along the coach cars. He stopped and peeked inside each one until he saw Ford and his party.

"Chechen come vue se ye hong lot," he said.

"We speak hill," Sark stated.

"Pardon," the elf said. "I said, a very light load today to the ruins it seems." He looked at a small pocket clock. "We embark in ten minutes. Make yourselves comfortable."

Each of them got on board and found a seat.

"Let's have a look at these clothes," Ford said dipping into the box.

Pulling out a package marked *Ford*, he tore open the brown paper wrapping.

"He does good work," he said holding up a red shirt.

"Let me look at that," Sark said as he fished out a round piece of glass from his pack. "I'll be…"

Sark looked on with an expression of amazement.

"It's made of magic silk."

He quickly found the package with his name on it and tore it open.

Each member of the party did the same and soon they were all marveling at the craftsmanship and quality of the clothes.

"While this is all well and good, I mean nice quality, what good are clothes made of magic silk?" Sean asked.

Sark laughed. "You must be kidding me!" He shook his head. "Magic silk provides lasting wear, it's much stronger than regular silk, and when woven right, is impenetrable by bladed weapons."

"Oh, is that all?" Sean asked.

"Actually, no. You can also imbue it with properties. If this shirt is empty of a magic imprint, I can theoretically load it with a spell. Something juicy, I think, like an electrical discharge if someone touches me."

"How would you do it?" Han inquired.

"Well, I mean it would take some thinking of course… but the possibilities are boundless!" Sark was almost as giddy as a child.

"All on board," shouted the elf outside the coach.

A moment later the doors closed and the car moved forward then dipped down at almost a ninety degree angle. They rushed down a high cliff toward jagged rocks, leveled out and made an angled turn toward the setting sun.

The coach quickly plunged into a dark green mangrove, and Ford felt uneasy. He imagined the device breaking free from the rail and plummeting down a cliff, or flying into the forest where the four armed creatures would have their way with his broken body.

Harigan slapped him on the back and smiled.

"You don't have to worry. The fall would most likely kill you before the horrible monsters laid hands on you." He laughed.

How did he know? Ford thought.

Harigan laughed louder, and moved to another chair. The car emerged from the forest and ran along the broken coast line for some time, then passed over a smooth, level beach. It slowed and came to a stop.

The door came open, and a large muscular goblin looked in.

"Dolche!" he called.

Looking around as he exited the car, Ford saw the golden sands, the red setting sun, and the forest that hemmed in the beach.

"Do you smell that?" Sean asked. "The smell of the sea is in the air."

"Do you by chance know where the ruins are?" Ford asked the goblin.

He looked thoughtful and put his scaly green finger to his chin. His yellow eyes were transfixed on the sky for a moment, as he produced what Ford thought was a smile.

"Yer from the hills? No matter. Of course I know. I work here for the park."

He pointed at a patch on his uniform.

"It's in that direction down the path three hundred yards. Once you leave the trees and enter the beach you'll see the ancient port of Neonbo," he said.

"Be careful. Blood fish are out this time of year, so don't go swimming in the surf without bathing trunks." He chuckled. "If you know what I mean…"

"Did you say the park?" Sark asked.

"Aye, my little friend. The Preserve and Parks Society, also called the PP and S," he said while eyeing them.

"You're not from the hills are you?" He looked at them in what seemed some curiosity.

"No," Ford interjected. "We're touring the island."

"From Deerback, or maybe the continent of Ver? I mean, you speak hill very well, but it's not the right dialect."

"Ford, we should be going," Sark interupted.

"Please excuse us; we're in a bit of a hurry."

"On vacation and in a hurry?" The goblin again grinned.

"You wouldn't happen to have heard of a chap named Raven Hill, would you?" Ford asked.

"Raven Hill? He's a guest of the Count. He visits this island from time to time. Comes here to pick up mage components from what I hear. Not very liked around these parts; barking orders, issuing commands. You know, like he owns the place. If you take this path here you'll come to Tower Shore. From there you can see the Count's island and castle where Raven Hill stays."

He gestured toward the walkway.

"Thank you for that bit of information," Ford said, as they took to the path.

He led the way through the forest along a wooden boardwalk. The sound of the sea grew louder as did the briny scent.

Large green and yellow leafy plants grew in every conceivable place, and the trees were ladened with the yellow liquor fruit. Much of the foliage seemed tightly intermixed.

Vines entwined in trees that were covered with moss and ferns, and large broad leafed plants all lined the trail. Turning a corner, Ford came to a stop near an outcropping of large black boulders. The trail ended.

Climbing over the boulders, he circled around some rocks and towards the sound of surf and the sea breeze. He pushed his way through a large leafy bush, and a dozen gigantic black rabbits, the size of horses, bolted.

For a moment he was shocked, not knowing what to say or if to tell his companions. The huge creatures hopped this way and that.

"Gigantic rabbits," he casually said over his shoulder.

"I'm sorry," Sark said, as he came through the plant.

"Gigantic rabbits, loping and hopping about. I mean they're really large," Ford said.

"Really?"

Sark fell into deep thought.

"Are you sure?"

"Quite!"

"Interesting," Sark added. "There's a legend from the Lake Elves that says, 'In boats they ventured long and hard, over rivers and through bogs; into the blue they traveled so, upon the new land they met dragons gold. On island green of leaf, where fruit steals mind like thief; rabbits large loom in dark, to ride these creatures kept for stock'."

He paused.

"'They sailed long night and day, toward the sun and then away; only one returned to tell the say, what was lost and what was saved.'"

"Nice," Ford complemented him.

"What does it mean?" Han asked.

Sean chuckled. "Nothing, it's a children's rhyme. We all had to learn it in school. I think it had something to do with lost expeditions long ago."

"Perhaps more than just children's rhymes," Sark hypothesized.

"Come on," Ford said.

Moving forward, he made his way down to a clearing near a stream, and dropped his backpack to the ground.

"I can feel raw power pulsing in the air," Sark said surprised.

Sean stopped in his tracks.

"Look at that."

A tall tower was visible as if behind frosted glass.

"And that," Ford said pointing toward the ocean and a distant island. "The Count's castle."

Sark took out his spyglass and extended it.

"It must be the castle of the Count. I can see a damaged ship moored by a set of docks.

Sark approached the tower.

"It seems that it stretches up into the sky to infinity," he said.

"Leave off the tower. The real question is how do we get over to the castle?" asked Ford.

Sean approached Sark.

"The tower doesn't appear to have any doors or windows."

"I'm afraid it's making me feel ill," Hugh said.

"Admiring the necromancer's tower?" an old man said, as he slowly walked along the brook just down the treeline.

"I'm Ford, and these are my friends. We're from the hills."

"I heard you speaking the hill talk, but yer not friends, nor are you from the hills." He smiled a broad grin. "What ye doing here is of no business of mine. I've fished these waters for nigh on eighty years, and met a many a strange fellow on this beach."

He smiled at them, bent down and filled a wine skin in the brook.

"So, yer from the continent and on tour I take it. Most folks think that because you speak hill talk yer from the hills." He chuckled and stood up. "Enjoy your holiday." He turned to leave.

"Wait!" Ford approached him. "You said you're a fisherman?"

"Yup, been doing it since I was a boy with my father."

"Could you take me and my... associates over to the island?"

The old man scoffed. "Count Dulopolis does not take kindly to trespassers."

Ford reached into his pouch and produced five gold coins.

"Not even for this?" He held it out.

"Gold does motivate," the man said. "Very well, be down at the beach in an hour. But remember… even though the Count throws a ball once a year, that doesn't mean he likes uninvited guests to show up. He likes his privacy and would care of it if you were to be found out."

"What's your name?" Ford asked.

"Yull Hargrove, captain of the fishing vessel the *Semidry*."

"Semidry?" Sean chuckled.

"Aye, because the deck is always wet from work."

Yull fostered a wry grin, turned and walked back down the brook.

"I'm quite delighted," Sark said, staring at the tower.

Ford looked over at him.

"Why are you delighted?"

"Do you know what this tower is?" Sark asked, with a dreamy lilt in his voice.

"The necromancer's tower?"

"This is a sarum para farum," he said with what sounded like almost a boyish giggle.

"And that is important why?"

"A sarum para farum is a leftover relic from the age of Tohm. The age before people; when the vale between our universe and the next had fractures in it. This is one of the gateways between."

"I did some research concerning this many years ago, and concluded that all the gates were somewhere at the bottom of the seas. But now I see I was wrong. I must make a record of this"

He dug into his pack and pulled out a large blue gem attached to a silver necklace. Putting it on, he nodded his head,

"There, now I can make an image of this and study this all later."

"So, how does one get in a sarum para farum?" Sean asked.

"By using a vin key," Sark said.

Ford looked at the other members of the party. They were looking back at him. He shrugged his shoulders.

"What's that?"

Sark dug into his pack and pulled out what looked like a gold ring on a chain.

"I happen to have one right here. To get access, one must utter in the Tohmish language the access phrase. Unfortunately, no one knows what Tohmish sounds like," Sark said with a frown.

The forest burst forth and a massive black rabbit emerged.

"You've all bitten at my heels to oblivion, and I have had enough," shouted Raven Hill from atop the beast.

He swung a flaming sword and narrowly missed Sean.

"You'll not ruin my plans!

Ford leapt to his feet just as the rabbit trampled him and knocked him into the water. Raven Hill, his sword slashing left and right rode roughshod over the top of the party.

The rabbit lashed out with its hind feet knocking Harigan and Han to the ground. Sean was mowed down by the monster.

Hugh's sword was in his hand and he smashed into the side of the beast, but the rabbit was immovable as it knocked him to the ground and hopped with some contempt towards the tower.

Raven Hill lifted his head and in a strange baritone melody called out. A flash of lightning erupted and a hole appeared in the distortion around the tower. The rabbit made straight for the hole.

Sark, unfazed by all the commotion planted his feet wide and extended his hand as if grabbing something in the air. He called some words and was dragged in the sand for a few feet.

Raven Hill's hand was pulled back; he screamed in pain nearly falling from his rabbit. It was clear that the man was enraged, and he screamed a litany of curses.

The rabbit and Raven Hill vanished into the darkness of the tower and were gone as the distortion reformed.

"There," Sark said loudly as he walked towards the tower, reached up and plucked the bloody finger and vin key from the air.

"Now, we have his key."

Ford climbed up onto the sandy bank of the creek. His face betrayed his shock at Raven Hill's appearance.

"That was unexpected," Harigan laughed. "A gigantic bunny. What next, a hoard of armored fairies?"

Sark pulled the finger from the key.

"He's not going to forgive me for this."

"Not much good it will do us, we couldn't repeat those words, and we don't know how he triggered it," Ford said solemnly.

"Give me a few hours and I'll have both answers for you," Sark said, as he pointed at the crystal hanging from his neck.

"I got this on an expedition to the ruins of the elf city of Gorn many a year ago. The crystal makes visual and audio records. Don't worry; it is highly unlikely that Raven Hill will get out of there without his key."

CHAPTER

24

Friends in High Places

Sean came up from the beach along the path. He carried a stringer filled with fish.

"The blood fish are out in force tonight," he said. "I'm lucky to have gotten these all intact."

Stopping at the fire, he sat down and laid the fish on a hot stone to bake.

The sound of the jungle intensified as the hour ticked by, and Harigan offered him some food from his magic dish.

"You'll get parasites from eating those. Here, have a nice cut of meat," he offered.

"I didn't spend an hour fishing to just eat off your magic plate," Sean told Harigan.

The smell of roasting fish filled the air. Sean reached and flipped a few before they could burn.

"They should be ready to eat in just a moment."

Sark approached from down the creek.

"What news?" Ford asked while taking a fish from the stone. He took a mouthful of flesh from the bony creature.

"Good news and bad news." Sark gave a wily grin.

Ford looked annoyed. "Get on with it."

"I need more time to master the words. The good news is that Yull is down by the beach with a rowboat."

"An ally is waiting for the light bringer," Harigan said.

"Light bringer?" Ford asked.

"Why must you question?" Harigan looked over at Ford.

"It's important that you understand that we will take the boat to the castle, but Raven Hill is not whom we seek there."

"What are you talking about?" Ford questioned.

Harigan was silent, stood and began walking down to the beach.

"Let's try the castle then," Ford said, as he followed Harigan.

Once on the beach, they climbed into Yull's dingy, pushed off into the surf, and rowed out to the sailor's fishing boat. Onboard, they quickly put Sean in a bucket and into a tub of water.

The island was not far; two miles at most. The waves were large, and both Sean and Yull mentioned that the two moons were getting close to an eclipse period. On that day, the seas would become very turbulent.

The Semidry plowed the waves as curious sea beasts looked on. Sean's feet rested in the bucket. He looked up to see two sea harpies fly overhead.

"Probably looking for a handout," Yull said, as he took a fish by the tail and threw it high into the air.

One of the creatures swooped and caught it with its talons. The other followed as the creatures flew back toward the castle.

"They're vagabonds really," Yull remarked, as he spun the wheel and the ship sailed toward a high cliff with a wide cavern below. "I'll put ye a shore here. No windows or battlements on this side… I suppose ye'll want me to pick ye up here too?"

"Aye," Ford affirmed.

"I'll be back here at daybreak. If you're not here by seven bells, I'll head back to port on Bri Zeel. The sun will be growing dark, and woe be it to any ship on the seas for that three hours."

"Understood," Ford said.

They put ashore and Yull rowed back to his boat. He weighed anchor and sailed back toward Bri Zeel.

In the sky, four harpies followed the ship into the darkness. Slowly, Ford and his party made their way up the jagged rocks and into the gaping mouth of the cavern. The stench of rotted seaweed and stagnant sea water was strong.

"Unpleasant," Harigan said.

"Smells like death," Han added.

The waves crashed against the broken cliff walls behind them making a sound like thunder. The noise passed them, reverberated from the back of the cave and back past them.

Harigan raised his cudgel and a golden light emitted from it. Broken island rock lay strewn about mixed with piles of rotted seaweed and animal bones.

"The light," a voice in the darkness said. "The light… can it be the light bringer as foretold in the prophesy? Bring it forth."

They all froze. Harigan waited for a moment, then maneuvered past Ford. Thirty paces ahead, the light illuminated a creature. The thing was taller than twenty feet, six arms, and a head like an octopus.

Its yellow eyes looked down on them as it came forward. The sounds of chain rattled behind it, and it came to a stop.

"The light – I have craved a moment in the light," it said. "Now you come. Bring it forth, and with your company. It has been a hundred years if a day that I've had company. Tell me of the world outside."

Harigan approached the thing and examined it closely. He then examined the chains and how they were anchored to the cavern wall.

"What name do you go by, creature?" he asked.

"When I was young the Thomlins called me Tequatill."

Sean came up the path.

"What happened to you?"

"Imprisoned here for helping the Thoms defeat the Incubites. I was betrayed and chained here. I could not communicate with the Thoms any longer, and so I've languished here for thousands of years.

"But, as the chains were secured to me, the Incubite smith told me of a vision; a creature will one day bring the light, and salvation. I would then aid him in a quest to restore the universe to it's axis."

"You said we're the first company you've had in a hundred years?"

Sark came forward too.

Tequatill sat back on a flat stone.

"A dark creature came to me a hundred years ago. He was a necromancer who became a vampire. He brought light to me, and in return I imbued his skin with magic that would allow him to be outside in the sun.

"He tried to free me, but the chains are anti-metal, forged here in this cave by the Incubites. They cursed the stone and I was trapped." Tequatill stood again. "Oh, but for this moment of light I relish."

Harigan handed the creature his cudgel. "Keep it with you until we meet again."

"Again?" Tequatill held the light up high, and the cavern was completely illuminated.

"Yes, you will use my cudgel to free yourself, then bring it to me," Harigan said.

The massive chains disintegrated into dust. Tequatill flexed his fists, and stood to his full height, towering over the party.

"I see now who you are, and where you are going. When Gorg commands me, I shall come."

His tentacles waved about and a small ball of energy formed. He handed it to Harigan, who quickly tucked it into his shirt. "Keep it well, and close at hand, for I am connected to it, and like an egg, it shall spawn me forth when needed."

Hugh approached. "How is it that you speak our language?"

The creature made a sound that Hugh thought was a chuckle. "Your minds. I examined them and know all that was contained within," he said.

"Then you know Raven Hill's mind too?" Ford asked.

"Yes."

Sark cleared his throat. "What of the lantern?"

"He has it now in his workshop."

"We need to go," Ford said.

"The creature who calls himself Raven Hill can be found in the tall tower. His mind is full of malice and hatred. He seeks to enslave all peoples and become immortal."

"He hopes the Count will provide him the elixir of vampirius, and give him an army to rule your kind until you rot," Tequatill said. "But he does not understand what it is he has."

Harigan harrumphed once and began glowing. He walked up the path bathed in the golden light. Ford followed as did the others.

At the top of the stairs a round slab of stone lay on the ground. Cryptic markings, carved into it, began to glow. Harigan raised his hands, mumbled some words and climbed up on the disk.

"Come, you mortals, know the magic of old," he commanded.

"Bless my soul," Sark said. "That's Root-magic."

"Root-magic?" Sean asked.

"Yes, the basis of all power manipulation, the really old stuff."

"Is that good?"

Sark shook his head. "In the world, there are only two other objects known that pulse with such energy. It's at the base root of chaos magic. This is demigod stuff."

Ford climbed up. "Come on. Harigan may be mad, but he's given me much reason to trust him."

The others followed. All of them stood in the middle of the disk.

"I feel strange," Sark said.

"Me too," Sean agreed.

A swirling light engulfed them. Ford grabbed out and latched onto Harigan's arm. For a moment he felt like he was tumbling head over heels.

He was in a great white hall, and many strange-looking creatures stared back at him. Again he felt as if he was tumbling. He opened his mouth to say something; monstrous slug-like things reached out of the light and slathered him with slimy mucus.

As he spit out the gooey slime, a terrible and loud sound vibrated his very core. The light flashed, and he was standing on red, dusty aggregate.

Ford cleared his throat. "I think we're not in the cave anymore," he said and pointed at a tower, that seemingly stretched into infinity. "That's the tallest tower I've ever seen," he added.

"Where do you think we are?" Sean asked.

"Look in the distance, beyond the haze," Harigan said getting to his feet. "Mountains and an iridescent red glow."

"This place resembles the fabled Netherworld," Han said. "It's well described in several tomes for the dead."

"We're somehow inside the field of the tower," Sark added, while he pointed back at a shimmering image of green forests and sandy dunes.

"Let's have a look at this tower," Ford stated.

As he got closer he saw it was made of some form of metal, riveted into place and overlapping like dragon scales. At the base was the only opening, a tall door.

The door was large, but not massive, appearing to be made of wood and riveted iron straps. Patterns were inlayed in the surface and each glowed softly, pulsing from the bottom up along the tower to the invisible top.

Sean reached for the door.

"Don't' touch it!" Sark shouted in a panic. "These things are typically booby trapped."

"Okay, what do you suggest?" Han asked, coming up next to them.

"I can test it for electric shock, heat and severe cold," Sark said, as he once again opened his satchel. "Let me have a moment."

He pulled out a brass disk and attached it to a small copper rod. Placing the rod into the ground, he took a thin wire and dropped it onto the latch. Nothing happened.

"Should we be worried?" Harigan asked.

"No. It appears not to be loaded with electricity, heat or cold." He seemed surprised as he replaced his tools.

"How do we get in?" Ford asked.

Harigan pushed, and the door swung inward. "It's open," he declared. "And I thought this was going to be hard." He laughed as he stepped through the doorway and vanished.

"This is troubling," Han said, as he put his finger to his chin. "An open door and no traps?"

"I didn't hear any screams," Sean concluded, and stepped through himself.

Ford emerged into a room that was very large and lit with sconces on the walls. The ceiling was nowhere to be seen and there was a strange smell, almost sweet like perfume.

Harigan stood in front of them, his arms crossed over his chest.

"Strange place," he declared.

Ford saw that they stood on large tiles of polished white and black marble. The chessboard pattern reflected the flickering torch light.

"I don't think I like this," Ford whispered.

"Hello," called Harigan loudly. "Guests have arrived."

Ford looked at Harigan with a withering stare. Harigan formed a dunce-like smile. Turning back, Ford nearly leapt from his skin.

Standing right in front of him was a fifteen-foot-tall ogre. The beast was muscular, large and well-dressed. In fact, the creature was wearing a fashionably tailored shirt secured at the cuffs with gold links and a black leather belt around his dark brown breeches.

White tights disappeared tucked neatly into soft leather house shoes. The scent of perfume wafted over the party.

In one hand the ogre held a large black skillet, and in the other a massive wooden spoon. He extended his face just a little as he stared down at them. Ford saw what appeared to be flour on the tip of his nose.

"Guests?" the ogre said. "Oh yes, wonderful… guests!" He danced a funny little jig. "Oh, I can't tell you how wonderful this is to have visitors.I was just making a pie and I was thinking, Gorg, you need to have some guests by for tea and pie. And now here you are."

Gorg turned and rushed away a few steps then stopped and turned back.

"You must all tell me your names and all the news you know. This will be just splendid." He clapped the spoon and the skillet together with excitement, making a gong-like sound.

He again turned and sped away past giant chairs and an equally enormous table.

"Yet, another disturbing thing since we've been on this quest," Sean said. "I nearly soiled myself."

"I would have thought he'd smash us with that large skillet," Sark added.

"And bake us into that pie he was making?" Ford asked.

Harigan shook his head.

"You mortals are all alike, see little, worry lots."

"I, for one, am glad he's friendly," Hugh said. "Not like that Raven Hill; constantly trying to kill us."

Lurching from the darkness, Gorg was again among them.

"Did you say Raven Hill?" he asked.

"Do you know of him?" Ford asked, feeling a bit unnerved.

Gorg made a dour face. "I ask because Raven Hill has been most rude these past years. Refuses to attend any of my tea parties, not even for Royal Tea! A strange chap, really. Constantly asks me about the old tools and how they work. I can't say that I like him much."

"Could you possibly tell us how you know him?" Ford asked.

"As the guest of the Count, he's come to visit me through the portal. The castle and this tower are connected." He smiled. "I met Raven Hill several years ago when I had to deliver a parcel to the Castle. It was a large box containing something that was warm." He frowned. "Raven Hill took it, and didn't even invite me in for supper. I was aghast at how rude he was."

"The tower is linked to the Count's castle?" Sark asked.

"Oh yes, a teleportal. Let me see, where is that map? It can be dangerous if you don't have one."

"Why is that?" Han asked.

"I see you aren't familiar with a teleportal hyper-tube. How do I explain? The tube is actually a bubble—"

"That can have limitless space and dimensions within it," Sark cut in.

"Yes! I see that you do know." Gorg grinned. "Excellent! Then you know why it can be dangerous if you wander without a map."

"Yes," Sark said. "One can end up anywhere and nowhere. You could starve to death a jump away from a feast, and die of thirst a jump away from a river."

"Exactly," Gorg affirmed. "I assure you, there are much worse things than that though." He laughed. "Many worse things, but there are many amazing places to visit also…. Three thousand, five hundred and seventy-one, times ten, to the power of three thousand, five hundred and seventy-one from this tower alone. But before I get you a map, you must sit down and have tea with me."

"Sure, we'd be delighted," Harigan agreed.

The cheery ogre laid out a table fit for a king. Harigan stood on a chair so he could see the food. At the end nearest him he saw pastries filled with whipped cream, giant sugared cherries, finger sandwiches the size of pillows, and a teacups, of which he could fit his head into.

Gorg came from the kitchen, a blue cooking apron around his waist. In one hand he held a steaming teapot the size of a beer keg, and in the other a large clear bowl of what appeared to be some type of milk.

"The biscuits should be done shortly," he said with a toothy grin.

"Gorg?" Sark began. "What exactly do you do here? I mean other than cook?"

"Oh, young sub-creature, I do many things. I keep the Bowlrage clean and tidy... I offer visitors my hospitality, and I oversee many of the day-to-day functions."

"The Bowlrage?" Han looked intrigued.

"Oh, sorry, Bowlrage is the name of the hyper-tube. Each level of the Bowlrage can be a separate universe or just a room, or sometimes it is both."

Sark cleared his throat. "How do we transition between these places?"

"Through the portal-doors, or as we used to call them, *gates*. If nothing else the Builders were interested in keeping things simple."

Gorg looked thoughtful.

"How did you like your walk here? It's a lovely place filled with lush gardens, enigmatic fountains, lusty red skies." Gorg waxed on with a near orgasmic expression. "And, the forest creatures such as the mischievous centaurs, the frolicking minyagatares, the playful water nymphs, and darling fluttery harpies."

He paused to pour the tea. Steam rolled up from the pot into the darkness overhead. Gorg moved from cup to cup, filling each about halfway to the top.

"We did not see any of those things, though we just walked directly to the tower," Ford stated.

"Really?"

Gorg put down the pot on a large cozy and proceeded to place a pastry, sandwich, and cherry on each plate. Next he offered cubes of sugar, and dollops of milk.

Once finished, he took up the seat at the head of the table and smiled warmly at everyone.

"Well, I've not been outside for some time."

"Gorg, how long has it been since you've been outside the Bowlrage?" Ford asked.

"Hmm... let me see." He paused for a moment and looked up towards the absent ceiling. "Well, I closed the main portal when the Thulnour Flanopolis was besieging the Vestibule of Light. That was a messy affair from what I've heard."

Ford looked around the table; everyone seemed just as confused as he.

"How long ago was this?" Ford pressed.

Gorg looked sheepish. "Well, I don't exactly know what you're asking me. The Bowlrage doesn't really cater to measurements of time. So, let's discuss something else. Let's talk of matters trivial rather than concerting." He raised his tea cup, pinky out, and sipped it gingerly.

"Why don't you start?" Sark suggested to Gorg.

"Most kind of you. Where is it that you little folk come from? Are you constructs of the Delincock? Oh, let me guess, you're products of the Filinthrop?"

"We're not familiar with any of those things …" Hugh trailed off.

"We don't know those names," Sean said.

"You don't know from where it is you come, or the property you keep? Most curious." He sipped his tea again. "Does it have purple grass?"

"No," Sark said.

"Is there a plant that floats in the air?"

"Not that I know of," Ford stated.

"Then it's not Shir'remore. Perhaps you'd like to take a look at my spatial globe? It shows all the dimensions and their adjacent matter clumps. I'll tone down the frequency so you don't get it all in one shot."

"We'd love to," Sark said excitedly.

"I'll go and warm it up. But first, tell me what the world looks like where you are from?"

Gorg sat forward and put his elbows on the table, cradling the cup in both hands.

"It's green," Sean began.

"Green?" Gorg interrupted. "Oh, that could be Hig'tight the ringed planet, or Pilsh'twin that has two suns, or Greegle'pete that has one moon, or it could be Seroland the globe of the two moons—"

"We do have two moons," Sean said. "What do you know of our world?"

Gorg broke out into a deep trembling laugh.

"Quite a lot. My kind did connect the many places of the Bowlrage."

He rose and checked each person's cup, refilling where needed.

"It was quite an effort to negotiate with the world-makers and bubble heads; gods, I think you call them. They are a stubborn breed, but similar in makeup to the Pepitaydes. The most violent we found were the Bohls. They are three monstrous world makers who rule the spatial Eliad of Granilin. They found access into the Bowlrage and began taking over other worlds. Very unreasonable and cruel, but they were subdued by a sub-creature. It's a funny story, really."

"Who subdued three gods?" Hugh asked.

"A little fellow from Seroland, your world. It was no easy feat, but a sub-creature called Golium Huld Yammer made a device that trapped them within."

"They have since been absent from the Bowlrage and all maps. I'm not sure what ever truly became of them," Gorg mused.

"Light of Smith Hammer?" Sark said.

"Yes, in your language it is that," Gorg smiled.

"Just because you've not heard from the Bohls in a while, doesn't mean they're gone." Harigan said, as he grabbed the pastry on his plate with both hands and consumed as much as he could in a single bite.

Harigan swallowed, took a drink then wiped his mouth with his sleeve.

"Surely you failed to contain Aor the great god?"

"No need to. He negotiated right away, and my kin supplied him with all that he wished. He was left to maintain his authority."

"He negotiated?" Harigan said loudly, his mouth hanging open as if in shock. "Allowed to keep his authority?"

"Yes. A very reasonable and shrewd creature. A real bubble head," Gorg assured them.

"How does each of the towers work?" Ford cut in.

"Oh, quite simple... the Bowlrage is a medium, or rather a transducer, that is composed of some complex energy fields and subatomic waves. Once activated each individual transducer creates a bubble that displaces an existence and sets up a shield or isolator wave that protects the hole from intrusion or extrusion. Time-space of one place is not intrusive on another."

He took a sip of tea. "When we made a universe or partitioned one, we realized that it was programmed with the sequence of possible combinations that allows the formation of biological components. Those things evolved into living creatures.

"Each hyper-tube is given a sequence of numbers, scribed in the coded script, and can only be activated with the right vibratory phase signature."

He stopped and looked around the table.

"Forgive me, I do prattle on."He again lifted his tea cup and sipped it.

"We eventually ran into ourselves from a completely different spatial construct who were doing the same thing that we were doing. We joined together linking the many reclusive towers. Then, our other selves decided we should all close down the connections. It was rumoured that they ran into themselves along another path, and those selves were somewhat evil"

He paused and passed around a plate filled with four large pastries. "More tea dainties?"

"We'd love to remain here with you, but we really need to find Raven Hill. He and the Count are mixed up with a plot to destroy our civilization," Ford said.

"Nonsense. The Count is a wonderful neighbor."

"I assure you that he is in league with Raven Hill," Sark assured him.

"What could be his motivation?" Gorg's eyes narrowed.

"Raven Hill is going to open the portal to the Bohls," Ford declared.

Gorg stood up. "What are you talking about?

"Raven Hill has the Light of Smith Hammer. He intends on releasing the Bohls," Ford repeated.

"That is disastrous. The Bohls will make war."

"It's possible he doesn't know what he has. Will you help us?" Ford looked desperate.

"Yes, of course," Gorg said. "Raven Hill is a bitter pill anyway." He reached into the pocket of his apron and produced what appeared to be a scroll. "I brought one of my many guides for you. If you take a wrong turn, you may end up somewhere you would prefer not to be. The map is easy to follow; you'll see a glowing golden line that will lead you to Raven Hill." He held up the immense scroll.

"That's too large for us to carry," Hugh said.

"Then I must make it smaller," Gorg said as he lifted the scroll, put it between his two hands and squeezed it down in size. Handing it to Sark, he smiled.

"This should do the trick."

Taking the scroll, Sark followed Gorg down a hallway until he came to a red door. Gorg opened it and motioned for them to go inside.

"Use the map… don't try to navigate without it. The portals are painted so you should have no trouble. Too bad you couldn't stay longer and look at the spatial globe."

Harigan motioned for Gorg to bend down. He whispered into the creature's ear, and Gorg nodded.

"It seems I will see you again," Gorg said, as he handed Harigan something. He bowed and stepped out of the room.

Ford looked around him. Doors of varying colors along the walls pulsed with light. The ceiling was absolute black, and the floor was pure white.

Sark unrolled the scroll, and a three dimensional image of the room appeared. On the page were six small blue dots. Harigan moved to one of the doors and listened.

Sark watched one blue dot move to one of the doors.

"Looks like we're the blue dots," he said. "Pretty smart document," he added. "And the thin golden line seems to mark our path."

"It's also on the floor," Ford said, pointing at the golden line leading to a green door.

He moved to the door. "Well?" Ford asked. "Shall we?"

"I'll go first," Hugh said, as he took up the position. "I'm the best protected of us all."

Hugh opened the door and looked in; only a flat sheet of darkness appeared. He stepped through the doorway, and a flash of light blinded him.

He stumbled a few feet and stopped. Lifting his visor, he looked around. He was in a room that was decorated in a *mid-age* style. The room was long, wide, with a lush and thick golden rug on the floor.

Two beautiful women were at the opposite end; one was washing the other in a sunken tub. Steam was rising from the water, and the woman within tossed her golden hair back, looked over and saw Hugh.

She screamed, and both women fled the room.

Ford, Han, Sark, Harigan, and Sean all stumbled in.

"Now where?" Sean asked.

"Follow the golden line," Sark reiterated.

A thick carpet obscured the line.

"We'll have to pull it up."

Harigan and Han grabbed onto opposite edges and heaved. It was heavy, and dust filled the air. Below it, a golden line lead to a tapestry at the opposite end of the room.

Ford pulled down the decoration and opened the door. Without hesitation, he walked through.

The smell of the sea filled Ford's nostrils as he stepped out onto a cliff overlooking a vast purple ocean. He walked across a narrow ledge to three doors embedded in the face of the cliff. Each one pulsed with energy.

"What a strange place to put these doors," Harigan said as he appeared behind Ford.

"Who knows what lurked in the minds of the builders?" Ford said.

Sark, Han, Hugh, and Sean came onto the ledge.

"Sark, what does the map say?" Ford asked.

Sark pointed at the yellow door in the cliff side. "Through there," he said.

"Aor be praised," Harigan said, as he opened the door and stepped through.

A debris-filled room came into view. Harigan immediately shoved a wooden bench and an old table to the side. Another three doors were visible.

In the corner of the room was a pile of bones. He approached and knelt down. The creature was surely not human, for the skull was far too irregular. Remnants of clothing were still visible, and at each side were strange weapons.

Sark appeared, followed by the others. Sark looked at the map and pointed at the left most door.

"The white one," he said.

Sean walked over to Harigan and looked down at the bones.

"Another of Gorg's visitor's maybe?"

"Come on, we've no time to waste," Ford chided, as he moved to the white door and pulled it open. "This way," he said as he went through.

Instantly, Ford's boots stuck to the floor. He was unable to move.

Looking around he saw an alchemist's laboratory, filled with bubbling glass beakers of colored fluids and glass tubes twisted in coils leading from one boiling liquid to another.

Ford was captivated by the strange and mysterious blue glow emitting from the walls. Willowfern stood there twenty feet away near one of the bubbling glass containers. Her eyes met with his, a surprised expression upon her lovely face.

"Willow?" Ford said.

"I didn't think you would make it here," she replied.

"Oh, good, you're here," Raven Hill said, as he came from the shadows his hand bandaged and missing a finger. "I wasn't expecting you, but prepared for your arrival anyway. You see, I know more of this tower than some would believe."

He twirled around once causing his velvet blue cape to fly about.

"Lovely, isn't it? The color I mean." He bowed and tipped his floppy blue muffin-cap. "What do you think of my ensemble? Note my regal and ruffled blue poet's shirt neatly laced to the top with a bow, my black breaches and blood red boots. An outfit fit for one on the verge of immortality."

Harigan landed next to Ford and stuck fast. As quick as lightning he lunged at Raven Hill, who took a step back.

"Please, Mister Harigan, your attempt is not becoming your station and lends itself to absurdity," Raven Hill said.

"Come a little closer, I'm a bit hard of hearing," Harigan baited.

"I'm quite fine here."

Raven Hill walked to one of his experiment tables and picked up what looked like a long metal box.

"Here it is, and as close to the prize as you'll get, Ford."

Sean and Han landed on the floor. They, too, were stuck and unable to move.

"Good… more the merrier says I." Raven Hill laughed.

Hugh landed with a thud. He attempted to move but found he could not.

"What happened?" he asked, as he pulled at his feet.

"What indeed?" Raven Hill mocked. "You are nearly at the end of your quest, and I might add lives also."

He moved from the table towards them. "You see this?" He held up the box.

"It's a box," Sean said angrily, as he pulled at his legs.

"Mister Efferguard knows what this is," Raven said with a smirk.

"It's the Lantern of Dern Blackhammer." Ford sighed.

"That?" Sean cried out. "What a disappointment."

"Disappointment?" Raven Hill was incredulous. "You stand here in the shadow of the greatest relic in our world and you're disappointed? Ford, why do you surround yourself with such fools?"

He set the box down on the table.

"I'm about to open the case and break the matrix. I will drink in the energy and soon, all shall call me god!"

He unlatched the box and lifted the cover off. "You all will bear witness to my glory and my power."

"You'll unleash the trapped gods," Ford cautioned.

"Once I break the matrix I shall be bathed in the chaos light, made unto a god and the master of all!"

"I'm afraid that is not what the lantern does," Ford said.

"Willowfern told me you were a clever one. You're not impressing me at the moment, though," Raven scoffed. "You are just stalling, and it'll do you no good. All of you are dead, as sure as I am standing here."

Willowfern said nothing. She looked on with no outward delight. She approached Raven Hill and spoke in his ear.

He looked bemused and turned to her.

"Are you mad? They must all perish! Don't overstep your place, my darling." He focused again on Ford. "Once my transformation is complete, you will want to prepare to cross over to the land of the dead."

He retrieved the lantern.

Willowfern turned with a dagger in her hand, took two steps, and struck at Raven Hill. The man moved like a coiled snake. He sidestepped and struck back, driving a jeweled dagger into Willowfern's heart.

She fell, her head looking toward Ford. Her once vibrant eyes gray with death. Ford instinctively reached toward her, but in his mind her voice rang out clear and bold.

"Waste not this time I've given you!"

Sark landed on top of Harigan, rolled over onto Sean, then onto Hugh, and fell to the side of the party. He stood up to see the surprised eyes of Raven Hill fall upon him.

Sark raised his hands and pointed. The lantern case blazed orange, blasting off a heat wave that singed the hair of all in the room.

Raven Hill screamed, dropped the lantern to the floor, and rolled around on the ground to put out his flaming clothes. Smoke filled the air.

Falling on its side, the case popped off and the lantern emitted an eerie silver glow like moonlight. Raven Hill got to his feet, his face a mask of fury.

Hugh thres something at Raven Hill.

Raven Hill's hands and ankles became shackled with orange light. He looked on the men with malice and mortal rage.

"And, a Justice Knight thinks his ancient tricks will keep such as me in bondage?"

The mage closed his eyes and the shackle-light grew with intensity until it blinded all in the room with a flash.

"Kill him," Ford shouted at Sark.

Sight returned to the party. A wand was in Raven's hand and the tip was glowing red. Sark stepped forward feeling the power surging through him, as he imagined the atoms forming into a weapon of energy.

A sound of drums echoed, and Sark saw his magical energy sucked into the lantern.

Raven Hill's eyes were filled with murder.

"I'm afraid the time of your death has come," he said, as he moved the wand about his head.

Raven Hill grinned malevolently. "I consign you to burn to ash!"

Suddenly, Raven Hill sneezed, and sneezed again. His hand shook, and he doubled over sneezing without a pause.

"What just happened?" Han asked.

Ford pulled off his boots and jumped over the sticky floor.

"A child's trick brings down the great Raven Hill," he taunted and rushed toward Raven Hill.

"You, sir, stole my father's life!" Ford landed a right-cross, sending Raven back a step. "And now you murdered Willow!" He slugged him in the gut causing Raven to double up. "I'll have you atone for it all!"

Raven Hill stopped sneezing. His eyes were bulging with rage; his nose was streaming bloody viscous goo.

"You'll not be the one to undo me," he said, blocking Ford's next blow and darting to the lantern. He picked it up. "Let the heaven's crack wide."

He pulled the lens cap off and the room filled with a red light. A foul stench filled the air. From the lantern came a crackling of static power.

Sark fell to his knees. All the party groaned in pain. The lantern fell to the floor and bounced once, landing face up. A beam of energy hit the roof, and a black hole appeared and began expanding.

Raven Hill dropped his wand and looked horrified. It appeared as if he was encased in a cloudburst; drops that hit him caused him to slowly dissolve.

"It is time," Harigan casually said.

Gorg appeared from a corner of the room. "You, follower of Aor, release the orb-of-travel as I call upon the Lost One!"

Harigan pulled forth the orb and Gord said loudly, "Tequatill."

The orb grew in size and intensity.

Tequatill appeared and placed one hand on Sark and pointed Harigan's cudgel at the lantern. Sark shook violently.

Magic flowed from Tequatill in bright orange streams of power.

Gorg began pressing lighted stones along the walls in rhythmic patterns.

Ford watched as the room bent and his vision darkened. Several creatures slithered by, then wrapped around him. Multiple eyes gazed from the darkness, and he cried out in pain.

His arms and legs were being pulled from their sockets as were his eyes. Fire licked his skin and the stench of burnt hair made his stomach lurch. He blacked out.

"Ford?"

Ford's eyes came open and he realized that he was looking at Gorg's face.

"What happened?"

"You took a nap, I think," Gorg said.

"Where's the rest of the party?"

"Mostly awake also. You little people are susceptible to sleep it seems." Gorg helped Ford to his feet. "They're over there by the expired one." He pointed at Willow's body.

Sark was standing and talking with Harigan. Sean lay on the floor and struggled to sit up. Han and Hugh were sitting, but silent.

"Ah, Ford, it's good that you're conscious," Sark said, as he walked over to him with the shielded lantern. "I'm still not sure what happened, but I think between Harigan's heavenly contact, my channeling of chaos magic through Tequatill, and Gorg's help we seemed to have sealed the breach in the matrix."

"Sealed it?"

Sark put the lantern onto one of Raven Hill's chemistry tables.

"Yes, I think that Gorg did something special, but I'm not sure what that was,"

Gorg laughed.

"Yes, of course I did. I used the power of the Bowlrage to rebuild the chaos matrix. We were lucky that Raven Hill did not destroy it completely."

"How so?" Sean said getting to his feet.

"Well, if the matrix were to have collapsed, in a matter of hours this world would have been pulled into a singularity and torn to shreds." He smiled. "Not to mention that the Bohls would have become free to build another universe in their image. Glad that didn't happen."

"Where's Raven Hill?" Ford looked around.

"Gone, into the matrix of the crystal. He's lost." Gorg patted the lantern. "He'll not bother anyone anymore."

"Where's Tequatill?" Ford didn't see him.

Sark shrugged his shoulders. "Gone too."

Han got up. "What now?"

"I suggest that we have brunch," Gorg replied.

*   *   *

Raven Hill's vision slowly came back to him. His eyes were nearly blinded by the light, but now, aside from a few green circles in his vision, he could see.

Taking a step, he heard the crunch of gravel under his boot heel. He was on a road, paved with white gravel that stretched for miles along a lush, well-manicured countryside of rolling green hills.

Looking up he saw the drab overcast of a gray cloudy day. The air was moist and he began walking, more out of curiosity than inclination.

Looking back, he saw the place where he'd arrived; two boot prints in white gravel, none trailing, as if he just jumped from the sky and landed there.

"Teleported? That damned Sark is more powerful than I thought," he said. "Where did he send me? Perhaps the hills of the Midlands?"

He walked for what seemed like an hour. The countryside was clean, lacking both fauna and fences. The smell in the air was crisp and fresh, and he began feeling strong and highly aware of a strange energy that seemed to flow around him.

Ahead he saw a large hill rising up. The path forked at the base, one leading around the hill, the other up to some unseen destination.

Get to higher ground and have a look at the surrounding area, he thought.

At the base he drew in a deep breath and began the climb. Up he went following the switchback trail.

In the distance he heard a faint sound, like that of a black smith driving his hammer atop an anvil. The sound grew as he came closer to the crest.

Rounding the top, he saw a massive tree, like that of the oldest of oaks. Its girth was such that a hundred men could not have encircled it. A large creature working a red glowing forge near its thick gray bows did not look up.

Looks like an overripe troll, he thought.

Its muscular arms drove the hammer against the anvil cracking the air with each impact. In the creature's other hand he held pincers, that in turn held a brightly glowing red hot billet.

The metal was placed on the anvil. The hammer fell in a rhythmic fashion, and a final product emerged from the sparks.

A large nail? Raven Hill thought. *For what purpose?*

The beast doused the nail in a barrel of water; steam filled the air. This was repeated over and over again as Raven Hill watched intently.

Rain began falling in heavy droplets smashing into the leaves of the tree and making a slapping sound. Raven Hill began to inch his way forward towards the beast.

In his mind he was rehearsing a caustic spell that would unleash a cellular disrupting blast. He envisioned in his mind the necessary atoms and particles. If the creature wished to be unreasonable, he was ready to use deadly force.

Within twenty feet he stopped, and the creature halted its forging. The creature's back was broad like a granite wall. The hammer was held aloft over the red-hot iron as if frozen in time.

"You, what is this place?" Raven asked, ready to unleash his spell at the slightest provocation.

The creature made no sound or movement.

"Didn't you hear me?" he chided. "I'm talking to you!" His anger was growing.

The creature again slammed the hammer on the iron, quickly shaped it into a long black nail, doused it in the bucket of water, and threw it onto a pile of nails.

Raven Hill's ire was up. The creature was most rude.

Perhaps it's a pet, he thought.

With unimagined speed, the creature moved and seized Raven Hill by the arms lifting him from the ground. With lightning swiftness, he was forced against the tree, and with four strokes of the hammer secured there with four of the long black nails.

He was dazed by what happened. Screams of someone in the distance came to his ears, as if all the tortures of the damned were being vocalized. After a moment, he realized it was he who screamed.

Unable to concentrate for the pain, he writhed against his nailed arms and legs. The wounds felt like fire burning his limbs until he was awash with the savage agony; the un-sated savage pain.

Several gray creatures slithered around him, as a mirthful and mocking laughter echoed in his head. Beyond the laughter, somehow he heard the rhythmic clanking of a hammer… somewhere in the bleak darkness of his broken mind.

CHAPTER

25

All and Moore

Goldworm stood at the base of a long set of marble stairs. At the top was an elf dressed in black wool trousers, a red waist coat, and green silk shirt.

Ford stood next to Goldworm, his thumbs tucked neatly into the blood-red sash that was tied around his midsection. He was just beginning to wonder if his choice of a long-coat was too gaudy when a trumpet blared and the man at the top of the stairs came slowly down.

"Steward of Moore Mister Pol Underborn," shouted a baritone voice hidden by the top of the stairs. The Steward stopped just in front of the assembled party and looked at all.

"You who are all assembled, give your undivided attention to the Steward of Moore," the disembodied voice called. "Keeper of the peace, head administrator, and lord of the artists!"

Goldworm held up the box containing the lantern.

"It's safe with us now!" he said.

"We thought you were gone for good!" the Steward said to Ford. "A half year you've been gone. But, we are pleased that you're not dead."

"Your Gace," Ford said, bowing slightly.

The Steward waved over a young Paige and pointed at the lantern.

"Take that and turn it over to the dragons. They'll know what to do with it."

The Paige looked concerned. "Dragons?"

A withering look from the Steward sent the boy running with the lantern tucked under his arm. A complement of two Black Guards followed him.

The steward turned to Ford and Goldworm.

"Let us all pay homage to the Brood, and particularly Ford Efferguard. He has again come through for the city of Moore."

Ford looked over at the two dozen members of parliament, and city officials standing just a few feet away. Some clapped, others smiled, and a few did nothing at all. He heard a few voices saying such things as, "commendable work," or, "well done."

The Steward brushed the front of his coat and smiled broadly.

"I see that those of your party survived as well. Come close and receive your rewards."

Sean came forward. The Steward looked at Goldworm, who realized he was expected to introduce the man.

"This is Sean Friggand, Captain," he said.

"Oh, yes, the cursed ship captain," the steward said. "The curse is a result of a witch called Bobka Yoshka."

He clapped his hands together and several Black Guards came from a side yard pushing in front of them the witch, her chains dragging on the ground. Sean was shocked and stood dumb as she was brought before him.

"The only way to break the curse is to kill its master," Goldworm said to Sean.

"You can't just remove it?" Sean was clearly uncomfortable.

"I'm afraid not. The magic that witches practice is called exact bonding. Neither she nor any other can remove such a curse once it is placed. It's powered by the witch's life force thus, once the host of the spell dies so does the infecting curse. You must kill her."

He handed Sean a dagger.

Sean took the weapon, but looked back at the men he had grown to know. Ford shrugged his shoulders.

"If you must, then do it," he said.

Han looked away. Sark nodded his head in agreement, and Harigan drew his finger across his throat.

"To do so is not justice," Hugh said shaking his head.

Sean lifted the knife into the air.

The witch cowered.

"Master, do not undo me!" she cried out.

"Remove this curse or I shall strike you dead," Sean ordered.

"I cannot," she hissed. "Witch's magic is irreversible forged from exact bonding, very black magic."

He prepared to bring down the dagger. His hand shook then he lowered the blade to his side.

"I can't do this."

She stood up and jumped for joy with a near shout of triumph. Dancing around in a circle she stopped and looked Sean up and down.

"Very well, you little whelp," she said and waved her hand.

Sean felt his skin ripple and the hair on his body stand up.

"It's done. I have modified the original spell," she said begrudgingly. "If you remove your boots when aboard a ship, it will not sink."

"Spare her life, and send her far from the known lands and kingdoms," Sean said.

"Take her away and see that she is released far to the east in the Scablands," Goldworm commanded.

The guards led the witch away.

"Now, Osara Han. Come hither and reap your reward."

Han came forward and stood before Goldworm.

"Your reward is this," Goldworm said handing Han a scroll.

Opening the scroll, Han shook his head in amazement.

"It's a writ that commissions my school to reopen," he said. "It's signed by the Emperor Ching."

"He understands that good relations with Moore are to his benefit. He knows that we value your talents, and he would like to also," Goldworm said.

Han stepped back.

"Now, for you," Goldworm pointed at Hugh.

The Steward smiled broadly. "Now, for your mother who languishes ill… Take this gift to her and mix it with warm ox milk. Dissolve it in the milk, and make her drink it all. In two days from that moment, she will rise and shed her ill manner. But take heed…it is the last of this type of medicine. Do not lose it."

A guard in black armor brought a clear bottle filled with white powder, handed the bottle to Hugh, turned abruptly, and walked back to his post.

"Sark," called Goldworm.

Sark approached.

"We have sent the lantern to the dragons – the only place we know it will remain safe. You may have access to it upon request, but you will have to travel to their lair," he said.

"The dragons are notoriously stingy with their hoards," Sark stated.

"We have an understanding," the Steward reassured him. "You will have access, but only there. It is not to be removed."

"I understand," Sark said and stepped back.

"Father Harigan. It is your time," Goldworm summoned. "I have chosen you for last, since your reward is the most difficult."

The Steward signaled for two elves in long brightly-colored robes to approach. One in a green robe carried a large black sack.

Reaching into the sack he produced a silver hoop six feet in diameter. An elf in a yellow robe came forward and gripped one side of the hoop. They hefted it up high and motioned for Harigan to come stand in the middle.

Laughing, Harigan took up a position directly under the ring.

"Do your worst," he said with a snicker.

"I will," the fellow in yellow said, as the hoop was passed over Harigan's shaggy head and down to his boots.

The two robed men chanted several mantras as they shook the hoop. The area within the diameter of the hoop filled with white smoke that swirled around Harigan.

"I don't understand!" the man in yellow said. "This should have blocked the connection to the curse. Fetch the mirror," he ordered the man in green as they both put the hoop down at Harigan's boots.

Quickly moving to the black sack, the man in green pulled forth a highly polished gold mirror. He brought it over and handed it to the man in yellow.

Holding it up to Harigan, he jumped back with shock and puzzlement.

"No wonder this didn't work, he's not cursed!" he exclaimed.

"And that's what I've been telling you all," Harigan said.

"What does that mean?" Ford asked.

"There is nothing to remove, or block... I mean to say he is simply not cursed," the elf in green said.

"So, I'm incurable?" Harigan asked.

"And incorrigible," Sark added.

"Aor and I are one and the same," Harigan stated. "Your silly mortal tools will have no effect here."

"Well, whatever you are, you're not cursed," Goldworm added.

The Steward looked at the assembled men.

"Your payments of coin have been delivered to your banking houses as requested, which I might add made them very happy indeed. But... we have another problem.This one will also affect you and your loved ones. If you are in agreement, perhaps you might serve Moore one last time as the party to which you have become?"

"What is it?" Ford asked.

"It's not too difficult a task," Goldworm said. "We just need you to enter the ancient buried city of Moore and acquire the codpiece of the Un-dead White Elf King Gormeron!"

Ford turned to his friends.

"Moore is built atop the ancient city. The White King is said to still roam down there with his army of undead. No one really knows where the entrance is, except the city sewer engineers."

"Is that an issue?" Sark asked.

"I have a feeling they'll not be too helpful," Ford replied.

"Then where do we start?" Sean asked.

"With getting the key of course," Ford said.

Other titles by this author are –

In the World of Hyboria Book 1 Grim Determination, and Book 2 The Ties that Bind

In a time of wizards and barbarians, forces are at work that threaten to undo the lands of Hyboria.

Grimface the wizard stands ready to have his revenge against a rival, who in days long past destroyed his kingdom, family, and life.

To ensure his success he's drawn into his plot two witless barbarians, who join him in seeking a magic item so powerful, it once belonged to a god-king.

Can he resist the lure of such power? Will he have his vengeance against his mightiest foe? Will the drunken, brawling, cavorting, Cimmerians help him, or get him killed?

Find out in the two book novella titled In the World of Hyboria Book 1 Grim Determination, and Book 2 The Ties that Bind.

Thadius

Thadius has long since put away his pilum, scutum, and gladius for the serenity of retired life. His days have been spent gardening, telling and re-telling tales of old with his friend Dominus.

But, the gods do not seem to be finished with the old war dog, as his life transforms into a pursuit of a serial killer, and the reawakening of an old secret that is sure to get him killed.

Sawbones

Carrigan LeRoy arrives in the United States just as it falls into bloody conflict. He's a trained surgeon from London, and steps up to use his skills to mend the broken bones and torn flesh of the Union Army.

Along the way, he is thrust into an intrigue; a plot to alter the eminent outcome of the war. Villains lurk in the woods of Virginia, and Carrigan, and his two colleagues find themselves the only three men that can take action to stop a bold and desperate scheme.

If you liked this author's work, you may like his other works. Try them out when you get the chance.

U.S.A $15.99

FANTASY FICTION

Lawrence BoarerPitchford

ISBN 978-0-9850647-9-2

www.ingramcontent.com/pod-product-compliance
Lightning Source LLC
Chambersburg PA
CBHW031420240626

47154CB00001B/124